continued ...

Whisper's Edge

A CRICKET CREEK NOVEL

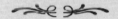

LuAnn McLane

A SIGNET ECLIPSE BOOK

SIGNET ECLIPSE
Published by the Penguin Group
Penguin Group (USA) Inc., 375 Hudson Street,
New York, New York 10014, USA

USA | Canada | UK | Ireland | Australia | New Zealand | India | South Africa | China

Penguin Books Ltd., Registered Offices: 80 Strand, London WC2R 0RL, England
For more information about the Penguin Group visit penguin.com.

First published by Signet Eclipse, an imprint of New American Library,
a division of Penguin Group (USA) Inc.

First Printing, May 2013

ISBN 978-0-451-41557-8

Printed in the United States of America
10 9 8 7 6 5 4 3 2 1

The book is dedicated to my son, Dave. You are a shining example of how hard work and dedication turn into success.

Acknowledgments

I want to give a heartfelt thanks to the editorial staff at New American Library. Putting a book on the shelf is a big team effort, and from the gorgeous covers to the detailed copy-edits, I couldn't ask for more. I want to give a very special thank-you to my editor, Jesse Feldman. The two scenes that you wanted me to add are my favorite. Because of you I no longer fear but welcome revisions!

As always, I want to thank my wonderful agent, Jenny Bent. You have given me confidence in my writing from the moment we sat down together. I wouldn't be able to navigate this changing world of publishing without you.

Thanks so much to my loyal readers. I hope that my stories bring a smile to your faces and joy into your hearts!

1

Wet Willie

"WILLIE! NO! DON'T JUMP!" THE LOUD, DESPERATE PLEA frightened social director Savannah Perry into sprinting toward the pool at Whisper's Edge. Willie's dangerous plunge attempts had been happening all too often. "Oh baby, please don't! It isn't worth it!" Although the tearful wail had Savannah picking up her already swift pace she did manage to notice a sleek sports car parked in front of the main office. The sun glinting off the silver hood piqued Savannah's curious nature but a splash followed by another wail of distress kept her placing one flowered flip-flop in front of the other. The thongs adorned with daisies were the result of last Wednesday's craft workshop but were not very good for running shoes. "Doggone it!" Savannah nearly tripped as she hopped over the curb but she refused to slow down. Willie was not a strong swimmer.

Breathing hard, Savannah pushed open the gate that should have been latched and looked past umbrella tables and lounge chairs. "On no!" She spotted eighty-year-old Patty Parsons teetering precariously close to the edge of the water at the deep end of the pool. "Please back up," Savannah warned, but hard-of-hearing Miss Patty was further hampered by the pink bathing cap covering her ears.

"I'll rescue Willie!" Savannah tried again, but Miss Patty's attention remained focused on her sinking dog.

"Oh, Willie, swim harder!" Miss Patty wrung her hands together as she watched her beloved basset hound trying to capture a yellow tennis ball that bobbed just past his nose. Willie's ears fanned out over the surface of the water and, although he doggy-paddled at a furious pace, his short legs and rotund body were no match for gravity. He sunk a little lower.

"Baby, forget about the danged ball! I'll buy you a dozen!" Miss Patty wailed but Willie was on a mission and paid his master no heed. Then, to Savannah's horror, the spry little lady pointed her hands over her capped head and bent her body toward the glistening water. "I'm coming for ya!" she promised, but although Miss Patty was in great shape for her advanced age, Savannah knew from experience that without her flotation noodle she'd sink like a stone.

Savannah was about to have quite a situation on her hands. She cupped her fingers at the corners of her mouth and shouted at the top of her lungs, "For the love of God, don't dive in, Miss Patty! I'll save Willie!"

God must have been listening because Miss Patty suddenly straightened up and looked at Savannah across the width of the pool. With wide eyes she put a hand to her chest. "Oh, praise the lord! Child, pul-ease save my Willie!"

Savannah kicked off her flip-flops, losing a hot-glued daisy in the process. "I will," she promised and, while holding her nose, she jumped fully dressed into the pool. Although she'd cranked up the heat for afternoon water aerobics, the sudden plunge still felt shockingly cold. Ignoring the discomfort, Savannah bobbed to the surface. She lunged for Willie and managed to wrap her arm around his midsection.

"You got him," Miss Patty shouted, but her glee was

short-lived. Although Savannah kicked with all her might, she and her canine buddy sank beneath the water. Willie, apparently sensing doggy death by drowning, wiggled away. With a gurgled protest, Savannah followed in swift pursuit but Willie swam like a manatee while under water. He didn't, however, manage to paddle his way back up to the surface and started sinking closer to the bottom.

Although her lungs protested, Savannah knew her only hope was to get beneath Willie and push him upward. She lunged forward and gave his furry rump a huge heave-ho, repeating the action while using her legs as a springboard off the bottom. The old, Olympic-sized pool was deep and Savannah was short so by the time she and Willie reached the side of the pool Savannah was struggling. Her lungs burned but she somehow managed to give Willie one last hard shove closer to where Miss Patty was bent over paddling the water as if that would somehow help.

The effort sent Savannah sinking backward but she pushed off the bottom and stroked as quickly as her tired arms would allow. Savannah broke surface and took a huge gasp of much-needed air. Wet hair obscuring her vision, she dipped under the water to slick the long dark red tresses back from her forehead. Just as she raised her head above water another splash had her cringing. Not again! Savannah was flailing around in a circle trying to get a bead on where Willie landed when, to her surprise, a strong arm snaked around her waist and pulled her against a hard body.

"Don't worry. I've got you," the owner of the hard body said next to her ear. Savannah tried to twist to see his face but his firm grip prevented her from budging. "Stay calm and put your arms around my neck. I'll get you over to the edge."

Savannah obeyed but then felt silly. The words *I'm not drowning* formed in her head but the exertion, coupled with the lack of oxygen, scrambled Savannah's brain. She attempted to talk once more but unfortunately only a breathy *drowning* got past her lips.

"Don't worry. I won't let you," her knight in soggy clothing promised in a whiskey-smooth voice laced with a touch of the South. Savannah loved accents because they represented a sense of home, and roots, something she'd never had until landing the job at Whisper's Edge. "Hang on and you'll be just fine."

"Okay," Savannah managed. She tightened her hold, forgetting that she didn't really need assistance.

"We're almost there." His warm breath near her ear sent a delicious tingle down her spine, and when he tilted his head back Savannah was able to see his tanned face. "Don't worry." He gave Savannah a reassuring smile that was utterly gorgeous. In that brief moment when their eyes met, Savannah felt an unexpected flash of longing she couldn't quite explain. He must have felt something similar because his gaze dropped to her mouth and lingered. Time felt suspended and unfolded like one of those slow-motion movie moments that needed Maroon 5 music in the background. Savannah tilted her face slightly closer but before she could do something incredibly insane like lean in and kiss a perfect stranger, he turned his head and started swimming toward the ladder. "Thank God . . ." *Damn . . . didn't mean to utter that out loud.*

"Almost there," he assured her in a soothing tone of voice.

Savannah could see the hot pink silk zinnias adorning the top of Miss Patty's flip-flops. Several of the ladies had squabbled over favorite flowers during craft time, and Savannah had had to make them draw straws.

"Here you go." With firm hands circling her waist he gently guided Savannah to the rungs of the ladder. She could feel the heat of his body pressing against her back and the urge to lean against him was almost too strong to resist. Luckily, Willie's deep bark startled some sense back into Savannah's befuddled brain. With a quick intake of breath she gripped the metal handrails and hoisted herself up while hoping that her wet sweatpants clinging to her body didn't make her butt look big. Belatedly, Savannah realized she wore a swimsuit beneath her clothing and wished she had taken the time to shed it before rescuing Willie. Too late now . . .

Trying not to think about her butt, Savannah sloshed her way up the ladder but when she tried to stand, her shaky legs gave her trouble. To her acute embarrassment she stumbled sideways like a drunken sailor.

"Whoa there." Her handsome hero placed a steadying arm about her waist. "Are you okay?"

"Yes." Her voice, which had a low timbre to begin with, came out sounding like a croak. Could this possibly get any worse? It wasn't until she pushed her wet hair from her eyes that Savannah realized that they had quickly drawn a small crowd of elderly lady onlookers, most of whom were dressed in swimsuits and clutching colorful foam noodles for water aerobics.

Apparently, her day could indeed get worse.

"She's fine," her lifeguard assured them, earning a collective sigh of relief, but then turned to her. "Aren't you?"

Savannah, who didn't trust her voice, opted for a smile at him and a wimpy little wave at the class. After an awkward moment of silence Savannah searched for what to say. *Thanks, but I wasn't really drowning. Sorry that you're sopping wet. Who are you, anyway?* None of those thoughts seemed appropriate for the current situation so she was going to go with a simple thank-you when Willie sat back on his haunches and barked.

"Just hush. You've caused enough trouble now, don't ya know?" Miss Patty wagged a finger and Willie had the decency to hang his head.

Savannah wanted to be angry with Willie but his sad basset hound face melted her heart every time his rump landed in trouble. When his big brown eyes rounded upward and gazed sorrowfully at Savannah she barely refrained from reaching out and patting his head.

"Thank you both so much," Miss Patty tearfully told

them. She started clapping and then glanced back at the
water aerobic class who stood behind her in a neat row.
Most of them had color coordinated their bathing caps,
foam noodles, and flowered flip-flops. "Ladies?" At Miss
Patty's nod they joined her applause by clapping their
hands against their noodles, causing a low thumping sound
that Savannah found funny. She snuck a sideways glance at
her hero but her smile faded when she noticed that he wore
a watch and most likely had a wallet and cell phone in the
pocket of his khaki pants. A dark blue polo shirt molded to
a very nice chest and clung to wide shoulders and impressive biceps. The only thing he managed to shed before his
plunge was expensive-looking leather loafers lying on their
sides near the grass. Savannah swallowed hard. Oh boy . . .

"It was no big deal," he said smoothly. When he glanced
at Savannah she looked down at her toes. She wondered if
his demeanor would change if he knew that his heroic efforts weren't actually needed and then decided that there
was no real reason to clue him in on that particular detail.
"I'm just glad that I was here to help."

Before she could come up with a reply, all the bathing-
capped heads turned in the direction of Clyde and Clovis
Camden entering the area. The seventy-eight-year-old iden-
tical twin brothers who resembled George Hamilton in
both looks and demeanor were the resident hotties. The
brothers were blessed with full heads of salt-and-pepper
hair, a rare sight at Whisper's Edge, and their arrival sent an
audible feminine flutter through the row of bathing beau-
ties.

The dapper duo had donned old-school white tennis
shorts and matching polo shirts. Orange headbands and
wristbands added a shot of color, and gold rope-chain neck-
laces glinted against tanned skin. Savannah wondered if
dressing the same ever got old but they seemed to enjoy
fooling people with typical twin gags. Miss Patty, however,
didn't seem at all happy to see them. She pointed to a yellow tennis ball that Clovis clutched in his hand. The only

way Savannah knew it was Clovis was that he had a slightly crooked nose that must have once been broken. Miss Patty narrowed her eyes. "Once again, y'all almost caused the demise of my dear Willie."

"Now, Miss Patty, we can't help that the tennis courts are next to the pool," Clyde countered smoothly. "My wicked backhand sometimes sends balls sailing over the fence." He flexed a muscle, causing more swooning.

Miss Patty pursed her lips and then raised her chin. "I fully understand the close proximity to the pool, but it's the fact that after you sashay over here to retrieve your balls you fail to close the gate after your departure, putting my dear Willie in danger! To him an open gate is an open invitation. Willie simply cannot resist jumping into the pool when an enticing tennis ball comes sailing over the fence! It happened yet again!"

Clovis arched one eyebrow. "Perhaps you should have Willie on a leash. I do believe it's in the rules."

"He has a point, Patty," Joy Potter piped up and was rewarded with a slight smile from Clovis. Joy returned the gesture with a coy eye flutter.

Miss Patty silenced Joy with an I-can't-believe-you're-siding-with-them glare and then turned her attention back to the twins. "A leash chokes Willie. Per my request he has been exempted from the resident leash law." She looked at Savannah, who quickly nodded her agreement. Although Willie's nonleash exemption slid through the Whisper's Edge council by a narrow margin, a free Willie was indeed legal. "Under normal circumstances Willie remains obediently by my side."

"Then, may I suggest taking a different route?" Clyde asked.

"You may not!" Miss Patty clearly did not like Clyde's suggestion. She narrowed her eyes. "Closing and latching the gate would solve the problem. It's clearly stated in the pool rules." Miss Patty pointed to the sign posted on the far wall and then looked to her lady friends for support but they all dipped their colorful capped heads downward as if in a synchronized swim move. At Miss Patty's audible intake of breath most of the ladies remained staring at the flowers on their flip-flips, clearly not willing to rant against the Camden brothers. "Well, I'll be . . ."

If Savannah hadn't been in her soggy state of embarrassment with the handsome stranger dripping at her side she would have jumped in with some sort of compromise.

At the continued silence Miss Patty finally sighed, and then rolled her eyes. "And if that's not bad enough Savannah had to rescue Willie again. Not to mention that her water aerobics class is going to start late, running into lunch!" She waved her hand in an arc in front of the twins. "See what your negligence has caused?"

Savannah felt her silent hero nudge her arm. "You can swim?"

Oh no . . . busted.

After a sideways glance at his incredulous expression Savannah gave him a slight nod followed by a tiny smile.

His brown eyes widened further. "Wait. So I jumped into the pool fully clothed for nothing?"

"It was a nice gesture," Savannah said softly but felt heat creep up her neck. "Truly . . ."

"A nice *gesture*? I *thought* I was saving your life," he muttered darkly.

Savannah looked up at his face, which remained arrestingly handsome despite his stormy expression. "I'm sorry," she added lamely, but when his expression failed to change, she quickly added, "Although . . . your heroic rescue will make for a funny story, right?" Savannah looked over at the line of ladies for colorful head bobs but they clutched their noodles and blinked back as if not quite sure what the protocol was for this kind of situation. At least the bickering between the Camden brothers and Miss Patty had died down, so that was something. "Sure to get a laugh, don't you think?" She raised her eyebrows with hope.

"Not especially," her reluctant hero answered in a

clipped tone that put Savannah's teeth on edge. Okay, so he was wet. It wasn't the end of the world.

"Hey, I didn't ask you to jump into the pool," Savannah said a bit tightly.

"That's the thanks I get for attempting to save your life?"

"Thank you," she primly replied.

"For nothing."

"Look." Savannah put her hands on her hips. "I'm sorry I didn't need to be saved. So sue me!"

His lips twitched at her comment. "You could have mentioned that little detail."

"I tried." Savannah remembered her instant attraction and felt the heat go from her neck to her cheeks. "I was out of breath from saving Willie. Besides, you had already jumped in so it really wouldn't have mattered, now would it?" Savannah prided herself on being pretty levelheaded but he was getting under her skin in more ways than one. "Look, I'm very sorry that you got wet but are you made of sugar?"

He shook his head. "Ah . . . no."

"Then you're not going to melt."

"Well, true, but I have an important meeting to attend in a little over an hour." He raked his fingers through his dark, wet hair and grimaced. "And I'm not exactly presentable."

"Oh, look, I truly am sorry for the confusion." Savannah felt her anger evaporate but then frowned when she recalled the sleek sports car parked in front of the office. Her heart suddenly started to thud. "Excuse me, but may I ask . . . who are you?"

A dark eyebrow shot up. "Tristan McMillan."

Oh no . . . "Related to Maxwell McMillan?" Although she had never met the man, it was the name signed on her paychecks. Rumor had it that Whisper's Edge was struggling and without a buyer would be sold on the courthouse steps. Her heart pounded. Was he here to deliver bad news?

"As most of you know, my grandfather has retired to

Florida for . . . uh, health reasons. I've purchased the property from him."

Savannah's eyes widened and she heard a ripple of excitement go through the crowd. Bathing-capped heads bobbed like floating balloons and the Camden brothers stopped bouncing tennis balls. Even Willie seemed to sit up and take notice. The fact that Whisper's Edge was for sale wasn't a secret. But although no one really talked about it, the residents lived in silent fear that the retirement community might close down if a buyer wasn't found.

Miss Patty's face broke into a wide smile. "Well then, young Mr. McMillan, it appears as if you truly are a hero!" When she started applauding, everyone joined in, including Savannah. But when Savannah looked up at Tristan she noticed that, although he smiled back, something flickered in his brown eyes that gave her pause. A cold shot of fear slithered down her spine but when she saw the radiant faces of the senior ladies whom she dearly loved, Savannah decided she was being overly cautious. Whisper's Edge had a buyer! Her prayers had been answered and it was time to celebrate! Savannah turned to her new boss and smiled. "Congratulations, Mr. McMillan. Whisper's Edge is a wonderful community. I haven't had the, um, pleasure of meeting him but I'm sure your grandfather is proud and happy that you're keeping Whisper's Edge in the family."

"I was more than happy to do it," Tristan answered but there was a wry tone to his voice that Savannah didn't miss. She'd also heard stories about Max McMillan, and not all of them were good. "While I grew up in the northern part of Kentucky near Cincinnati, I spent some time here as a kid."

"Well, we're grateful," Miss Patty said. "No disrespect, but your grandpappy has been an absentee owner for quite some time now. His signature is about all we ever see of him."

"I intend to make some major improvements. In fact—"

"Hear, hear!" shouted Clovis, raising his tennis racket skyward. Clyde joined him and was quickly followed by the women raising their noodles. Somebody started singing "For He's a Jolly Good Fellow" and the crowd joined in, ending with more applause.

Savannah noticed that Tristan seemed a bit flustered by the cheers. He shifted his weight from one wet-socked foot to the other and said, "Please, applause isn't necessary."

"On the contrary," Miss Patty announced and got nods of approval. "We've been worried that we'd soon be out of house and home. This is really grand news! We can't thank you enough, Mr. McMillan."

"No, really . . ." Tristan raised his hands while giving them a shake of his head.

Savannah thought his humbleness was rather sweet, and silently acknowledged that she had misjudged him. "Mr. McMillan, allow me to formerly introduce myself." She extended her hand and beamed at him. "I'm Savannah Perry, social director and Girl Friday to Kate Winston, whom I'm sure you've already met. I do my best to schedule fun events and help keep daily operations running smoothly." She squeezed his hand. "I'd like to give you a warm . . . instead of *wet*, welcome!"

2
When Pigs Fly

"*T*HANK YOU," TRISTAN REPLIED. SAVANNAH'S GRIP FELT surprisingly strong for such a little thing, and although he wasn't easily charmed, Tristan found her sweet smile to be infectious.

"Sorry I was so snarky earlier." She pressed her lips together and gave him a small shrug. "And you know, that you jumped into the pool and all that."

"Don't worry about it." Tristan found himself grinning. "I'm not going to melt, as you pointed out."

"Sorry 'bout that . . ." she said with a wince. When she tilted her head to the side, sunshine glinted off her auburn hair, which was starting to curl as it dried. Nutmeg-colored freckles dusted a perky nose. She was pretty in a wholesome girl-next-door kind of way—totally not Tristan's type and yet he felt a tug of awareness when her fingers slipped out of his grasp.

"Like you said, gives me something to talk about."

"So true." Savannah's laugh was a throaty, pleasant sound that made Tristan want to tell a joke just to hear it again. She glanced at the onlookers, who watched with rapt interest. "And the main subject over the dinner table at Whisper's Edge. Am I right?" Nods and the tinkle of giggles followed Savannah's question. Tristan couldn't help but notice that the assembled crowd looked at her with fondness, making him believe that she really did excel at her job. "See?" She put her hands on her hips and grinned.

"I do." Tristan felt a flash of guilt. If things went as planned, Savannah's position wouldn't be necessary. But as he frowned, her lively expression dimmed.

"We are a close-knit community," she explained uncertainly. "News travels fast here."

"I don't mind being the topic of conversation," Tristan assured her. "Believe me, it's happened many times." In this very town, he thought with dark humor.

"Oh, well, good," she said with a smile but the uncertainty remained in her eyes. "I guess . . ."

Tristan found himself laughing. "Not always," he acknowledged. His laughter seemed to put her at ease. "I'm not one to care much what people say or think about me." Not that he wasn't above making his grandfather eat crow. The judgmental old coot had caused him and his mother a lot of heartache.

"Good for you. Be true to yourself," Miss Patty chimed in, and Tristan found himself getting yet another round of applause.

Savannah leaned close and stood on tiptoe. "Looks like you've already won them over," she said as near to his ear as she could manage. Although short in stature, Tristan knew from recent up-close-and-personal experience that Savannah had an abundance of curves in all the right places. He wouldn't soon forget the feel of pulling her out of the water. Sweet yet sexy came to mind and Tristan forced himself to rein in his thoughts in order to concentrate on what Savannah was saying. "Good for you." Savannah gave his forearm a squeeze but then quickly dropped her hand as if she thought she might have overstepped her bounds. When she took a step away from him Tristan had the odd urge to pull her close once more. "Now, let's get you out of those clothes."

"I ... uh ..." he stuttered as an instant image of her undressing him popped into his mind. For a lawyer with a hard-nosed reputation, he wasn't usually at a loss for words, but Tristan suddenly found himself feeling terribly tongue-tied.

"Cat got yer tongue?" one of the tennis-clad twins inquired and then elbowed his brother.

No, the thought of Savannah removing his clothes got his tongue. "Excuse me?" Tristan managed to ask.

"I meant your ... you know ... your *wet* clothes." Savannah blushed and shot an I-can't-believe-you look at the twins. "I can round up a robe or something for you to wear," she assured him. Her cheeks were flushed a pretty shade of pink.

Miss Patty shook her head. "Don't pay any attention to those two yahoos. Their minds are always in the gutter."

Savannah cleared her throat, drawing Tristan's attention. He tried not to notice how her wet clothes were clinging to her curves and pretty much failed. Although his demanding career had left him with little time for romance, the women he'd dated had been reed thin. But suddenly he found himself wondering what had been the attraction of skin and bones.

"Mr. McMillan, what I was trying to say is that I have a dryer."

Tristan blinked at her for a moment. Wow, she had amazing green eyes.

"I'll be happy to dry your clothing so you can be presentable for your meeting."

Tristan suddenly realized that everyone was looking at him expectantly. He reeled his wayward thoughts back in. "Oh, sure, thanks."

"It's the very least I can do." Savannah smiled and then turned to the group awaiting water aerobics. "Joy, would you lead the class while I dry Mr. McMillan's clothes?"

A woman stepped forward. "Certainly, Savannah." She

raised her chin and plunked her noodle down in front of her like a wizard's staff. "I'll give these girls a workout. Now, you two run along."

"Thanks, Joy." Savannah waved at the ladies and then turned back to Tristan. "Follow me, please."

"Sure." Right now, he would follow her anywhere, he thought as he hid a grin.

Savannah darted over and retrieved his loafers and held on to them with her fingertips. "I don't suggest putting them on until I dry your socks," she explained with a wry smile. While he peeled off his socks she slipped her own feet into her flip-flops and then frowned at the one missing a daisy.

Tristan glanced around and spotted the yellow flower at the edge of the grass. With a chuckle, he walked over and picked it up. "I think this is yours."

"Thanks." Savannah accepted the flower with a soft smile. "We made these in craft class." She raised her adorned flip-flop and wiggled her foot.

"You're the instructor?" Tristan asked as they fell into step together. "You must be artistic."

Savannah arched one eyebrow. "Well, I spent a lot of time in camp while growing up so I know tons of easy things to make. This particular project turned out to be a big hit."

"I could see that." He followed her down the sidewalk past mobile homes of various shapes and sizes. Although none of them appeared expensive or flashy, Tristan could feel the residents' sense of pride in their small but immaculate yards and patios. Flags depicting summer scenes, sports mascots, and the stars and stripes cheerfully waved in the gentle breeze. Gurgling fountains, bird feeders, colorful gnomes, praying angels, and dressed geese might be cheesy, but to Tristan's surprise he found the homespun decor rather charming. Music, conversation, and laughter filtered their way, and every single person they encountered smiled and waved. To the left a group of men were pitching a lively game of horseshoes while several women looked on, chatting away.

"This is nice." Tristan nodded, and drew a curious look from Savannah.

"I agree, but you seem surprised. Surely you knew what the grounds looked like?"

"My mother was born in Cricket Creek but I was raised north of here. I haven't actually been back to Whisper's Edge in years."

"So a lot has changed?"

"Well, when I was a kid this was more of a fishing and boating community. Not all of the permanent mobile homes were here. I didn't realize how many people actually lived here year-round." The realization bothered him. Uprooting people wasn't part of his plan. He remembered Cricket Creek as being a sleepy little town. "I guess a lot of things changed after Noah Falcon built the baseball stadium."

Her eyes widened and she pulled up short. "You're kidding? I would have thought you'd have visited before buying."

He shrugged. "I was looking for an investment. With the recent growth along the riverfront this seemed like a no-brainer," he explained. "Besides, after eight grueling years of practicing law with a big firm in Cincinnati I was eager for a change. A nice case settlement has allowed me to try something different." *And show my grandfather what I'm made of*, went through his head but he kept that little tidbit to himself.

"Oh . . . Savannah nodded and seemed to be digesting his comment. She finally angled her head and gave him a questioning expression. "So you decided to quit the firm and move to Cricket Creek, Kentucky, to run a retirement community? I realize that my question might be bold—but do you think you'll be challenged enough by this?"

"I'm not offended. The only way to get answers is to ask questions."

"I'm curious by nature."

"Not a bad trait."

"So . . . do you?"

"Think I'll miss my job?" When she nodded, Tristan inhaled a deep breath. In truth, although his job had been stressful, going on a sabbatical ended up being more difficult than he bargained for. Leaving behind friends and colleagues proved to be more of an issue than he imagined, leading Tristan to immediately question his decision. And although, as always, his mother had put up a brave front, moving several hours away from her had made Tristan feel guilty. It didn't help that she'd made it clear that, as a seasoned real estate agent, she thought Tristan's vision for Whisper's Edge was smart, but she didn't like his core motive for buying the property from her father. And although she hated the long, grueling hours he put in at the firm, she also wasn't sure he should take leave from a successful career that he'd worked so hard to establish. Although he left the door open to return she remained skeptical.

At his silence, Savannah put a hand on his forearm. "Hey, I'm sorry. I'm being too nosy. I'll quit prying."

Tristan tried to put her at ease with a smile. "Savannah, I pry information out of people for a living. And while I found satisfaction in winning settlements for deserving clients . . . to put it bluntly, I was just tired of long hours of research and arguing for a living." Tristan knew he hadn't really satiated all of her curiosity, but he wasn't ready to divulge his plans for Whisper's Edge yet. There was no reason to alarm her or the community when most of his ideas were still in the planning stages.

"Oh . . ."

To divert her attention, Tristan put his lawyer hat on and decided to ask some questions of his own. "So, were you born here in Cricket Creek?"

"No." When she resumed walking down the sidewalk he fell in step beside her.

"Where then?"

Savannah gave him a slight shrug followed by a small smile. "Maybe someday I'll find that out. I've lived here longer than I lived anywhere else and I can't imagine leaving. This is home."

Tristan gave her a sideways glance but she averted her gaze and kept on walking. Although he longed to probe, Tristan knew from much experience that silence could sometimes lead to more information than questions. He waited patiently, but when she failed to elaborate, he considered asking more. Before he had the opportunity, though, she stopped in front of a cute, pale blue bungalow-style mobile home and pointed.

"Here we are," she announced and pushed open a white gate attached to a picket fence. "The washer and dryer is a small stacked version but it does the job."

Just like you, ran through his head and Tristan grinned but kept his thought to himself. "So you live and work here in Whisper's Edge?" he asked as he followed her up a brick-paved sidewalk that led to matching steps.

"I'm allowed to bypass the fifty-five-and-up rule because I'm an employee. Plus, it makes my commute to work a piece of cake." Savannah flashed a grin and then opened the front door. "A humble home, for sure, but it's all mine and I like it."

Tristan took a look around. "I can see why. It's bigger inside than I would have guessed."

"I know." Her smile boasted pride in ownership. "But believe me, this place sure needed some tender loving care and a whole lot of elbow grease."

"Well worth the effort, I'd say." The neat-as-a-pin main interior consisted of one big room that abutted a breakfast bar in front of a galley kitchen. To the right, he noticed a small hallway that he guessed must lead to a bedroom or two and a bathroom. Shiny hardwood floors gleamed against ample sunshine streaming through the front bay window. The furnishings were a mix-and-match variety that felt cozy but without too much clutter.

"So you like it?"

"Yes, I do." Tristan found the surroundings warm and inviting. "I appreciate your sense of style."

"Garage-sale chic?" She tossed her wavy head to the

side and gave him her throaty laugh, which he didn't think he could ever get tired of hearing.

"Call it whatever you want. I think it's pretty cool."

"Well, thank you. I'm guessing it's very different from your own place. You seem like a modern-furniture kind of guy."

"Mmm . . . yeah, I suppose," he answered but had to think for a minute. What was his style? An interior decorator furnished his high-rise condo overlooking the Ohio River in Cincinnati. "Flying pigs," he finally stated, drawing raised eyebrows from Savannah.

"Excuse me?"

Tristan chuckled. "My interior decorator decided that I needed a theme throughout my condo."

"And she chose flying pigs?"

"I asked her the same thing. She got all snooty on me and explained that Cincinnati used to be called Porkopolis because of the farmers who used to transport pigs through the city. It was the pig capital of the country or something, and evidently herds of pigs traveled through the streets."

"Oh wow." The expression on her face said that she was imagining pigs wandering through town. "Interesting."

Tristan chuckled. "The history of the river and pigs remains strong in the city to this day. They even have a yearly marathon that's called The Flying Pig."

"Oh." Savannah shrugged. "Well, I guess she was trying to tie in local flavor." She grinned and said, "Everything's better with bacon. Don't you agree?"

He laughed. "Totally. Now you're making me hungry."

"If you had more time I'd fix you some lunch. But go on . . . Why the flying pigs?"

"I guess she did it because my place looks out over the river and the city but every other day I would find a new flying pig somewhere . . . on towels, coffee mugs, salt and pepper shakers. People started thinking I *liked* flying pigs, and the collection that I didn't want kept growing. It took on a life of its own."

Savannah laughed. "So I guess birthdays and Christmases are full of flying pigs."

"Come here." Tristan held out a wet sock and winced. "Look closely."

Savannah crossed the space between them and peered at the sock. "Oh my gosh, there are little winged pigs all over your socks!" She put a hand to her chest and chuckled with delight.

"It's not funny. I have ties, a watch . . . you name it."

"Did you ever tell anyone differently?" When she looked up at him he noticed flecks of gold in her green eyes.

Tristan hesitated. He had never divulged this to anyone and he had just met Savannah. But her sweet smile and inquiring eyes made him keep talking. "No, I didn't because my mother made it her mission to find flying pigs to add to my crazy collection."

"Ah . . ." Savannah glanced at his socks and then back at him. "And you couldn't find it in your heart to disappoint her."

"I'm wearing boxers riddled with flying pigs," he answered drily. "Does that answer your question?"

"It does and I think it's so sweet." When her eyes misted over, Tristan felt another shot of guilt.

"I'm a hard-nosed lawyer. Not many people would think of me as sweet."

"Oh well, I've got your number." She leaned in closer. "But I won't tell."

"Thank you," he said and had to grin. In less than one hour Savannah Perry and the people of Whisper's Edge thought Tristan was some kind of hero. In his thirty-two years of living he had been called many things but *never* a hero and certainly not sweet. Not even close.

Damn, he sure did like the feeling. Too bad he didn't deserve it.

3

The Naked Truth

NOT WANTING TRISTAN TO SEE HER BLINKING EMOTION FROM
her eyes, Savannah quickly turned away and hurried
over to the closet hiding the washer and dryer. How embarrassing! First she caused her new boss to jump into the
swimming pool for no reason; then she snapped at him, and
now she was getting a bit emotional because of something
as silly as flying-pig boxers. "I'll just get the dryer ready."

"Thanks," Tristan replied. "Arriving sopping wet to a
meeting isn't something I usually do," he continued with an
edge of humor in his deep voice. "You need to change into
something dry too."

"I will as soon as I get your stuff loaded in the dryer."
Savannah wanted to turn around but kept her back to
Tristan, hoping he hadn't noticed her getting a little choked
up. She had learned at an early age not to show weakness
or you'd get preyed upon, but lately her emotions had been
getting the best of her and she didn't like it one bit. Just the
other day Kate had discovered Savannah dissolving into a
puddle of tears over a television commercial involving a
puppy being chased by a chubby-cheeked toddler.

"What in the world is coming over me?" Savannah had wanted to know.

"It's your biological body clock ticking away," Kate had explained in her slow, Paula Deen Southern drawl. "Child, you're knocking on the door of thirty and your hormones want you to have a baby."

"It would be a good idea to have a boyfriend first."

"Point taken." Kate had looked up over reading glasses. "This is precisely why you need to get away from Whisper's Edge once in awhile!" Every word had a few extra syllables. "We could go to Sully's Tavern where all of those Cricket Creek baseball players hang out. I'll be your . . . What do they call it?" She snapped her fingers and pointed. "Your wingman."

"Maybe *you* need a wingman," Savannah had shot back.

"I'm fifty-five, almost fifty-six. That ship has sailed."

Savannah had waggled her eyebrows. "You could be a cougar for a Cricket Creek Cougar," she teased and they had both laughed. In truth, though, Kate didn't look anywhere near her age.

"Look, we can't both be the wingman. It doesn't work that way." Kate had slanted Savannah a pointed look. "But seriously, Cricket Creek has livened up in the past couple of years. You need to get into town and take in a game or hang out at Wine and Diner or Sully's . . . *whatever*. Girl, just get out and socialize, and I don't mean playing shuffleboard."

"I will," Savannah had promised but without real conviction. On the other hand, her instant attraction to Tristan might have proven Kate's point. With that thought she took a deep breath and willed her cheeks not to turn red when she turned to face him. "We'll have those clothes dry in no time." Savannah gave him a quick glance and then turned back to her task.

"Good deal," Tristan replied.

"Just give me another minute to rearrange some things here." Having to move a stack of folded clothes out of the way gave Savannah a quick breather to get herself under control. Having been tossed from one foster home to the next, Savannah had lived a less than perfect childhood, and one would have expected her to end up one tough cookie. In many ways she was, but lately she'd had to hide emotion when it came to the mention of family, especially the kindness of someone's mother.

Although she didn't have a clue as to who or where her blood family was, to her delight, many of the residents of Whisper's Edge treated her as if she were their very own granddaughter. To her way of thinking, feeling treasured made up for the lack of a raise in salary in the past five years. Of course she would welcome more money in her wallet, but for now Savannah simply felt relieved that Tristan bought the property from his absentee grandfather.

When there remained nothing left to fiddle with, Savannah turned around and gave Tristan what she hoped was a businesslike smile. "Well, what do you say we get those wet clothes dry?"

He put down a framed photograph he was looking at. "I'd say that's an excellent idea, Savannah, but I think I'd better have something to change into." His slow grin made her suddenly feel warm all over, despite her damp clothing, and she had to fight the urge to fan her face like Kate did during a hot flash. Her clothes just might steam dry on their own.

"Oh . . . yes, what was I thinking?" She tried her best to sound businesslike. "I'll be right back." Savannah pivoted on the balls of her feet and hustled out of the room but then stopped in her tracks. What in the world did she have that would fit him? The robe she had suggested earlier wouldn't fit over those wide shoulders, although picturing him in it made her grin. While nibbling on her bottom lip, she frantically searched in her cluttered closet but came up empty-handed. "There!" She finally grabbed a giant-sized orange beach towel and hurried back into the living room. "This is all I could come up with." She tossed him the towel and then pointed to the hallway. "You can change in the bathroom to the right."

"Thanks, I'll be back in a minute."

After he walked away Savannah hurried back into her bedroom, anxious to get out of her own clothes. She peeled off the jogging suit and then wiggled out of the bathing suit before quickly tugging on dry panties and a bra. After pulling on jeans and a random T-shirt she made the mistake of glancing at the mirror over her dresser. "Oh dear lord," she muttered at her disheveled appearance. As usual, unless tamed, her hair had taken on a life of its own. Auburn curls framed her flushed face and tumbled over her shoulders. Because of water aerobics class Savannah had skipped the foundation she usually used to cover up her freckles. "I look like I'm twelve. Well, except for my boobs." She groaned and then reached up to try to smooth her hair, even though she knew it was pointless. "Oh well, I am what I am. Such is life." After a deep breath she headed back out into the living room, but when she reached the doorway she stopped in her tracks and swallowed hard. All she could think was . . . *wow*.

Tristan stood in front of the tiny laundry closet with his back to her . . . make that his bare back. *Oh my* . . . Savannah's gaze traveled over wide shoulders, down tanned skin to a narrow waist. The orange towel hugged a nicely rounded butt that deserved a very firm squeeze. While she knew she should speak up and let her presence be known, the only bodily function that seemed to be working was her libido. Seriously, Savannah found herself fighting the urge to walk over there and run her hands up his tanned skin and sink her fingers into his dark hair. Instead, she curled her fingers into fists and took another deep breath. Words had almost made it to her vocal cords when Tristan placed his pile of clothes in her laundry basket. When she saw him reach up and open the dryer Savannah's eyes widened; she had forgotten that she had tossed in one last load. Before she could stop him Tristan reached inside the dryer and pulled out a handful of panties and thongs. He looked down at the lace and silk dangling from his fingers just as Savannah found her voice.

"Oh no!"

Tristan whipped around at the sound. "Uh, didn't know these were in there." He thrust his handful of colorful panties toward her and looked at Savannah as if he had been caught with his hand in the cookie jar. "I, uh, was just trying to be helpful." She wanted to say something but the sight of his sculpted bare chest prevented words from forming. She should have told him to wear the towel like a toga. "I'm sorry," he continued, and wiggled his hand. "Please, take them," he pleaded but the movement sent several wisps of lace and silk fluttering to the floor.

"S-sure." With her face flaming, Savannah hurried over to him but just as she reached his side, Tristan dropped another thong. They both bent over to pick them up at the same time and bumped heads. With a yelp, Savannah lost her balance and reached forward to grab onto Tristan to keep from falling to the floor. Unfortunately, she grabbed a handful of towel and staggered sideways, whipping it from his hips so fast that they were both caught by surprise. "Oh!" She covered her face with her hands before she caught an eyeful ... well almost before she caught an eyeful. "Sorry!" she squeaked in a voice muffled by her palms on her lips.

"You can open your eyes now."

"Are you decent?"

"Well, halfway."

Savannah lowered her hands and was relieved to see the towel knotted at his waist. "I want you to know that was an accident," she said.

"Sure it was."

Savannah's eyes widened, but when he started laughing she joined him. "I should get those clothes dry," she said, but a moment of awareness hung in the air between them. She gave him a shy smile. The feeling was a bit foreign but she liked the warm rush of excitement. Swallowing hard, she turned toward the dryer.

A moment later she checked to make sure he had removed his wallet and then tossed his clothes into the dryer on low. Luckily there was no sign of a ruined cell phone and she sure hoped that his watch was waterproof, not that she was about to ask. "This won't take long," she promised without looking at him, although the sight of his splendid naked body would remain branded in her memory for quite some time. Perhaps forever.

"Savannah?" The unexpected firmness in his tone made her cringe. Perhaps he wasn't as amused as she thought he was?

"Yes?" Savannah inhaled a deep breath, and wondered if she was about to be fired. Emotion pooled in her throat and her eyes burned. Not even the sight of his flying-pig boxers tossing in a circle, making the pigs look as if they were truly flying, could make her smile.

"Are you going to turn around and look at me?"

"I think I might have already seen way too much," she answered, hoping that a touch of humor might soften him up. She had learned from Kate that laughter was often the best medicine and prayed that it worked this time.

4

Wishful Thinking

KATE WINSTON FROWNED WHEN SHE SPOTTED TRISTAN MC-
Millan's fancy-looking cell phone lying on her desk.
He'd taken a phone call just before telling her that he
wanted to check out the grounds, including the community
center and the pool. She'd offered to accompany him but
he'd politely refused, saying only that he wanted to see a
few things and it wasn't necessary for her to leave her desk.

Kate picked up a pen and toyed with it. She found it odd
that Tristan wanted to tour Whisper's Edge on his own and
had to wonder if there wasn't something more to his purchase of the property than he was letting on. While tapping
the pen against her cheek she reviewed in her head what
she knew about the relationship between Tristan McMillan
and his grandfather.

"Not much," she mumbled as she racked her brain for
clues. Max McMillan's only daughter, Maggie, had been several years behind her in school. Although Kate only knew
Maggie in passing, news had traveled fast that after only
four months into her freshman year in college Maggie
turned up pregnant. Word on the street had it that Max,

already a bitter man after his wife's descrtion, had a falling-out with Maggie, who ended up leaving town.

Kate thought for another minute and then frowned when she remembered that a battle with breast cancer is what had brought Maggie home one summer when Tristan was just a kid. Other than that, Kate remained clueless. Kate knew that Tristan's return would surely stir up local gossip, so if she kept her ear to the ground perhaps she would come up with some answers. She only hoped that his intentions were good.

Kate inhaled a deep breath and willed her thoughts not to go down that path. Worry had been her middle name since Max McMillan started letting the conditions of the grounds slide. She'd heard that the old sourpuss had made some poor investments in Florida and teetered on the verge of bank-ruptcy. While the riverfront property had gone up in value with the revitalization of Cricket Creek, Kate had also heard it through the local grapevine that Max was so far upside-down financially that it didn't make a lick of difference. The bank had been waiting in the wings to swoop down and seize the property, but although Tristan had kept mum on details, he did divulge that there was a legal clause allowing him to purchase it from his grandfather before the bank stepped in.

Kate sighed as she looked over at the stack of unpaid bills piled high on her desk. As the property manager she'd learned to pinch pennies and call in favors but the past year had been stressful. Savannah Perry, bless her heart, hadn't had a raise in who knows when and never complained, even though she worked her little tail off. Kate dropped her pen and rubbed her temples. Not everyone was so gracious. Over the past six months she had gone through three main-tenance men, and the current one had just given his notice a week ago. Kate massaged her temples. She was becoming desperate. Duct tape could only go so far.

Although Kate could put an ad in the paper it might be weeks before finding another replacement. The baseball stadium complex and new strip mall were doing well and Cricket Creek continued to flourish. Competition for em-

ployees was fierce and she simply couldn't match the sala-
ries offered to skilled workers that other businesses were
giving. Kate could sweeten the pot by offering living accom-
modations but not everyone wanted to reside in a retirement community. Kate sighed. She could only hope that
Tristan would soon change all that.

With that thought she looked down at his cell phone,
which kept making all kinds of weird blinks, dings and
beeps. Either he'd left the phone by mistake or he simply
wanted to get away from the constant noises and vibrations.
"Where did he go for this long?" she murmured, and bent
the blinds down to see if his snazzy car was still parked in
front of the office. "Still there," she said and leaned back in
her weathered swivel chair.

Kate rested her head against the cool leather and closed
her eyes in an effort to remain calm. Insomnia had been a
constant companion for the past few months and she
thought she would just rest her weary eyes for a moment or
two. The low hum of the air conditioner soothed her nerves
and after a minute Kate drifted off to sleep . . .

Ding, *ding!*

The sudden sound cut through Kate's peaceful slumber
and jarred her awake so fast that she grabbed the arms of
her chair and spun in a half circle. With a little yelp she
stopped the spin by slamming her feet to the floor. Breathing hard, she glared at Tristan's fancy phone and considered
tossing it out the window. Kate shook her head, thinking
that she couldn't fall asleep in the comfort of her bed but
could doze off in an instant in a fully lit office while sitting
straight up in a chair. Go figure . . .

"Oh dear lord," Kate grumbled when beads of sweat
suddenly popped out on her forehead. She stood up and
went over to the thermostat to check the temperature. "Just
what I thought. It's me." Kate picked up a magazine and
started fanning her face. Even though she cut corners, she
kept the office at meat-locker temperatures to battle the
hot flashes that plagued her on a daily basis, but nothing

seemed to help. Poor little Savannah had to wear a sweater even though it was summertime. Although she had teased Savannah about her biological clock hormones, lately it was Kate who was no stranger to mood swings and crying jags. And although Kate had a closet full of weirdly named herbal remedies, nothing seemed to give her much relief. And seriously, something with a name like black cohosh just sounded scary. She'd rather sweat. Well, maybe.

"Menopause sucks." After putting down the magazine she opened an extra button on her cotton blouse and plucked at the collar to let cool air slide down her damp neck. Light, cotton clothing composed most of her wardrobe. She'd even had her shoulder-length blond bob snipped into a short layered cut to help ward off the heat, but she continued to suffer. "Surely to God, I'm going to melt from the inside out." She walked over to stand beneath the paddle fan. "Ahhh," she said, breathing. With a grateful smile she tilted her face up, stretched her arms akimbo, and let the cool breeze bring blessed relief.

"Interesting pose." At the sound of the deep male voice Kate jumped and let out a silly-sounding squeal. "Yoga?"

"Ben! You scared the daylights out of me!"

"Sorry." His laugh was a rusty but pleasant sound that Kate realized she rarely heard.

"No, you're not." Kate moved her hands to her hips and hoped the sweat had dried.

Ben leaned one shoulder against the doorframe. "Guilty."

"At least you're honest."

"To a fault."

As Kate already knew, Ben was a man of few words and the words that did come out of his mouth tended to be on the grumpy side. She also knew that even though she might be in full-blown menopause, there was nothing wrong with her eyesight. Tall and rugged, with piercing blue eyes, sandy blond hair, and a thick lumberjack build, Ben Bakersfield, at sixty years old, could still turn female heads. Not that he seemed to notice or care. It was widely known that Ben had lost his wife to a sudden aneurism five years ago, and he carried around his grief like a shield of armor. He mostly kept to himself, tinkering with his boat and making a few extra bucks as a local fishing guide but only if the spirit moved him, which wasn't often. "So what brings you here?"

He folded his arms across his impressive chest. "You."

"M-me?" Kate's heart kicked up a notch and the need to fan her face had nothing to do with a hot flash. Okay, so she'd had a fantasy or two ... okay or *ten* about Ben that started out much like this but ended very steamy. But she wasn't prepared for the real deal. Oh, why hadn't she shaved her legs?

"You called me," he slowly explained.

"Ohhhh, yes, yes, I did." Kate waved her hands and tried to act as if she hadn't been thinking in a totally different direction, about something other than wrapping herself around him like kudzu. She cleared her throat and nodded briskly. Ha, not that she really *wanted* to have a fling with Ben, anyway. She didn't need a man to make her happy or complicate her life. She didn't want to suffer that heartache ever again. Besides, she had her hands full keeping Whisper's Edge from falling apart. "Right, I called you ..." Damn, she was having a senior moment.

"And?" Ben pushed away from the doorway and took a couple of steps into the room.

"Uh ..." Damned if his nearness didn't send another warm flutter sinking into regions hoping for male attention and made her train of thought jump the track and derail. It didn't help matters that he managed to make a faded work shirt and worn jeans look sexy. Or that the sleeves were rolled up to the elbows, revealing muscled forearms. Ben was one of those Liam Neeson types of men who just got better with age. It wasn't fair.

"I ... um ..." Kate inhaled a deep breath to clear her head but inhaled the subtle male scent of his aftershave. Kate dug deep to stay focused. Oh, she remembered. "Look, I know you're a jack-of-all-trades, right?"

He nodded slowly. "Some might say that."

"Some, meaning a lot of residents here at Whisper's Edge."

He merely shrugged.

"Ben, I know that you've done a lot of plumbing and electrical work around here for free."

"Keeps me busy."

"I'd like to make it official and offer you a job."

Ben remained silent but reached up and rubbed his chin, drawing Kate's attention to the tawny stubble gracing his cheeks. She wondered what it would feel like to have that slight abrasion against her own skin and swallowed hard. Her hormones, she decided, were seriously out of control. "I don't mind helping out a neighbor but I really don't want to have the responsibility of a real job. Sorry."

Kate's heart sank. "Look, Ben, my last maintenance man quit a week ago. I haven't had any luck replacing him. Could you just do it for a while? Until I find someone else? I can't pay more than twelve bucks an hour but I can throw in your boat storage fee for free."

"It's not about the money, Kate. I like my time to be my own."

"Okay." Kate nodded sadly and then backed up so that she could rest her hips against her desk. "I can respect that." The stress, coupled with her female reaction to him, was making her legs a bit shaky. "Thought I'd give it a shot," she said, but when she tried for a smile her lips trembled and she had to sniff. Horrified, Kate blinked so as not to shed an embarrassing tear. "Damned allergies." She reached for a nearby box of tissues and plucked one from the slit at the top. *Damned hormones* echoed in her head and she faked blowing her nose.

Ben gave a long look that indicated he didn't totally believe her.

"Everything's bloomin'." When she tried to fake a sneeze it came out more like a sob. Damn!

After a sigh he said, "Okay, I'll do it."

Kate stopped dabbing at her nose and looked up at him. "Really?"

"You're making it pretty damned difficult for me to refuse."

"It's the ragweed."

"Right."

"But you'll do it? For real?"

"Yes, but only until you can find someone else."

"Agreed!" With a smile, Kate pushed up from the desk and stuck out her hand for him to shake but the tip of her flowered flip-flop caught in a jagged piece of linoleum that needed to be fixed. When she stumbled slightly Ben quickly came forward, causing her to land against his chest.

"Whoa there." Two big hands caught Kate around the waist and held her steady. She could feel the heat of his skin beneath his shirt and the solid thud of his heart against her palm. It took everything in her might not to lean against the strength, the comfort. She wasn't sure if it was wishful thinking, but when his touch seemed to linger and she looked up, she thought she saw a hint of longing in Ben's blue eyes. But before she could be sure, he abruptly released her and backed away. "I guess I'll have to fix that," he said and smiled.

Smiled.

"Yeah." Kate smiled back.

His gaze suddenly dropped from her face as if he felt guilty for something. He pointed to her flip-flops. "What's up with everyone wearing those?"

"The flip flops? Oh, one of Savannah's never-ending crafts," Kate explained.

"Oh, I should have guessed."

"Yeah, well, they should be called trip-flops."

Ben laughed. Broody Ben was sexy in a dark and mysterious way, but his smile was killer and she wished it would remain. When he looked at her with amusement in his eyes she wanted to swoon.

"Ben . . ." she began, but his smile faded and she saw a muscle twitch in his jaw.

"I'll get to fixing it first thing tomorrow," he said briskly and then jammed his hands in his pockets.

"Thanks," Kate replied. "I really appreciate you doing this, by the way."

"I do like staying busy. But remember, it's only temporary." His mood shifted and he nodded solemnly before he turned and walked out the door.

Kate stood there for a minute and watched him retreat. With a sigh she turned around and looked at her desk in an effort to remember what she'd been doing. Oh yeah, wondering where in the world Tristan McMillan had wandered off to.

5

Slow Southern Smile

*T*RISTAN FROWNED WHEN SAVANNAH FAILED TO TURN
around. His initial irritation at the unnecessary jump
into the pool had evaporated like rain on a hot sidewalk
and he was actually finding the entire situation sort of
amusing. He had only been teasing her with his comments,
but he guessed he was about as good at joking around as he
was at flirting. He might work out and keep fit but he was
still an awkward geek at heart.

"Um . . ." Tristan tightened the knot on the towel and
stood there uncertainly. "Remember, I'm decent now." He
searched for something more to say but came up blank. Although his serious nature suited him well as a lawyer, his
mother was forever urging him to lighten up. Tristan admired that, in spite of her unhappy childhood and her
narrow-minded father, his mother remained one of the
most positive people that he knew. She made damned sure
that he never felt unloved or unwanted. He had been terri-
fied when he almost lost her to breast cancer. He only
wished he had been old enough to take care of her during

her illness instead of her having to return to Whisper's Edge and her coldhearted father for help.

Tristan shoved his fingers through his hair and pushed the memory of that horrible summer from his head. Instead, he focused his attention on the cute little redhead who refused to turn and face him. "Savannah? Would you please turn around?" He noticed that her shoulders tensed at the sound of his request, and he had the urge to walk over there and place reassuring hands on her arms. "Look," he began, but before he could finish his sentence she whirled around.

"Please don't fire me."

"Fire you?"

She nodded.

"Why on earth would I fire you?"

"Well for the . . . the pool incident for starters." She took a deep breath. "And for, you know, yanking your towel off and causing you to be naked in front of my very own eyes."

"So you looked?" When her eyes widened and she turned a pretty shade of bright pink, Tristan realized that his attempt at teasing had failed once more.

"No! Well, I mean yes, but I wasn't trying to! I closed my eyes right away," she insisted and then nervously licked her lips.

"Savannah . . ." he tried but she was on a roll and gaining momentum.

"For the record I most *certainly* did *not* yank the towel off for the purpose of viewing your naked body. I was merely attempting to stand upright."

"Okay!" Tristan put his palms up in surrender. "I really do believe you. Seriously."

She blinked at him. "So can I have my job back?"

"I di—"

"I know it must seem like I am the queen of incompetence but I actually work hard and there are lots of people who would miss me." She paused briefly to consider her statement. "I think. Well, I would miss everyone, for sure."

"Are you finished?"

"I believe so." She fell silent and looked at him with soulful eyes.

"Savannah, for the last time . . . I was only teasing."

"Teasing? Are you kidding me?"

"Yes. I mean, no, I'm not kidding you . . . not *now* at least. I was before." Wow, for a lawyer he was sure sucking at this explanation.

"Wait." She tilted her head forward and gave him an incredulous look. "Pardon me for saying so but you should not tease a person about firing them."

"Who said *anything* about firing you?"

"Oh . . ." She nibbled on the inside of her lip. "So I just gave that big, long speech for nothing?"

"Pretty much." Tristan took a step closer. "What gave you the impression that I was going to give you the boot?"

Savannah gave him a slight shrug. "I just, I don't know, get feelings that I can't always explain," she admitted in a serious tone that made Tristan want to peel away the cheerful layers and get to the heart of Savannah Perry. She shrugged once more but then grinned slightly. "Go figure . . ."

"I understand more than you might think," Tristan told her, but when she raised her eyebrows as if wanting him to elaborate, he clammed up.

After a moment of silence Savannah looked a bit confused but then said, "Your clothes should be dry in a few minutes." He could feel her putting distance between them and Tristan was fine with pulling back. He was already getting too close, and he needed to keep his mind clear. Buying Whisper's Edge was an investment that he could simply turn over for a nice profit without risk or develop into an amazing riverfront hot spot. Either option could make him wealthy enough to ensure his mother never had to work another day in her life. And, of course, there was the added attraction of showing his grandfather what he was made of. Tristan wasn't yet sure which way to go but he did know one thing . . . getting emotionally involved never boded well. He'd learned that valuable lesson the hard way.

"I feel the need for a glass of sweet tea. How about you?"

"Yes, tea sounds great." He wasn't really all that thirsty, but it gave Savannah something to do and filled in the sudden silence.

"Feel free to have a seat." She gestured toward the sofa and then turned on her heel.

"Thanks." Tristan sat down on plump floral cushions and rested one elbow on the armrest. But as Savannah made her way over to the small kitchen he couldn't stop himself from watching her progress with male appreciation. *Keep your distance*, slid through his brain. With an inner groan he pulled his gaze away from her cute butt and looked down at the array of magazines on the coffee table. Most of them were about arts and crafts, but several travel magazines caught his attention. He picked one up and was paging through it when she returned with the tea.

"So you like to travel?" he asked as he took the glass from her. He noticed it held a cheerful sprig of mint and a thin slice of lemon. She seemed to like small touches that made something ordinary a little bit special. Nice, he thought, and then checked himself. It was just tea . . .

"I don't know." She sat down on a wingback chair to the left of the sofa.

"You don't know?" Tristan put the magazine down and gave her a quizzical look.

"I haven't had much of a chance to go anywhere." She flicked a glance at the coffee table and sighed. "But a girl can dream." She gave him a slow Southern smile that went straight to his gut. "Don't ya think?"

"Oh . . . sure." Duh, she lived in a small mobile home in a retirement community. He guessed that traveling wasn't part of her budget. He sucked at small talk!

"I've never been anywhere really exotic or foreign." She grinned, clearly not offended. "But I do have a passport that

I'm just itching to use. Kate talked me into getting one. That way I can go to the places on my bucket list."

"Wait. Bucket list? You mean the things to do before you die?"

"Yeah. You know, like the stuff that Jack Nicholson and Morgan Freeman did in that movie where they find out they're going to kick the bucket." She frowned. "But I don't want to skydive. I'm afraid of heights."

"Savannah, how old are you?"

Her face fell a little. "Knocking on the door of thirty," she admitted in a low tone. "And having a bit of trouble with it."

She looked even younger. "I think you have plenty of time left."

"Well . . ." She put her glass down on a coaster and held her hands far apart. "I have a long list of places to go on my bucket list, so it will take a while, especially at the pace I'm able to save up."

Tristan felt a flash of guilt.

She sighed. "I might not make it to every one of them, well, or most of them, but I sure do have fun window shopping in the magazines."

He looked at the coffee table. "You do a lot of window shopping."

Savannah shrugged. "Keeps me out of trouble."

"Yeah, you look like a troublemaker."

She laughed. "I guess part of the interest in seeing the world came from listening to the stories of people who live here." She shook her head. "They might look like Grandma and Grandpa, but boy, oh boy, have I heard some grand adventures from the residents. I want to have some of my own to tell someday."

"What's your number one destination?" he found himself asking.

"Oh that's easy. I won't get to use my passport but I'd love to go to Hawaii!" She leaned over and pointed to a glossy cover. "All of the islands would be cool but Maui in particular. It's called the Magic Isle. They say there are too many waterfalls to count on the road to Hana. That's on the rain forest side of the island." She leaned back in her chair. "Have you been there?"

"To Maui, yes, but not to Hana," he admitted. He had been with his girlfriend at the time and although he'd wanted to explore the island all she had wanted to do was lounge poolside, something they could've done anywhere. Dating her had ended after the trip. Unbidden, the thought ran through his mind that traveling with someone like Savannah would be a blast.

"I bet you've been to a lot of amazing places." She looked at him with interest.

"Not as often as I would have liked," he admitted, and realized that it was true. "Law school was demanding and my work schedule after that was brutal." He took a long swig of the cold tea. "There are a lot of lawyers out there. If you want to succeed you have to put in the time."

"So you made a lot of money but didn't get to enjoy it."

"Pretty much."

"That's too bad," she said with such sincerity that Tristan had to smile. She was such an upbeat, caring person. No wonder the residents loved her. "You need to stop and smell the roses."

"You're right. My mother says the same thing to me."

"Smart woman! So you must be close."

"We are." Tristan nodded slowly.

"That's nice." The wistful look in her eyes made him want to ask about her mother but he refrained.

"So what's on your bucket list, Tristan?" She put a hand to her chest. "I mean, Mr. McMillan."

"Call me Tristan."

She shook her head. "You're my boss."

"Please." He rolled his eyes. "You call Kate by her first name, don't you?"

"Yes, well, okay . . . *Tristan*," she agreed a bit shyly.

"There you go." Tristan was used to bold, assertive

women, but he found Savannah's quiet confidence and softer nature to be a breath of fresh air. And she actually seemed interested in what he was saying. Nice ... he could get used to conversations like this.

"So what about your bucket list? And I don't mean business stuff. I mean fun ... adventure ..." She tilted her head and waited.

"I don't have one."

"You need one," she said firmly. "And they don't have to be big things like Maui. It can be something simple like a book you always wanted to read. Or seeing someone amazing in concert. Stuff like that."

"You've put a lot of thought into this," he said, dodging the question.

"Yeah, I have. And I actually check things off." She smiled at him. "But then it makes me feel as if the end is near so I add more things."

Tristan chuckled at her reasoning but it made a weird kind of sense.

"Don't you believe me?"

"Oh, I believe you," he replied, but then fell silent. Savannah was getting into personal territory and he was enjoying their simple conversation way too much. He glanced down at his watch and winced.

She grabbed the arms of her chair. "Oh my goodness! Your meeting!"

"Yeah, I've got to go."

"I'm so sorry. Me and my nonstop chatter." She pushed up from the chair and hurried over to the dryer. "The bell telling you that the clothes are dry doesn't work anymore," she explained over her shoulder. After opening the small door she reached up and started pulling his clothes out. "Yes, dry. I had them on low so as not to shrink anything." She shook out his shirt and then held it up for him to see. "No wrinkles! I think you're good to go." She folded the clothes into a neat pile and hurried over to him. "I even put a dryer sheet in there so you'll smell nice."

"Thanks," he said briskly, but when their fingers brushed he felt a warm tingle of awareness. He took a quick step away.

"You can change in the bathroom." She pointed to the hallway. "I hope you're not late."

He was but shook his head. "Don't worry. I'll make it."

"Good!" Savannah smiled. "I wouldn't want to keep you from something important."

"Then put your mind at ease," Tristan said before he headed down the short hallway. The rest of her home appeared as neat and tidy as the living area. A small office was to the right with a bathroom on the left. Out of curiosity Tristan paused at her bedroom door and peeked in. He was expecting something dainty and cute but the furnishings were made of smooth, sleek wood with very little clutter except for lots of pillows on the bed. It was almost as if she wanted to clear her head before going to sleep at night. The walls were painted a soft cream that set off the dark wood of the vintage-looking bed. The mound of colorful throw pillows hinted at the playful personality that Tristan already glimpsed in the short time he'd known Savannah.

Not wanting to get caught snooping, he ducked into the bathroom and changed into his dry clothes. After folding the orange towel he finger-combed his hair and headed back out to the living room.

As soon as he entered, Savannah stood up. "I hope the clothes are dry enough?"

"I'm good to go," Tristan assured her, even though he felt hesitant to leave her company. "And smelling fresh."

"After the rain."

"Excuse me?"

"The scent of the dryer sheets. I've always liked that clean, earthy smell," she said. "Here I am going on about nothing when you're in a hurry."

Tristan suddenly didn't want to be in hurry.

She shook her head. "Well, thanks, you know, for coming to my rescue."

"I didn't really save you, remember?"

"That's not the point," she said and then grinned. "Kinda like it's the thought that counts, you know?"

"I'll take being a hero by default."

Savannah's grin faded and she looked up at him with serious eyes. "Hey, you've saved Whisper's Edge. A lot of people are going to sleep easier tonight."

"Savannah—"

She raised a hand of protest. "Nope, don't play it down. I know this is just a glorified trailer park to some but to the residents it's home. It's my home too, for that matter," she added with a soft smile and a catch in her voice. "But I don't want to keep you." She cleared her throat. "You'd better get to that meeting of yours."

"Yes, I should go." Tristan nodded and managed a smile but once he was outside he immediately felt an odd wave of sadness mixed with guilt. *Stupid*, he said to himself. Developing this land would be another boon to the local economy. Jobs would be created and add enticement for more investors to come into the community. Sure, some residents would be displaced, but there had to be a price for progress. Right?

He was still pondering the question when he crossed the street to Whisper's Edge's office.

"So there you are." Kate peered at him over zebra-striped reading glasses. "I was getting worried."

"I had a little mishap," he told her.

Kate pushed her glasses to the top of her head and frowned. "Care to elaborate?"

"I have a feeling you'll hear all about it sometime soon," he said with a slight grin. "In the meantime I came back for my phone."

"Okay, I guess I'll have to be satisfied with that. Will you be back here soon? I have some paperwork and finances I need to go over with you."

Tristan nodded. "Feel free to e-mail anything to me to review but I'll head back here as soon as I get settled. I'm renting a furnished condo down by the baseball stadium so I won't be far away."

"I'll probably do that so you can get a handle on things here." She reached over and picked up his phone. "Here's your phone. It's been making all kinds of noises so you might have missed a message or two . . . or thirty."

"Thanks, Kate. It was nice meeting you," he said and then hurried out the door. But after a few moments he decided he was going to blow off the meeting with the mayor of Cricket Creek. He'd thought he was eager to get the ball rolling with city permits, but now he wasn't so sure. Instead, Tristan decided to head to a local tavern that he'd spotted called Sully's and grab some pub grub and a cold beer. While he ate he could jot down some thoughts and try to clear his head. Tristan had always been a note taker and a list maker, weighing the good, the bad, and the ugly of a given situation. He grinned slightly. And now he had beautiful to add to the mix.

6

Guess Who's Coming to Dinner.

"YOU'VE BEEN AWFULLY QUIET FOR THE PAST FEW DAYS, SAvannah. Something wrong?" Kate tilted her head in question.

"No, everything's all right." Savannah looked up from her computer screen and the expense account she was filling out. After a yawn she said, "I've just had a little trouble sleeping lately."

"Oh, sugar, I know the name of that sad tune. Damned night sweats wake me up and I cannot go back to sleep for the life of me. I've watched some really weird late-night reality TV and bought some strange items on HSN. At three in the mornin' a juicer seemed like somethin' I needed to have."

Savannah chuckled. "So, have you used it?"

"Hell to the no. Damned thing is still in the box. You want it?"

"Maybe." Savannah rarely turned down anything for free.

Kate waved a hand through the air. "Well, then, it's yours. Just remind me to bring it in." She angled her head and said, "But you're too young for night sweats so something else must be keeping you up. What is it, sugar?"

Savannah shrugged. "I don't know. I've just been feeling . . . restless."

"I'm tellin' ya, it's that biological clock of yours ticking away. You've got the big three-oh birthday coming up, you know." She made ticking sounds to prove her point.

Savannah rolled her eyes. "Don't remind me. And don't go throwing a big party, okay? I usually love birthdays but this one has me feeling a little bit uneasy."

"You're hardly over the hill."

Savannah shrugged.

"But you know what? We do need to get out of here more darned often."

"You could be right." She hesitated and then added. "I'm not sure how good of a mama I'd be, having never had one of my own."

"Savannah, you're one of the sweetest, kindest people I know. You'd make a wonderful mother. But look, if there's anything else on your mind feel free to bend my ear."

"Thanks, Kate," Savannah said, but she wasn't about to confess that thoughts of Tristan McMillan had been keeping her up at night. To add insult to injury, when she finally did fall asleep she'd often have dreams about the man. She'd hoped to get a glimpse of him again but had been disappointed thus far. Trying to keep her voice nonchalant she said, "Has Tristan McMillan been back to see you?"

"No, but I sent him some finances to look over." Kate gave her a measuring look. "Why do you ask?"

"Oh . . . I was just curious. You know how I am."

Kate pushed her glasses up and leaned back in her chair. "Handsome devil, isn't he?"

"I suppose," Savannah responded airily, but she could feel heat creep into her cheeks. "If you like that type . . ."

"Sexy as sin and successful? You mean that type?"

Savannah lifted one shoulder and tucked a stray lock of hair behind her ear. "I hadn't really noticed."

"Girl, you need your eyes checked. You need my glasses?" She looked around for them.

"On top of your head." Savannah laughed. "Okay, he's good-looking." *Especially in a towel.* "That's for sure."

"But not your type?"

What was her type? She didn't have one! "I like ... cowboys."

Kate snorted.

"Okay, I made that up." Savannah sighed. "It's a moot point, Kate. Even if I were interested in someone like Tristan, he would never go for a girl like me. Tristan McMillan is ... sophisticated. Super-educated and all that good stuff. I just bet he goes for tall, beautiful blondes with legs that go on forever and manes of straight, amazing hair. A Stacy Keibler kind of woman. Not short, curly-haired redheads with stumps for legs."

"Ahhh, so you've thought about it?"

"That my legs are stumps?"

"Savannah ..."

"Look, I'm just sayin'. The man is waaay out of my league." Savannah raised her palms upward. "And he's my boss to boot!"

Kate shook her head. "You sell yourself way too short."

"I am short."

"Savannah! I'm gonna throw somethin' at you. I've got a few new blonde jokes if that will help."

"You're blond!"

"And waiting to have more fun."

Savannah rolled her eyes. "Look, I'm being realistic."

"Whatever."

When Kate fell silent Savannah thought she was off the hook. She went back to her work.

"It's Friday," Kate suddenly stated.

"I know, Captain Obvious."

"So, what are your plans?"

"Well ..." Savannah looked up. "Trying out making these cute headbands that I saw on Pinterest."

"Now, what in blue blazes is Pinterest?"

"Kinda like Facebook only for crafts, travel, and such.

See, you follow people and pin things you like. You create your own boards that are like a collage. It's fun!"

"Sounds like a blast." Kate rolled her eyes. "Another Internet time suck." Although Savannah had finally convinced Kate to get a Facebook page, she still had that little cartoon head for her profile picture and, like, twelve friends.

"I needed something new for craft day and I was drawing a blank. After the popularity of the flip-flops I had set the bar pretty high."

"Those were fun," Kate admitted.

"Well, I think the headbands will be too. I bought the stuff I needed so I thought I'd give it a whirl tonight."

"You're kidding me."

"No, they're cute. . . . See, you wrap ribbon—"

"No, I mean you're kidding about *that's* how you're spending Friday evening on a gorgeous June night?"

"Well . . . yeah." Her chin came up defiantly. "But I'm eating at Ken and Betty's first."

Kate gave her a deadpan stare and then twirled her index finger in a circle.

"Oh, and Miss Patty might drop by and make a headband. You know, a prototype."

"Savannah . . ."

"You really need to stop saying my name in that weary tone. She said she'd bring a bottle of wine. A big one."

"Sounds like a wild night."

"So what are *you* doing tonight, Kate?" Savannah raised her eyebrows to match her tone.

"Going to Wine and Diner for dinner and then maybe heading over to Sully's to dance the night away."

Savannah's eyebrows fell back down to their rightful position on her face and her jaw dropped open. She clamped it shut and then narrowed her eyes. "Really?"

"Yep." Kate pointed at Savannah. "And you, my friend, are going with me."

"But—"

"No buts! Ken and Betty will get over it and Miss Patty

can drink wine with someone else. You have other plans," Kate said firmly.

"Well . . ." She thought about protesting, but although Kate might nag Savannah about getting out, to be honest, her boss wasn't much better about socializing. She didn't want to keep Kate from having some fun. "What are you going to wear?"

Kate's face lit up. "So you're going?"

"Do I have a choice?"

"No," Kate said even though they both knew that she did. "I think I'll wear black Capri pants and a sweater set. The nights still get a little bit cool near the river."

"True." Savannah started mentally going through her wardrobe. She really needed to stop in Violet's Vintage Clothing up on Main Street. Violet often held back clothing in rich, earthy hues of gold, olive, camel, and spicy orange that she said suited Savannah's deep red hair and green eyes. "I'll bring a light shawl or sweater with me."

"We can walk if that's okay? I don't want to worry about driving if we have one too many. And I hope we do."

"And have hangovers tomorrow?"

"Don't be a Debbie Downer. You're acting as old as the residents."

"Are you kidding? I had to ask the Camden brothers to calm it down the other night. Joy and Etta Mae made Jell-O shots for the last book club meeting! Some of these folks still know how to let their hair down."

Kate laughed. "So you're in?"

"Sure, and I don't mind walking. I've been sitting way too much today. I think when I stand up my butt might be glued to this chair."

"Super."

"No, I'll look silly with the chair stuck to my butt."

Kate laughed. "I meant super that you're going." She glanced at her computer screen and then back at Savannah. "It's almost four o'clock. Let's wrap things up."

"Cool," Savannah said with a smile. "Gives me time to get ready."

Kate leaned forward and gave Savannah a wink. You have some nice curves. Show them off."

Savannah grinned. "Why, thank you, I believe I will."

"There's the attitude! Show off what God gave ya!" Kate stood up and cupped her hands beneath her breasts and swung her hips back and forth. "Come on, girl, join me! Shake that moneymaker!"

Laughing, Savannah stood up and did the little ta-ta-booty dance with Kate just as Ben Bakersfield walked through the doorway.

"Uh, should I come back another time?" He jammed his thumb over his shoulder and looked at them expectantly.

"Noooo!" Savannah dropped her hands and giggled. "Oh, Ben, come on in." While she found the situation hilarious, she was surprised to see her boss blushing to the roots of her short blond hair. "We were just having some fun."

Ben hesitated. "Really, I can come back."

"Oh, get on in here," Kate assured him but looked as if she wanted to fan her face. "We're just goin' on. Havin' a little fun for shits and giggles."

"Okay," Ben said, but continued to look a little uncomfortable.

Savannah liked quiet Ben Bakersfield and was glad Kate had somehow convinced him to be the maintenance man. Not only did Ben do an excellent job at whatever needed doing, but he was also prompt and could be trusted. He tended to be a little bit on the grumpy side, but Savannah could usually make him laugh whether he wanted to or not.

"Now," Kate said in a brisk voice that was at total odds with her ta-ta-booty dance. The color remained high in her cheeks but she sat down on the edge of her desk and folded her hands in a businesslike manner. "What can I do for you?"

"I need to run a few expenses by you. Pavers for the walkway in front of the rec hall for starters."

"Um, Kate, I hate to interrupt, but do you mind if I leave?" Savannah asked. "I want to get ready for our big night."

"Sure, Savannah. Call me when you're ready. We can meet here."

"Hey," Ben said, "I really can come back tomorrow."

Kate waved a dismissive hand at him. "No . . . no, you're fine. Savannah and I are just going to Wine and Diner for a bite to eat and then maybe to Sully's for a bit. No big deal," she added lightly as if it were typical for them to head out on a Friday night. "Maybe do a little dancing."

"Is that what you were practicing?" Ben looked alarmed.

"No!" Kate and Savannah said together.

"Oh . . . all right then," Ben said quietly, and although there wasn't anything in his tone to suggest it, Savannah thought he seemed lonely and she felt sad for him.

"You should come," Savannah suddenly piped up without really considering that she should've asked Kate first. The invitation just sort of popped out of her mouth. Maybe it was because she thought that Ben could use a fun night away from Whisper's Edge. They all could.

Ben looked a little stunned at the suggestion. "Well, I . . . have some work I should do," he said slowly but glanced at Kate as if to get a bead on her reaction.

"Like what?" Kate challenged.

"I . . . uh . . . like being the maintenance man that you talked me into."

When he stuttered, clearly stuck for a valid answer, Kate said, "Oh . . . come with us. We'll talk business and I'll expense it to see what Tristan McMillan is made of. Now that we've been bought we can breathe a sigh of relief and celebrate a little bit. Come on, we deserve it."

"We'd like for you to join us." Savannah gave him an encouraging smile. They both stood there and waited for Ben to answer.

"It's okay if you already have dinner plans," Kate said casually, but Savannah saw a flicker of hope in her eyes. It suddenly occurred to her that Kate might have a thing for Ben. "Do you?"

"No," Ben said in his straightforward way.

"Well then?" Kate asked.

A muscle worked in his jaw for a second and then he said, "Actually, I've got a hankerin' for some of Jessica's pot roast. I haven't been to Wine and Diner in a while."

"Then it's a date," Kate announced, but then looked as if she wanted to swallow her tongue. "Not a *date* . . . date. Just, you know, I'm confirming that you're going with us." She pointed to Savannah and then swung her finger in a circle. "All of us."

"Confirmed," Ben said, and Savannah might have been mistaken but she thought she saw amusement flash in his eyes.

"Great! It's all settled!" Savannah said and waved to them. "I'll see you guys soon."

After calling Miss Patty and Betty to let them know she was going out tonight, Savannah made a beeline for the bathroom. Forty-five minutes later she had showered, shaved her legs, and carefully applied her makeup. Antifrizz products tamed the curly mane that she had scooped back into a loose bun, allowing a few locks to frame her face. She had even painted her toenails a soft, shiny rose. Now came the hard part.

What should she wear?

She walked over to her closet and started trying things on. A floral sundress felt too dressy. The denim skirt showed off too much leg. The white skort worked but she hated the stupid shorts-beneath-the-skirt feeling. "Why did I even buy this?" She wiggled out of it and tossed it onto her bed and groaned when she found the same thing in green. Okay, how about shorts? No, too casual. Jeans? Too tight? "Must have shrunk in the dryer," she said with a laugh.

With a long sigh Savannah looked at the mounds of discarded clothing strewn all over her bed. After a few more minutes, piles started to flow over onto the floor. "Oh, it must be nice to be tall and willowy," she moaned. "I have nothing to wear. You are what you are, Savannah Perry. Just put something on and be done with it," she grumbled. She

didn't usually take such pains with her clothes since she
grew up wearing whatever she was lucky enough to find. To
this day she paid very little attention to fashion trends, and
her favorite place to shop was Violet's Vintage Clothing.
Deep down she knew why she was so flustered today. What
if she ran into Tristan McMillan?

"Stop it!" Savannah said firmly, wishing she at least had
a dog to talk to. Over the many years of living alone she'd
developed a habit of talking to herself or to the television.
"You're not likely to see him and if you do who gives a flying fig?" She lifted her chin and picked up an olive green
camisole top with a built-in bra. The snug material was
meant to slim and she buttoned up a billowy blouse one
shade darker over it. The color flattered her hair and the top
hid a multitude of sins. She tugged on stretchy white skinny
jeans and added a thin silver woven belt she'd found at Violet's. After slipping on strappy sandals with a wedge heel
that, thank God, made her taller—and a matching purse in
gunmetal gray, she felt ready to head out the door.

"Oh . . . dear lord." Her reflection in the mirror showed
a good amount of cleavage peeking above the gauzy blouse.
This just might be showing off a bit more of her curves than
she wanted to! In a panic she turned back to the mound of
clothing but a glance at the digital clock on her nightstand
said that she couldn't take the time to try on anything else.
With a quick intake of breath she grabbed a loosely woven
white crochet poncho that Miss Patty made for her birthday.

"I made one for my granddaughter and she loved it,"
Miss Patty had explained. "I thought you might too. She
said seventies stuff is back in style."

Savannah smiled at the memory. While her social life
outside Whisper's Edge might be lacking, she sure did love
living where people fought over her company instead of
having the horrible feeling of being invisible or worse yet,
feeling in the way. Still, nights could be lonely.

Who was she kidding? Nights *were* lonely.

She gave her appearance one last critical once-over in

the mirror. "It's only dinner and drinks in Cricket Creek," she whispered with a shake of her head. But as she walked out the door into the breezy evening her heart kicked up a notch. Maybe it simply felt good to be dressed up and getting out be but as she strolled toward the front office there seemed to be a hint of anticipation hanging in the air.

Silly, she thought as she waved to people here and there. The Camden brothers whistled and winked as she passed their yard where they grilled steaks and sipped cocktails. "Come on over for a Manhattan, Savannah!"

"Sorry, boys. Have to take a rain check."

"Don't wait for it to rain!" Clyde called out. Or maybe it was Clovis.

"Woof!" Willie looked up from his perch between Miss Patty's feet where she lounged in a white wicker chair while reading a paperback novel on her front porch. One would think that Miss Patty would enjoy cozy mysteries but she favored gritty detective suspense stories. When Savannah waved, Miss Patty called back, "Have fun tonight!"

"Thanks!" Everything was as it should be at Whisper's Edge, making Savannah smile.

But when she rounded the corner and spotted Tristan's sleek sports car parked in front of the office her heart thudded, and butterflies started fluttering in her stomach. She slowed her pace, half hoping he would leave before she reached the front door. Eyeing a big oak tree, she wondered if she could hide behind it. Um . . . no. Not even close. She wanted to see him . . . and then she didn't. A part of Savannah longed to turn on her heel and run back to her quiet little home, to have dinner with Ken and Betty and make headbands with Miss Patty. Her life, she realized, had become easy . . . *safe* and she liked the comfort of consistency.

But she wasn't a coward. So Savannah put one wedged sandal in front of the other and willed herself not to stammer and blush in front of Tristan. Perhaps he was simply dropping something off or bringing the paperwork over that Kate had given him. Surely he wouldn't linger long and would go on about his business.

As she approached the front door Savannah could hear voices filtering through the open window. Kate made one of her usual wisecracks followed by two sets of deep male mirth. Savannah had to smile. Kate could make anyone laugh. She had managed to keep her sense of humor intact through the recent tough times at Whisper's Edge.

Relax, Savannah told herself as she opened the front door and walked inside.

"There you are," Kate said and pressed a cold Corona with a jaunty lime sticking out of the top into Savannah's hand. "I was just getting ready to call you."

"I couldn't decide what to wear," Savannah answered honestly. After poking the lime down the neck of her bottle she gave a shy nod to Tristan and Ben.

"Well, that olive shade of green suits you." Kate nodded with approval. "You look great."

"So do you." Savannah smiled before taking a swig of her beer.

"I clean up well," Kate said with a chuckle. As promised, she wore the black Capri pants and had opted for a sweater set in a soft shade of lavender. Kate's hair sported a bit more fluff than usual and a soft shade of coral lipstick brightened her normally low-key makeup. Kate was a naturally pretty woman on any given day but tonight she looked sassy and stunning in a Sharon Stone kind of way. Surely Ben thought so too? If Ben's lingering glances were any indication, he was well aware of Kate's beauty. "Tristan stopped over to bring me some paperwork he had been going over."

"Oh," Savannah said and wished she could think of something clever to say. "I hope you've gotten a chance to see some of the town this week?"

"Not really. I've been pretty busy," Tristan answered. "I finally just shut my laptop and got out of the condo. It's too nice of an evening to work."

"I agree." Savannah nodded and then took another swig of her Corona.

"Me too," Kate chimed in. "That's why Tristan decided to come out on the town with us."

Savannah tried to swallow her beer but of course the knowledge that Tristan was coming along, making this sort of like a double date sent the swallow down the wrong pipe. To her horror she started sputtering and coughing. She wasn't sure but a piece of lime pulp might have flown out of her mouth. Dear God, she hoped beer didn't come running out of her nose.

"Are you all right?" Tristan asked, rushing over to her side, but seeming to be at a loss as to what to do.

"Give her a pat on the back," Kate instructed.

"Okay," Tristan said and gently patted between Savannah's shoulder blades. "Better?"

When Savannah nodded, Tristan removed his hand but the tingle of his touch remained. She immediately missed the warm, soothing way he was rubbing her back and thought about adding another round of coughing. "Thanks." She accepted the tissue offered to her by Ben and dabbed her mouth in case any of the lime pulp was stuck to her generous application of lip gloss. "Wrong pipe."

"It happens," Tristan said with a grin. "Even though we really only have one pipe."

"For some reason I feel the need to make a fool out of myself whenever you're near."

Tristan tossed back his head and laughed. "I have to admit that there's never a dull moment around you, Savannah."

"You mean that in a good way, right?" she asked with another little cough.

7

Dangerous Territory

"OF COURSE, SAVANNAH . . ." TRISTAN DREW OUT HER NAME and widened his eyes in mock innocence. "I enjoy coming to your rescue for no real reason."

"At least you didn't get wet this time," Kate pointed out before tilting her Corona up to her lips.

"Or naked," Tristan added. *Oh crap, why did I say that?*

"Naked!" Kate swung around to face him so fast that droplets of moisture flew from her bottle.

"Tristan!" Savannah sputtered. His comment brought two spots of color to her cheeks.

"What?" He tried to keep things light and teasing in order to hide the effect she was having on him. When he'd patted her back the feel of her warm skin beneath the thin fabric of her blouse sent a hot jolt of awareness humming through his veins, taking him by surprise. If a mere touch could do that what would it be like to have her in his arms?

"Oh, sugar, don't leave us hanging," Kate pleaded.

"I tugged a towel off him while I was drying his clothes."

"Well, now." Kate wiggled her eyebrows.

"It was because he had a handful of my panties."

"That explains a lot." Kate rubbed her hands together and shot Tristan a look. "This is gettin' good."

"Un, maybe we shouldn't be discussing this," Ben said slowly but Kate shushed him.

"No, wait . . . I wasn't *wearing* them," Savannah explained.

"Like I said," Ben tried again.

"You sly dog." Kate turned and raised a palm at Savannah. "No wonder you yanked his towel off. High five."

Savannah automatically started to high-five Kate but then drew her hand back. "It was an ac-ci-*dent*." She looked imploringly at Tristan.

"It was," he admitted.

"Ohh, Tristan, have a heart and tell them what happened!" Savannah pleaded.

"Okaaay." Tristan chuckled and then briefly explained what really transpired. "Totally embarrassing, but innocent," he finished.

"Thank you!" Savannah said with a sigh.

"I'm just messing with ya," Tristan promised in a bigbrother tone, but the sight of her amazing breasts peeking out over the silky fabric had him feeling anything but brotherly. He wasn't the teasing type but Savannah had a knack for bringing out a playful side in him that he hadn't known was there until now. His mother would be stunned. His mother would also adore Savannah.

Stop! This line of thinking was getting him into the dangerous territory that he wanted to avoid. He was in Cricket Creek to prove himself as a businessman, not for romance or making friends.

"Why does everybody like to see me get worked up?" Savannah raised her hands upward.

"Because it's so easy and so much fun," Kate replied, drawing laughs from them all. "I knew the story was going to be something like it turned out to be or I wouldn't have egged you on. Sugar, I know you better than that." She looked at

Tristan. "And I really shouldn't be going on like that with my boss." She held up her bottle. "Blame it on the beer."

"We're all off the clock," Tristan assured them. "And trust me, I could use a fun night out."

"Oh boy." Savannah shook her head. "Tristan, you're being an enabler. Kate will be unstoppable."

"You're in for it now." Kate laughed. "But listen, we really should head up to Wine and Diner. Fridays can get busy in Cricket Creek, especially on a gorgeous night like this. Let's finish our drinks and head on up the road," Kate suggested.

Tristan nodded but thought maybe he should think of an excuse to bow out. He shouldn't have agreed to come with them, but after sitting all day, he'd needed fresh air and wanted some company. Friday nights back in Cincinnati meant happy hour and laughter, and he just didn't feel like sitting alone one more night. He'd used the excuse of bringing paperwork to Kate to get him out the door. If he was being honest he had been hoping to run into Savannah, and the unexpected invitation to join them was too hard to resist.

Still, he was already enjoying himself way too much. He felt more at ease and relaxed than he'd been in a long time . . . not good when he needed to make some serious business decisions in the very near future. Becoming close to these people, or romantically involved with Savannah, could potentially cloud his clear thinking.

As they walked out the door he told himself to simply enjoy the warm summer evening, but after tonight he vowed to find entertainment in Cricket Creek that was not connected to Whisper's Edge.

"I just love late spring when everything is in full bloom," Savannah said as they strolled through the community.

"Yeah, I enjoy it too. I always wanted to have a few tomato plants on my terrace but never seemed to find the time."

"Really? I started a garden club and give awards for the best something or other every week." She chuckled. "Boy, oh boy, these ladies are competitive." She pointed to planters laden with blooms. "Best flower pots caused quite a stir. Next week it's hanging baskets. So be prepared to see lots of baskets swinging from front porches," she said with a grin, and it was damned near impossible not to grin back. "Each basket bigger than the one before."

"Looks like you'll be installing lots of heavy-duty hooks," Kate said to Ben.

"Yeah, having a flower pot fall on someone's head would not be a good thing," he said.

"Maybe you should have size limits," Kate suggested.

"That rule would be broken for sure," Savannah said.

"I'll keep an eye on things," Ben promised as they turned the corner.

It didn't help Tristan's resolve when the narrow sidewalk outside Whisper's Edge forced him to fall into step side by side with Savannah when Ben and Kate took the lead. While he sure sucked at small talk, Savannah filled in that gap with ease. Her bubbly personality made it difficult to remain detached.

"The river looks so pretty tonight. There's something soothing about the water, don't you think?"

"Yeah," Tristan agreed. "I've always enjoyed boating."

"Do you have one?"

"I had a cabin cruiser for a while but my schedule was so busy that I finally sold it."

"Oh, that's too bad."

Tristan shrugged. "Not really. I have friends with boats and it sure is a lot less hassle to be a passenger rather than the captain."

"Never thought of it that way but I guess you're right. But I do think it would be cool to own a boat."

"Maybe you will someday."

Savannah rolled her eyes. "Not likely, but I do get the chance to go out with some of the residents. Several of them have boats and I like to drop a line in the water every now and then. We usually have a fishing tournament or two to raise money for charity."

Tristan nodded. "That's very commendable."

"Yeah, I have a running list of local charities that need volunteers. Keeping active is important for the physical and mental health of the residents. So many people retire and think it's going to be all rosy but they soon get bored."

"Makes perfect sense."

"I read somewhere that happy people are those who wake up with a sense of purpose." She shrugged. "I try to have activities scheduled that make them want to put their feet on the floor in the morning and get the day started. And, of course, helping the community is always a good thing. Even though Cricket Creek is thriving, there are still plenty of people in need."

"A win-win situation," he commented lightly but he couldn't help but be impressed. While he had a lot more formal education than Savannah did, she had a quiet confidence that must come from living and learning on her own terms.

"I know how it feels to be down and out," Savannah stated simply, and then shrugged. "I've come a long way and I count my blessings every day."

Tristan thought of her modest home and the pride she so obviously took in it and had the sudden urge to take her hand and kiss it. He had never had the urge to do such a thing . . . *ever* and it shook him up a little bit.

"I guess this small-town atmosphere is a far cry from city living." She glanced up at him in question.

"Yes and no. The view from the condo I'm renting is similar to the one I lived in back in Cincinnati. My terrace overlooked the Ohio River and Great American Ballpark. The smaller city across the river in Covington in Kentucky actually reminds me a little bit of what I've seen of Cricket Creek. Old buildings, lots of shops and restaurants."

"But Cincinnati was full of skyscrapers, right?"

"True. My office was located in a beautiful old building called the Carew Tower. It was built back in 1930 and is actually on the list of Historic Landmarks. The art deco architecture was used as a model for the Empire State Building."

"Wow, that's pretty darned cool."

"Yeah, I was too young to remember but my mom said that back in the 1980s there was a giant inflatable gorilla hanging from the side of the Carew Tower."

"Ah! I get it! King Kong! Somebody on city council had a sense of humor. Too funny."

"The inside is pretty sweet too."

"Wow, I bet."

"Yeah, the cost to build it was over thirty million, which was a fortune back then. The metalwork and lights are old school and gorgeous, especially on the first three floors. It would have been even more amazing but the building was finished right before the stock market crash that led to the Great Depression . . . and I am probably boring you to tears."

Savannah placed a hand on his arm. "Not at all. Did you forget that I want to travel and see the world? I'm sure the building is amazing and I'd love to see it."

The thought flashed through his mind that he'd love to take her there.

"Of course, I'd probably walk around with my jaw hanging open wide enough to catch flies."

Tristan laughed. "Well, I studied history as my prelaw major so I enjoy reading the background of just about anything. When you know the history of something I think it makes it all the more interesting."

"We can learn from our past, for sure," she said, but her smile faded a bit, making Tristan wonder what was going through her mind. He remembered asking her about where she was from and her answer had been cryptic. "If walls could talk, huh?"

"Wow . . ." he said and then immediately wished he hadn't said that out loud.

"Wow . . . what?" She looked at him when they stopped at a curb. Ben and Kate were in deep discussion about the shade of brick pavers to use and didn't turn around to save him from answering.

"Nothing, it's just that I think about that a lot. When I'm in a historical building I always envision what it would have been like to have been there in the heyday." Tristan didn't think he had ever divulged that to anyone. "They have this thing in Cincinnati every so many years called Tall Stacks where the river is flooded with steamboats. Makes me wonder what it would have been like to have lived back then." He chuckled, a little bit embarrassed at his admission. "I guess my view of the river makes my imagination run wild."

"Hey, no, I understand completely. Books and magazines do that for me as well." She reached out and touched his arm again. "They transport me to that place and time, even if it's fiction. Books are my escape. They always have been."

"So what do you like to read?" he asked as they started walking again. The small talk that he sucked at started coming easier.

"Oh, I read a bit of everything. I'm a regular at the local library and there's a new and used local bookstore that recently reopened up in town."

"And your favorite genre?"

She caught her bottom lip between her teeth, but then said, "Romance novels."

Tristan raised his eyebrows. "The kind with those racy covers?"

"Don't judge a book by its cover," she warned and gave his side a gentle nudge with her elbow.

"Fair enough, so what do you like about romance novels?"

"That there is always hope," she answered simply.

"Hope about what?" He knew he should be pulling back but Savannah was sucking him in with her sweetness.

Savannah looked away and at first he didn't think she was going to answer. "Well, I suppose it's the hope that against all odds, love will win in the end." She gave him a jerky shrug. "I know. I'm silly."

"No." Tristan pulled up short, even though Kate and Ben kept walking. "There's nothing silly about believing in something, Savannah."

"So . . ." She looked up from the ground that she was staring at and he knew what was coming. "Do you believe?"

"In Santa?" He tried to joke but she shook her head.

"No, silly, in fairy-tale endings. You know, happily ever after."

"I . . ." He had heard the saying about drowning in someone's eyes and thought it was a bunch of bull but damned if he wasn't feeling it right now. He swallowed. He knew that she was really asking if he believed in everlasting love. "Honestly, I've dated here and there but I've been too focused on my career to get involved in a serious relationship."

"That's not what I was asking, Mr. Lawyer. You sure are good at dodging questions."

"Guilty." Ah, she was on to his tactics. He started walking slowly, hoping she'd give it up. After his brief silence she did.

"Oh, listen to me goin' on about fairy tales. You must think I've got my head stuck in the clouds."

"Not at all. You're way too short."

"Ha-ha," she said and wrinkled her nose at him.

"I'm joking. Truthfully, I think you're very levelheaded."

"You're being too kind. Well, in any case, please forgive my curious nature. It tends to get me into trouble." She started walking at a quicker pace.

Tristan fell into faster step beside her. They had almost caught up with Ben and Kate when she stopped in her tracks so fast that he was surprised there weren't skid marks on the sidewalk.

"I wasn't hitting on you or anything."

Once again she had him at a loss for words. Nothing that came out of her mouth was expected. As a lawyer, Tristan was always careful about how he worded things. Her honestly and candor took him by surprise. "Okay . . ." He wasn't quite sure how to respond.

"I'm just sayin'."

"I didn't think that you were hitting on me, Savannah."

"Good. Since you're my boss and everything."

He didn't quite know what the "everything" part meant but he simply nodded. "I understand."

"I'll just be quiet now," she said and started walking again. Of course her resolve didn't stay strong for very long. Not that he wanted it to. But this time instead of asking anything remotely personal she became his tour guide for Cricket Creek. "I didn't grow up here but I've come to love Main Street. Over there is Grammar's Bakery. Cheese Danish to die for. Oh, and the butter cookies. Rumor has it that they are Noah Falcon's favorite and it was his first stop when he returned to Cricket Creek."

"Yeah, he's been the pride and joy of this town for a long time. Small-town boy makes it to the major leagues. I do remember that. And my mom watched him on some soap opera."

"Yeah!" Savannah pointed across the street to a theater with an old-fashioned marquee. "Noah came back here after he was killed off on the soap opera and starred in a play written by Madison Robinson, daughter of Jessica, who owns Wine and Diner. He fell in love with his costar Olivia Lawson, a local English teacher."

"Really?" Noah was a talented player that he'd admired as a kid. The summer Tristan had stayed here his grandfather bragged about Noah Falcon being from Cricket Creek.

Savannah leaned in as if she were telling a huge secret. "Olivia tutored him in high school! She had a crush on him way back then, and when he found out she'd never been asked to the prom the entire school re-created her prom night for her, and Noah was her date. Is that not the most romantic thing ev-er?"

"Must have taken some doing."

Savannah nodded. "The whole school and most of the town was in on the secret." Savannah put her hand to her chest. "I saw the play they were in together. Well, the entire town did and I cried like a baby. So did Kate!" she called loud enough for Kate to hear.

Kate stopped and turned around. "What did I do?"

"Cried at *Just One Thing*, the play that Olivia and Noah starred in."

"I did not!"

"I'm guessing it was allergies," Ben wanted to know.

"Most likely," Kate said with a lift of her chin.

"She did," Savannah said in a stage whisper.

Tristan laughed. They caught up to Kate and Ben, who were looking in the window of a local hardware store.

"Is that the kind of leaf blower you were talking about?" Kate pointed inside the store.

"Yep." Ben nodded. "I tried to repair the old one again but without any luck this time. I can rake, but it will take me a lot longer and since you pay me by the hour it makes sense to get a new blower, Kate."

The conversation added another shot of guilt to Tristan's mounting list. The finances given to him by Kate showed that she had been running Whisper's Edge on a shoestring, robbing Peter to pay Paul and doing some creative shuffling around to keep the community from going under. No one, including Savannah, had received a raise in several years, and after an assistant had to be let go, Savannah had had to take on that position along with her other duties. "Was a leaf blower on the list of equipment you requested, Kate?"

"I'm afraid not," she replied with a sigh.

"Well, add it." The words came out of Tristan's mouth even though he knew it was pointless to purchase equipment for property he planned to either sell or develop. He just couldn't help himself.

"My wish list is already pretty long," Kate reminded him.

"I understand, but Ben has a good point. It will pay for itself in a short time frame."

"Thanks, Tristan," Kate responded with a grateful smile.

"It's no big deal." "For He's a Jolly Good Fellow" started playing in his head.

Damn. This was going to be a lot tougher than he ever imagined.

8

Angel Food Cake

"WHY DID THE BLONDE SPEND ALL DAY IN THE SHOWER?" Kate asked when they stopped to wait for the traffic light to turn red.

"I don't know," Ben replied and tried not to smile. He was suddenly glad that he'd made the decision to come along.

"Savannah?"

"Hey, I'm a redhead."

Kate arched an eyebrow at Tristan, who shrugged. "The shampoo bottle said 'rinse, lather, repeat.'"

"Groan," Savannah said but Tristan and Ben both chuckled.

"Okay, why did the blonde climb up on the roof?" Kate asked and waited. "Ben?"

He shook his head. "You got me."

"She heard that drinks were on the house."

Ben laughed hard at that one. "Are you sure these jokes are politically correct?"

"Do you seriously think it matters to me?" Kate asked.

"No." Ben kept laughing. He couldn't remember the last

time he had felt this good. *When Anna was alive*, slammed against his good mood. Ben braced himself for the hot pain of his loss, followed sharply by guilt for smiling, but before the feeling seeped into his bones, Kate nudged him.

"Okay, one more," Kate announced with a grin.

Savannah moaned. "Will this light ev-*er* change?"

Kate ignored her. "Why was the blonde excited when she finished the jigsaw puzzle in four days?"

"Because the box said four to six years," Savannah answered with a roll of her eyes, but Ben and Tristan laughed again. "You already told that one to me."

"Well . . ." Kate pursed her lips. "How about this one, smarty-pants? What do you call a redhead with an attitude? Well, Savannah? Huh?"

"I don't know."

"Normal," Kate said smugly just as the light changed.

"Very funny," Savannah said but grinned.

"Why do you tell blonde jokes when you're a blonde?" Ben asked.

"Because she's a blonde," Tristan said and they all laughed again.

"Hey, I know plenty of lawyer jokes too." Kate arched an eyebrow at him.

"Probably not one that I haven't heard before," Tristan responded with a sigh. "I have pretty thick skin so fire away," he challenged as they approached the entrance to Wine and Diner.

"Why don't sharks attack lawyers?" Kate wanted to know.

"Professional courtesy," Tristan answered in a bored tone.

"You're no fun," Kate said glumly.

"Because he's a lawyer," Savannah quipped but then her eyes rounded. "Oh, that wasn't a one-liner, was it?"

"It is now," Ben said and they all laughed once more. The comment came out naturally but Kate looked at him with a bit of surprise.

"Good one," Kate conceded.

"I have my moments."

"You don't say . . ." When Kate looked at him with raised eyebrows, he shrugged.

"Not a whole lot," Ben quipped and she smiled at his unexpected show of humor. "Maybe we shouldn't rattle our new boss's cage," he said loud enough for Tristan to hear.

"Like I said, my skin is thick," Tristan assured him.

They might not believe it, Ben thought, but he used to be a happy-go-lucky kind of guy, living for the day. He labored with his hands, made an honest living working up a sweat, and then came home to a woman he adored. He loved to fish, and Anna often came with him in his boat and read endless novels, bird-watched, and sometimes knitted. It might sound like a line in a country song but to Ben, it didn't get any better than that. The only snag was that he and Anna had wished for children that never came. In return they became the aunt and uncle that their nieces and nephew adored. But Anna's untimely death sucked the life right out of him. Unable to live in the home they once shared, Ben had sold everything, hit the road, and ended up in Cricket Creek, Kentucky, where he fished and mostly kept to himself.

Until now.

"You're in luck," Kate said, bringing Ben out of his thoughts. She pointed to a chalkboard easel perched beneath an awning leading to the front door of Wine and Diner. "Jessica's pot roast is tonight's special. Comes with glazed carrots and mashed potatoes. I just might have to order that too."

"Sounds delicious," Savannah agreed, "but I have chicken potpie on my mind. Jessica's crust simply melts in your mouth," she gushed to Tristan. "I just hope I can save room for dessert."

Tristan nodded. "I've had both breakfast and lunch here but I've wanted to try dinner. I think I remember when this used to be called Myra's Diner?"

"Myra is Jessica's aunt," Savannah explained. "During

the tough economic times here in Cricket Creek the diner started to struggle. Jessica came back from where she was a chef in some fancy Chicago restaurant to help Myra save her restaurant. She was only supposed to stay here for a while but fell in love with Ty McKenna, manager of the Cougars, and the rest, as they say, is history."

"They have a little toddler that's cute as a button," Kate added and then looked at Ben. "I do believe his name is Benjamin too!"

"Oh ..." Tristan said as if he were trying to digest all of the information.

Kate chuckled. "Tristan, this is a small town. Everybody knows everything about everybody."

"I'm starting to get that," Tristan said. "I was lucky to know the names of my neighbors in my complex much less their pasts."

"Welcome back to Cricket Creek," Kate said and winked at him

"After you." Ben opened the door for Kate to enter. He suddenly wanted to put his hand at the small of her back and usher her in but he didn't dare. Instead, he held the door for Tristan and Savannah as well and then followed them inside. For once he wouldn't be asking for a table for one or sitting at the counter trying to avoid small talk.

Bella, the perky little hostess, gave them a bright smile. "Well, hey there, Kate. I haven't seen you in a while. How many?"

"There are four of us," Kate answered. She pointed at the necklace Bella wore. "One of your mother's creations?"

Bella lifted the bold coral and silver necklace from her chest. "Yes, Designs by Diamante is doing fabulous. In fact, Mom is having a difficult time keeping up with the demand. I help her out when I'm not working here or watching Logan play baseball, but unfortunately I didn't get the creative gene."

"Good to hear business is brisk but I'm not surprised," Kate said. "I really need to pop in there soon."

"I'm sure she would enjoy that," Bella said. "So, will it be inside or outside tonight?"

"Anyone have a preference?" Kate asked.

"I'll let you ladies decide," Ben replied. "If that's okay with you, Tristan?"

"Sure, I'm fine either way," Tristan replied, but Ben noticed that he looked at Savannah in question. Damn, this was feeling more and more like a double date.

Bella picked up four menus. "It's gorgeous outside with no wait, if that helps you make your decision."

"I enjoy dining outdoors," Savannah said. "And the patio is so pretty this time of year."

"Sounds like the patio?" Bella asked. After the nods of agreement she said, "Oh, and we will have some live music later this evening. A duo from Lexington. They're fantastic. We can even push back tables to make a dance floor if you're so inclined."

Ben couldn't help it. "Well, ladies, you could do an encore of your earlier dance routine."

"Do I want to see this dance?" Tristan asked.

"Um . . . no," Savannah said but Kate grinned. "I think we'll pass."

"Ya never know. The night is young," Kate warned as they followed Bella through the double doors out to the outdoor seating.

"Oh boy," Ben said with a slow shake of his head. For a moment he felt like his old fun-loving self. "Heaven help us," he added as they sat down, but the word *heaven* reverberated in his head. Was Anna watching? He used to feel her presence almost like a tangible thing and hear her lovely laughter as if she were in the room with him. Sometimes, he swore he could smell her perfume and feel the warmth of her smile. But lately he found himself going for days without thinking of her and it frightened him. Would he forget what she looked like? Sounded like? Would the memories fade and curl up on the edges like old photographs?

"Ben?" Kate asked softly. "Bella wanted to know if she could go ahead and take our drink order."

"Oh ... I ..." Ben stuttered and glanced up at Bella. "Sorry. My mind drifted away there for a second. I'll have a Manhattan," he said, hoping the strong cocktail would dull the sudden shot of sadness.

"No problem! Happens to me all the time," Bella said with an understanding wave of her hand. "Especially at the end of a long week. But hey, it's Friday"—she looked at her watch "and still happy hour for twenty more minutes!"

"I say we suck 'em up," Kate announced and ordered a glass of house Chardonnay.

"Will I like that?" Savannah wanted to know, "I'm not much of a wine drinker," she explained with an apologetic little wince.

"Maybe you should give it a try," Tristan said. "Dinner is on me tonight, so have some fun exploring new things."

"Thanks, I think I'll try the wine," Savannah declared with a determined lift of her chin. Ben had to grin. He had grown fond of Savannah over the past few years. Her sweet smile and easy demeanor had often chased away his sorrow for at least a little while. She was one of the few people Ben actually would talk to for more than a few minutes. He could also sense that although Savannah was beloved throughout Whisper's Edge, there was loneliness beneath her cheerful exterior.

"Bring the ladies a bottle to share," Tristan requested. "Do you have a recommendation? The only one I really know is Kendall Jackson."

"Jessica is always adding something new and she was just talking about the Bogle Vineyards from California. The Chardonnay is rich and buttery with a lime finish." Bella put a hand to her chest. "I personally like a new wine from Cupcake Vineyards called Angel Food."

"Ladies?" Tristan asked, but Ben noticed that his gaze once again landed on Savannah and lingered. Oh, it had been a long time, but Ben recognized that look. If he wasn't mistaken, the boy was smitten.

"Oh, the Angel Food sounds scrumptious," Savannah said and Bella nodded. "Good choice."

"For you?" Bella asked Tristan.

"Well, since we're walking I think I'll join Ben with a Manhattan, Woodford Reserve, please. I enjoy an old-school cocktail once in a while."

"Nice choice. We only serve top-shelf bourbon here," Bella told them. "Jessica's daughter, Madison, is bartending tonight. She steps in once in a while and loves to mix drinks. The last time she was at Sully's she challenged Pete to a best martini competition." Bella shook her head and chuckled. "That would be something to behold! Your server will be back with your orders in a few minutes. Hope you enjoy your evening."

"Thanks for treating us to dinner," Kate said, but then winced. "Although, I had considered expensing it, anyway."

"I would have approved it," Tristan said. "After looking over the finances, I have to say that my hat's off to you, Kate. Whisper's Edge is still up and running largely due to your ingenuity."

"Thanks, Tristan," Kate said but shook it off. "We're pretty tough here in Cricket Creek. We don't give up without a fight. Whisper's Edge is important to a lot of people. It's definitely worth saving."

Ben watched Kate's eyes get a little misty and had the urge to reach over and cover her hand with his. It hit him hard that he missed tender moments like this in life, but he toyed with his napkin instead. Ben also noticed that her comment made something flicker in Tristan's eyes. Tristan McMillan seemed like a straight-up kind of guy, but Ben had a sudden inkling that there just might be something more to his buying Whisper's Edge than he was letting on. The retirement community wasn't exactly a cash cow, but Ben just bet that the riverfront property itself must be worth a mint with the addition of the nearby baseball park, coupled with the new strip mall. He certainly hoped he was wrong. But before he could think much more about it their server came over with the bottle of wine.

"Hey there, I'm Sunny and I'll be your server on this lovely night." She flashed them a smile as bright as her name. "I have a bottle of wine for the ladies and the Manhattans are coming right up." She showed the bottle to Savannah. "This is what you ordered, right?" After Savannah nodded, Sunny took a corkscrew out of her apron and deftly opened the bottle. She then poured a small amount into Savannah's glass. When Savannah's eyes widened a bit Sunny said, "Try it, please?"

"Oh . . . okay." When Savannah swallowed hard, Ben had to hide his grin.

Ben remembered being green around the ears like that when he'd first started dating Anna. She had come from an upper class family and knew about all that stuff. Ben was the son of a construction worker and didn't know a good wine from a hole in the ground but he had quickly learned. Ben believed that when you loved someone you learned to enjoy their favorite things too. He learned to appreciate a fine wine, and Anna went fishing.

Savannah looked at Tristan. "Maybe you should do the . . . uh . . . honors."

Tristan shook his head. "It's for you to decide if you like it or not, Savannah."

Ben watched the exchange with a lump in his throat. He remembered feeling like a fish out of water in this kind of situation but Anna always put him at ease until he eventually felt comfortable in any setting. He leaned forward and said, "Savannah, my wife loved her wine and I watched her do this many a time. She called them the five S steps . . . see, swirl, sniff, sip, and savor."

"Oh . . . so what do I do?"

"Pick up the glass. Look at the wine," Ben instructed.

Savannah nodded. "Pretty? Now what?"

"Swirl the glass to get the aroma going and then take a deep sniff."

Savannah obeyed but then appeared confused.

"What did you smell?" Ben asked.

"Um . . ." After sniffing again Savannah tilted her head and frowned but then her eyebrows shot upward. "Oh . . . apples? Like, tart ones."

"Granny Smith," Kate supplied.

"Yes!" Clearly warming up to the process, Savannah took another sniff. "Oh . . . ah, vanilla! Yes, definitely vanilla!" Her eyes rounded. "Wow and it does remind me a bit of the sweet smell of Angel Food cake. Amazing! Can I take a sip now?" She looked up at Sunny, who stood there patiently and nodded. Ben thought it was cute that Savannah looked at everybody for a moment, building the anticipation before taking a sip. After she did, Savannah shook her head. "Well, now . . . the wine does have the subtle flavor of tart baked apples and vanilla but with a toasty kind of aftertaste, you know?"

"So, you approve?" Sunny asked with a slight smile.

"Yes!" Savannah said with a laugh. "I guess I wasn't supposed to take so darned long, huh?"

"Not at all." Ben shook his head while Sunny poured more Angel Food into Savannah's glass and then filled Kate's. "It's part of the fun."

Kate looked at Ben with a sense of wonder. "You surprise me once again."

"I'll bring a bucket of ice and those Manhattans," Sunny promised.

Savannah grinned. "Well, that was pretty darned cool." She took another sip and rolled it around on her tongue.

"My mother enjoys attending wine tastings," Tristan said. "Personally, I'm more of a craft beer kind of guy but I can see where it would be interesting."

"Kate, I think we should do wine tasting at Whisper's Edge." Savannah looked at Ben. "You and Kate need to go shopping for some wines. I wouldn't know what in the world I was doing. We can charge a cover fee and have, you know, cheese and crackers and all that stuff. What do you think?" she turned to Kate and asked.

"I think it's a great idea, Savannah. It's something different, that's for sure. Maybe you could put the word out and see if there's any interest," Kate said and then turned to Tristan. "Do you have any thoughts?"

Tristan waited while Sunny delivered their drinks and topped off the glasses of wine. "I guess you'll need a few minutes to look over the menu or would you like to start off with an appetizer first."

"The artichoke and spinach dip is good," Ben said, drawing a surprised look from Kate. "What?" he asked her with a grin.

"I had you pegged for a buffalo wings kind of guy," Kate answered.

"Actually, I am," Ben admitted. "But I guess there's more to me than meets the eye."

"Then we should share an order of both," Tristan said with a nod to Sunny.

"Coming right up," Sunny said and hurried off to place the order.

Over appetizers they chatted about the wine-tasting idea. Ben felt himself becoming more relaxed and joined in by suggesting that they add craft-beer tasting to please the men who might not enjoy sampling wine.

"I agree," Tristan said with a nod. "And we'll have to do some sampling of our own first."

"For the sake of the event of course," Ben said after scooping up some dip with a chunk of pita bread. He tried to convince himself that it was the Manhattan that loosened his tongue but in truth he knew it had a lot to do with the company.

"We'll do a raffle for charity," Savannah said. "I'll hit up Mia Monroe over at the Cougars' front office. I haven't begged for baseball tickets in a while."

"Didn't her daddy marry Bella's mama?" Kate asked.

Savannah took a sip of her wine and then nodded. "I heard it was an autumn wedding held right here beneath that gazebo. It must have been gorgeous. Cricket Creek is so pretty in the fall."

"I have to agree with you," Kate said with a glance toward the large gazebo at the far end of the patio.

Sunny returned to refill the wineglasses and take the entrée orders. They all opted for the pot roast special except for Savannah, who was determined to have her potpie. After it arrived conversation continued in between bites and moans of appreciation for the food.

"I remember eating a burger and fries here with my mother when I was a kid," Tristan said, but then shook his head. "But wow, this food is off-the-charts good."

Savannah nodded. "I think Guy Fieri should pay Wine and Diner a visit."

"Who is he?" Tristan asked.

"Host of *Diners, Drive-Ins and Dives*," Ben explained and got another raised-eyebrow look from Kate.

"Who knew that you were such a foodie?" Kate asked with a shake of her head.

Ben chuckled. "What can I say? I like to eat." When he reached for his glass of water his elbow brushed against Kate's arm. It was just an innocent touch, not even against skin, but the soft material of her sweater sent a shot of male longing straight through him. He sucked in a breath, trying to clear his head but the subtle scent of her perfume befuddled him further. Ben took a quick swallow of the cold water hoping to cool his ardor but when he moved in his seat, damned if his leg didn't press against hers.

He waited to feel guilty but he didn't. He felt alive.

If she noticed, Kate didn't react or at least she did a damned good job of hiding it. Of course, perhaps the attraction was one-sided. The only indication that she felt anything was that while Tristan and Savannah chatted about flying pigs of all things, Kate remained silent and seemed to be concentrating on cutting her pot roast. Throwing caution to the wind, Ben decided to test the water and, this time, with his heart pounding, he subtly allowed his leg to brush up against hers. But as soon as he did it, he felt silly and immediately pulled his leg away from any and all contact.

What in the hell was he doing? He decided to concentrate on his food as well but risked a sideways glance at Kate. How was it that he had never noticed how pretty she was? Sassy, funny . . . smart but never pretty.

And sexy as hell.

The realization was more intoxicating than the bourbon in his Manhattan.

When the sun sank lower in the sky, shadows danced on the brick wall opposite of where they sat. Suddenly, twinkling lights woven through several trees came on and illuminated the patio with a soft glow. Candles flickered in the evening breeze, which carried a hint of the nearby river and sweet summer blossoms. As Bella promised, a duo set up shop in the far corner.

The tall, gorgeous woman flipped her long dark hair over her shoulder. "Welcome to Wine and Diner!" she announced in a smoky voice that sounded destined for singing. "I'm Rita and this is my husband, Rick. We're the Watsons but we go by simply Rick and Rita. We take requests and we'd love to see y'all get up and dance." Rita nodded to Rick on the keyboard and grabbed the microphone. They started out with a medley of Captain and Tennille songs that had many of the patrons tapping their feet and singing along.

"They're really good," Ben leaned over and said to Kate.

Their shoulders touched, but just when he was about to pull back, Kate leaned even closer and said in his ear, "I've heard them before. Rita has an amazing voice. I'm so glad that we came here tonight."

"Me too," he said knowing that he wouldn't muster up the nerve to ask her to dance but something inside of him shifted, softened. And when Kate briefly touched his hand, Ben closed his eyes and swallowed. Maybe he could finally find the courage to start healing.

9
Lucky Dog

NO MATTER HOW HARD SHE TRIED, WHICH AT FIRST WASN'T very much at all, Savannah could not stop thinking about Tristan McMillan. After the dinner on Friday, sleep eluded her pretty much the entire night. She'd tossed and turned for hours, getting all twisted up in the bedclothes while thinking about the way he looked, the way he smelled—which was very nice by the way—and the warmth of his smile. Savannah had chuckled in the dark while recalling funny things he'd said after he'd loosened up. She smiled at the memory of the promises he made to help Kate manage Whisper's Edge.

Tristan had seemed to have a good time with them, laughing easily as the night wore on and even walking her to her door. He'd asked for her phone number, and for one heart-pounding moment Savannah even hoped he might kiss her! Or at the very least ask to do this again sometime. He hadn't.

Yes, okay technically he was her boss, but Savannah decided to ignore that little detail.

Savannah wondered if thoughts of her were keeping Tristan awake. Would Tristan call or text to let her know?

She thought it would be incredibly sweet to talk softly to each other while lying in bed.

But her phone remained stubbornly silent.

When Savannah didn't hear from Tristan on Saturday morning she cleaned every inch of her little house in an effort to keep him off her mind, but as she ran the sweeper, polished the furniture and, yes, even washed windows, his face kept sliding into her brain and refused to budge. Oh, and doing the laundry brought back such vivid memories that she finally had to walk away from the washing machine and go outside to cool down.

Now, here it was Sunday afternoon. Savannah had the day off and damned if thoughts of Tristan weren't keeping her from getting into a perfectly good book that she had been dying to start reading.

"Well, hellfire!" Savannah grumbled, using one of Kate's expressions. She tossed the book down onto the glossy magazines littering her coffee table, crossed her arms over her chest, tapped her toes that barely reached the floor because her legs were so doggone short, and well . . . she pouted. At least until she realized that her unconventional childhood meant she had never mastered the fine art of pouting, and after a few moments she felt silly and gave it up.

She glanced down at the coffee table and considered giving the book another try. But the shirtless guy on the cover sort of looked like Tristan and she groaned in pure exasperation. "This is stupid." She needed to talk to somebody; get her mind someplace else. This was getting . . . weird.

Knowing all she had to do was walk out the door to find somebody to chat with, Savannah went in search of her tennis shoes. Of course she couldn't find them and then remembered they had gotten muddy when she pulled weeds yesterday evening. Yes, she had weeded her garden on a perfectly nice *Saturday* evening.

Savannah put her hands on her hips and started to get well and truly grumpy. "I sure could use a glass of that Angel Food Cake wine," she mumbled beneath her breath and finally slipped her feet into her flip-flops, even though one was still missing the daisy. Of course, even *that* brought back memories of the day she met Tristan.

Savannah thought about changing from her tattered blue gym shorts and worn white tank top but failed to muster up the energy. Who knew that having an obsession would be so draining? Because Savannah wasn't a down-in-the-dumps kind of person, this mood felt strange but for the life of her, she just couldn't shake it.

"What in the world is wrong with me?" After a long-suffering sigh she looked at her reflection in the mirror above her dresser. "Mercy." Swallowing hard, Savannah reached up and touched the messy braid that was supposed to keep her hair tame but was losing the battle with curls that had worked their way loose. Without makeup her freckles stood out like sprinkles of nutmeg on custard, and there were dark smudges beneath her eyes, courtesy of her sleepless nights. "I am one hot mess."

Savannah let her gaze slide down her body and then put her hand on her stomach, wishing it were flat as a pancake. After another sigh she turned and checked out her butt. "Not as big as Kim Kardashian but still . . ." She pivoted and cupped her full breasts but then had to smile ever so slightly at the memory of the crazy boobs-and-booty dance she and Kate did on Friday.

Savannah took a step back and frowned at her reflection. Having always worried about important things like putting a roof over her head and food on the table, she'd never worried much about her appearance.

Until now.

Oh, she'd dated here and there, mostly stemming from a grandson of someone who lived in Whisper's Edge. Before landing the job she'd struggled to make ends meet, much less date. One dead-end job had led to another, and, thinking she needed another change of scenery, Savannah had packed her one suitcase and hit the road until she ran out of money.

Savannah remembered with a hot flash of shame that Kate had found her sleeping in this very mobile home, but instead of kicking her out or calling the cops, Kate had fed her a huge meal and they'd hit it off as friends right away. And after an acknowledged background check, Kate had offered her the social director's position, which had morphed into Girl Friday when Kate's assistant went back to college when the budget got tighter. The money wasn't great, but having a home of her very own was a dream come true with the added bonus of home-cooked meals from residents who soon adopted her as their own.

Savannah gave her reflection a wobbly smile. Comfort food stuck like glue to her waistline but there wasn't a night that went by that she didn't fall to her knees and thank her lucky stars and heaven above that she'd stumbled upon this vacant home while on the never-ending road to nowhere. From that day forward her life had changed for the better. Kate turned out to be a mom and friend rolled into one. Miss Patty doted on her, and there wasn't a home in the community to which Savannah hadn't been invited on more than one occasion. And holidays? Savannah grinned. All of the Christmas mornings without presents and birthdays gone unnoticed were trumped by the showering of gifts that she received from the good people of Whisper's Edge. She glanced at her bulging closet and had to chuckle. There was one entire rack packed with ugly sweaters and she wore each and every one. A gift, no matter how big or how small or unnecessary, Savannah wore it, used it, or consumed it with lavish praise. She never, *ever* regifted.

"Oh boy . . ." She brushed away a sudden fat tear at the thought and then sniffed hard. She didn't allow herself the luxury of tears very often, and the recent frequency of her eyes misting over was becoming alarming. Savannah sniffed again and shook her head. She'd spent a lifetime tamping down her emotions and pushing away fear. With a lift of her chin she swallowed the hot moisture gathering in her throat. "Just think happy thoughts," Savannah said sternly. "Oh,

Tinker Bell, sprinkle me with pixie dust!" What in the world was going on with her restless, blue mood, anyway? She flopped down onto her bed and stared up at the ceiling fan that Ben had kindly installed for her a few weeks ago. She inhaled deeply and tried to think things out.

Was it hormones? The biological-clock-ticking theory that Kate kept spinning didn't really resonate with Savannah. Having a child of her own wasn't something Savannah ever daydreamed about. The only babies she had ever been around were other foster care children, so she never felt that tenderness or longing. Rather she mostly felt annoyance at the messes they made. She'd only had one baby doll. It had been tucked into one of those random bags of Christmas gifts received from the kindness of some charity with tags labeled *girl* and *age*. Not quite knowing what to do with the doll, which was supposed to burp and cry, she had traded it for a book. Even as a child, books had been her escape. Her library card was still her passport to worlds of wonder and she gobbled up books and then hurried back for more.

Savannah's thoughts went back to babies, and she frowned as she stared at the fan. Having only had the basics of food and clothing, Savannah had no childhood memory of being cuddled, rocked, or cared for. And she had learned early on that any show of weakness meant getting picked on, so she learned to stand her ground no matter how hard her knees were knocking. Perhaps it was the feisty redhead in her, but she got pretty adept at staring down bullies despite her small stature. "Sugar, what doesn't kill you makes you stronger," Kate announced one afternoon when she and Savannah were having a particularly stressful day.

"Well then, I should be able to bench press a boulder." With a small smile Savannah grabbed a throw pillow and hugged it to her chest. She darned well knew the reason for her blue mood. Tristan McMillan. She wanted him to notice her as a woman. She wanted him to drag her into his arms and kiss her senseless. Ah, she would thread her fingers through his hair, which she imagined would feel soft and silky, and then he would carry her off to bed and make wild and passionate love to her! She could have sworn he'd been making eyes at her too at dinner, but of course it could have been the alcohol. "Guess he had his beer goggles on," Savannah mumbled with a lifeless laugh.

Still, she continued imagining a steamy kiss but then inhaled sharply. Dear lord. She put the back of her hand to her forehead and suddenly felt warm all over. She was glad for the slowly moving fan. She considered getting up to tug the chain for more of a breeze but that would require moving and she couldn't muster up the energy. She needed one of those remotes, but the fan had been purchased second-hand and had one of those old-school chains, which she always tugged more times than needed or not enough.

Savannah wondered if someone like Tristan could ever fall madly in love with her like the heroes in so many of her favorite books and movies. "Not likely," she whispered, giving in to a tired sigh, but she grinned slightly thinking that, hey, this was her fantasy so she might as well go all the way. What I need is a fairy godmother, Savannah thought, and then turned onto her side, still hugging the pillow. Oh yeah, and a generous sprinkling of pixie dust.

Savannah yawned. Maybe she would just stay inside after all. She guessed that her lethargy had been brought on by her lack of sleep, and she suddenly felt very tired. Blinking, she decided a little cat nap might restore her energy and hopefully her good humor. Like she'd already told Kate, Tristan was light-years out of her league, and unfortunately there wasn't a magic wand that could change that situation. I'm not Cinderella, she thought, and my life sure isn't a fairy tale, even though she loved reading them. But in reality, wishing on a star, like giving in to tears, was wasted energy, which was why she supposed she was so darned exhausted. Of course, it could have something to do with the massive housecleaning she did yesterday—if she had silver, it would have been polished. Combine her cleaning frenzy with lack of sleep and it was no wonder she was bone tired.

Savannah yawned again and then hugged the fluffy pillow closer, squishing it against her chest. A wave of loneliness washed over her and her eyelids suddenly felt heavy. *Think happy thoughts* filtered into her brain, and she tried, but after a few moments she drifted off to sleep. . . .

Savannah dreamed that Peter Pan landed on her windowsill but she refused to *believe* and so he and Wendy flew away, leaving her behind calling after them. Not to be outdone, Savannah hoisted herself up to the windowsill and decided that she would fly by herself but Kate came along at the last minute and saved her from surely breaking her leg or worse. She was just about to convince Kate that they should at least give flying a whirl when the bed moved and then something soft and wet tickled her cheek.

"Mmm?" Savannah sort of woke up but decided this might be a delicious dream involving Tristan so she kept her eyes closed and dearly hoped the dream would continue. This was likely as close as she was going to get to the real thing so she sighed and waited for another moist kiss. Maybe a sweet nothing murmured into her ear. The warm tickle happened again but felt more like a tongue licking across her chin. This didn't seem like a very Tristan-like thing to do and, oh god, his breath needed a good freshening up. . . . Wow; this dream sucked, she thought, and it happened again but this time across her nose.

Savannah opened her eyes and was suddenly face-to-face with brown eyes, a big mouth, and there came the tongue again! "No!" she yelled and sat up so fast that her pillow buddy went tumbling to the floor. "How on earth did you get in here?" she shouted.

"The door was open."

"What?" Savannah looked over to see Tristan standing in the doorway to her bedroom. He was holding a bottle of wine and looking concerned. Wait. Was this still a dream? Her answer came when Willie farted. "Ew, Willie!" She pinched her nose with her thumb and finger. "That was Willie," Savannah said in a nasal tone, wanting Tristan to be sure that the dog was the culprit.

Willie, the guilty licker and farter, sat there staring at Tristan with a solemn basset hound expression but then edged closer to Savannah, as if staking his territory.

"You smell."

"I assure you I showered."

"I was talking to Willie."

Tristan raised his eyebrows. "I guess I should be relieved."

"People talk to dogs, you know."

"You seem to take it to a new level."

"My rather loud vocal reaction was in response to having my face licked," she explained but then felt heat creep into her cheeks. "I have no idea how he ended up in my bed." She gave Willie an accusing look but he stood, or rather sat, his ground.

"Lucky dog."

"I . . . uh . . ." Savannah stuttered. Was he flirting with her?

"I can answer for Willie," Tristan said. He leaned one shoulder against the doorframe looking all calm, cool, and handsome as all get out. "Your back screen door was ajar."

"Oh, the latch is broken and the breeze blows it open once in a while. I guess you thought it was an open invitation," she said to Willie, but then looked over at Tristan. "I guess you did too."

"I'm sorry." Tristan shook his head. "I'm not usually in the habit of entering uninvited but your car was in the driveway and after several knocks you failed to answer the door."

"Sorry. I didn't hear you. I was . . . resting." Savannah flipped what was left of her braid over her shoulder. God, she must look a sight. And he of course had to stand there looking amazing in khaki shorts and a baby blue golf shirt that stretched across wide shoulders and hugged his biceps.

He looked fit and energetic, and she had been caught napping in the middle of the day. She felt like a slug. "I guess I dozed off for a minute."

"Don't look so guilty. I love a good nap."

Savannah swallowed when his innocent comment made her imagine him all sleepy and ruffled and shirtless in a big bed.

With her in it.

Dear lord. Savannah prayed that what she was thinking wasn't written all over her face. She cleared her throat and tried to think of something to say . . . but what does one say in a situation such as this?

"I'm really sorry for intruding." Tristan straightened and showed her the bottle. "I was bringing you this. It's Cupcake wine but called Red Velvet. I thought you might like to sample it. You know, since you're thinking of doing a wine tasting here."

Savannah put a hand to her chest. "Oh . . ."

"Seriously, I wouldn't have barged right into your home but I heard you yell 'no' and then 'how did you get in here?' and I got worried that you were"—he grinned slightly—"once again in peril. I had my karate chop ready."

"You know karate?"

"Hell no, but I was willing to bluff my way for your safety." Tristan gave Willie a nod. "I think I could take him."

"Willie's a licker not a fighter." She patted his head and then glanced at Tristan, who looked as if he wanted to say something but then thought better of it. "See there?" Savannah patted Willie's head. "You got me in trouble again."

Willie looked at her with his usual sorry but somehow innocent expression. She imagined if Willie could talk he would sound just like Eeyore from *Winnie-the-Pooh*.

"Were you chasing after another tennis ball, Willie? You'd better skedaddle on *home*." When she gave Willie a pointed look he scrambled from the bed, taking a few pillows with him. For such a short-legged, hefty dog, he managed to leap with some agility, even though he grunted when he landed not-so-gracefully with a tuck and roll, and looked up at them as if to say, "I meant to do that." When Miss Patty called Willie's name the naughty dog picked up the pace and hurried on his short legs past Tristan, who watched the dog's progress with a grin. "You'd better hustle!"

"See, you're talking to Willie again."

"Yeah . . ." Savannah grinned. "And I talk to myself, to the television, to my plants."

"Does it help them grow?"

"I think so," she answered earnestly, but then shook her head at his amused expression. "I guess I'm some kind of crazy."

Tristan chuckled. "Well, don't change," he said and then held out the bottle as if he needed to remind Savannah of the reason for his visit. "I'm really *not* in the habit of entering without an invitation. But in my defense you did seem in distress."

"Um, yeah, I was! Willie's breath is not one bit sweet." She shuddered. "I almost needed an oxygen mask."

When Tristan laughed Savannah joined him, but he then stood there for an awkward moment. "I'll just leave this on your kitchen table. Let me know if you like it," he said, pausing just long enough to make Savannah think he might want to stay.

"Have a glass with me," Savannah offered before her nerve took a flying leap out the window. "Unless . . . you know, you have somewhere to go," she added in what she hoped was a nonchalant tone. Her heart pounded.

"Um . . ." He hesitated for a fraction, making Savannah want to pull the covers over her head. God, she must have read him all wrong.

"I thought you'd never ask."

"Really?" Oh great, she thought, *that* was sophisticated.

10

Going with the Flow

"REALLY." TRISTAN KNEW FULL WELL THAT HE SHOULD leave the wine and walk out the door, but seeing Savannah in the middle of her bed looking sleepy-eyed and sexy had him jumping all over her invitation. It was all he could do not to slide right into bed next to her. She'd been invading his thoughts ever since Friday, even though he knew he should stay the hell away. He'd actually almost called her a number of times but had put the phone down, knowing it was best not to, and yet here he was standing in the doorway of her bedroom. Go figure. "I had actually gone to the liquor store for a six-pack of beer, but saw this Cupcake wine on an end cap and thought you might like it."

"Why, thank you, Tristan."" She gave him an easy smile that he found adorable.

"No problem." Tristan excelled at making a point and winning an argument, and he prided himself on his prowess in the courtroom, but he found everyday interaction with people more of a challenge. Savannah, on the other hand, exuded a natural kind of confidence that he admired. He could definitely learn a thing or two from watching her in action.

"That was very thoughtful of you."

Tristan gave her a slight shrug, again a bit at a loss for words. He also left out the part that the trip to the store had been last night and he'd almost come over then but somehow managed to talk himself out of it. Well that, and a phone call from a partner in his firm that had delayed him an hour. They were already gunning to get him back in Cincinnati. The conversation had left him feeling unsettled and so he had given up on the idea of heading over to see Savannah.

"I'll go round up some glasses," she said and scrambled from the bed. Her hair was a mess, she didn't appear as if she had a trace of makeup on, and was in ratty clothes . . . and damned if she didn't look sexier than he had been imagining all weekend long. As he followed her down the short hallway he couldn't keep his eyes off her very nice ass. Tristan had also tried to convince himself that bringing the wine over was another excuse to walk around in Whisper's Edge and get a bead on what he wanted to do with the property but he knew he was kidding himself. He wanted to see Savannah, plain and simple.

He'd been drinking a bit on Friday, and to be honest, he wanted to know if seeing Savannah would have the same effect when he was stone-cold sober. Because, really, she was completely different from the other women he'd dated. Tristan had been living in a world of sharp angles and glossy veneer, and Savannah oozed an earthiness and sweet honesty that felt like a soft place to land. Her bright smile and laid-back demeanor had a calming effect on him that made being with her simply feel good.

Tristan watched Savannah pull open a drawer stuffed full of all kinds of gadgets. Somehow she didn't strike him as a gadget kind of person.

"I know I have a corkscrew in here somewhere. More

than one, I imagine," she mumbled as she pushed things around.

"That's quite a junk drawer. Do you use all that stuff?"

"No." Savannah chuckled. "I don't know what most of this stuff is for," she admitted, and then found a corkscrew. "Here we go! Would you do the honors?"

"Sure," he said and then cut through the foil.

"I get lots of gifts from the residents," she explained. She reached in and pulled out a tiny little scoop. "This is to make melon balls. I've never made melon balls. I don't think I want to make a melon ball." She showed him a weird-looking little tube. "An olive stuffer."

"How does it work?"

"Don't have a clue. Let's see, here is a celery slicer. I used it once but it was more effort than it was worth, just like this egg slicer. Oh, and here's a lemon press." She frowned as she turned it over. "I think."

Tristan popped the cork. "Why do you think they give you all of that stuff?"

Savannah shrugged, but then grinned. "Well, some of it is regifting. Many of them are of the age that their kids don't have a clue as to what presents to buy them for holidays and birthdays so they get some random, weird stuff. I can't ever go for a visit or dinner that I don't come away with something in my hand." She chuckled. "Some of it is stuff they buy from catalogs or online and then never take out of the box." Her smile softened. "And some of it is just pure kindness. A thrift-store find or something on sale that reminds them of me. And don't get me wrong—I love it. I might not ever use some of the gifts but I'm always touched by the thoughtfulness. Kind of like your flying pigs." Savannah raised an eyebrow at Tristan and gestured toward the drawer. "But this is the small stuff."

"You're kidding."

She raised her hand and started ticking off items. "Nope. I have a yogurt maker. A bread maker. A FryDaddy." She tapped her cheek. "Let's see, oh, and an iced-tea brewer.

And of course, a George Foreman grill. Some of the stuff comes from Kate, who suffers from insomnia and buys wacky things in the middle of the night. I will soon be the proud owner of a juicer."

"And you never kindly say, 'thanks, but no, thanks'?" he asked, and watched with some male appreciation when she had to go up on tiptoe to reach for some wineglasses.

Savannah came back down on her heels and turned to face him. "Well, when you grow up with nothing, you never turn down anything for free." She angled her head. "And I do use some of it . . . granted sometimes only once, but the main reason is to see the joy on their faces when I oooh and aaah over something. Kindness goes a long way, in my book. I just don't get mean people, do you? I mean, what's the point?"

"No, I don't get meanness." Tristan thought about how his grandfather had hurt his mother. "No, not at all. I have a reputation for being tough but I've seen people get really vicious in my line of work."

"I bet you have. Well, I imagine the pace is much slower here. I hope you can kick back and relax."

"I'm going to try." Damn, he was starting to like Savannah even more. When she smiled and went back up on her tiptoes Tristan walked over to her. "Here, let me get those for you." He put the wine bottle on the counter and reached up above her head, bringing his body up next to hers. A tendril of her hair brushed against his chin and the soft, feminine touch sent his senses reeling. Maybe it was because he'd been thinking about how much he wanted to see her, to touch her, that the reality of it hit him hard, but whatever the reason, Tristan couldn't recall ever having a reaction this intense over a slight touch. He quickly stepped backward, nearly dropping the glasses, and then tried to regain his composure.

"Are you okay?" She gave him a curious look, but her cheeks were flushed, making Tristan wonder if she felt the same way.

"I stumbled sideways."

She grinned. "I'm usually the one with that problem."

"And we haven't had wine yet," he tried to joke. He was used to feeling sure of himself, of what to say and what to do in the courtroom, but in this kind of setting he was completely thrown off balance in more ways than one. He never liked the sensation of not knowing what was going to happen next. Tristan wasn't impulsive. He was a planner, a note taker. He lived his life as if it were a chess game, pondering his next move way before making it. He thought about his purchase of Whisper's Edge long and hard before making the final decision. Even so, leaving the firm had astounded his friends, and they predicted he'd be back before summer's end.

For the past few weeks he'd been studying charts and graphs while considering his options for Whisper's Edge. His mother had recently suggested that it might be less of a risk to spruce it up and leave it as a retirement community. Of course, he'd quickly told her that wouldn't make sense financially. She'd sighed and said that life didn't always have to make perfect sense.

"Mercy, what's going on in that head of yours?" Savannah asked, making Tristan realize that he had been quiet while she poured the wine. She smiled as she handed him a glass, but her voice sounded a little breathless.

"Thinking." Tristan shrugged. "Sometimes I think way too much, but since it's a big part of being a lawyer it's pretty difficult to turn it off."

"Well, let's go outside on my patio and think about nothing but enjoying the wonderful weather."

Her simple statement immediately put him at ease. "Sounds like a plan." He followed her out the back door to a small but immaculate garden. "This is . . . pretty." He didn't use the word often but it fit.

"Thank you," she said but her voice held a measure of pride in it. "I enjoy it out here. It always feels . . . I don't know, somehow peaceful. This lot is a little ways away from the other lots that are situated much closer together."

"Nice that you have a bit of privacy."

"I agree." They sat down at a white wrought-iron bistro table with a cheerful potted red geranium sitting in the center. "Can we take a sip of wine or should we swirl and smell it first?"

"Swirl and smell and then savor," he replied with a smile.

"Good; I wanted to, but didn't want to feel silly unless you did it too." She glanced down at her shorts. "Although I must say that I look pretty darned shabby for sipping wine. I look more like I should be chugging cheap beer."

"Hey, it's my fault for dropping by unannounced."

Savannah brushed it off. "I have residents drop in on me all the time. Don't give it another thought."

"Thanks, but I'll call next time," he promised, and then realized that he was telling her he'd be coming back. He knew that he would too. His staying-away plan just wasn't working out. Although he barely knew her, the thought of never seeing Savannah again on a personal basis was not something he thought he wanted to contemplate. He watched her swirl the wine and almost spill it over the rim of the glass.

"Whoa, I think I need some practice."

"Not a problem. I could do this every evening," he admitted. Catching himself, he chuckled so that she thought he was joking—even as the thought went through his mind that having someone to share evenings like this would be nice. He watched her take a sniff. "What do you smell?"

She frowned and then said, "Blackberries?"

Tristan sniffed and then nodded. "Yeah, I agree."

After she took a sip her eyes widened. "Wow, it is intense."

"Don't like it?"

"I'm not used to red wine." Savannah tilted her head and then took another sip. "I taste . . . berries." She frowned, "A hint of coconut? Am I crazy?"

Tristan sampled the wine. "Yes, blackberry and . . . mocha?"

Savannah sipped and then let it roll on her tongue. "Oh . . . yeah." She nodded. "How did I miss the mocha?"

"This would taste great paired with a good steak or burger."

Savannah lifted one shoulder. "I have a grill. It's old-school charcoal but works like a charm."

Tristan gave her a slow smile. "Are you inviting me for dinner?"

She gave him another shy smile. "I do believe so."

"Well, then, I accept. Maybe dropping in unannounced wasn't such a bad idea, after all." He took another sip of the wine.

"If you go for the main course in a bit, I'll rustle up some side dishes. I have charcoal. Besides, it will give me a chance to get a little bit cleaned up."

"You don't have to do that," he assured her, but Savannah looked down at her shorts and rolled her eyes.

"There's a mom-and-pop store not far from here called Wilson's. They carry just about anything a person could ever need and then some. But for now let's enjoy our Red Velvet wine."

When she lifted her glass, Tristan leaned over and tapped his glass to hers. "To lazy Sunday afternoons."

"Cheers," Savannah said and then laughed.

"So, did you do all of this yourself?"

"Pretty much." Savannah nodded. "This backyard was in about the same condition as the house. Needed a generous amount of tender loving care, but I didn't have a lot of money to work with." She looked at him over the rim of her glass. "Actually, I had no money to work with." She formed her fingers into a zero and chuckled.

"So what did you do?"

"I rescued plants from the living dead. When I was caught taking a brown and brittle hanging planter from a garbage can sitting out for pickup, the residents here started bringing me their castoffs." She swung her arm in an arc. "Pretty much everything you see has been salvaged."

Tristan looked around at the abundant flowers and plants, all looking vibrant and healthy. "You have a green thumb, Savannah."

She tilted her head sideways and laughed. "I had an empty wallet. I had no choice. This table was set out for the garbage too . . . so I sanded, primed, and painted it."

Tristan looked down at the patio. "The pavers?"

"Ben helped me . . . well, correction, I helped Ben put in the bricks. They were salvaged from an old building that was torn down on Main Street. I got them for free."

"He did an excellent job."

Savannah nodded in agreement. "I argued but Ben wouldn't take any money for doing it. Now he brings me stuff that he thinks I might use." She pointed to a rustic ladder that was now a plant ledge. "I take just about anything."

"That's cool, Savannah. Repurposing has become the in thing to do. Very green . . ."

Her eyes lit up. "I have to admit, finding new ways to use old junk has become a fun hobby. One of my favorite things is using crazy containers for planters."

"Are those tomato plants?" He pointed to a small patch against a flagstone wall.

"It's a small salsa garden. Tomatoes, cilantro, peppers, and onions. I showed the garden club how to do it in a big planter. When we harvest we'll have a huge salsa-making day." She winked. "And maybe a few pitchers of margaritas."

"Sounds like fun."

"It will be." She took a sip of wine. "Wow, this tastes better as you drink it."

Tristan laughed. "It's all good after the first glass. So, what else have you done in the garden club?"

"This year we started seedlings in old egg cartons." She laughed. "We were like little kids when the seeds started sprouting."

"You're very good at your job."

Savannah shook her head. "I appreciate the compliment but it's truly a labor of love."

"Still, you deserve to be compensated more for all of the time you put in," Tristan said, but the comment was a reminder that he was the owner and she was the employee, and he wished he had kept his mouth shut. He also felt another flash of guilt that he wasn't being completely honest with her. What would she do if she knew he had other plans for the property? The thought bothered him more than he wanted it to, and for the first time he had to wonder if his mother had a point about life not having to make perfect sense. He looked down at the red wine and sighed.

"Um, I wasn't trying to score brownie points," Savannah said with a bit of uncertainty.

Tristan looked at her worried expression and damned if he didn't feel like an ass. "I know. I'm sorry. I just have a lot on my mind."

"Well, Tristan, you're right. You think way too much. Just go with the flow. . . ."

"I'm adjusting from working seventy-hour weeks but I'll try." Tristan looked at the sincerity in her green eyes and he was touched. Here was a woman whom he sensed came from nothing and cared about everything. While by rights she could be edgy and hard, instead he sensed determination and resiliency, her toughness buffered by an inner softness that he was finding damned hard to resist. "I'm a thinker. A planner." He poured another glass of wine for them both and then grinned. "Looks like I'll have to bring another bottle of wine. But yeah, in a few years I could have been a partner in my firm."

"Do you worry that you made the wrong career choice by coming here?"

"Sometimes," he admitted, but then smiled.

"Well, Kate always tells me to just go with my heart and my gut."

"And has that worked?"

Savannah leaned forward in her chair and nodded slowly. "Every single time."

Tristan angled his head to the side and then sighed. "I

wish I could be more like that but it's in my nature to over-think and worry."

"Worrying doesn't change anything, just causes unnecessary stress."

Tristan smiled at her. "You're very wise, Savannah."

She raised her eyebrows. "Are you serious?"

"I am. You have a great attitude and unique perspective on life."

"Well, I never really thought about it that way, but thank you." She shrugged. "I suppose my outlook on life comes from living here with people who are in their twilight years. They know that every day they have left on this earth is a gift so why sweat the small stuff, ya know?"

Tristan lifted his glass. "I'll drink to that," he said, and when she laughed, relief washed over him. "I suggest that we finish this bottle with our steak, what do you say?"

"You don't have to come back for dinner," Savannah said softly. "I kind of roped you into it."

When Tristan stood up, her eyes widened. He knew she would stand too, and for the first time since he could remember he decided to act on impulse. He pulled her into his arms, lowered his head, and kissed her. And, oh God, he had imagined what her lips would feel like, what she would taste like, and the real thing was so much better. Her mouth was soft, *pliant*, and she kissed him back with a combination of tenderness and pure sexiness that changed what was meant to be a simple kiss into something much more. She seemed to sink into his arms, and when her fingers threaded through his hair Tristan felt as if he were melting into the ground. When he finally pulled back she blinked up at him.

"What was that all about?" she asked breathlessly.

"Going with the flow," he answered with a slow grin. "I like it."

Savannah smiled back, but then shyly put her fingers to her lips as if not believing what had just happened.

"I'll be back in a bit with a couple of nice steaks and another bottle of Red Velvet. Do you need anything else?"

She shook her head mutely. As he walked away he had a goofy smile on his face and felt, well, positively giddy. When he reached the sidewalk he wanted to do one of those kick-your-heels-together moves, but spotted a neighbor and decided against it. But he felt like it, and that was more than enough.

As he drove away he turned on the radio and started singing along with the Black Eyed Peas. Yeah, *tonight's gonna be a good night . . .*

11

A Table for Two

KATE KNEW SHE WAS BEING NOSY, BUT SHE SIMPLY COULDN'T help herself. Every few minutes she peeked through the blinds of her front bay window and looked down the street to see if Tristan's car was still parked in front of Savannah's little house. This time when she peeked, his fancy silver car was gone. Damn. She'd hoped Savannah might have invited him to dinner. She'd have to have another talk with that girl!

But then again, maybe she should mind her own business.

Savannah was sweet and trusting, and if Tristan McMillan was anything like his jackass grandfather it would be bad news for her to get involved with him. Tristan sure didn't come off that way, especially after all of the generous improvements he'd promised to approve at Whisper's Edge, but Kate remained wary. The last thing in the world she wanted to see was Savannah get hurt—something Kate was all too familiar with and didn't recommend. The end of her marriage had been the result of the classic executive husband cheating with his secretary. To make matters worse,

Kate had just discovered she was pregnant, and when she lost the baby she'd wondered if it had been due to the stress of the divorce.

Never wanting to become dependent on a man again, Kate had become a successful sales rep for a pharmaceutical company. But years of longs hours and travel took its toll, and when she came home to Cricket Creek to call on an account, returning to a simpler way of life seemed like a smart thing to do, and she applied for the job at Whisper's Edge. The only family she had left in Cricket Creek was her sister's family but they were busy running a farm, and she didn't see nearly enough of them. "It's my own damned fault for getting into such a rut," she grumbled beneath her breath.

Kate sat down on her sofa and stared at the flat-screen television that had been a Christmas gift to herself last year. The purchase had been a Black Friday door-buster deal that had her up before the crack of dawn, even though she didn't really need to pinch pennies. But unlike the stupid juicer, the television was something she would at least use. While Kate knew she could find a better paying job elsewhere, she enjoyed running Whisper's Edge and the freedom from facing stressful sales quotas and endless hours on the road.

With a sigh, Kate picked up the remote to click the sound back on, but she'd seen *Love Actually* too many times to count, and it was coming to the Joni Mitchell song scene where she always cried and so she changed the channel. "A million channels and nothing to watch," she grumbled and turned on her old standby, the Food Network. Bobby Flay was grilling some amazing-looking black-and-bleu burgers, and Kate's stomach rumbled in protest. "Oh, that looks so darned good." She turned the sound on and listened to the instructions for how to cook the perfect backyard burger. Bobby was so right ... you've got to have a really quality bun.

Kate made a mental note to pay Grammar's Bakery a

visit this upcoming week. The only problem was that Kate
knew she'd leave the bakery with way more than a dozen
burger buns. Hell, she gained a pound just entering the fra-
grant shop. Visions of cinnamon cake danced in her head,
and her mouth watered. She was getting really hungry but
didn't have the gumption to fix anything, and the prospect
of going out to dinner by her lonesome simply didn't appeal, especially after the fun she'd had on Friday night.
Sometimes a table for one just sucked.

Feeling glum, she walked into the kitchen and opened
the fridge, knowing full well that there wasn't going to be
anything in there that would interest her after seeing that
damned juicy burger perched on the golden, toasted bun.
The jar of pickle spears mocked her. Damn, she craved a
burger.

Sully's Tavern served some pretty good burgers and his
French fries were hand cut with the skin still on, just the
way Kate liked them. But then again, his onion rings were
crispy bites of deliciousness. Not exactly heart-healthy, but
if she walked, she wouldn't feel so guilty about eating bodacious but bad-for-you bar food. Besides, Kate reasoned, all
she'd had to eat all day long was a bowl of Honey Nut
Cheerios, so she could splurge on a few extra calories.
Right?

Right! Oh, she could justify with the best of them.

Her decision made, Kate hurried to her closet and
changed from her sweatpants to a pair of white Capri pants,
but instead of going for her usual sweater set, she opted for
a soft blue button-down blouse that she'd bought last year
but had never worn. Not quite satisfied, she added a simple
silver cuff bracelet and slipped into a new pair of white
Clark's sandals that she had been saving, for what reason
she'd never know. Kate had an entire closet full of clothes
she was saving for a special occasion that never seemed to
arrive.

"There," she said, but then scowled at her image in the
mirror. "When did I go and get this damned old?" she

grumbled, and felt a lump form in her throat. She headed with angry steps into the bathroom and started rummaging through the makeup that she rarely took the time to use. Friday had been the first time in a long while she'd made an effort, and Kate had to admit that it felt good to have a reason to care about her appearance.

After a few minutes of primping she examined herself in the mirror. "A little better." She fluffed up her short layers until they framed her face. But after she sprayed on some perfume, Kate suddenly wondered why in the world she was going through all the trouble since she was once again flying solo.

"Oh, to hell with it," she said and toed off her sandals. Her stomach rumbled in protest but she ignored it and sat down on the bed so hard that she actually bounced. But really, eating alone sometimes just sucked so badly. She'd have to buy a newspaper or something because, really, where do you look when you're sitting there all by yourself? She sometimes played with her phone, even though she had no clue as to what most of the bells and whistles were for. Kate inhaled sharply and then decided that maybe Savannah would go with her. Besides, she really wanted to get the scoop on why Tristan McMillan had paid her a visit.

Kate reached into her purse for her phone but before she could scroll down for Savannah's number, it rang that annoying cheerful tune that she didn't know how to change.

"Kate!" Savannah said, sounding as if she were in a state of panic.

"Oh, sweetie, what's wrong?"

"Tristan is coming back here to eat dinner with me. What am I going to do?"

"Um, feed him?"

"Very funny," Savannah said, but something in her tone gave Kate pause.

"Savannah, I know you can cook, so what aren't you telling me?"

There was a moment of silence and then, "Nothing."

"Savannah, just spill. You know I'll get it out of you in due time anyway."

"He might have . . . Oh, Kate!"

"What?" Feeling a flash of alarm, Kate sat up straight. "He might have what?"

"*Kissed* me," Savannah replied in a stage whisper.

"Kissed you?" Kate sank back down with relief.

"Maybe . . ."

"Maybe?" Kate smiled. "Sugar, there doesn't seem to be a lot of gray area here."

"Okay, he did."

"And?"

"I am in full-blown off-the-charts panic."

"Savannah, he is just a boy, and it was just a kiss."

"No . . . and hell to the *no*!"

"So it was more than that?"

"Kate, he's my *boss* and the *kiss* knocked my socks off."

"So it wasn't just a little peck?"

"Nooo!"

"Savannah . . ."

"It must have been the wine."

"Wine?"

"He brought a bottle and we had a glass of it on my patio. No, wait. We had two."

"And one thing led to another?" Kate looked up at the ceiling and smiled.

"No! Nothing led to anything. We were just talking and he was going to leave, but then, well, he suddenly just, well, kissed me. I did not egg him on or flirt one little bit."

"Maybe he's been thinking about you as much as you've been thinking about him."

"Kate, you don't understand. I am a flipping mess. I said I'd cook for him! What was I thinking? Huh? Have I lost my ever-loving mind?"

"Like I said, you can cook. And quite well, I might add."

Savannah groaned.

"What are you fixing?"

"We're grilling steaks. Oh damn, I've got to light the charcoal."

"He'll do the grilling. It's a guy thing. All you need is some baked potatoes and a tossed salad. Do you have all that stuff?"

"Yes," she answered in a small voice.

"Then stop freaking out."

"I can't! Kate, I'm sweating. Sweat-*ing*!" She drew out the world for at least ten seconds. "There's not a deodorant in the world that could handle my armpits right now. Kate, it's not about cooking in general. It's about cooking for Tristan McMillan."

"Calm down. Put on something cool like that cute yellow sundress that you bought at Violet's but haven't worn."

"But my hair is crazy as usual."

"Put your hair in a bun."

"Okay . . . okay, now what?"

"Are you actually taking notes?"

"Maybe."

"Put on a little makeup and your favorite perfume."

"And?"

"Relax!"

"I can't."

Kate had to chuckle softly. Somewhere, in the back of her mind where a door was firmly locked, she remembered what it was like to feel the excitement of a first kiss. Falling in love was such a heady feeling . . . like floating on air. She wanted that for Savannah. She deserved to be loved and treasured.

But Kate knew the pain of loss and she put a sudden hand to her chest. After all these years the feeling could still steal her breath and cause physical pain. She didn't want that for Savannah.

"Kate?"

Kate cleared her throat. Yes, falling in love was exhilarating. Breathtaking.

Heartbreaking.

But worth the risk! Her heart pounded at that frightening thought.

"Just breathe, Savannah. Enjoy. We can't choose who we're attracted to or who we fall for. Forget about anything other than you like being with him. Just go with the flow."

"That's exactly what I told him and look at the mess I'm in."

Kate chuckled. "You can do it."

"Easier said than done but I guess I should practice what I preach. Wait. What *you* preach!"

Kate chuckled again. "I want a full report tomorrow."

"Okay, I think I've calmed down. A little. I just hope I can eat. This was just so . . . unexpected."

"That's how life is. Now go get ready, would you please?"

"Okay . . . but—"

"But nothing! Like I said, just have fun and be yourself, Savannah. Remember, I said a full report tomorrow." Kate ended the call and frowned. Now who would she have dinner with? "Well, there goes that plan up in a puff of smoke," she grumbled, but had to smile for Savannah's sake. But then her smile wobbled at the corners, and she thought she'd just open a damned can of soup or heat up a frozen dinner. But the vision of Bobby Flay's burger made that idea very unappealing. Kate inhaled a cleansing breath and looked down at her new sandals. After a moment she slipped them back on and lifted her chin. Hot emotion filled her throat but she swallowed hard and shrugged it off. Dinner for one again . . . so what?

Kate put a hand over her stomach and felt the pain and hollow loss wash over her again, but then inhaled another breath and grabbed her purse. With determined steps she headed for the door. *Feeling sorry for yourself will get you back on a long road to nowhere.* With great effort, Kate pushed the past from her mind and decided she'd treat herself to a dinner out on the town. Anything was better than being caught up in her own head like this.

Sunday night would be low-key at Sully's but still have

some music and laughter, which would hopefully make her feel alive instead of going through the motions.

Oh, but it didn't help that Cricket Creek Park was filled with families picnicking beneath shelters. Music and laugher filtered her way and her heart suddenly ached with longing when she passed the swing sets on the playground. If Craig hadn't cheated, her life would have been so different. Would she have had more children? She hadn't told anyone of her miscarriage, not even her family. Instead, she had packed her bags and taken her pain with her on the road and channeled all of her efforts into making money.

Oh . . . so much anger, so much pain, so much sorrow.

Kate's legs suddenly felt like they were made of jelly, and she had to sit down on a park bench. Why oh *why* had she let her thoughts go down this path? It was pointless and yet it seeped into her brain when she least expected it.

Kate knew why. Menopause made her emotional in more ways than simply the imbalance of hormones. The stark reality was that she was getting older . . . old enough to be a legal resident of Whisper's Edge. She was beyond middle age and heading into her twilight years. While many of the residents were robust and living a full life, some of them had serious health issues, and Kate had seen the death of many of them over the years. Each time it hit her hard that life was very quickly passing her by.

Kate closed her eyes and inhaled the scent of charcoal, summer blossoms, and sunscreen. She heard the giggles of children, the laughter of teenagers, and the crack of a bat hitting a ball. She longed to be sitting at a picnic table laden with casseroles and desserts, chatting with moms while the dads grilled and kids played. With a jolt, Kate realized that she could very well have been a grandma by now. What would it feel like to hold a grandchild in your arms; a child that was the image of your own?

Kate wanted to get up and make a beeline for home, but sorrow held her rooted to the wooden bench. Grief that she'd held pent up for years suddenly bubbled to the surface and it was all she could do to hold herself together. Dear God, this was not the time or the place to have a meltdown, but her body didn't seem to care one iota.

"Kate?"

She heard her name as if through a fog and looked up to see Ben standing next to the bench. His big body blocked out the sun and Kate hoped she didn't look as stricken as she felt.

"Are you okay?"

Well, so much for that hope.

"Yeah," she managed in a strangled voice that didn't even sound like her own. She swiped at a tear.

"Allergies?" he asked, and sat down beside her.

"Ragweed," she choked out.

"Thought so. You look nice."

"Not many people would say that I'm nice." She reached deep for her humor.

Ben chuckled. "Let me try that again. You look pretty."

Kate narrowed her eyes at him. "Have you been drinking? Got your beer goggles on?"

Ben held up an index finger. "One beer while I waited for my takeout at Sully's." He pointed to a white plastic bag sitting between his feet.

"That wouldn't happen to be a black-and-bleu cheeseburger with extra crispy bacon, would it?"

"No."

"Good for you because I was going to grab it and run like hell," she joked, and to her relief her voice only cracked a little bit.

Ben laughed, and damned if it didn't almost chase away her blues.

"And you wouldn't have had a chance in hell of catching me."

He laughed harder, and for some reason, hearing his laughter gave her ... hope. Why, she didn't know, but she couldn't explain her recent emotions to anyone lately. But Ben was making her feel better so she clung to that. "It's called the Cowboy with bacon and barbecue sauce."

"Ahhh bacon. Good enough. Will you share?"

"Hell no."

"Well, you could have at least thought about it, or at the very least pretended to consider my request, anyway."

"I thought about stopping by your place to see if you wanted to go grab a bite to eat with me."

"W-what?" His admission took her by surprise.

Ben shrugged slightly. "I wish I would have."

"Oh. I was actually headed to Sully's but got . . . a charley horse in my . . ." Where in the world does a person get a charley horse? "My ass," she finally said, since she knew he wasn't buying her bull.

"And had to sit down?" He nodded and was polite enough not to call her out on what was an obvious lie. "So do you want to?"

"Yes." Oh, that question held so many hidden meanings. "Wait a minute. Do I want to do . . . what?"

"Go back to Sully's and get you a . . . What was it that you wanted?"

"A black-and-bleu cheeseburger. Blame it on Bobby Flay."

"Kate, why did you say yes before you knew what the question was?"

Kate hesitated, but when his eyes held her captive she decided that honesty was the best policy. "Because the question didn't really matter."

Kate saw his very nice chest rise and fall and she wanted to reach over and see if his heart was pounding as hard as hers was hammering against her ribs. She wouldn't have been surprised if her shirt was lifting with each heavy beat.

"Then I think we'll just share the burger and save room for a little dessert."

Mercy. Was he thinking what she was thinking? She looked at the hot intensity of his gaze and swallowed hard. The answer would be yes.

"S-sounds like a plan," Kate managed to say and prayed that her legs would carry her home.

12

From This Moment . . .

$\mathcal{B}$EN NOTED THAT THEY MADE THE NORMAL TWENTY-MINUTE
walk back to Whisper's Edge in almost half the time
but damned if it didn't feel as if it took forever. As they
walked through the streets, residents waved or shouted
from front porches but Ben didn't even consider stopping,
and if someone needed something fixed it was going to have
to wait.

He was a man on a mission.

When he glanced at Kate's flushed face, Ben knew that
they were on the same page, and the thought sank straight
to his groin. But the fact that he was taking Kate to his place
felt surreal, like he was trapped in one of the daydreams he
had been having about her for a while now, but he knew
one thing . . . he didn't want it to end. When he spotted her
sitting there on that park bench looking so alone and so sad,
he knew that must be how he appeared most of the time,
and it was about damned time that it ended.

What he did know was that Kate had taken young Savannah under her wing and had given her a fresh start. He'd
witnessed her kindness to the elderly residents and admired

her tenacity in keeping Whisper's Edge going when times had gotten so tough. Her quick wit kept those around her laughing but Ben recognized the sadness in the depths of her eyes ... sorrow that she tried to keep hidden.

"You okay?" They'd hoofed it pretty quickly but she hadn't seemed to mind the fast pace.

"I'm fine," she said as they rounded the bend and closed in on his small home. "I'm in pretty good shape for an old broad," she joked but her smile had an edge of shyness to it.

Ben realized that she must be feeling much of the same kind of emotion that was gripping him and he felt his heart kick into high gear. But then worry suddenly slipped into his mind and threatened his good mood. What if things got a little steamy? He hadn't kissed a woman for such a long time. . . . What if he sucked? And damn, did he forget that he was sixty? All kinds of what-ifs started slamming into his brain and he suddenly wondered what the hell he was doing.

This was insanity!

But in truth he'd been attracted to Kate for a long time, even though he'd fought it tooth and nail. If he wasn't mistaken, she felt the same way. He sure as hell hoped that he wasn't mistaken. When he'd walked in on her cooling off beneath the ceiling fan with her shirt half unbuttoned he'd about lost it right then and there. The vision had stuck in his mind and invaded his brain at all hours of the day and night. He thought about it now. . . .

And that was all it took.

When they reached his home Ben opened the front door for her. Even though his heart was beating like wild, he calmly walked over and put the bag of food onto the round table in the breakfast nook in the corner of the room. And then, just as calmly, he walked back over to where Kate stood. He looked deep into her eyes to make sure she was feeling the same thing.

And that's where the calm ended.

Her purse hit the hardwood floor with a soft thud when

Ben pulled her into his arms. He dipped his head and captured her mouth in a kiss that was like striking a match to dry timber. The feel of her soft, moist lips had him deepening the kiss, needing more. She moaned against his mouth and gripped his shoulders, pressing her body closer. Ben wrapped his arms around her and slipped his hands beneath the silky blouse, eager for the feel of her skin.

He wanted her beneath him, in his bed, naked with her legs wrapped around his waist.

But it was too much, too soon. . . . Or was it?

She kissed him back with hot passion, and when she tugged his shirt from his pants Ben eagerly awaited the sensation of her hands sliding up his back. He explored her sweet mouth, kissing her deeply, thoroughly, and loving ever second. When his mouth moved to her neck she gasped, pressing her body even closer, as if she couldn't get enough. Well good, because neither could he.

"All these damned clothes are in the way," he grumbled.

"True."

"I want you in my bed," he said into her ear. "But—"

"Then take me there," she answered in a sexy, breathy voice that made him groan. He looked down at the tent in his pants. Yep, all of his parts were working.

"No problem." When he scooped her up in his arms she yelped and then laughed as he carried her down the short hallway to his bedroom. His house was small and his furnishings were simple but Ben kept everything clean and neat even though he rarely had company. The blinds were pulled shut but fingers of waning sunlight bathed the room with a soft glow. A paddle fan turned in a lazy circle but did nothing to cool Ben off. He let Kate's long legs ease to the floor and then kissed her again. "I need some skin," he pleaded.

"Me too." Her tone was husky, needy. When she fumbled with the buttons on his shirt he chuckled softly and then helped her. When he was shirtless she ran her hands over his chest. "You're gorgeous. All that muscle makes my knees weak. It would make my day when you would mow your lawn in nothing but gym shorts. I made a point of having to pass by your house but pretended not to stare."

Ben chuckled. "I had no idea."

"I fully confess that I find you gorgeous and sexy as hell." Her fingers fumbled again this time with his belt and when she brushed against his erection he sucked in a breath. God, he hoped he could hold it together. "And it evidently makes me clumsy."

Ben laughed. He stepped back and toed off his leather sandals before making quick work of his pants and underwear.

"Dear God." She reached out and grazed her fingers down his chest, sending a hot shiver down his spine. The female admiration in her gaze made him even harder, and when she lightly touched his cock Ben had to swallow a groan. "You are one gorgeous man."

"So you say."

"I mean it."

"Why do *you* still have your clothes on?"

"Good question," she joked, but Ben sensed hesitation.

He tilted her head up with the tip of his finger. "Are we going too fast?"

"No, it's just that . . ." She swallowed hard. "I haven't been naked in front of a man for a long time and—"

Ben smothered her insecurity with a hot kiss. "You're beautiful, Kate. And, um, as you can tell you turn me on something fierce."

"You haven't seen me naked yet," she joked, and Ben felt emotion gather in his throat. The humor was her shield, her guard.

"Well, I'm about to remedy that." He made quick work of the belt and then tugged the billowy shirt over her head. He took in the sexy sight of her standing there in a cream-colored bra before reaching behind her to unhook it. When she reached up to cover her breasts he beat her to the punch, cupping the lush fullness. "You are one beautiful woman."

"So you say," she teased him with his own line but her voice was breathless.

"So I mean it," he said softly but firmly.

She opened her eyes as if to see if he was telling the truth.

"You are." When he brushed her nipples with his thumbs, her eyes closed and they sank backward onto the bed.

"I'm no spring chicken," she protested.

"Neither am I but I swear you make me feel like I'm eighteen again." Ben quickly pulled off her sandals and tugged her pants off until she was naked except for a pair of cream silky panties and he wanted to lap it up. "Those are hot."

She laughed low in her throat. "And I'm damned sure glad that I shaved my legs," she joked, but her breath hitched while he explored her soft skin.

When she shivered, he asked, "Are my hands too rough? I have callouses."

"God no, you have the hands of a workingman. I love the way they feel on my body." Youth might have passed them by but there was a certain beauty that comes with age. She moaned when he caressed the silk fabric between her thighs until she felt hot and moist. "I need to taste you, Kate."

"Ben!" she protested but he tugged her panties down and buried his face between her thighs. "Oh . . ." She pushed at his head but he laved and teased with his tongue until she tugged his hair and arched her back. "God!" she gasped hoarsely but he could feel her giving in to the pleasure. He wanted to please her, to pleasure her until she couldn't take any more. He loved the taste of her, the feel of her, and when he reached up and caressed her breasts she cried his name.

Unable to wait any longer Ben scooted up and covered her body with his. He groaned at the sheer pleasure of skin on smooth skin. Her alluring, feminine perfume filled his head and the texture of her curves fitting perfectly against him made his senses sing. Ben dipped his head and kissed her, and when she parted her thighs he entered her silky warm heat.

God, it felt amazing.

"Oh!" Kate moaned and then wrapped her legs around him. He rocked against her, moving slowly, savoring each stroke, wanting to make this last. He kissed her neck, loving the sweet sensation of being sheathed inside her body. But when she arched her back and pressed her hands to his ass and squeezed, he stroked faster, went deeper. "Oh, Ben!" When he heard her soft gasp and felt her body clench Ben thrust deep and climaxed with hot pleasure that seemed to erupt from his toes.

"God . . ." He pressed his forehead to hers and then chuckled softly. He shuddered. "That was . . ."

"Amazing? Stupendous? Incredible?"

Ben pulled back and looked into her eyes. "Yeah . . . all those things." He dipped his head and kissed her gently and then rolled to his side and pulled her close, enjoying the warm afterglow of their lovemaking. "And more." He could feel the fast beat of her heart and he smiled. He kissed the delicate slope of her shoulder and then sent a warm trail of kisses up her neck before hugging her close. She sighed, and he smiled again at the sound of her contentment. Relaxed. As it should be. They spooned for a while, not speaking, neither of them wanting to break the spell.

"Are you hungry?" he finally asked.

"Famished."

"Sorry we had dessert first."

Kate rolled over and faced him. "Dessert? I thought that was just an appetizer."

Ben laughed and he felt something ease inside him. Kate was melting the hard ball of pain that had been lodged in his gut for a long time. Ben was starting to feel more like his old self.

And it felt good. No, it felt great.

Kate smiled, and Ben was pleased to see that the sad, haunting look in her eyes had vanished. Life, as he well knew, sometimes threw you curveballs, and it was hard to keep your head in the game. But Ben suddenly felt recharged. He had no idea how long the feeling would last, or where this would go past tonight, but he refused to think about anything and, instead, simply live in the moment.

13

There's Something About Savannah

"HOW DO YOU KNOW WHEN THE CHARCOAL IS READY?" Tristan waved his hand over the coals but wasn't sure.

Savannah finished lighting the citronella lanterns and then walked over to stand beside him. "When it turns an ash gray and looks as if it's glowing red from the inside."

"Oh." Tristan examined the mound of charcoal she had fashioned in the Weber grill, and then nodded. "I think we're almost there."

Savannah picked up a stick and poked a briquette. "I do believe you're right. Haven't you used charcoal before?"

"No, only the gas kind of grill."

"Sweet. Well then you're going to be pleasantly surprised."

"I like those kind of surprises the best."

Savannah chuckled. "The flavor is so much better. Lots of the folks here in Whisper's Edge use old-school charcoal. It was all they knew back in the day." She pointed to the grill. "Of course, this relic was left here by the previous owner, looking all crusty but I brought it back to life with some elbow grease."

"Is there anything here that hasn't been salvaged?"

"Hmmm . . ." She tapped the side of her cheek. "Not much, I suppose and I guess in a way even I fall into that category." Savannah peered down at the charcoal but then glanced back up at him and winced. "Sorry that it's taken so long for the coals to get hot. I should have gotten it lit a while ago but . . ." She paused and rolled her eyes. "I was too caught up in deciding what to wear." She looked down at her yellow sundress and shrugged. "I think I'm over-dressed. The outfit was Kate's idea."

Tristan loved her honesty. "Well, you look very pretty, Savannah," he assured her with a firm nod.

"Thank you, Tristan," she said, but then ducked her head and gazed down at her toes. "An improvement over what I was wearing earlier, I suppose?"

Tristan chuckled. She sure would be surprised if she knew that he'd found her sexy as hell in her tattered shorts and tight tank top. But surely she'd been told that she was pretty before? He could tell that she was nervous, and he wished he could put her at ease. Of course, he guessed he'd be jittery too if his boss had come over for dinner, and he hoped she didn't regret her invitation. Maybe she was only being polite? He hoped not. But although Tristan didn't really feel like her boss, he was well aware of the fact that he held her future in the palm of his hands.

"Would you like another beer?" When she titled her head up Tristan had a hard time not closing the gap between them and kissing her.

"Yes, please." He handed her his empty bottle, and the slight touch of her fingers brushing his sent another jolt of longing through his bloodstream.

"Coming right up." She gave him that shy smile of hers that made him want to drag her into his arms and kiss her. But then again what didn't? All it took was a look, a touch; even the sound of her husky laughter turned him on. Now that he knew what it felt like to kiss her, he wanted her in his arms even more. The kiss was sort of hanging in the air between them, creating a sexual tension unlike any he'd felt before. But it went beyond attraction. There was just something about Savannah that made him feel ... protective of her. This basic male instinct wasn't something he was used to experiencing and it took him by absolute surprise.

He looked over at her and watched her open the bottle of beer. Maybe it was because she had a vulnerable softness and he was used to hard edges. *Or perhaps I'm already starting to care about her* tiptoed into his reasoning but he pushed that thought away.

Tristan already knew that coming here with a bottle of wine was going against everything he'd told himself to do. And cooking dinner with her in the moonlight wasn't smart either. But where Savannah Perry was concerned Tristan didn't seem to have one ounce of self-control.

"Thanks," he said when she pressed the cold beer into his hand and then peered over his shoulder. "I think we should give it about ten more minutes and the coals will be perfection." She gave him an okay sign with her thumb and index finger.

Tristan nodded. "I always go for perfection when given the option."

"So you're a perfectionist?"

Tristan stepped away from the heat of the grill. "You sort of have to be in my line of work. A minor missed detail could cost the client lots of money or even the case."

"That must have been stressful."

"It was, especially when you're poring over details at all hours of the day and night. I needed a break."

"I can't even imagine."

When he sensed she would have asked more, Tristan decided it was best to change the subject. "Let's sit down while the coals burn. Unless you have something I can help you with in the kitchen?"

"I don't think so." Savannah shook her head. "Those

amazing steaks you brought are seasoned and coming to room temperature. The potatoes are baking in the oven and the salad is tossed and chilling in the fridge. I even have some emergency dessert in the freezer."

"Emergency dessert?"

"Mint chocolate chip ice cream. I keep it on hand for my sweet-tooth cravings and for when I'm having one of those days."

"I have a stash of Reese's Cups for that."

"Excellent choice!"

Tristan smiled but he hated to imagine Savannah sad and in need of ice cream in order to cheer her up. He suddenly wondered if she had any friends her own age that she hung out with or if she dated. Although they'd had a blast at Wine and Diner, Tristan got the impression that she was a homebody. The thought somehow bothered him. Savannah deserved to go out on the town and have fun on a regular basis. "Well"—he raised his eyebrows—"sounds like you have everything under control. You must like to cook."

"I've learned a lot from watching seasoned cooks in the community. Since I'm often invited to dinner I pitch in and help. My senior friends cook a lot of comfort food that likes to stick to my bum." She lightly patted her backside and groaned.

Tristan chuckled as they sat down at the bistro table, but he thought her bum was quite nice. The sun had set but the lanterns cheerfully flickered in the background and there was just enough light coming from the kitchen to cast a soft glow over the backyard. Savannah had replaced the geranium in the center of the table with two fat candles and added two place settings. An end table held a small galvanized bucket of beer chilling in ice. Little did she know that she was the perfect hostess and that her simple patio and lush garden could easily be featured in one of those decorating magazines that were stacked on her coffee table.

"Would you like some music?" Savannah asked.

"No, I don't think so right now." He shook his head. "Our conversation is enough for me. Do I hear water gurgling?"

Savannah nodded. "Yeah, it's a tiny pond with a waterfall in the center over there in the far corner of the yard. The water attracts birds and sometimes a frog or two will appear. It was a DIY project gone way wrong until Ben came to my rescue."

"The sound is soothing."

"Oh, I know. I leave the windows open until it gets too hot to take. I like hearing bullfrogs from the river, the wind in the trees, and the chirp of crickets. The sounds of nature put me to sleep in nothing flat."

"I can imagine. All I heard from my condo was the hum of traffic on the highway, horns honking, and an occasional siren. Not exactly music to my ears."

She took a sip of her wine. "I know I've already asked but I can't believe that you really don't miss the city?"

Tristan tilted his head. "Ah, some things, for sure. And at the risk of sounding like a mama's boy, I do miss my mother."

Savannah's eyes widened. "Oh, don't *ever* apologize for missing your mother." She leaned forward. "And don't ever take her for granted. People do, you know." She suddenly sat back and looked up at the sky. "Oh, sorry for sounding so bossy! I guess you just hit a nerve."

Tristan had to ask, even though he was pretty sure of the answer. "Are you an orphan, Savannah?"

"Not technically, but kind of like that," she answered quietly, but then gave him a slight grin. "But I sure looked like Orphan Annie. All that poufy red hair! I just never had Daddy Warbucks to rescue me or a cute dog named Sandy to keep me company," she joked, but he wasn't buying the humor.

"So were you raised in an orphanage?"

"No." Savannah shook her head. "There really aren't orphanages like that anymore. Foster care is supposed to create a 'family atmosphere.'" She used air quotes.

"And I'm guessing it didn't?" he asked gently.

Savannah shrugged. "It's an overcrowded and flawed system for sure. There are way too many kids and not nearly enough homes to place them." She shook her head. "Foster parents are supposed to be trained and certified. Qualified. And don't get me wrong, I think many of them offer their homes for all the right reasons but sometimes it turns out to be more than they can handle and they drop out of the program. Unfortunately, others are in it simply for the money. There is abuse and neglect. It's sad, Tristan."

"Are there social workers who check up on things?"

"Not nearly enough. Those jobs are low-paying and difficult at best. The stories you might have seen on the news were things I witnessed with my own eyes."

The vision of his mother reading bedtime stores to him at night filtered into his head. He couldn't imagine not having that in his life. "So were you given up for adoption at birth?"

"No, I'm told that my parents were declared unfit, so they didn't give me up, just didn't take care of me. I was removed from their care at about the age of two. Sometimes I wish I remembered them but I guess in a sad way I'm blessed that I don't recall the conditions that led to me being taken away. Couldn't have been good, that's for sure."

He reached over and covered her hand with his. "I'm sorry. My comment about being a mama's boy was callous."

"You didn't know," she said. And when he squeezed her hand she said, "You gotta play the hand you were dealt."

"That's true." Tristan thought once again about his own childhood without a father figure and a grandfather who resented him. But still, he'd always felt loved by his mother. "But you know what they say: it's not the hand you were dealt but how you play the game, right?"

"Yeah, buddy, and I sure had to do some bluffing along the way." She remained thoughtful for a moment and then said, "There was one year when I had seven different addresses."

"Wow."

"It was my normal so I just dealt with it. I didn't have a clue as to what it felt like to have a real family. I could only go by books and television, so my idea of the whole thing was probably a little bit unrealistic. There weren't shows like *Modern Family* back then."

Tristan nodded. "I never knew my dad so I could have used a show like that too."

"I'm sorry, Tristan. Here I am going on and on. We all have our story, that's for sure."

"Not that I'm comparing it to your situation."

"Like I said, it was my normal," she replied, but then something flickered in her eyes. After a moment she said, "Oh, but going to those adoption fairs was not my favorite thing."

"Where prospective parents come to adopt?"

"Yes." Savannah nodded. "When I was really little it was just a fun afternoon of activities usually held at a park or something like that. I had no idea what was really transpiring. Later on, the whole thing just made me nervous and ultimately disappointed."

"I'm sorry."

"It was like speed dating for kids."

Tristan found that concept unsettling. "That had to be difficult."

"It was horrible for me but lots of cute kids got adopted so it is a method that works."

"I guess so, but seriously, I would have thought you would have been chosen right away."

"Are you kidding?" Savannah rolled her eyes. "I was born extremely pigeon-toed so I had to wear braces on my legs for a couple of years. Of course *now* they say braces don't even help and that the condition would have corrected itself. To top it off, remember I had this neon orange curly hair." She pointed to her head. "I looked like Orphan Annie on a good day and a Carrot Top mini-me when it rained. I was teased like crazy."

"I'm really sorry to hear that."

"Ah, don't be." Savannah waved a hand at him. "Kate says that whatever doesn't kill you makes you stronger." She laughed. "I guess I'm pretty damned strong." She bent her arm and flexed a muscle. "Maybe even have superpowers that I haven't discovered." She took a sip of wine and shrugged. After another minute she said, "*Aging out* is the hardest part."

"Aging out?"

"When you're too old to remain in the system. You're kind of just like shoved off into the big, bad world."

"That doesn't seem fair." Tristan felt his anger rise.

Savannah toyed with the stem of her glass. "What other choice is there? The sad thing is that lots of kids end up getting into drugs and land in jail. Pregnancy . . . poverty. It's a cycle that starts all over again. I, at least, finished high school and I tried so hard—I *really* did—but couldn't support myself. It was tough to make ends meet on minimum wage. I didn't have a car at first so getting to work was an issue. I finally bought this old heap of junk that lasted for about six months and then croaked." She paused for a second. "I'm embarrassed to admit it but I ended up homeless and just started . . . wandering. Kate found me here when this place was empty." After her quiet admission she lowered her gaze and fell silent.

Caught off guard, Tristan searched for something comforting to say. But having trained himself to stay emotionally detached, he remained at a loss for words. He liked to stick to graphs, charts, and reports and hard data. But when she took a sip of her wine he noticed a slight tremble in her hand, and it was his undoing. "You have absolutely nothing to be embarrassed about," Tristan said firmly. "Look at you, Savannah. You do a lot of good around here. You're one of the ones who broke the cycle."

She glanced over at him. "Thanks for saying that, but I was fortunate that Kate took me under her wing. Who knows what might have become of me."

Tristan had a sudden urge to reach over and take her hand but refrained. "I have a feeling you would have made it. I'm just sorry that your journey was such a tough one."

"Well, the journey led me here and I'm grateful. Hey, I have a nice home and lots people who care about me. I enjoy my job. Not everyone can say that."

"I really do admire your positive attitude."

"It wasn't the best of circumstances growing up, for sure, and boy, I saw some crazy stuff over the years, no doubt about it, but all in all I feel pretty lucky. Some of the other kids came from hideous abuse and acted out." She shuddered as if from the memory. "I just tried to stay away from trouble." She gave him a crooked smile. "Let's just say that if I could have had a superpower it would have been invisibility."

Something inside him rushed up to defend her. "Again, you don't give yourself enough credit! Sounds like you made your own luck."

She lifted one shoulder and looked at him. "Don't we all?"

"To a degree, I guess." Tristan watched her while she traced the rim of her wineglass and looked out over the yard.

After a moment she turned to him and smiled. "Well, there's always an upside to everything if you look hard enough."

"A silver lining?"

"Yeah, the cool thing about being poor is that you're so thrilled with such little bitty things. And my escape was always reading. The library was free! I spent a lot of time there as a kid. My afternoons weren't filled with playing soccer or at Girl Scouts meetings. I still visit the library whenever I can get the chance. It doesn't take much to make me happy and I appreciate everything I have. And, wow, that was a long speech."

"Savannah . . ."

She laughed. "Oh, don't look at me like I'm some kind of saint. I have my moods. Just ask Kate. I can moan and groan with the best of them." She made a big show of moaning and groaning until Tristan laughed with her.

"Okay, I get the picture," he said, but when her eyes suddenly turned serious again he asked, "Hey, what's wrong?"

"Well, it's just that . . ." She shook her head but then put a hand up to her lips. "Nothing."

"Savannah? Seriously, did I say something wrong?" The thought that he could upset her hit him like a sucker punch. "Tell me."

"Well, there is one thing that I don't like about working here."

"What? Is it something I can fix?"

"I wish."

"Savannah, I'll try. What is it?"

She sighed deeply. "Well, this is a retirement community, you know. People here are up in age." She swallowed hard. "It's tough when we lose someone or something serious happens like a stroke or heart attack. That's why I always try to have lots of exercise and activities."

He thought about the water aerobics class. "I'm certain it does a lot of good."

"I know but it still sucks. Sometimes leaving a spouse behind who has a hard time coping is just so painful to witness. I don't know if there is such a thing as dying of a broken heart but I've often seen the surviving spouse go not long afterward. And I know that there are lonely seniors living up in town. I wish we could make room for more of them." She rolled her eyes. "Oh, would you listen to me going on again? I'm so sorry!"

"Don't be, Savannah."

"Well, thank you, but you must think I'm one hot mess."

"No, I don't. I think you care. There's nothing wrong with that."

"Thank you, even if you're not being completely honest."

"I've been honest about everything I've said to you tonight," he answered, even though the word *honest* bothered him. "I guess seeing people living here in their twilight years makes you appreciate life more. I know it's cliché but I suppose it makes you remember that we're only here for a short time and that we should try to make the best of it."

She sat up straighter. "Oh, that is completely true! Now you know why I have a bucket list." It looked as if she was about to say something else but suddenly shook her head. "I've gone and talked your ear right off! You're probably bored to tears. I think that charcoal is darned good and ready. What do you say we put those steaks on the grill?"

"Sure." Tristan nodded, but when she rose to go inside he reached out and grabbed her hand. "Savannah, I enjoy talking to you. I'm not one bit bored."

"I'm glad," she said with a smile, but as she pulled her hand away Tristan held on just tightly enough to allow the contact to linger. He really couldn't remember when he had enjoyed the company of a woman more.

Tristan sighed as he watched her walk into her house, wishing that Savannah wasn't connected to Whisper's Edge, especially after hearing her story. He thought about the meeting he had later in the week with Mitch Monroe, who was one of the partners in the Cricket Creek stadium project and the developer of Wedding Row, the strip of shops near the river. In Tristan's recent research he'd read that with the success of the Cricket Creek Cougars, Mitch Monroe was hoping to add a convention center and perhaps a hotel in the future. Tristan's hope was that Monroe would either want to purchase the property as part of the development or perhaps have an interest in investing in the marina that Tristan had in mind. Either way it could be a lucrative deal and add to the satisfaction of making his grandfather eat crow.

He should be over-the-moon excited.

But Tristan just wasn't sure he could handle seeing disappointment in Savannah's expressive eyes. Whisper's Edge meant so much to her and to the residents who lived here. How in the world could he take that away?

14
Midnight Confessions

"WOW, SAVANNAH, YOU'RE RIGHT," TRISTAN COMMENTED after he swallowed his first bite of steak. "The flavor of real charcoal is amazing."

Savannah watched him dig in with relish and felt a sense of satisfaction that he was enjoying the meal. "Yep, my little ole grill isn't fancy but does the job. Sometimes simple is better. No bells and whistles need apply."

"Mmm . . ." Tristan nodded in agreement as he happily chewed on another bite and then pointed to his plate with his fork. "No-frills baked potato and a nice crisp salad is one of my favorite meals. Thank you."

Savannah shrugged. "There's nothing too fancy about me, Tristan. I'm pretty straightforward."

"You sound as if you're apologizing for that." He shook some salt onto his potato and then looked at her. "Believe me, I find your candor incredibly refreshing."

"Thank you." Savannah accepted his compliment but she wasn't quite sure what *candor* meant. She kept the smile on her face, even though she felt a quick stab of insecurity poke her in the gut. He was a lawyer. He went to school for a million years. She had been lucky to finish high school. If they got into an intellectual discussion about something like politics or art she was going to be toast.

"So have you needed to rescue Willie lately?"

Ah, a safe subject. Savannah breathed an inner sigh of relief. "No, the Camden brothers have been careful about keeping the gate closed. They might have acted all huffy about the situation, but Miss Patty pretty much rules the roost for the most part."

"That's good to hear."

"Oh, not so fast. Willie did, however, dig up Etta Mae Baker's petunias a couple of days ago. Well, I should say allegedly. Miss Patty tried to blame deer, but they tend to eat flowers and not dig them up. Etta Mae was madder than a wet hen! She was yelling really loud since Miss Patty is a tad hard of hearing, or so she says. I sometimes think it's selective hearing on her part. Anyway, I had to come between the two of them and attempt to smooth their ruffled feathers."

Tristan grinned. "And how did you do that?"

Savannah put her fork down and said, "Well, as you already witnessed, Miss Patty can be pretty stubborn and protective where her dear Willie's concerned. When Etta Mae demanded new petunias, Miss Patty wanted to know if there were any witnesses to Willie's said destruction of her flower bed."

"And was there?"

"No, but Etta Mae threw out there that every other dog must adhere to the leash law so it must have been Willie."

Tristan angled his head. "But that doesn't mean that another dog couldn't have gotten loose."

"That's what Miss Patty said in a snippy tone that totally ticked Etta Mae off even more. At that point Etta Mae even hinted that the destruction was an attempt to keep her from winning the best flower bed award for the week. That comment blew the lid off any niceties, and, Tristan, they got nose to nose. Etta Mae was pointing her finger and shaking her

head so hard that I was afraid that her false teeth were going to go flying out of her mouth. Lordy, I thought I was
going to have a dire situation on my hands!" She leaned
forward. "That's when I had to *literally* get between them,
and it was a tight squeeze."

"So what happened?"

"One of the Camden brothers, I think it was Clovis,
yelled 'cat fight,' from where they were observing the tussle
from across the street, drawing Etta Mae's attention. She
tried to lure them over with a sweet smile. I swear she even
showed them some leg."

"Are you kidding?"

"Nope, she used to be a dancer and her legs are still in
great shape. She shows them off at every opportunity, ticking the other women off something fierce."

"So she was hoping to get the Camdens on her side?"

"Exactly. I took the brief opportunity to lean over and
advise Miss Patty to just give in and replace the petunias to
avoid having the possibility of having Willie's no-leash freedom revoked at the next council meeting."

"Did she agree?"

"Yes, but very reluctantly. Then there was the added dis-
pute of who would plant the petunias. Miss Patty would not
offer to do the planting but Etta Mae knew she was pushing
her luck and gave in pretty fast on that one."

"Good job, Savannah. You're a good mediator."

"Thanks. I guess I get plenty of practice."

"So, I have to ask . . . off the record, of course. Do you
think Willie was the culprit?"

Savannah started slicing her steak. "Well, like Miss Patty
pointed out, there weren't witnesses but, yes, most likely.
Willie likes to bury bones here and there and when the
spirit moves him he runs off and digs one up and then eats
the dirty ole thing."

"And do you think Miss Patty knew it was Willie all
along?"

"Oh, without a doubt, but admitting it might also get

Willie's wings clipped. I knew she'd never come clean in a million years. And of course only Willie knows for sure and he isn't talking."

"Well then, you did an excellent job. Nice legal work, Savannah." He reached over and gave her a high five.

"That's quite a compliment coming from you." Savannah looked closely at his expression to see if he was teasing but he seemed sincere.

"Well, you're a natural. I wouldn't want to face you in court."

The thought that he really did admire her made her feel pretty proud. "I'll fully admit that keeping the peace sometimes takes some doing. We have our fair share of grumpy old men, angry disputes, and . . . dare I say it?" She nibbled on the inside of her lip and remained mum.

"Oh, come on, don't leave me hanging."

Savannah put her fork down and leaned closer. "Love triangles," she told him in a stage whisper.

"You're pulling my chain."

Savannah pressed her lips together and shook her head slowly. "Nope, the men here are outnumbered two to one so it's slim pickings for the single ladies."

Tristan chuckled. "I guess you do have your hands full."

"Sometimes it's like dealing with elderly teenagers but I love each and every one of them. I have a bird's-eye view of aging, and at least I know that growing old doesn't have to be boring. I swear I could write a book."

Tristan angled his head. "Well, then, you should."

"What?"

"Write a book."

Savannah waved a hand at him. "Oh, I was just joking."

"I'm not." He took a swallow of his beer and looked at her after setting it down. "You said you were an avid reader. Writing would probably come naturally. Have you ever tried it?"

"No . . ."

"Then you should."

"Oh . . . Tristan," she scoffed but a flutter of excitement went through her stomach. "I wouldn't know where to begin."

"Jot down some anecdotes or vignettes."

"Good, idea," she said, nodding.

"Savannah, you're creative, smart, and funny. You just might be on to something."

She thought she should remind him that she had only been joking but he seemed serious and so she nodded. "Maybe . . ."

"You could show that growing old doesn't have to be a bête noire."

"True," she agreed but then tried to piece together in her brain what that could possibly mean. "I could go that route . . . but I have to confess that I have absolutely no clue on God's green earth what bête noire is."

Tristan chuckled. "It means something you dread. And hey, only a geek like me would use that term."

"Well then, now that I know the definition I'll use it in conversation tomorrow and show off my superior knowledge." Even though Savannah felt a little bit better at his admission she still knew that they were worlds apart. To think that anything could come from a dinner and a kiss would be foolish. Lyrics from the Taylor Swift song "White Horse" filtered into her head and she reminded herself once again that *I'm not a princess and this ain't a fairy tale.*

But as she looked across the small table at Tristan's handsome face she decided to give herself tonight. If she fell a little bit in love, no one would ever know.

With her resolve firmly in place, Savannah allowed herself to relax. She soon had Tristan laughing at more tales of Whisper's Edge residents. "You might not believe it but there is rarely a dull moment around here."

"Oh no, I believe it. Seriously, you should consider the book suggestion."

"I could go on forever," she admitted with a laugh.

"I could listen forever," Tristan said, but instead of laughing he looked at her and gave Savannah a bone-melting smile that made her feel as if she might slide from her chair and dissolve into a warm puddle right there in the middle of the patio.

There was a sudden silence, an awareness that passed between them making Savannah long to push the table to the side, stand up, and press her body against his. She wanted to dance in the moonlight, and throw caution to the doggone wind! But most of all, she wanted to be kissed again.

Dangerous, she thought and cleared her throat. "Um, can I get you anything else?" she asked to break the silence, but her darned voice came out breathless. She felt the heat of a blush steal into her cheeks when she realized that her breathy question somehow sounded suggestive. Or then again maybe it was just the steamy images that kept coming into her brain every time she looked at him. "Coffee?" She decided to be more specific.

"No, thanks. I'm good."

Oh, I bet you are, said the devil perched on her shoulder.

"Well, if you change your mind let me know," she offered in a fairly steady voice but felt heat remain in her cheeks. She really needed to rein in her racy thoughts before one of them came shooting right out of her mouth. "I don't mind brewing some."

"No, that's okay. It keeps me up at night."

"Oh," was all that she could muster since his up-all-night response conjured all kinds of sexy images. Savannah wasn't one to have these kinds of thoughts but her imagination decided to run wild. *Please don't blush*, she thought but gingers were the world's worst at controlling blushing, and she felt another one coming on.

Damn!

Savannah decided to blame her flaming face on something else other than her acute embarrassment at picturing him twisted in the sheets, naked. "Whew, yes, it's too warm of a night for hot coffee," she said and fanned her face.

"What was I thinking?" She hoped the dim light would hide her sudden glow.

"You were simply being a good hostess."

Of course, a cool breeze that threatened to make her shiver had to go and blow right through the yard strongly enough to make the candles flicker. She willed herself not to hug her arms across her chest and rub the goose bumps from her bare skin. "Well, I wish I had something sweet to offer you for dessert," she said and then wanted to cover her face with her hands. Every single thing that came out of her mouth seemed to sound suggestive. She decided she'd be better off keeping her mouth shut, but if the conversation ceased he would leave and Savannah realized that she didn't want the evening to end. She wasn't ready for the coach to turn back into a pumpkin just yet.

"You're frowning."

"Am I?"

"I'm sorry, Savannah."

"Sorry? Whatever for?"

"It's late and I'm sure I've overstayed my welcome. Let me help you clean up."

"No . . . no, I'll do it." Not knowing what else to do, she stood up.

"I insist." He pushed back his chair and picked up his plate. "Besides, cleaning up gives me the excuse to stay a little while longer," he admitted, and then gave her that smile that made her legs feel as if they were made of salt-water taffy on a warm summer day.

Now, just how was she going to walk on saltwater taffy legs? Very carefully.

Savannah took a step and, to her horror, swayed just slightly but of course he had to notice.

"Are you okay?" He sat down his dish and put a steadying hand on her elbow.

"Must be the wine," she lied.

"You didn't have that much."

"I guess I'm a lightweight."

"We'll find out," he said and then without warning scooped her up into his arms.

"Tristan, what in heaven's name are you doing? I meant, like, figuratively."

"I'm carrying you into the house."

"I don't need for you to carry me!"

"It's just a precaution."

"You're going to hurt yourself!"

"I'm not as weak as I look."

"I didn't mean that you look weak."

"Good, I wouldn't want all those hours in the gym to be for nothing."

"I'm too heavy. You'll blow a disc or something horrible."

"Savannah, you're not heavy in the least."

"I eat a lot of meat loaf and mashed potatoes. And pie. You're gonna hurt yourself. This is crazy."

"I feel a little crazy when I'm around you."

"You mean that in a good way, right?"

"Yes! I like feeling . . ."

"Spontaneous?" she provided.

"Yes."

Savannah smiled. "It's about time that I provided a word for you and . . ." She tapped his chest but when his gaze lingered on her lips she forgot the rest of what she was going to say.

"Now, stop being silly and put your arms around my neck. I promise I won't drop you." He demonstrated by carrying her with apparent ease, making her feel girly and feminine. She was relieved that he didn't grunt or seem to strain himself. "I'm going to put you on the sofa and then go back out to blow out the candles and bring in the dishes. You stay put."

"I can't let you do that," she sputtered. "I'm not about to let you wait on me for goodness' sake. Seriously, I can't let you do this."

"Oh, yes, you can." He turned his face toward hers just

as she was going to protest further and *oh dear lord* their lips brushed.

And that was all it took.

Tristan let her slide down his body and then captured her mouth with a hot kiss that had Savannah clinging to him in order to stay upright. She'd always thought that the weak-in-the-knees thing that she read about was a bunch of bologna.

She was wrong.

His lips felt firm but deliciously soft, and when his tongue touched hers Savannah felt a hot shot of desire slip down her body and had her toes curling. Any minute she was going to do the knee-pop thing and point her toes toward the ceiling just like in the movies. She threaded her fingers through his hair and kissed him back like they had just invented kissing and there would be a law against it tomorrow. He slanted his mouth across hers and kissed her on and on. And there went her knee, *pop* . . .

Savannah felt her feet float and wondered if the walking-on-air thing was true too but then realized he was half carrying her across the living room to the sofa. He tumbled backward, taking her with him without breaking where their lips were fused together. His warm mouth finally moved to her neck, making her gasp with pleasure at the hot tingle that traveled down her spine. She pressed her body to his shamelessly, and when Tristan slid his hands up her legs to her butt she moaned with the sheer pleasure of it all. He tilted her body against the back cushions and turned his attention to her breasts, caressing one while he kissed where she spilled out of the top of her dress. Savannah arched her back, and when he slipped her straps down her shoulders she didn't protest. Not one little bit.

She simply couldn't. She was putty in his hands.

Savannah sighed when he showered her with warm kisses. Although Savannah longed to rip her dress off and drag him into her bed, there was just enough sense left in her befuddled sex-drugged brain to realize that as much as she wanted to make wild, passionate love to him, she probably shouldn't. Oh, but she wanted to. Maybe he'd twist her arm a little bit. All it would take is another kiss and she'd be a goner.

Tristan must have dug for his last shred of reason at about the same point of no return because he slowly pulled back. Savannah kept her eyes closed, drunk with passion, but as the heat of the moment wore off she started to feel a bit embarrassed at her wild, wanton behavior.

"Hey," Tristan said gently, and then ran his fingertip down her cheek.

Savannah nodded slightly but refused to open her eyes and look at him.

"Savannah?"

She opened her eyes. "Yes?"

He gave her a slight grin, but even in the dim light she could tell that his eyes were serious. "I pride myself on having self-control but when I get around you my control goes for a ride and never comes back."

"Why do you think you have to control yourself around me, Tristan? Why can't you just be yourself?"

"Because I guess I don't really know who that is, Savannah," he answered softly, but something flickered in his eyes. He was holding something back and she wondered if this was a gentle way of letting her down without telling her that she was beneath him in so many ways.

"I understand," she said and was glad that her voice remained fairly steady.

"I'm so sorry."

Her heart dropped to her toes. "Hey, we got caught up in the moment. The wine . . . the moonlight. It happens."

Just not to her.

Tristan scooted back and gave her the opportunity to adjust her clothing. She did so with flaming cheeks. "Don't beat yourself up about it," she offered, but he turned on the cushion and looked at her with gentle but troubled eyes. "Hey, I didn't exactly put up a fight."

Tristan reached over and cupped her chin in the palm of his hand and it was all Savannah could do not to tilt her head and lean into his caress. For a moment she thought he was going to say something to put her heart and insecurities at ease but he cleared his throat and remained silent. Finally, he said, "You're a sweetheart, Savannah. And I'd better go before I kiss you again." He rubbed his thumb across her bottom lip and then dropped his hand.

And what would be so wrong with that? She wanted to ask that simple question but she knew the answer was complicated. Instead, she gave him a slight smile to let him know that she was going to be okay. But as she watched him walk out the door every fiber in her being wanted to run after him and drag him back into her arms. But throwing herself at her boss might not be the best decision and so she refrained.

Savannah glanced over at the digital clock on the microwave and chuckled darkly at the irony.

It was midnight. Go figure.

She walked on wooden legs to her closet and took off the sundress that she might not ever be able to wear again. After putting on the ragged shorts and tank top that she'd worn earlier she headed outside, cleaned up the forgotten dinner plates, and then came back out to blow out the torches and candles.

With a long sigh, Savannah sat down in the moonlight and listened to the sounds of the night. The gentle gurgle of the fountain soothed her sadness and she finally inhaled a deep, shaky breath. She wasn't one to dwell on things. She'd given herself the night and she'd keep it in her memory vault and bring it out for review now and then. Savannah knew how to capture bits and pieces of happiness when it presented itself. This was a night to remember. And she would.

But after she crawled into bed she felt so alone that she ached with it. Oh, how she wished she had someone to hold her, to spoon her . . . to love her like there was no tomorrow.

But there was tomorrow. She thought of the Orphan Annie song but couldn't quite muster up a smile. Yes, the sun would rise and she would take on another day with a smile on her face.

She was a survivor.

And maybe, just *maybe* . . . someday her prince would come.

15

God Gave Me . . . You

KATE TOSSED HER ZEBRA-STRIPED READING GLASSES DOWN on her desk and looked over at Savannah. "Girl, are you gonna tell me who pooped in your Cheerios?"

"Ew—Ah, that is just so gross. Seriously."

"So is that pinched frown on your pretty face."

"I am merely concentrating on the tutorial I'm reading about on how to hook rugs from old T-shirts. I don't want to do a craft that would be too taxing on the ladies that suffer with arthritis."

"You can't fool an old fool, Savannah. You've been in a blue funk for the past few days. What gives?"

"Nothing," Savannah insisted, but when her eyes went back to the computer screen Kate persisted.

"Okay, I'll just say it. Seems to me the blue mood started after you had dinner with Tristan. Care to elaborate?"

"There's nothing to explain, Kate."

"Uh-huh. Right. I believe that one. Sure I do."

Savannah sighed. "You're not going to let this go, are you?"

"Not on your life."

Savannah gave her a long-suffering look and then said, "Okay, I might have allowed myself to enjoy Tristan's company a bit too much."

"Did he kiss you again? I've been dying to ask."

"Yes."

"I thought kissing him was amazing?"

"It was."

Kate barely refrained from rubbing her hands together. "So why so glum?"

"Because, Kate, nothing can come of it."

"And you know this . . . how?"

Savannah shot her a grave look. "Okay, then let me put it this way. It won't. Tristan let me know at the end of the evening that he didn't mean for things to get . . . you know."

"Steamy?"

"He didn't use that term but yes."

"But it did and that's all that matters."

"Kate, I haven't heard a peep from him since."

"Grow a couple and call him."

Savannah's mouth dropped open. "Are you out of your ever-lovin' mind?"

"Sometimes you have to jump out of the chute and enter the rodeo even if you might get tossed off."

"My life has been a wild enough ride. I think I'll pass."

"And sit in the stands?"

"Can we quit with this bull-riding analogy?"

Kate looked at her for a long moment.

"What?" Savannah finally asked. "I know that look and I'm pretty sure the answer is going to be a very big no."

"My nephew Jeff is coming into town."

"No! I am so done with blind dates."

"You've met him so it isn't blind. He's cute."

"The answer is still no."

"We're going to Sully's later on. It's karaoke night."

"I can't sing worth a lick and you know it."

"Jeff can."

Savannah sighed. "Kate!"

"Ben is going to go, and Jeff said he doesn't want to feel like a third wheel."

"He did not say that."

"Okay, no, but Jeff did ask about you. He said you're hot."

"He didn't say that either. You're making this up."

"Yes, he did."

Savannah gave her a look.

"Okay, I asked him first but he said yes."

"As I recall he is several years younger than me."

"So? He's twenty-four. Single and getting better lookin' every time I see the boy. He's been in Nashville going after his dream of having a country music career. My sister is trying her best to bring him back to Cricket Creek. I told her to let him give it a shot but she wants him to stay and work the family farm. It's been weighing on his mind. A fun night out would do the boy a world of good."

"And just how do I fit into the picture?"

"I might have said that I would get you to come along."

"Kate!"

"Have a heart. The boy needs some cheering up."

"You're not playing fair."

"So will you? Ben wants you to come too."

That admission squeezed a small smile out of Savannah. "So what gives with you two?"

Kate shrugged. "We've been . . . hanging out." And having wild and passionate lovemaking sessions that left Kate physically drained but seriously satisfied. "You know, enjoying each other's company." In every room of the house.

"That's good to hear. He seemed to have such a nice time that night we all went out," she said but then gave Kate a closer look. "Why haven't you told me?"

"You haven't exactly been talkative here of late." Kate really wanted to tell Savannah more but she and Ben had decided to keep their relationship or whatever it was on the down low. Tongues wagged in Whisper's Edge and until she knew where this was going with Ben she wanted to keep her personal life under wraps. Ben was perfectly fine with the situation. He liked his privacy too. But coming home from his place in the wee hours of the morning was proving to be dangerous since she took the route through backyards rather than be seen on the street. This morning, half asleep and worn-out from lovemaking, Kate had tripped over a garden troll and had landed facedown in the dewy grass. Tonight it was going to be Ben's turn to sneak home in the dark. "So, we'll pick you up around seven? Eat dinner at Sully's and then do a little dancing and karaoke?"

Savannah hesitated.

"Come on, don't be such a fuddy-dud."

"I'm not a fuddy-dud!"

"Great, I'll take that as a yes. See you at seven sharp," she insisted and got a sigh for an answer. She'd take that as a yes too. "You'll have fun, Savannah," Kate added gently. She hated to see the young woman appear unhappy.

"My life was just fine and dandy until you decided that I needed to start going out."

"Was it?" Kate challenged and wished she would have bitten her tongue. But then she thought about how taking a chance with Ben had improved her life and shook her head.

"Why am I getting that look?"

"Because I care about you like you were my very own daughter," Kate said and then felt tears well up in her eyes. She rolled her chair back and stood up. "Come on." She gestured toward Savannah. "Get on over here."

When Savannah walked over to her side Kate wrapped her in a bear hug.

"I wish you *were* my mama," Savannah said in a choked voice. "I do . . . I really do."

Kate kissed the top of her head. "Savannah, you might not be my flesh and blood but I love you dearly. I will always be here for you come what may, do you hear me, child? Don't ever be afraid." A tear slid down her face when Savannah nodded. Kate had known from the moment she'd discovered Savannah huddled against the cold and hiding

out in the abandoned mobile home that she would do anything in her power to help her. Oh, those pretty green eyes
had looked so big and lost in her pale face. She'd felt an
instant bond, and the maternal love that had been living
dormant in her soul was put to use that day and lived on in
her heart. She pulled back and looked Savannah in the eye.
"I am hereby officially adopting you."

"Oh, Kate . . ." Savannah blinked at her for a moment
and hugged her again. They clung to each other until they
both burst into laughter.

"Would you just look at us?" Kate said. "You are coming
out tonight, right?"

"Oh, like I could refuse after this?" Savannah's laughter
came out husky and a bit gurgled but it was music to Kate's
ears. She wanted to see Savannah smiling and happy.

"Good, now that we've got that settled, let's get back to
work so we can get the hell outta here."

Savannah smiled but there was still a haunting quality to
her gaze that troubled Kate. Jeff really was a good kid and
he just might be what Savannah needed to bring her bubbly
personality back to where it belonged. Kate felt guilty that
she'd encouraged Savannah to have dinner with Tristan. She
guessed that Tristan McMillan thought he was above getting involved with someone like Savannah. Kate was usually pretty spot-on at reading people, and she'd thought she
saw something good in the McMillan boy but she guessed
she had been dead wrong.

Well, so be it. There are other fish in the sea, and although she might be a tad prejudiced, Kate thought Jeff
would be a very good catch. And once Savannah heard her
handsome nephew croon a soulful ballad she just might forget all about Tristan McMillan.

16

Cowboy Up

TRISTAN ENJOYED THE FRESH SCENT OF THE SUMMER breeze as he made his way toward Sully's Tavern for his meeting with Mitch Monroe. He was glad that he'd decided to walk instead of driving to the tavern. After sitting all day long going over graphs and crunching numbers, it felt good to stretch his legs. Since the meeting was at Sully's Tristan had opted to wear his favorite pair of Lucky Brand jeans and a Western-cut plaid shirt, hoping to make the statement to Mitch Monroe that he fit in with the locals.

The flags were up at the Cricket Creek baseball stadium, indicating an evening ball game, and Tristan made a mental note to take in an outing sometime soon. Back home he'd lived near Cincinnati's Great American Ballpark, and although he hadn't had time to go to many games, he found himself missing the atmosphere of a baseball park.

Tristan grinned, remembering going to Cincinnati Reds games with his mother. Tristan had been such a bookworm that his mom decided they needed to attend sporting events in order to make him a more well-rounded kid. Although she didn't say so, Tristan also knew now that it was her way of getting him to go to "guy" things, and since he didn't have a father figure in his life, it was up to her to include sports in their lives. She'd boned up on her sports knowledge and attending baseball and football games had become a favorite way to spend time together.

Tristan sighed as the aroma of hot dogs and popcorn drifted his way. Maggie McMillan had been quite the vocal spectator, cheering on her favorite players and sometimes riding the umpires after a bad call. Tristan had been more comfortable cracking peanut shells and keeping score. He'd sometimes wondered if he'd inherited his unknown father's personality. Coincidentally, his mother's upbeat demeanor was nothing like her surly father's disposition, making Tristan sometimes wonder what his grandmother had been like. And what kind of woman abandoned her husband and child? Tristan was the kind of person who demanded answers and these unanswered questions often bothered him. Something didn't add up.

In his line of work Tristan had learned that human nature was difficult to predict but that the answers were always lurking there somewhere if you dug deep enough. He was convinced that his grandfather knew exactly why his young wife left, and although Tristan thought that his mother deserved to know, he also feared that the answers could be harder to live with than remaining in the dark. He was also pretty sure he could track down Miranda McMillan but unless his mother was on board with it, Tristan would leave well enough alone. But Tristan had trouble even broaching the topic with his mother. The few times he'd brought up the subject the usual light in her eyes would dim, and as much as Tristan wanted answers it wasn't worth seeing his mother troubled or unhappy.

Tristan sat down on a park bench and looked out over the glistening Ohio River and let his mind wander back over his childhood. No matter what had transpired between his grandparents, it certainly didn't give his grandfather any right to be downright mean to his mother for getting pregnant or to treat Tristan with disdain for merely existing. Tristan had been to college and law school at the University of Kentucky. He was all too familiar with college partying. He wondered if his small-town mother had been an easy target at a frat party and her trusting nature had landed her in trouble. Her total lack of memory of a party she had attended that night made Tristan think that she'd been slipped a drug into her drink. He hated to think that his mother could have been a victim. Tristan shut his eyes and gripped the edge of the wooden bench. Regardless, she had needed sympathy and support instead of nasty accusations against her character.

Tristan ran a hand down his face and sighed. There might still be unanswered questions but he knew a hell of a lot more about his family tree than Savannah did, and his own childhood had been stable and happy. He marveled at Savannah's positive outlook on life despite the adversity she'd faced. Tristan shook his head. Ah, there she was again ... sneaking into his thoughts and invading his dreams. Try as he might, he couldn't stop thinking about her. And he was trying his damnedest.

After glancing at his watch Tristan knew he had to get moving or risk being late for his meeting. He stood up and rolled the tension out of his neck before he resumed walking. The paved path along the banks of the Ohio River led all the way to Sully's Tavern. Couples strolled by, joggers pounded the pavement, and young mothers pushed strollers. A group of teenagers joked and laughed, bouncing a basketball on the way to the nearby court that was just up ahead. Music and laughter coupled with the pleasant weather made for a lively feeling that seemed to linger on the edge of the breeze.

People here, he'd learned, loved to be outdoors. Pickup trucks and camouflage were abundant, and Tristan had overheard tales of bass fishing and deer hunting when he ate breakfast at Wine and Diner. But that being said, the local theater was critically acclaimed and a nearby liberal arts college added an artsy flavor to the town. It suddenly occurred to him that Cricket Creek might be a small town but it had many of the amenities he'd enjoyed in Cincinnati, just at a slower pace and on a smaller scale.

Tristan could tell by the shiny trash cans and decorative benches that there had been recent improvement along the riverbank. Cricket Creek was still on the upswing of an economic recovery and all signs indicated that the small town was ready and poised for a boom.

The cove where Whisper's Edge was located was a perfect location for a marina. Tristan has already gotten interest from a boat dealer and he knew that a riverfront restaurant would also go over well. The possibilities were endless and he told himself again that the added jobs would be a good way to keep the local economy growing and thriving. The loss of one small retirement community would be well worth it. He had to keep that in consideration and keep his mind off the disappointment the project would surely cause Savannah.

Oh, and how sweet it would be to turn his grandfather's failing business into a gold mine and to reward his mother, who'd scrimped and saved to put him through law school. What should have been her retirement had gone toward his education. She'd put away money during the boom in real estate and if all went well, Tristan could give her an early retirement from selling homes and send her on a much-deserved vacation. Living well was always the best revenge.

He sighed. All of this was good, so where was the excitement; the overwhelming sense of joy?

Tristan had learned a long time ago that to conquer something challenging, you simply had to meet it head-on and knock all of the obstacles out of the way one by one. He knew what he had to do. If the meeting went well with Mitch Monroe, Tristan needed to sit down and tell Savannah about the possible plans he had for the Whisper's Edge property. Surely she would understand and realize that the progress was necessary for the greater good.

Clinging to that positive thought, Tristan headed up the sidewalk to Sully's Tavern. The marquee advertized that today's special was all-you-could-eat spaghetti and meatballs and that karaoke started at eight o'clock. Tristan shook his head. No, thank you! Although he had a decent voice, the notion of singing in front of anybody scared the crap out of him. While he loved music, singing in the shower or sometimes along with the radio in his car was as far as he would go. The spaghetti and meatballs, however, sounded pretty darned good.

When Tristan opened the big front door the delicious aroma of marinara and garlic made his stomach rumble. He'd worked right through lunch and hadn't realized how hungry he was until now. The food here, as he already knew, was good, much better than standard bar fare. The local tavern catered to a wide demographic of customers, offering everything from home-cooked comfort meals to live entertainment. The atmosphere could be vastly different depending on what time of the day you entered the building.

"Welcome to Sully's," greeted the bubbly little hostess. "Just one tonight?"

"Actually, I'm meeting someone," Tristan replied. After scanning the room he spotted Mitch Monroe seated at a booth near the back of the dining room. Although they'd never met in person, Tristan had found out that Mitch Monroe had an office in the building next to the stadium. After speaking to him at length on the phone Tristan had snagged a meeting. It hadn't been difficult learning Mitch Monroe's impressive history. Articles and pictures about the tycoon were abundant online. "Oh, I see him, thanks."

"You're welcome." She handed him a menu. "Enjoy your dinner."

Tristan made his way to the booth. "Mr. Monroe?"

"Yes, and you must be Tristan McMillan." He extended his hand and gave Tristan a firm handshake. "Nice to meet you. Have a seat."

"Thanks, same here," Tristan said and slid across the smooth leather bench.

"Oh, and call me Mitch, please. I feel old enough as it is."

"Will do," Tristan agreed, but except for neatly trimmed gray hair that gave away his age, Mitch Monroe appeared to be in great physical shape. Even dressed casually in Dockers and a blue golf shirt, Mitch Monroe still had an air about him that commanded attention. Perhaps it was the arresting light blue eyes that seemed to take in everything, but he reminded Tristan of going before a seasoned judge who demanded no bullshit.

"Sorry to meet you so informally but I've been so damned busy that I decided I'd better combine our meeting with grabbing a bite to eat. Hope you don't mind?"

"Not at all," Tristan said. "I skipped lunch so I'm famished."

"Good. Everything on the menu is, as my daughter Mia would say, pretty legit. And surprisingly, Pete Sully makes a kick-ass martini if you're interested."

Tristan was tempted, and although he wasn't sure that he should order something quite so strong, he was glad to see that Mitch had a drink in front of him. He needed a little something to take off the edge. He looked at the amber liquid in the snifter. "What are you drinking?"

"Kentucky Bourbon Barrel Ale."

"Really? That's beer?" He pointed to the glass.

"Excellent enough to be served in these." Mitch held up the snifter. "And it's damned smooth. It's aged in freshly decanted bourbon barrels, giving it the distinctive nose of a well-crafted bourbon. I love the stuff but you've got to be careful because it's got some kick to it." He grinned. "That's experience talking."

"I think I'll have to drink at least one," Tristan said and gave his order to the server. "Come to think of it, it seems like they had it when I was living in Lexington and going to law school but it wasn't available in stores and you had to get it in a beer growler."

"You won't be sorry you're trying it now . . . well, unless you drink several," Mitch added with a grin, but then as Tristan suspected he immediately got down to business. "I've always enjoyed craft beer and have considered opening a brewery someday. But enough about that. I looked over the proposal that you e-mailed to me. I have to say that I was impressed with your thoroughness, Tristan."

"It's the lawyer in me. I leave no stone unturned."

Mitch nodded slowly. "Me too, but then after that you have to rely on your gut."

"And what is your gut saying?"

Mitch toyed with the stem of his glass. "I have to admit that with continued high gas prices and an economy that's still in recovery your proposed project still has a high risk factor. It's a bit ambitious."

Tristan accepted his drink from the server. "You think so?"

"Yes, but that's not necessarily a bad thing. High risk often turns into high profit. Over the years I've made a lot of money but lost it too. Sometimes you just have to have the guts to take the plunge, knowing that there could very well be consequences."

Tristan knew he should be thinking in terms of numbers, but Savannah immediately came to mind. He took a sip of the ale to distract his thoughts. "Wow, this is fantastic. I can taste the bourbon."

Mitch took a sip from his snifter and sighed. "One of the perks of living in Kentucky. I swear if I moved back to Chicago I'd have to have this shipped to me."

"So you've moved here permanently?"

He nodded. "I have to fly to Chicago sometimes a couple of times a month but I live here."

"Don't you miss the bright lights of the big city?"

"There's something to be said for the moon and the stars. The sky is certainly different here at night."

"True."

"I would miss my daughter. And my wife recently opened a jewelry store here in Cricket Creek."

"Oh yeah, I've heard good things. Designs by Diamante, correct?" He had come across a few articles about the shop while researching Mitch Monroe.

"Ah, yes, Nicolina's long-awaited dream has finally come true."

"You mean marrying you?" Tristan asked with a grin.

"Ah . . . no, that, my friend, was quite the challenge. But well worth the end result." Mitch smiled softly and then took another sip of his drink. After a moment he said, "It took me a while, Tristan, to realize what I value most in life."

"And what is that?"

"I no longer worship money."

Tristan felt his hopes slip a bit. This didn't sound good. "So are you interested in the project?" He decided that with someone like Mitch Monroe he should come straight to the point.

Mitch chuckled. "Hey, I no longer *worship* money but I still like to make it. If I see a need or a worthwhile investment, I'll bite. I simply leave time to enjoy other things. Balance is the key. All work and no play and all that good stuff." He looked at Tristan keenly. "And I no longer feel the need to prove anything to anybody. It makes a big difference when that kind of pressure doesn't play into the big picture. Letting go of the past took a big load off my shoulders."

Tristan nodded and took a swallow of his ale to hide the fact that Mitch had hit a little too close to the bone. He cleared his throat. "I read an article that said you're considering adding a convention center and hotel down on the riverfront. Don't you think a full-scale marina would enhance that project? Perhaps a restaurant as well? Steak and seafood?" He angled his head slightly and arched an eyebrow. "With a microbrewery?"

"You listen. I like that," Mitch said as he flipped open his menu. "One thing we both know for sure: Whisper's Edge is suddenly prime riverfront property. The question is just what to do with it."

Tristan nodded and felt a sense of relief that Mitch seemed to be warming up to the idea. They placed their order, Tristan ordering the special and Mitch opting for the grouper sandwich.

"No one makes pasta better than my wife, Nicolina, and I eat a lot of it," Mitch said fondly. "And the fish sandwich here is a monster." He patted his stomach. "I shouldn't have the fries, but oh, what the hell. I'll just have to hit the work-out room over at the stadium." He grinned. "I'll just have to do it when there aren't any hard-bodied baseball players in there making me look bad."

"I've been meaning to pay a visit to your wife's shop. My mother's birthday is coming up and she loves jewelry."

"Tell Nicolina her color choices and a little bit about her personality and she will create a one-of-a-kind piece that I'm sure your mother will treasure."

"I'll do that."

"Make it soon because she's pretty backed up with orders. Mother's Day was a killer and now with June weddings she just hasn't stopped working." Mitch shook his head. "Nicolina was the one who advised me to stop and smell the roses and now she's busy all the time. I just might have to simply kidnap her this weekend. At least get her to sketch her designs poolside." Mitch sat back against the seat and sighed.

"Sounds like she's a dedicated, hard worker."

"I fully appreciate hard work, but the difference is that this was her dream. Her passion. It's not always like work to her, making it even more difficult to steal her away."

"And it sounds like her jewelry is more like a work of art." Tristan had read that as well.

"Exactly! Tristan, I had to convince her that her jewelry was worth a helluva lot more than what she was asking." He shook his head. "I'm sorry. I don't mean to go on and on. I'm just proud of her. And she put her dream on hold for her own daughter's sake while I missed so much of Mia's childhood." He looked across the room and grinned. "Speak of the devil," he said and waved. A moment later a gorgeous young blonde hurried over to their table.

"Daddy!"

"What are you doing here, sweetie?"

"I'm trying to get Pete Sully to put a buy-one-get-one discount coupon on the back of the Cougar's admission tickets. We called it Stub and Grub last season and it went over well."

Mitch winked at his daughter. "I'm sure you'll talk him into it again."

She grinned and held her thumb and index finger an inch apart. "I'm this close. I reminded him that business has increased twenty percent since he bought a billboard in centerfield."

"Excellent," Mitch said, and she seemed to beam beneath his praise. "Mia, I'd like you to meet Tristan McMillan."

Mia extended her hand. "Nice to meet you, Tristan. I think we're living in the same condo complex by the stadium? Do you like it there?"

"Yeah, I like the view of the river and the amenities are amazing."

"I thought I'd seen you over there. Welcome to Cricket Creek . . . and don't tell me we have another Chicago transplant?"

"Actually, I'm from northern Kentucky and live in Cincinnati, Ohio."

"Hmm, I thought I detected a bit of a Southern drawl in your voice?"

"Well, I've lived in Cincinnati for a while but my mother grew up here in Cricket Creek and I've always had a touch of the South in my tone. Going to school in Lexington added to that."

Mia nodded. "Oh, I know. I'm told that I'm starting to pick up a twang too." She wrinkled her nose at her father. "Dad laughs at me but I love it."

Mitch scooted from the bench and gave his daughter a hug. "Are you staying for karaoke?"

"Hmm ..." She nibbled on the inside of her cheek. "I *should* get back to the office and do some paperwork."

Mitch frowned. "Noah has you working too many hours."

Mia chuckled. "I bet you never thought you'd have to say that to me. Did you, Daddy?"

Mitch flicked Tristan a glance and grinned. "Nope."

"Actually, Noah chased me *out* of the office and told me to come here and have a martini and to put it on his tab." She shrugged and held up her glass. "I decided to multi-task."

"I can't argue with that," Mitch admitted. "But give yourself a break and have some fun, okay? I know you're missing Cam, and getting out will help."

"I probably will. Bella is helping Nicolina out at the shop, but she's going to come over later and wants me to stay. I texted Madison, and if she will take a break from the new play she's writing, she said she'll stop over too. Maybe we'll even sing." She wiggled her eyebrows and giggled.

"You need to get Nicolina to come over and hang out with you girls," Mitch told her. "It will do her some good. And Jessica and Olivia too, for that matter. Ty can babysit and bring Noah over to help. Surely the two of them can handle one small toddler."

Mia laughed. "Ty popped into my office the other day and said that watching his son was more tiring than playing nine innings of major league baseball but I'll try," Mia promised, and then smiled at Tristan. "It was nice to meet you, and I'll apologize for my singing in advance. After a couple of Sully's martinis I suddenly think I'm Adele."

"She's not," Mitch said.

Tristan smiled as Mia walked away. "Your daughter seems like a sweet girl."

"I'm a lucky man," he said in a suddenly husky voice. "But let's get back to why you're here." They discussed various possibilities for the riverfront property, pausing only when his tossed salad and Mitch's coleslaw arrived. Tristan found Mitch Monroe's insight and knowledge fascinating and soaked up everything he said like a sponge. Over their entrées Tristan realized that not only did Mitch have a keen sense of business savvy but he threw in some life lessons as well. He also had a dry sense of humor, which kept Tristan entertained, and he was thoroughly enjoying himself until he looked across the room and spotted Savannah.

Since Tristan and Mitch were in a pretty much secluded booth, Savannah hadn't spotted him, but as he watched her walk over to a high-topped table with some dude in a cowboy hat, Tristan was hit with a big dose of white-hot jealousy. Kate and Ben sat down with them but his attention was focused on Savannah and the cowboy. When the cowboy said something close to her ear that made her laugh, it was all Tristan could do not to stomp over there and drag her away from the table like some sort of crazy caveman.

"What's her name?" Mitch asked, drawing Tristan's attention.

"Who?" Tristan tried to fake but Mitch wasn't having it.

"The pretty redhead that you're staring at."

Tristan pulled his eyes away from Savannah and looked across the booth at Mitch. "Savannah Perry," he said.

"And?"

"And what?"

"I definitely think there's much more to it."

"How did you know?"

"Well your tone for starters and the fact that you've held that bite of food inches from your mouth for the past few minutes. Like you forgot it was there."

"Okay . . . busted." Tristan put down the fork that still had spaghetti neatly twirled around it. "She's the social director at Whisper's Edge. That's Kate Winston, the manager of the community, and Ben Bakersfield, the maintenance man, sitting with her."

"And the cowboy?"

"I don't know the . . . *cowboy*," he answered tightly.

"So, you've got a thing for Savannah." He didn't ask but

stated what must be the obvious so Tristan didn't even bother to deny it.

"Yeah." Tristan then told Mitch a much abbreviated explanation of how the residents had basically adopted her as their collective and shared granddaughter.

"Oh boy."

Tristan nodded and then flicked a glance over to the table in time to see the cowboy flash a white-toothed grin at Savannah.

"And she has no idea that you're planning to redevelop the community into something other than what it is?"

"Not a clue." Tristan paused to take the last swallow of his ale. Although he knew it wasn't a smart business practice to disclose any of his personal life, Mitch sort of compelled him to do so. Plus, he was already busted, anyway. "To be fair, I wasn't sure what I was going to do with it so I didn't feel the need to worry anyone."

"And it gets worse, doesn't it?"

Tristan gave Mitch a level look, and then sighed. "They're all under the impression I've bought my grandfather's failing business and saved it from foreclosure, thus saving their community."

"And you are the big hero?"

"Uh, yeah. Mitch, they sang 'For He's a Jolly Good Fellow.'"

"Ouch."

"I know."

"Which nobody can deny . . . but you."

"And I didn't."

"And gorgeous little Savannah looks at you with adoring eyes."

"Pretty much." Tristan nodded slowly. "That's why I'm trying to keep my distance."

"And how's that working out for ya?"

"Not well." Tristan waited, hoping that Mitch would tell him that all is fair in business and that—like he had already justified to himself—the development would be for the greater good of the community. He felt compelled to mention that last part to Mitch, hoping that he would agree wholeheartedly and even expound upon the notion. "Advice?" he finally asked.

Mitch looked at Tristan with those piercing blue eyes and sighed. "If you had asked me this question a few years ago I'd have told you that business is business and not always easy. Sometimes you have to be tough to the point of being just shy of ruthless, but you were a successful attorney in a big law firm. You already know that."

Tristan nodded. "I do."

"I would have also advised you to remain emotionally distant and to keep your eyes on the prize."

"But you're not telling me that now?"

"Not exactly. Keep your eyes on the prize, Tristan," he said slowly and firmly. "But the question is: what is the prize? Consider what you really want out of life." Mitch angled his head. "It took me a long-ass time to figure it out and I can tell you one thing for sure."

"That it isn't about money?"

Mitch chuckled. "Eh . . . like I said, I still *love* making money. I just love other things . . . people, that is, more."

Tristan frowned. "Then, what is the *one* thing?"

"It's simple Tristan. Just do what makes you happy. Once you figure that out the rest is pretty damned easy."

"I guess figuring it out is the hard part."

"If you let it be." Mitch nodded. "Yep, I'm a living, breathing example of throwing myself into what I *thought* would bring me happiness and satisfaction. I was dead-ass wrong because I had blinders on. Whatever you decide, Tristan, do it for all the right reasons. Clear as mud?"

"Uh . . . yeah."

Mitch grinned. "Take the blinders off and see the whole picture. There's more around you than the finish line."

"I'll try."

"Well, I'll muddy the waters even more and tell you that I am interested in the marina project and buying the property outright. I'm not sure which one but the interest is definitely there."

"Thank you." Tristan mustered up a smile, but he was annoyed with himself for letting his personal life enter into a business discussion. But after Savannah had come in with the damned cowboy his good sense flew out the window.

Mitch looked down at his watch. "I'd better head on out. I'm going to try to get Nicolina to come out with the girls and take a breather and I think it will take some doing."

"I've got the tab," Tristan said when Mitch reached for his wallet.

"Thanks, Tristan. I'll be in touch," he said as he slid from the booth.

Tristan stood up and shook his hand. "I appreciate your time and the advice. It was truly a pleasure meeting you."

"Same here. Good luck."

After Mitch left, Tristan sat back down and ordered another Bourbon Barrel Ale. He knew he should probably leave but he couldn't bring himself to do so. Instead, he nursed his drink, watched Savannah having fun, and brooded.

Just when he thought it couldn't get any worse, the karaoke started, and after a really horrible but funny version of Shania Twain's "Man! I Feel Like a Woman," the cowboy who seemed to be on a date with Savannah walked up and stood behind the mic. Tristan couldn't help hoping he sucked.

"Turn on the music and let the lights down low . . ." the cowboy crooned in a deep Josh Turner voice.

He didn't suck. People actually stopped eating and conversation ceased. Tristan saw Kate nudge Savannah with her elbow, and Savannah nodded and smiled before turning her attention back to the cowboy just as he sang, "I wanna be your man. . . ." Tristan swore he looked directly at Savannah.

"Hit a sour note," Tristan said beneath his breath and then felt like a jackass for hoping something so petty. Plus, his wish wasn't granted. Oh no, when the cowboy finished the song the crowd roared for more.

"Let's hear it for Jeff Greenfield," the disc jockey needlessly shouted. "Fresh from the recording studio in Nashville, Tennessee!"

Oh great. Of course . . .

"Will we hear you on the radio soon, Jeff?"

Jeff tipped his cowboy hat and looked humble. "I've got some demo tapes out there so keep your fingers crossed for me," he said in a deep voice that sounded like honey-laced Southern Comfort.

"Mind if I ask for requests before we open the floor back up?" the disc jockey asked.

"'Firecracker'!" a woman shouted, and Jeff looked at the disc jockey.

"I've got that one," he said, referring to another Josh Turner song that really got the crowd going. People actually got up and started dancing. When they wouldn't allow Jeff to sit down, he went into the old-school Randy Travis classic "Forever and Ever, Amen."

If Tristan hadn't been so damned jealous he would have enjoyed the performance. Although he preferred classic rock he had a deep appreciation for country music. He glanced over at Savannah. Apparently so did she . . . well at least a deep appreciation for the singer.

Tristan sat there for a long moment, wondering if he should stay and be tortured or leave and be tortured. Should he go over there and say hello and hope for an invitation to sit down? Or maybe ask a girl to dance and try to make Savannah jealous? He didn't even bother reminding himself that he was supposed to keep his distance. That plan just wasn't going to work.

Leave it to him to fall for a girl who was probably going to end up despising him.

Jeff the cowboy started singing again and Tristan swore that the women in the audience collectively sighed. Okay, scratch the last make-her-jealous plan of attack. Tristan drained his beer and decided to just pay his tab and leave.

Tristan was halfway out of the booth when the cowboy walked back to his table and put his hand on Savannah's back while he leaned in and said something to her. She tipped her head sideways and laughed. The cowboy's hand remained there and when he rubbed her back and then squeezed her shoulder Tristan scooted back into the booth. Enough was enough.

Game on.

17

A Wing and a Prayer

"YOU HAVE AN AMAZING VOICE," SAVANNAH SAID AFTER THE applause finally died down.

"Thanks." Jeff tipped his hat and flashed a humble grin. "I'm glad you liked it." He gave her shoulder a final squeeze and then sat.

"You've surely got a bright future ahead of you," Kate said, and Ben nodded his agreement.

"I wish. But it's a tough, competitive industry. There's a lot of talent out there. I'm just one of thousands." He glanced over at Kate and a look passed between them.

"I, for one, hope you don't give up," Kate said firmly.

"I don't think you're the only one who hopes that," Ben chimed in with a grin. "I swear, the ladies in the crowd were swooning." He fanned his face, getting a chuckle from Jeff. "What's your secret, you know, other than youth and talent?"

"It's the hat." Jeff touched the brim of his black Stetson.

"I think I might have to get me one." Ben wiggled his eyebrows at Kate. "What do you think?"

"You could definitely rock the hat." Kate gave his shoulder a playful shove.

"Why, thank you." When Ben reached down and put his hand over Kate's, Savannah felt a flash of surprise at the open show of affection and had to hide her reaction by taking a drink of her beer. They both seemed so happy and Savannah hoped with all her heart that whatever was developing between them grew stronger and deeper.

"Hey, I have an idea," Kate announced over someone singing a loud but very bad cover of "Friends in Low Places." Luckily the crowd didn't seem to care and joined in. "Jeff, would you mind coming over to Whisper's Edge sometime soon to perform at the community center? Savannah, we could plan a country music night. Have a barbecue? Do some two-steppin'?"

"That's a great idea!" Savannah agreed. "Jeff?"

"Sure, I'd love to." Jeff smiled at Savannah. "Just give me a date and I'll keep it open."

"I'll do that," Savannah answered and noticed that he had a very cute dimple when he smiled. "We'll charge a cover that will go directly to you."

"Ah, not necessary." Jeff was positively gorgeous in a sexy, country-boy way and she couldn't help but be flattered that he was giving her all of his attention when he could have any girl in the room.

"That's very generous of you, Jeff," Savannah said. "I'm sure the event will be a big hit."

"I'll do my best." Jeff's laid-back but playful demeanor made him very likeable, and the man had a mouth made for kissing. His aftershave wafted her way, woodsy and clean, and she waited for the tug of desire to hit her that she always felt when around Tristan. So far, it was a no-show. Still, she was having a good time. Perhaps the attraction was simmering beneath the surface. She just needed to give it a little bit more time.

"I don't know why I didn't think of it before," Kate added.

A moment later Pete Sully walked over to their table with a bucketful of Bud Light dangling from his beefy hand.

"I come bearing gifts," he announced in his big booming voice that matched his imposing body. He was, however, a gentle giant and well liked throughout the town. After plunking the bucket down in the center of the table he said, "Jeff, how would you like to have a singing gig here on the weekends?" Sully tugged on his beard and waited for Jeff's answer. "You'd get a generous portion of the cover charge and drink for free," he added.

"He's concentrating on Nashville, Pete," Kate interrupted and got a nudge from Ben.

"Are you his road manager, Miss Kate?" Pete asked.

"No, just an interfering aunt," Ben answered for her.

"Hey, I'm just sayin'," Kate said.

"That so?" Sully handed Jeff a cold beer. "You headin' back to Nashville?"

"I'm not really sure. I've been singing in Nashville at the honky-tonks for tips for a while now." Jeff twisted off the cap and shrugged. "And I've got some demos out there making the rounds but I thought I might stay here in Cricket Creek for a few weeks and sort things out. So, yeah, at least for the time being I would be happy to sing on weekends."

"Sweet," Pete said and gave Jeff a slap on the back. "You'll pack the place, son!"

"I hope so." Jeff raised his bottle. "Thanks for the beer."

"My pleasure. Come on over tomorrow for lunch and we'll talk details. I'm making a pot of my soon-to-be-famous chili."

"When are you gonna give me that recipe?" Kate wanted to know.

"If I tell you, I'll have to kill you," Pete said with a low chuckle. He gave them all a salute before turning on his cowboy boots and heading back to the bar.

Kate narrowed her eyes. "I've tried to duplicate that danged chili for years now but there is some elusive ingredient that I know I'm missing. I just can't put my finger on it."

Savannah nodded but she was only half listening. Instead, she was pondering why she kept thinking about

Tristan McMillan when she had Jeff Greenfield sitting right next to her. Although Jeff was a little bit younger, he was much more suited to her than high-powered lawyer Tristan. Jeff was a homegrown Cricket Creek son of a farmer. He drove a pickup truck and wore Wrangler jeans. He was sweet and handsome and seemed totally into her and not to mention that he could sing his face off.

What was her problem?

Savannah sighed inwardly. If Jeff couldn't take her mind off Tristan, then nobody probably could. Perhaps she should redouble her efforts at flirting with cutie-pie Jeff and see where the night took her? Jeff could be just the antidote for her unrequited feelings for Tristan. Maybe a kiss would do the trick. It was worth a shot.

Then again, perhaps she should just throw caution to the wind and follow her heart? Even though Tristan was everything she wasn't . . . perhaps in the end it really didn't matter. Ugh! Her head was spinning. She just wasn't used to all of this man trouble.

"Are you okay?" Jeff asked.

Savannah looked up into his frowning face. "Sure, why?"

"You just groaned."

"I did?" How embarrassing.

He looked at her oddly and nodded. "As if you were in distress."

"Oh." Savannah felt heat creep up her neck. "I . . . um, think I might be a little bit hungry."

"Well, now." Jeff smiled. "We can fix that easy enough. What would you like to eat?"

"How about we share some hot wings?" She wasn't sure she wanted wings but it was the first thing that popped into her mind. Damn. Wings were messy. What was she thinking?

Jeff nodded his agreement. "I love wings. The hotter the better. How about you?"

"Oh, yes," she agreed and was rewarded with one of his dimpled grins. Surely if he kissed her . . .

"Sounds like a winner." He looked over at Kate and Ben. "Y'all want to order us up a mess of wings?"

Kate raised her eyebrows at Ben, and Savannah had to hide her smile. In all the years that Savannah had known Kate she always just answered for herself without hesitation. The mere fact that she looked to Ben for approval spoke volumes.

"I think wings would hit the spot," Ben said. "And maybe some potato skins too."

"All right, then," Jeff said. "I'll flag down the server."

"If you'll excuse me, I think I'll go to the ladies room before the food arrives." Savannah looked across the table. "Kate, do you have to go?"

"Sure," Kate answered, drawing a chuckle from Ben.

"Why do y'all have to go together?" Ben shook his head at Jeff, who raised his hands in question.

"I've always wondered the same thing."

"So we can talk about you," Kate answered with a wink.

"Ah, the answer to the age-old question," Ben said. "Hurry back or I'll eat all your wings."

"Don't you even dare," Kate warned him.

After they reached the ladies room Kate pushed open the door. After bending over to peer beneath the stalls to see if they were alone she eagerly pounced on Savannah. "So, what do you think about Jeff?"

"He's cute."

"That's all?" Kate turned to the mirror. She fluffed her hair and primped, which was something she probably wouldn't have done if not with Ben.

"He's really nice."

"*Nice*?" Kate looked at Savannah in the mirror.

"And talented." Savannah tried harder. "Really talented."

"Oh, girlie . . ." Kate applied some coral lipstick and then turned to Savannah and sighed. "Fess up. It's Tristan, isn't it?"

"No!" Savannah protested with so much conviction that

it sounded phony even to her own ears. "Of course not," she added adamantly, and started applying her own lipstick.

"Then it won't bother you that he's here."

What? Savannah felt her heart rate rise, and her tube of lipstick dropped in the sink with a *clunk*. "No, why should it?"

"You tell me."

"Are you messing with me, Kate?"

Kate blotted her lips and then shook her head slowly. "No, sugar, I'm surely not. I spotted him earlier in a booth behind us in the far corner. You had your back to him. I think he is still there."

"Oh, Kate, I'm with the cutest boy in town and all I can do is think about someone totally, *totally* wrong for me."

"Don't start that he's-out-of-my-league bullshit. I'm not havin' it."

"Okay, but still, you can't deny that we are worlds apart in so many ways."

"I'll give you that."

"What in the world should I do? He uses words that I have no clue as to what they even mean."

"Follow your heart."

"My heart is being stupid. Leading me in the wrong doggone direction."

Kate gave her a tender smile. "I hear ya. Now, why don't you give Jeff a shot, anyway? Give your stupid heart someone else to think about?"

"I'm trying really hard."

Kate put her lipstick away and then placed her hands on Savannah's shoulders. "I know I should keep my nose out of this but I care about you." She swallowed and then shook her head. "You're my daughter now, remember? Butting my nose in is my job."

Savannah felt a hot lump form in her throat. "I've waited a long time for someone to say that to me."

"Ahhh, sweetie." Kate hugged her hard and then pulled back and tugged a couple of tissues from a box on the vanity. For a moment they both dabbed at their eyes. She chuckled. "Here come the waterworks again."

"I know." She blew her nose and sniffed. "We're quite a pair."

"Look, as much as I would love to see you and Jeff get together, I don't want to push you in the wrong direction."

"I hear a *but*."

Kate gave her a level look. "But tread carefully with Tristan."

"What do you mean? Don't you trust him?"

Kate pressed her lips together and then said, "My instincts tell me that he's a good person even though his grandfather is a class-A jerk. But that being said, I just have this feeling that there's more going on than what he's sayin'. I can see it in the boy's eyes."

"Like what?"

Kate shrugged. "I don't *know* and it might just be crazy ole me being overly protective of you. Just be careful, okay?"

Savannah nodded. "I will."

"Good, now we'd better tinkle and get back out there before they think we fell in," Kate said with a laugh.

It took all the willpower in the world not to look over her shoulder to see if Tristan was still there as she headed back to the table but Savannah somehow managed. Kate, bless her heart, gave her a discreet he's-still-here nod, making Savannah's heart skip a beat. The wings and skins had arrived, and although she really didn't want any food, she accepted the little white plate that Jeff handed to her. "Thanks."

"I didn't know if you wanted bleu cheese or ranch with the celery so I ordered both."

"I like it all as you can probably already tell."

"What do you mean?" He unscrewed a beer and placed the bottle in front of her.

"I'm short but certainly not tiny."

Jeff leaned in close to her ear. "I think you look amazing, Savannah."

Savannah felt a blush warm her cheeks. She could certainly get used to this kind of attention.

"I'm just stating a fact," he said before biting into a wing.

"Whew, holy cow these are spicy hot!" Kate reached for a stick of celery and dipped it in the cup of bleu cheese dressing.

"Just drink more beer," Ben advised and got a laugh from them all. Savannah was amazed at his recent transformation. He now smiled often instead of frowning all the time and Savannah said a silent prayer that it continued.

"I like how you think." Jeff clinked his bottle to Ben's.

Maybe it was the beer or the laughter but Savannah willed herself to stop thinking about Tristan and to just relax and enjoy the rest of the evening. She even tried to flirt with Jeff, but just when she thought she was succeeding his name was called to head up to the mic again.

"Aunt Kate, did you put my name in?"

"Who me?" She innocently put a hand to her chest. "And would I have you singing 'Honky Tonk Badonkadonk'?"

"Are you kiddin' me?"

Kate shrugged. "What can I say, I like that song. And you have that Trace Adkins kind of voice."

"I'll get you back for this," Jeff promised, but the crazy song got the crowd singing along. Savannah laughed and joined in. Jeff followed up by singing another Trace Adkins hit, "Just Fishin'," before heading back to the table.

"That was fun," Savannah told him. "And you had the audience eating out of your hand."

"If you have something you want to hear, just let me know, okay?" Jeff gave her a big smile when she nodded and his gaze lingered on her lips. "I'll sing it just for you."

"Why, thank you." Savannah hoped that he was thinking that he'd like to kiss her and not that she had sauce on her lips. She'd just go on with her earlier plan and let him. Surely a kiss from someone as cute and sexy as Jeff Greenfield would make her toes curl like they did with Tristan. It wasn't like she had a lot to compare to anyway. Maybe her reaction to Tristan was merely her annoying biological clock causing her to melt like cheese on a burger and want to drag him into bed and have her way with him. Well, she damn sure was going to find out if Jeff could make her hot and bothered too. With that thought in mind she vowed to devote the rest of the evening to enjoying Jeff's company and to do her best at flirting.

Savannah found herself relaxing and tapping her toes to the music. Kate kept them in stitches, and it did her heart good to see Ben smiling. When Jeff leaned in closer, pressing his arm against hers, Savannah smiled. "I'm having a great time."

"I'm glad." His grin showed off his sexy dimple. "I'm having a blast too." He leaned in closer to her ear. "And I'm glad that Aunt Kate is getting out. When she moved back here we thought we'd see her more often but she's always kind of kept to herself. I hope that is changing."

"Oh, I think we all needed to get out and have some fun."

"You got that right," Jeff agreed, and clanked his bottle to hers. A moment later someone got up and actually started singing a pretty good rendition of George Strait's "If I Know Me." Savannah was swaying to the song while Kate tried to talk Jeff into singing an Elvis medley.

And then Savannah's heart suddenly dropped to her toes and bounced like it was on a bungee cord.

There was Tristan . . . *slow* dancing with a tall, willowy blonde wearing painted-on jeans. She was clinging to him like Saran Wrap on a tuna sandwich. Savannah wondered if they were going to have to pry her off Tristan, not that he seemed to mind one little bit.

Savannah's teeth ground together. Jealousy ripped through her like a tornado and she gripped her beer bottle so hard that she was sure it might shatter. She dearly wanted to take a healthy swig but her body felt frozen to the spot while she positively seethed. Savannah knew she had absolutely no right whatsoever to feel that way.

But she did. And it wouldn't go away.

So she simply sat there and continued to seethe in sad silence. The only thing that made her feel a little bit better was when Ben and Kate headed to the dance floor and started swaying in each other's arms.

"Do you want to make him jealous?" Jeff whispered close to her ear.

"What?" Savannah asked innocently but felt as if she had been caught with her hand in the cookie jar. With an effort she pulled her gaze away from Tristan and cling-on Barbie. "Who are you talking about?"

"The guy that you're staring daggers at." Jeff nodded toward the dance floor.

"Oh him? I'm not—" she began, but Jeff put a gentle silencing fingertip to her lips.

And then, next to her ear once more, said, "It's okay. Look, you were staring so hard that you didn't even hear me ask you to dance the first time I asked." His smile held a hint of sadness. "So, sweet Savannah, do you want to dance with me and make that dude jealous?"

She managed a small smile. "The only thing that would actually do would be to make all of the girls in the room jealous of me. Besides, he's the lawyer who is the new owner of Whisper's Edge."

"You're avoiding the question."

"Come on, Jeff, look at who he's dancing with."

"What do you mean?"

"A tall, slender, blond Barbie doll."

Jeff shook his head. "Wow, would you do me a big favor and come out on the back deck with me? It's not so loud out there and I'd like to tell you something."

"Okay." She'd had her fill of watching Tristan and cling-on Barbie anyway. Savannah grabbed her purse and then took his extended hand. Once they were out on the back deck the music was muted and the cool air helped to cool her anger. Because the night had grown a bit breezy, no one else was outside, giving them the privacy that Jeff had requested. He walked over to the railing and then turned to her.

"Oh boy, Savannah." He shook his head.

"What?"

"You really don't understand how gorgeous you are, do you?"

"Oh, come on." Savannah rolled her eyes. "On a good day when my hair behaves I can pass for . . . cute." She frowned and then blew a curl away from her forehead. "Wait. My hair never behaves. Scratch the cute part."

Jeff chuckled. "Why in the world would you *ever* want to tame those sweet-ass curls?"

Savannah shrugged and looked down at her shoes.

"Hey," he said and gently tipped her head up. "Savannah, you might not be the Barbie-doll type, but girl, you are some kind of wonderful."

She grinned. "Wait. Isn't that a song?"

"Yeah, old-school Grand Funk Railroad. I can't help it, my brain thinks in song lyrics. It would suit me just fine if life was one great big musical."

Savannah laughed.

"Hey, the song could have been written about you."

"Really?" Savannah snorted and then started ticking off all of her flaws while pointing to each one. "I'm short, I have freckles, wild hair, pale skin, a big butt—"

He whipped his cowboy hat off, pulled her close, and shut her up with a kiss.

Savannah was taken by surprise and, oh, the kiss was nice . . . warm and pleasant. Enjoyable, even.

But not knock-your-socks-off-bone-melting-head-spinning *awesome*.

Jeff drew back slowly. "Sorry, but I did that for two reasons."

Savannah swallowed hard and waited.

"First, because you are definitely some kind of wonderful but some kind of crazy too. Savannah, look, whether you believe it or not you're gorgeous and supersexy. Not in a conventional way, but gorgeous nonetheless."

Savannah didn't know what to say. This was new territory for two very different but very sexy men to think that about her but she managed a soft, "Really?"

"Yeah, you remind me of that cool redheaded actress, um . . ." He paused and then snapped his fingers. "Emma . . . Stone. You even sound like her with that low, sultry voice and funny way about you. Damn, girl, don't you get it? You're the whole package and you don't have a clue."

All Savannah could do was shake her head.

"And all you women think you need to be skinny. Well, here's a news flash for ya." He grinned at her. "I *like* curves. So there, Savannah Perry."

Savannah laughed softly. "Are you finished?"

"No, here's reason number two." But this time Jeff gave Savannah another sad smile. "Because I've wanted to kiss you from the moment I met you, and I figured this would be my one and only chance."

"Now, just why is that?"

He tilted his head toward the building. "Lawyer guy in there."

"I think lawyer guy in there might be a lost cause."

Jeff put his arms around her waist. "Is it crappy of me that I hope so?"

Savannah chuckled. "No, flattering." She went on tiptoe and kissed him on the cheek.

"Oh no, not a cheek kiss!" He tilted his head up to the sky and groaned.

Savannah giggled and then said, "I must be out of my ever-lovin' mind."

"Keep telling yourself that." He looked at her for a long moment and then stepped away and put on his hat. "I should get back in there and sing the Elvis medley for Aunt Kate. I told her no way but I'm sure she put my name in anyway. Do you want to make lawyer guy jealous first?"

"No," Savannah shook her head. "I think I'll just head on home."

"I'll walk you, then."

Savannah put a hand on his chest. "Thanks, but I'll be fine. There are streetlights the whole way through Cricket Creek, and Whisper's Edge isn't far."

Jeff frowned. "I don't like you walking by yourself."

Savannah waved him off. "I do it all the time. And tell Kate not to worry. I'll text her when I get home." When Jeff hesitated she gave him a shove. "Get back in there and please your fans."

He tucked a finger beneath her chin. "I'd much rather please you," he said, but then backed away. "Pretend I didn't just say that. Seriously, I'm not usually so cheesy, I promise." He sighed. "I'm going to get back in there before I attempt to kiss you again."

"Thanks for the fun evening, Jeff. I'm looking forward to having you sing at Whisper's Edge."

"Me too." He looked at her as if he was about to say something else but then tipped his hat and then turned away.

When Jeff was back inside Savannah took a moment to gather her wits. She grabbed the railing and gazed up at the inky sky dotted with glittering stars. The moon was nearly full and the soft breeze carried the scent of honeysuckle with it. Her mood felt . . . strange. Jealousy slid into sadness as she started the journey toward Whisper's Edge but then she shook it off when she reached her street.

This was home. People here really truly cared about her. It felt wrong to feel sad when she finally had so much more than she'd ever hoped for. How ungrateful was that?

Savannah shook her head but slowed her pace while she pondered why Jeff's kiss hadn't knocked her socks off. And when the image of Tristan dancing with the blond Barbie filtered into her brain she clenched her fists. She inhaled sharply, trying to control her emotions, but she just couldn't. Odd, because Savannah had spent a lifetime exercising her self-control and was pretty damned good at it. She'd learned to shake off hunger, stare down fear, tamp down anger, and live with loneliness. But white-hot jealousy was such a foreign feeling that she had no idea how to cope with it. Coping was usually her specialty. This felt weird.

Savannah sighed and wondered if she should have danced with Jeff after all. But then again, Tristan McMillan probably wouldn't have cared one little old bit.

With that crappy thought in mind, she decided that as soon as she got into the house she was going to make a beeline for the fridge and get into her stash of ice cream. The thought had her picking up the pace so fast that she didn't notice that someone was sitting in the shadows on her front porch until she was nearly on top of the intruder.

A scream bubbled up in her throat. She took a step backward and she was about to let the scream rip when the moonlight suddenly illuminated the handsome face of none other than Tristan McMillan.

18

Geek Gone Wild

"TRISTAN!" WHEN HER VOICE SQUEAKED WITH TERROR Tristan pushed up from the stoop and took two giant steps to her side.

"Savannah! I'm sorry! I didn't mean to frighten you."

"W-what are you doing here?"

Tristan suddenly felt like a jackass. He raked his fingers through his hair and cleared his throat. How could he explain something that he didn't fully understand himself? He decided to cut to the chase. "When I saw you walk outside with the crooning cowboy I decided to go home and brood but damned if my feet didn't lead me here instead."

"What if I'd been with Jeff when I arrived?"

Tristan didn't like the sound of his name on Savannah's lips. "I saw him come back inside Sully's without you."

"Oh. So you were watching me?"

Tristan looked down at her pretty face and sighed. "All night long with that country singer wannabe," he said testily.

"He's a great singer."

"Do I have to admit that?"

Savannah shrugged.

"So I guess you like him."

She nodded.

Tristan shoved his fingers through his hair. "Okay, I fully admit it. I'm jealous."

Her chin came up. "It didn't seem like it when you were dancing with the Barbie doll in the painted-on jeans."

He groaned. "A move I instantly regretted. She was drunk and I had to hold her upright."

"Oh . . . and were you trying to make *me* jealous?"

"Busted. It seemed like a smart idea at the time. I had some other lamebrain ideas up my sleeve as well. It's a good thing you left or one more ale and I might have even attempted to sing. And that would not have impressed you at all."

Savannah chuckled. "You were really going to sing? To show Jeff up?"

"Hell, no. I was desperate and hoping for the sympathy vote. I figured I could pull off "Family Tradition." My plan was to get the crowd singing along with me so they wouldn't know how much I sucked."

"Smart plan."

"I thought so."

"Ah . . . so you were truly jealous."

She sounded so pleased that he nodded and confessed again. "Yep. No doubt about it." He raked his fingers through his hair again. "Now I feel like a damned stalker. I guess my behavior would just about qualify. Although, I did think I would catch up to you on the way home. Waiting in the wings wasn't the plan."

"I lollygagged on the back deck at Sully's." She smiled. "Well, I'm inviting you in so you can squash the stalker theory."

"So you're not calling the cops." He gave her a fake sigh of relief. "This night is looking up after all."

She tilted her head up and there it was . . . that throaty laugh that made him want to drag her into his arms. "No, but you're lucky I didn't karate chop you. Or give you my three-sixty, one-legged Charlie's Angels kick."

"I just bet you know karate as well as me."

She laughed again. "Actually, I punch like a girl but I have a bloodcurdling, movie-worthy scream that would have, at the very least, brought ferocious Willie to my rescue. Maybe even would have brought the Camden brothers running outside in their pajamas."

"They wear pajamas?"

Savannah winced. "My brain will not picture anything else."

Tristan laughed.

"Miss Patty definitely would have come running and she packs."

"Packs?"

"Carries a gun."

"I'd ask if you were kidding but clearly you're not."

"Southern women are ones to be reckoned with."

"I'll keep that in mind."

"Luckily, I saw your face before I had a chance to scream."

"Ah, praise the lord. And for the record, I would have announced my presence but you were making quick strides for the door and were almost upon me before I could say anything."

"I was on a mission."

"Oh . . . damn, I'm sorry. For the bathroom?" Wincing, he stepped out of her way.

Savannah laughed. "No, I was making a beeline for the freezer. I was in some serious need for ice cream. And I'm talking a pint with a spoon. No dish required."

"Do you have two?"

"Spoons?" she asked.

"No, pints."

"Of course. I stay stocked up." She unlocked the door and flipped on a light. "What kind of girl do you take me for?"

Tristan couldn't keep from having a silly grin on his face
as he followed her inside. He hadn't known how she would
react when she spotted him sitting there on her front stoop,
and felt like a fool when he scared the daylights out of her.
This, however, was going much better than he planned . . .
well, if had planned any of this craziness to begin with. For
the first time in his life he was winging it.

Savannah tossed her purse down onto the table but then
snapped her fingers and reached for her phone. "Oh, I'd
better text Kate that I've gotten home safely before I forget. I wouldn't want her to worry."

"Good idea." Tristan nodded, thinking that Savannah
was so sweet and thoughtful.

"I'm going to get out of these jeans and into some ice
cream-eating sweatpants. Make yourself at home. I'll be back
in a minute."

"Okay, thanks." Tristan nodded and then sat down on the
sofa. Memories of making out with her came flooding back
so vividly that he picked up a magazine and started flipping
through it in an effort not to have to put a pillow over his
lap. He'd never been this crazy over a woman before and,
oddly enough, he was beginning to like the feeling. After
spending a lifetime disciplining himself to study, to work,
and to keep his cool, this out-of-control emotion felt . . .
well, rather exhilarating. He grinned, thinking that he was a
geek gone wild.

Savannah returned shortly, dressed in gray sweatpants
with the University of Kentucky Wildcats logo down one
leg. Her T-shirt matched but had REFUSE TO LOSE printed
boldly across the front.

"I approve of your choice of teams," he said with a
thumbs-up. I went to school there. I might have moved to
Cincinnati but I will always bleed Kentucky blue."

"It was a gift. There are a lot of Wildcat fans here in
Whisper's Edge. When they won the NCAA championship
a roar went up in the entire community. Believe me, they
bleed blue here when your Wildcats lose too." Savannah

shook her head. "I'd never seen anything like it in all my born days. I had to become a fan or else."

Tristan watched her walk over to the kitchen and snag two pints of ice cream out of the freezer and then, as promised, came back with two spoons. She plopped down onto the sofa and held both pints up. "Pineapple coconut or rum raisin? I'm out of mint chocolate chip."

"Rum raisin?" He wrinkled his nose.

"It is surprisingly delicious."

"No plain vanilla?"

"Are you serious?" She shook her head slowly. "Plain vanilla is only for à la mode with pie, on the side with chocolate cake, or scooped into a root beer float. I have my standards."

"I'll go for the pineapple coconut."

"Excellent choice." She handed him the carton. "There might be a bite or two out of it."

"Only a bite or two?"

"I was trying to diet." She rolled her eyes. "Fail."

She pointed her spoon at his pint. "I usually have vanilla Swiss almond chilling in the back of the freezer but that pint bit the dust last week along with the mint chocolate chip." She peeled off her lid. "I only splurge on Häagen Dazs when it's on sale and I really need to restock."

Tristan felt a sharp pang of guilt. She had to pinch pennies for ice cream? "You need to get paid more."

Her eyes widened and she put a hand to her chest. "Oh, Tristan, I wasn't fishing for a raise!"

"I know," he assured her, but left it at that. He knew that she struggled with the fact that he owned Whisper's Edge, and he decided to drop the subject. Instead, he took a bite of his ice cream. "Wow, pineapple coconut is really good."

"Sometimes you have to venture away from plain vanilla, Tristan. There's a whole new world of ice cream out there just waiting to be explored." He watched her take a bite of her rum raisin, and when she licked the spoon he almost groaned. "I didn't think I'd like this combination but now it's one of my favorites." She took another bite and seemed to savor the flavor. "White chocolate raspberry truffle was another pleasant surprise. And I hate it when I get hooked on a flavor that's a limited edition. Puff, just like that it's off the shelves. Cruel, I tell you."

"There should be a law."

"I know!"

"So you're a connoisseur of ice cream?"

She gave him a puzzled, slightly embarrassed look, and he wished he'd kept his mouth shut. "If that means I like it a lot, then yes."

"It means that you're an expert."

"Well, I'm an expert at eating it, that's for sure."

Tristan took another bite that contained a big chunk of frozen pineapple and then shook his head. "Oh no you don't, Savannah. You choose top-of-the-line ice cream and bold flavors. You have a much more discriminating palate than you give yourself credit for. Just like with the wine. You detected the subtle notes and nuances right off the bat."

She lifted her nose in the air. "But of course," she said in a French accent, and then gave her spoon a twirl.

"I'm serious." Tristan laughed. "May I have a sample of your rum raisin?"

She pointed her spoon at his pint. "Only if you give up some of your pineapple coconut. That's how it works."

"Deal."

"Okay then." She leaned forward and placed a bite in his mouth. She waited for him to swallow. "So, do you like it?"

Tristan raised his eyebrows. "Hmm . . . I'm not much of a raisin kind of guy but, yeah, surprisingly I do."

"It's all about flavor combinations. Two things that are good by themselves can be awesome together."

"You're so right." He looked at her for a minute, scooped up a generous dollop, and then leaned closer than he needed to in order to feed her a bite. "And sometimes so unexpected."

"Like peanut butter and banana?"

"Ew, no."

She giggled. "Don't knock it unless you've tried it."

Tristan slid the bite into her mouth and then drew the spoon from her lips very slowly. When she closed her eyes he watched her let the ice cream melt on her tongue. "Mmm . . . delicious." The act of feeding each other felt so damned seductive, and when her tongue darted out to lick coconut from her bottom lip Tristan couldn't hold back any longer. He put his mouth against hers and kissed her.

The coldness of the ice cream mingled with the heat of passion. The dessert was decadent but she tasted even better. After he finally pulled his lips from hers he quickly fed her again. She savored and then swallowed. When she opened her eyes and looked at him with such longing, Tristan melted faster than the rum raisin.

"That was scrumptious," she said softly.

"Better than the ice cream?"

"Definitely, and that's saying a lot coming from a *connoisseur* like me." She chuckled low in her throat. "I told you it was all about the combination of flavors."

"You and me?"

"Yeah, like that. Unexpected since we are so . . . different."

"How so?"

Savannah paused as if gathering her thoughts. "Well . . . I'm causal, live in the moment and . . ."

"I'm formal . . . stuffy." Tristan had a sudden vision of her laughing with the country singer. "Unlike jeans and a cowboy hat?" he asked, but when she raised her eyebrows he groaned and slapped a hand over his face. "Wow, that comment was uncalled for."

"Really? Because I happen to be totally flattered that you're jealous."

When he peeked through his fingers she laughed, but then he reached over and cupped her chin. "Look, I know I can be uptight and on the nerdy side sometimes. And I get it that there are other complications . . ."

"Like you being my boss?"

Tristan shook his head. "I own the place but I'm not exactly your boss. But, Savannah, the bottom line is that I can't stop thinking about you." When her eyes widened slightly he continued. "And yeah, we have our differences, but just like the crazy ice cream, some flavors just blend together as the perfect combination and sometimes the result is simply irresistible." He rubbed his thumb over her bottom lip.

"You think so?"

"I know so." When she swallowed hard Tristan gave her a slow grin. This sweet seduction should feel somewhat foreign to him but Savannah continued to bring out parts of his personality that he didn't know he possessed. Jealousy . . . passion, damn but the girl could get him fired up. And he liked it.

"Allow me to demonstrate." This time he dipped his finger into the carton instead of using the spoon. Her eyes widened once more but she understood and leaned forward. She let him slide the creamy goodness into her mouth. He groaned, loving the feeling of her warm tongue laving it off thoroughly, and then blew him away by slowly sucking his fingertip.

"That was so good." When she giggled low and sexy he did it again.

"My turn." She dipped a finger into her rum raisin and then into his mouth.

For someone who had never been a playful kind of lover, and was more of a straightforward kind of guy, this was . . . fun, sexy, and totally seductive.

"Yummy?"

He put his carton down and then gave her finger a lingering lick. "You bet." He warmed up to the idea even more and put a bit on her bottom lip and then licked it off. When she closed her eyes and moaned, it drove Tristan crazy. "Savannah, take your shirt off for me," he pleaded softly. She opened her eyes and met his gaze for a long, heated moment. They both knew that if she did there would be no turning back. They would make love. "Please . . ."

Savannah nodded oh so slightly and put her pint down, nearly missing the coffee table since her eyes remained focused on him. She tugged the hem of her T-shirt upward and over her head and tossed the garment to the floor. The movement dislodged more of the curls from her ponytail, framing her sweet face. Her pale skin turned slightly rosy and she licked her bottom lip as if unsure of what his reaction would be.

She had nothing to worry about.

"God . . . Savannah." A black satin bra seemed to have trouble containing full breasts that spilled out over the top of the lace trim. Freckles, sprinkled across her skin, seemed like an invitation to lean forward and lick. Taste.

A throaty moan escaped her when he cupped the silk-covered fullness in his hands and squeezed ever so slightly. She tilted her head back and to the side and closed her eyes. With a hammering heart Tristan reached behind her and unhooked her bra, exposing her breasts for him to feast his eyes upon. Creamy skin, rosy nipples . . . How could she not know that she was sheer perfection?

Tristan dipped his head and took one nipple into his mouth and sucked lightly. She gasped again and reached out to thread her fingers through his hair. He licked . . . teasing, toying, and then sucked harder, drawing a deep, sexy moan from her that seemed to slide over his body like thick, warm honey.

Then, he reached back and replaced the heat of his mouth with a cold smear of ice cream.

"Oh!" She arched her back, half groaning, half laughing.

"Delicious." He licked the ice cream from her skin, taking his sweet time doing so. Tristan repeated with the other breast while rubbing his thumb over her puckered nipple. She squirmed, moaned, and when Tristan gently pushed her back against the cushions she didn't protest.

Tristan dipped his finger into the rum raisin and painted a swirling trail of sweetness down her torso all the way to her belly button before licking it off. He repeated the action until her breath came in short gasps and her nipples puckered as if begging for his attention.

He gave it to them. First, cold, creamy ice cream followed by his hot, hungry mouth.

"Tristan!" She arched her back, giving him full access to her breasts and he took full advantage. He toyed, licked, sucked and when he nipped slightly she moaned. "Dear, God, you've got me hotter than a firecracker."

Tristan laughed. "Good." He just knew it would be like this with her. No pretense, no teasing, just sweet honesty. He tugged her sweatpants over her hips and then down her legs, tossing them onto the floor. He sucked in a breath. She wore a black lacy thong that just tore him up. He had already pictured her naked . . . oh, but he sure hadn't done her justice. Not even close.

"You're beautiful, Savannah."

"You certainly make me feel that way."

He gave her a half grin. "Hey, I was a geeky kid. Didn't dare sit at the cool table."

"So here we are." She smiled softly.

"Beauty and the geek?"

She laughed as she reached up for his belt, half-shy while trying to be bold, and it tugged at his heart. But her fingers didn't fumble. A moment later his jeans hit the floor with a plop and he tugged his shirt over his head. She grinned when she saw his flying-pig boxers. "Take them off too," she requested, and to his surprise she quickly tugged them to his knees before he got the chance. He did the rest for her. "Oh my . . ."

"Your fault." He was fully erect and hard as nails, but he wanted this to last, so he took a deep breath and said, "Let's go to your bedroom, Savannah. I want full access to every single sweet part of you and this sofa just won't do it justice." Plus, he selfishly wanted to sleep all night with her, and his game plan was to make love to her so thoroughly that she fell asleep in his arms.

"Okay." When she breathlessly agreed he scooped her up in his arms and carried her.

When she gasped and then opened her mouth as if to protest Tristan shook his head. "Don't even say it this time. You're not heavy and I might be a geek, but I work out."

"Oh, so you can read my mind?"

"I can read your beautiful but totally expressive face. I could beat your butt in poker every time."

"Ha," she said. "We'll see about that," she added, but shrieked when he spun her around and then carried her swiftly through the small hallway to the bedroom. He gently put her down in the middle of the mound of pillows and immediately covered her body with his. The feeling of his skin sliding against hers felt amazing.

Tristan kissed her deeply, moving suggestively in a sneak preview of what he wanted to do with her.

"I'm sticky," she said.

"I'll give you a tongue bath."

She giggled, but then gasped and shivered. Her hands played with his hair and then caressed his back while he licked, kissed, and explored her body from her head to her cute toes.

"Tristan!" She moaned and wrapped her legs around his waist, pushing up as if trying to get even closer than skin on skin. Tristan understood. She couldn't get close enough. Savannah's full breasts were crushed against his chest, and when he eased back and rocked against her body, her nipples grazed back and forth. His erection pressed against her belly, hot and hard against her cooler skin. Damn . . . he needed a condom.

"Baby, I need to go and get protection."

She looked at him through half-lidded eyes. "Okay . . . I don't have any . . . No wait." She grinned and then hurried into the bathroom. "Don't go anywhere," she said over her shoulder.

"No chance of that."

She returned, clutching a colorful handful of what

looked like lollypops. "The Camden brothers gave these out at our last Halloween party. They thought it was hilarious."

Tristan laughed when he realized the "lollypops" were actually condoms on a stick. The little break cooled his ardor enough to allow him to start kissing her at her ankles and working his way up her calves to her thighs. He teased her by kissing close to her mound but just shy of where she needed him. He wanted her hot and ready because he knew when he entered her he wouldn't last long. His heart hammered as he started a trail of soft kisses up her torso. "You still taste like ice cream."

She giggled low and breathless. "Then lick me again."

"Gladly and, believe me, I'll never look at ice cream the same way again." He licked his way up to one nipple and then sucked the other while toying with her silk-covered mound. She arched her back in silent plea while he moved his finger slowly over her thong. Finally, he slipped his finger beneath the triangle, feeling her moist heat. She was close.

Tristan tugged the silk to the side and slipped his finger into her folds and encountered her wet and ready. He dipped and toyed, moving in a slow circle while she moved her hips in an effort to get him to touch her in the right spot. Tristan teased a moment longer and then moved his finger over her clit and rubbed while he drew a puckered nipple into his mouth and then sucked hard.

She arched her hips and cried out his name gruffly before falling against the pillows. "Dear God . . ."

Tristan tugged her thong down her legs and tossed the wisp of silk from the bed. He paused—just briefly—to look at her flushed face and trail his fingers down her body. She shivered, pliant and satisfied.

Well, he was only beginning.

Tristan kissed her, barely refraining from the urgent need to be sheathed inside her. But he wanted to get her juices flowing again and wring another orgasm from her while he made sweet love to her. He caressed her breasts while kissing her deeply, stroking her tongue and then pulling back to lick her bottom lip. Her eyes were closed and her breath started to come in shallow breaths when he lowered his caress closer to her mound. Knowing she was still sensitive, he touched her ever so lightly, and when he drew another low moan from her, Tristan parted her thighs wider and then entered her with one delicious stroke.

"Mmm, Savannah you feel amazing."

"Yes, oh *yes*," she responded in a throaty, breathless tone that sent Tristan over the edge. Balancing on his arms, he moved his hips, pumping in and out in a slow rhythm that had her matching him until he quickly picked up the pace, moving faster, going deeper until she wrapped her legs around his waist tighter and crossed her ankles. "Give me all you've got," she said, half laughing, half moaning while clinging to him.

Tristan complied and made love to her with deep, steady strokes, holding nothing back. When he felt her begin to climax Tristan felt his own release with an intensity that he'd never experienced before. His arms trembled and sweat trickled down his back. But it wasn't just a physical release . . . no, he felt a hard tug on his emotions and pulled her against him. When she didn't speak . . . something she always did, Tristan smiled softly. She'd felt it too.

Could he be falling in love with Savannah? Was it possible to fall this hard and this fast?

Tristan kissed the top of her head. He knew one thing for sure. He couldn't imagine doing anything that would cause her any kind of hurt. He was in a helluva pickle but he would find a solution.

He had to.

Losing Savannah wasn't an option.

19

In Living Color

AFTER SHARING MORNING COFFEE WITH KATE, BEN TOLD her that he was going fishing. He was, but in truth he also had plans to stop up in town and buy her a present. It wasn't her birthday or a holiday but he knew that unexpected gifts were the best kind of surprise. Anna had loved it when he brought her home something out of the blue, and it didn't have to be expensive . . . simply thoughtful.

Anna. Ben felt a sad pang thump him in his gut but not the guilt of simply being alive that he'd endured for so many years. Oh, and sometimes he'd get so damn pissed at her for dying. Like either of them had a choice in the matter. For the first time since her shocking death, Ben gave himself permission to simply live his life and to be happy.

He'd never thought he'd get to this point, and he sure never thought he'd have another woman in his life but he did. He was tired of sneaking around with Kate and wanted their relationship to go public. It was time. Oh boy, not that it didn't scare the hell out of him. Coming out of his cocoon of sadness meant allowing for the possibility of suffering another tragic loss. But it was too late. Tonight, over dinner, hopefully fresh fish, he was going to tell Kate that he had fallen in love with her.

Ben gripped the steering wheel tighter to steady the slight tremble in his hands. Yeah, he was scared all right, but with the heavy cloak of loneliness lifted, Ben felt as if he were walking from darkness into sunlight.

Ben pulled into the parking lot of the block of shops called Wedding Row, and took up several spaces with his boat still hooked to his truck. He looked at the brick buildings that were new but could have passed for vintage brownstones. Along with Designs by Diamante, the jewelry store where he was headed, there was a florist called Flower Power and a bakery called Take the Cake, a spinoff from Grammers up in town. A sign advertised that there was a bridal shop opening soon. There were a few more storefronts up for lease but Ben thought it wouldn't be long before they too were filled.

A bell tinkled when Ben entered the jewelry store. Soft, soothing music played in the background and a spicy, sweet scent lingered in the air, nice but not too overpowering. Recessed lighting cast a bright, cheerful glow that glinted off silver and gemstones. Round, glass-topped tables were scattered throughout the shop, all of them laden with artfully displayed jewelry. He stood there for a moment and glanced around, suddenly feeling a bit uncertain. Where should he begin?

"Welcome!" greeted a pretty woman from behind the counter. "Come on in and have a look around."

"Thank you." Ben recognized Nicolina Diamante from a recent article about her store in the local paper. She had made news with her marriage to Mitch Monroe, the Chicago bigwig who had moved to Cricket Creek. Monroe had been responsible for much of the recent economic boom in town and apparently more was on the horizon.

"May I help you?"

"I hope so. I'm a bit out of my element."

Nicolina gave him a warm smile that eased his nerves. "Ah, shopping for a woman?"

"Yes." Ben approached the counter and looked down at the display case. The jewelry was gorgeous.

"Everything here is handcrafted," Nicolina explained. "If you don't see something to your liking, I will customize anything you wish. I do have to admit that I have a bit of a backlog, so it could take several weeks."

"I really wanted something today."

She nodded. "Well, describe your lady to me. First, what is your relationship?"

"Uh . . ." What should he call her? At their age, "girl-friend" sounded kind of silly. "We're uh . . ."

"In a romantic relationship?"

"Yes," he admitted.

"Is this a special day? Birthday or anniversary?"

"No, I want to show her that I appreciate her," Ben answered, and was met with another smile.

"Good for you! We all need to feel that way, that's for sure. Okay, that's a start. Now, tell me a bit about her tastes, her personality. Her favorite color." Nicolina waved her hands around in the air as she talked, reminding Ben of birds flying. "You know, is she a diva or down to earth, that kind of thing."

Ben rubbed his chin. "Well, she dresses pretty casual but with a touch of class, you know?"

"I do."

"She has blond hair that's . . . kind of a spiky mess but looks great on her."

"Ah, cool tones for fair skin." Nicolina nodded. "And something sassy."

Ben smiled fondly. "You betcha. Outspoken for sure . . . and funny. But a hard worker. Caring."

"Quite a woman. We need to find something that captures the essence of who she is so as to reflect her personality." Nicolina tilted her head to the side. "Well, it seems like you need something bold yet a bit whimsical."

"That sounds about right."

"What are her favorite colors to wear? We want something she can accessorize with most of her clothes."

"Mmm, she used to wear mostly black and white but she's started to add a lot of color lately."

"Ahhh." Nicolina put a hand to her chest. "Well personally, I love bracelets. Unlike a necklace, you get to look down and see the jewelry." She looked at him closely. "But then again, a ring is a strong statement, if you want to go that route."

A ring? Ben's heart thumped a little bit harder. "Let's go with the bracelet."

"Okay." Nicolina slid the glass door open and brought some bracelets up from the display case for him to look at. "These are all made with semiprecious stones like pearls, ivory, coral, jet . . . technically not really stones at all but used to make jewelry. I weave in sterling silver charms etched with powerful words or sayings that reflect personality or beliefs. Very popular now but I've been doing it for many years." She held up a bracelet. "This one is a whimsical variety of charms with bold color of turquoise, carnelian, and white jade." She held up another one. "This one is busy, bold, and jangly. The charms are etched with meaning. See, this one says *family* and this one says *hope*. I added colorful gemstones and rare antique trade beads."

Ben pointed to one that caught his eye. "What about that one?"

"Oh, a favorite of mine. I love the chunky coral and turquoise combination. It's called 'be strong.' Look closely and you'll see that the heart charm has *strength* etched on it. I only have the one silver charm on the bracelet because to me this represents that sometimes love hurts but the heart must remain strong. I stopped with only one, when in most cases I add several charms in between the beads."

Ben picked up the bracelet and examined it closely. It felt feminine and delicate in his big hand.

"The mother-of-pearl discs add a little whimsy and

soften the piece." She smiled. "Bold, beautiful, and strong. And perfect colors for a blond."

"Perfect," Ben said. "I'll take it." He didn't ask the price because it didn't matter. He already pictured Kate wearing it.

"It's one hundred twenty-five," Nicolina said in a rather apologetic tone.

"Worth every penny." Ben wasn't wealthy but well off enough not to have to worry. Splurging on Kate was a pleasure that he wanted to repeat. He didn't realize how much he missed buying presents.

Nicolina smiled. "I'll wrap it pretty for you!"

"Thanks," Ben said and handed her his debit card.

After Nicolina wrapped the bracelet she said, "Enjoy! I hope your lady loves it."

"I'm sure she will." After Ben was back in his truck he tucked the gift inside his glove box and locked it. He couldn't wait to see Kate's face when he handed her the package. Once he was out on the lake he even missed hooking several fish because all he could do was daydream about Kate and the evening ahead. He finally caught a few nice crappie to fry up that evening and called it an early day.

Later, after cleaning the fish, Ben took special pains with his appearance, shaving closely and then rustling up a bit of gel to put in his hair. He splashed on some aftershave and picked out his nicest pair of khaki shorts. He put on a light blue casual button-down shirt that he hadn't worn in years and then looked at the white box wrapped with a blue velvet ribbon. His heart thumped in his chest and for a moment he lost his nerve.

But the heart-shaped charm came to mind. "Love hurts but the heart must remain strong," he whispered. "Not easy." Ben closed his eyes and swallowed.

Love also heals.

When those words seemed to float into his head Ben had to smile. A tingle ran down his spine. "Thank you," Ben whispered.

Ben hadn't felt the presence of Anna standing next to

him for a long time. The first time it had happened he blamed it on the half bottle of bourbon he'd downed the night after her funeral. She chastised him for going that route and he'd never done it again. When it happened again the logical part of Ben chalked it up to his brain helping him cope with her sudden death. But in the end, whether the visits from his late wife were real or imagined ceased to matter. One way or another Anna found a way to calm him in his weakest hour and he was thankful.

Ben would have thought it was odd that Anna would pick the evening that he was going to profess his love to another woman to make an appearance but that was so like her. She had given him her blessing and that was all that mattered.

Ben closed his eyes again, and for the first time in so very long he pictured Anna with such clarity that it took his breath away. *Go! Hurry. Don't waste a precious moment.*

Love must transcend space and time. Because he loved another didn't mean he didn't love her. Anna understood. "Love is bigger, broader, and so much stronger than that."

A single fat tear slid from the corner of his eye and rolled down his cheek but the turmoil in his heart vanished and he felt a warm rush of peace. Whether coming from the hereafter or from his precious memories, the strength of Anna's love found a way to reassure and calm him.

Ben picked up the gift from the dresser and smiled. He was finally good and ready. There was no need to look back, only forward, and for the first time since he could remember the future looked bright rather than bleak. Ben felt as if he had started to live his life in color rather than black-and-white and it felt amazing.

After getting the bag of fish fillets out of the fridge he spotted a bottle of Bogle Chardonnay that Kate had come to enjoy. He grabbed it, put everything in a canvas tote, and smiled. The vineyard had become Kate's favorite and he kept it on hand for her. The thought occurred to him that living under the same roof would make things a whole lot easier, even though her place was just a short walk away. Still . . . the notion held appeal.

Ben whistled as he walked through Whisper's Edge. The sound of dishes clanking and the aroma of food wafted his way, making his stomach rumble in anticipation. He was suddenly very hungry for dinner . . . and a whole lot more.

20
Risky Business

KATE CRUMBLED THE CRUNCHY TOPPING OVER THE MAC AND cheese before sliding the glass dish into the oven. After washing a few dishes she sneaked a bite of the coleslaw that was already chilling in the fridge. "Hmmm." She added more cracked pepper and then tested it again. "There we go." She nodded with satisfaction, but after she put the slaw away she remembered why she had opened the fridge in the first place. "Whipped butter," she mumbled with a shake of her head. She wanted the butter to soften for the yeast rolls she'd picked up at Grammar's Bakery. Of course, she hadn't gotten out of the bakery before Mabel Grammar talked her into a scrumptious cinnamon cake for breakfast and a dozen of her famous butter tea cookies. All it had taken was a piece of cookie from the plate of broken samples and she'd caved.

Kate looked at the white paper bag containing the melt-in-your-mouth cookies and sighed. She'd eaten three of them on the way home. "Damn that Mabel anyway." Okay, Mabel hadn't really talked Kate into any of the purchases but that was her story and she was sticking to it. Luckily,

Ben worked the extra calories off her with evening walks around Whisper's Edge and down by the river, not to mention the lusty lovemaking sessions that left her breathless and limp as a rag doll. "Whoo-ee." Kate fanned her face at the mere thought and opened the fridge and stood there just to cool off.

After setting the kitchen table she tossed together some tartar sauce in anticipation of the fish fry. Ben had given her the easy recipe, and it tasted so much fresher than from a jar. Before Ben, cooking had been a mindless chore but it had turned into a labor of love. She bought his favorite things at the grocery store and stocked the fridge with condiments he enjoyed, like the hot sauce that he put on everything. It's a wonder the man had any stomach lining left. Something as simple as setting the table took on a whole new meaning when it wasn't just for one. After her divorce, Kate had shut herself off from the world and she suddenly realized what she had been missing.

After a quick peek in the oven at the mac and cheese that was just starting to bubble around the edges, Kate hurried into the bathroom to freshen up. Taking extra pains with her appearance was another change she had made since being with Ben. Kate grinned. Ah, but she'd noticed a difference in Ben too. Nowadays, he wasn't always dressed like a lumberjack . . . even though Kate found the look sexy as all get out, but Ben had either gone shopping or dragged clothing out of hiding because he was wearing clothes she'd never seen before. Kate suspected a little bit of both. But the best part was that Ben laughed and actually talked in sentences instead of giving one-word responses. She even saw him playing horseshoes and joking around with the men instead of keeping to himself.

Kate grinned at her reflection in the bathroom mirror. These days she positively glowed. The ship that she'd thought had sailed, as she'd told Savannah, had actually been stored in dry dock and *boy oh boy* was she glad to get back into the water.

Oh, not that Kate wasn't treading carefully in her budding romance with Ben. She was having the time of her life, and she wasn't about to ruin what they had by bogging down their relationship with declarations of everlasting love. Light and simple was what Kate wanted. Anything more than that would have her running for the hills, she thought with a lift of her chin. But when Kate's eyes stared back at her with a hint of *yeah-right-you-want-it-all*, she squashed it.

"Who needs all that heartache and drama?" she grumbled at her reflection. "Not me." And marriage? Kate shuddered at the very thought of giving up her independence. She refused to acknowledge that it was actually the fear of giving her whole heart that lurked in the shadows of her mind. Nope, she liked things just the way they were. She blotted her lipstick and tossed the tissue in the trash before giving her reflection a firm nod. Wanting more was asking for trouble and very well might push Ben right out the door. After the heartbreak he'd suffered in his life it was pretty unlikely that he would want to get serious. "If it ain't broke don't fix it," Kate said with a firm nod.

Kate tugged on a pair of denim Capri pants and a beaded turquoise tank, checking the wobble of her upper arms while wondering if she should get something with sleeves. But before she could decide she heard the screen door close with a metal bang. "Ben?"

"The one and only."

Kate grinned. They were to the easy point in their relationship where he came in without knocking if she was expecting him. "I'll be out in a jiffy," she called from her bedroom and checked the wobble once more. "Help yourself to a beer."

"You were reading my mind," he called back, making her smile again. The ease of their companionship was a soft place to land at the end of the day. Oh, and the incredible passion, at their age, was such an unexpected pleasure that Kate had to shake her head in wonder. She would never have guessed that sex could *ever* be this good. A teeny tiny part of Kate wondered if Ben had shared the same kind of passion with his late wife, but she'd never ask such a question. Kate also wondered if Ben could ever love her as much as he'd loved Anna, and she supposed that it was another reason she held back. And in an odd twist of where-the-hell-did-that-come-from, a part of Kate didn't want to diminish the cherished memory of his wife. Wanting the whole heart that had been given to another just felt . . . somehow wrong.

Kate, of course, had finally told Ben about her failed marriage and Craig's infidelity. She'd mentioned but not revealed how much pain her miscarriage had caused because it was so very difficult to go down that jagged path of her painful past. After that, they'd left the mention of Anna and Craig alone, preferring to stay in the present.

But the past was there and the scars were deep.

Kate slipped into her sandals and inhaled deeply, clearing those thoughts from her head but reminded herself that this was precisely why they needed to keep things fun and casual. It was better that way.

But not nearly as fulfilling slid into her brain but she pushed it right back out as she headed for the kitchen.

"Something sure smells good," Ben said and inhaled a deep breath.

"It's mac and cheese."

He turned around and nuzzled Kate's neck. "Mmm, nope, it's you."

"You ole flirt," she chided but his warm lips caused a hot tingle to slide down her spine.

"Better than being called an old fart."

"True." Kate laughed. "So you brought me some fish, did ya?" Kate asked with a smile.

"Yes, and a bottle of your favorite wine," he added. "I took the liberty of pouring you a glass."

"You didn't have to do that," Kate said, but accepted the glass of Chardonnay. She took a sip and sighed. "You've taught me that life is too short to drink the cheap stuff," she said and could have bit her tongue. What a stupid thing to say to a widower, she thought, and was about to say so, but Ben laughed.

"I agree. And we need to do some shopping for the wine-tasting night you and Savannah are planning. It will be fun. We could even take a drive up to some of the wineries. There are some pretty good ones. Elk Creek is a pretty long ride from here but they also have skeet shooting and that would be a blast, don't you think?"

"Sure," Kate agreed. "Sounds like fun and I could use a day off."

"I'll look into it." Ben's sexy smile caused a little flutter in her stomach. She sure hoped that feeling never went away.

Then Ben looked at her for a long moment, making Kate's heart thump against her ribs. She had a feeling he was about to say something substantial, but if he was, he suddenly refrained. She wasn't sure if she felt relief or disappointment. *Relief*, she told herself firmly and took another sip of the cold wine.

"Do you want to have our drinks out on the back deck while the mac and cheese bakes? It needs a little while longer."

"Sure," Ben said, but Kate thought she saw a nervous flash in his eyes.

"Let's go then," she said, but swallowed hard. He seemed in a good mood so she didn't think he had anything bad to tell her, but then again life was weird so who knew? She walked out onto the deck and was about to sit down when she spotted a lovely wrapped gift sitting on the round table. Her heart hammered and she turned around to face Ben. "For me?"

"Yes," he said softly.

Kate swallowed and put her wine down before her shaking hands gave away her sudden emotion. "This is a surprise," she said gruffly. "Is it an occasion I've forgotten? I'm bad that way," she joked even though she really wasn't.

Ben reached over and covered his big hand with hers. "No, I just wanted to get you a little something. No holiday, no special occasion, unless you count spending the evening with you. And I do."

"Oh . . ." She gave him a smile that wobbled a bit at the corners. Judging by the box, whatever was inside was going to be . . . something wonderful. Her heart hammered but then she suddenly remembered that the last unexpected gift she'd gotten from a man was an engagement ring. While the size of the box indicated something different in Kate's suddenly blown mind, it represented the same thing. Commitment. Declaration of feelings. Hope.

And then betrayal.

"Are you going to open it?" he asked gently.

"You really shouldn't have . . ."

"I wanted to, Kate. Go ahead. Open it up."

Kate nodded, but as she reached for the box she was suddenly overwhelmed. She felt hot, then cold and shaky. Dear God, like a panic attack.

"Kate, are you okay?"

"I . . ." Instead of picking up the box she turned on her heel and all but ran back inside her house.

"Kate!" Ben quickly followed but she kept on walking. Where she was going she didn't even know but aimlessly ended up in the corner of her bedroom. "What's wrong?"

Kate didn't turn around, but figured from the sound of his voice he was standing in the doorway as if uncertain whether to enter. She didn't blame him. This was stupid! Unfair to Ben! She needed to get under control but just couldn't.

Ben remained silent and all that could be heard in the room was the sound of her ragged breathing. After another few moments he asked, "Kate?" His voice sounded gruff, confused and hurt. He didn't deserve this.

She turned slowly and absolutely hated the look of sorrow etched on his handsome features. "Yes?" she whispered.

"What's come over you?" He took a couple of steps into the room but then stopped as if uncertain if he should come any closer. "Did I do something . . . say something *wrong*? If I did, I am so sorry. I can be a bonehead sometimes and not even know it."

Kate gave him a jerky negative shake of her head but couldn't find her voice.

"What then?" He appeared so upset but how could she begin to explain?

"It's just that I'm . . . I'm not . . . not ready to . . . be . . . serious."

"Oh." Hurt flickered in his eyes. "I thought we already were."

His quiet statement clawed at her heart but Kate shook her head. "No." Her voice sounded as sad as she felt." I'm sorry . . ."

"My mistake." If his tone had been harsh Kate could have handled it, but he simply sounded forlorn. Defeated. He stood there silently and Kate knew he was waiting for her to explain or even retract what she'd said but she didn't. Couldn't. He finally shoved his fingers through his hair and then said, "I guess I should go." Again, he looked at her with hope lingering in his eyes and she swallowed hard but remained silent. "Okay . . . guess that answers that." This time his disappointment held an edge of frustration. "Good night, Kate."

No! The single word screamed in her head but would not get past her lips. A moment later he was gone.

Kate's legs gave out and she all but fell onto her bed. She knew that she and Ben were being given the second chance at something wonderful. She knew that she was blowing it.

In the distance she heard the ping of the timer telling her that the mac and cheese was done. Tears welled up in her eyes as she walked on wooden legs into the kitchen and took the dish from the oven. She had ruined what could have been a perfect night. "You dumbass," she whispered fiercely. Kate balled her fingers into fists and tried to will her sorry-ass self into going after him. But cold, hard fear knotted in her stomach and kept her rooted to the spot.

Kate knew that happiness was within reach. All she had to do was grab it. But she knew the deep heartache of having joy snatched away. The logical side of her brain jumped in and reminded her that although she didn't say it, she was already in love with Ben, so what was the point? A sad smile trembled on her lips. Ah, because Ben was the type of man that she would fall more deeply in love with each and every day. Tonight was a glaring example.

Kate inhaled a shaky breath. Love was such risky business . . . like walking across a high wire without a safety net. And she just couldn't do it.

The aroma of the mac and cheese went from being enticing to cloying, and Kate's stomach rebelled. With a sigh, she poured a glass of sweet tea and took it out to the front porch so she could get some much-needed fresh air. But after she sat down in a rocker and sipped her drink, the cheerful sounds of the warm summer night reminded her of what she had just chased out of her life. Laughter and music drifted her way, making her mood even more melancholy. After a little while, Kate decided it was time to go in and watch television or maybe read. She knew she was in for a sleepless night and hoped that she didn't order anything too crazy from HSN. But just as she stood up, Kate heard a yell of distress.

"Stop! Get your ornery butt back here right this minute!"

Kate hurried to the edge of the porch and looked down the street. She shook her head when she saw Willie running down the sidewalk as fast as his short legs would allow.

"I mean it, Willie!"

Kate almost smiled, but when she saw Miss Patty running faster than a woman her age should go, she decided she needed to cut Willie off at the pass. She jogged across the yard and intercepted Willie just as he reached her front gate. "Gotcha!" Kate held on to Willie's collar and waited for Miss Patty to catch up.

"Thank you . . . kindly . . . Kate," Miss Patty managed to say in between breaths. 'W-Willie went chasing after a bee . . . of all things and he got a . . . a head start on me." She pointed a finger at her dog. "Now, just what were you going to do with a bee anyway? The danged thing would have stung your tongue."

Willie looked up and did that confused doggy thing with his eyebrows.

"Silly dog," Miss Patty muttered, still breathing hard.

Even though Kate didn't feel like small talk, Miss Patty looked as if she needed a cold drink. "Would you like to sit a spell and sip some tea?"

Miss Patty swiped at a droplet of sweat at her temple. "Oh, bless your heart. Yes, I would." She fell in step with Kate. "And he doesn't deserve it but would you get Willie a dish of water?"

"Sure thing." Kate gestured toward the rockers. "Have a seat and I'll be right back." A moment later she returned with water for Willie and a tall glass for Miss Patty.

"Thank you." While Willie happily lapped away, Miss Patty took a drink of her tea and then said, "Some good smells are coming from your house."

Kate lifted one shoulder. "Just some mac and cheese."

"Am I keeping you from dinner?" Miss Patty asked casually but her gaze was keen.

"No."

"Oh well. I saw Ben walking past my house a little while ago."

Kate nodded, knowing this was going to lead somewhere she didn't want to go.

"His hands were shoved in his pockets and his head was down. Didn't appear too happy. And since you seem down in the mouth I'm guessing something went wrong with you two?"

"We're just friends."

"Bull feathers. I've seen the way he looks at you."

Kate swallowed hard.

Miss Patty set her glass down on the small wicker table. "I would say that this is none of my business but I make everything in Whisper's Edge my business. And I care about you."

The lump in Kate's throat swelled.

"I'm not going to pry or ask for details, but I'm going to give you some sage advice."

"Okay," Kate managed gruffly.

"Don't let fear get in the way."

"Of what?"

"Of living your life the way you want to."

"I'm not afraid of anything," Kate scoffed, even though Miss Patty had hit the nail smack dab on the head of her problem.

"I can see fear in your eyes." Miss Patty arched one eyebrow. "And besides, why else would you let that handsome hunk of man walk away?" Miss Patty slapped her leg. "What's wrong with you, girl?"

Rather than deny anything, Kate merely sighed. What indeed?

"I'm just sayin'." Miss Patty fell silent and then drank the last of her tea. She rocked for a few more minutes and then stood up. "It's getting late. I'd better head for home." She reached over and patted Kate's shoulder. "Thanks for snagging Willie for me. Don't tell, but he was actually making a beeline for Etta Mae's petunias."

Miss Patty's admission managed to drag a chuckle from Kate. "No problem." She made a show of locking her mouth and throwing away the key.

"You take care now. If you need to bend my ear just give me a holler."

Kate smiled. "Thanks, I'll keep your offer in mind." After Miss Patty left she sat there for a few more minutes and then went to the backyard to retrieve the gift. She brought it inside and put it on the coffee table and looked at it for a long time.

Miss Patty was right. She had lived in fear since the end

of a marriage to a man she had loved and believed in with all her heart. It was about damned time that she took that power away from Craig. With trembling fingers she slowly and carefully removed the wrapping paper. After inhaling a deep breath she lifted the lid.

"Oh my . . ."

For a moment she simply admired the beauty of the turquoise and coral. But the silver heart-shaped charm beckoned her and she reached into the box and gently lifted the bracelet from the strip of cotton. When she saw the word *strength* etched in the center of the heart, Kate's breath caught in her throat. She pressed her fingers to the heart, until the cool silver turned warm beneath her skin. Letting go of fear took courage. "I have it in me," Kate said softly, and then smiled as she slipped the gift of strength onto her wrist.

21

Say Yes to the Dress

SAVANNAH LOOKED ACROSS THE OFFICE AT KATE AND frowned. She had been uncharacteristically quiet all morning. "I'm filling up the calendar of events for next month." When Kate didn't mention adding Savannah's upcoming birthday, she was surprised but hoped Kate was honoring her wish not to make a big deal out of her thirtieth. "The dates are filling up quickly."

"Good." Kate didn't even look up from whatever she was reading.

"I think I'll ask Jeff to perform on a Thursday since he's going to be singing at Sully's on Saturdays. Gives him a day in between."

"Mmmmhmmm."

"At first I thought I'd call it Whisper's Edge Hoedown, but I realized the Camden brothers would have a field day with that." Savannah tried for humor, but Kate didn't even crack a smile.

"I imagine so."

"I'm trying to figure out when to schedule the wine- and

beer-tasting event. I think the fall would be perfect. Have you and Ben already bought the wine for it?"

"No." Kate finally looked over at Savannah. "Maybe you and Tristan could work on that."

Savannah angled her head to the side. "Are you going to tell me what's going on? Did you and Ben have a falling-out?"

Kate hesitated for a second and then said, "Savannah, he bought me a present. And it's not my birthday or anything."

"And *that* put you in a bad mood?"

"Sure did." She lifted her chin as if daring Savannah to question her strange logic.

"Color me confused. Was the present crappy or something?"

"No."

"You're not making any sense."

Kate blew out a ragged sigh. "Damned if I don't know it."

"You want to bend my ear?" Savannah asked gently.

"Not especially." Kate's tone remained firm, but she swallowed hard and glanced away.

"Well, do it anyway."

Kate put her pen down but remained silent. Savannah had to wonder if this had anything to do with Ben's late wife. It was no secret how much he'd loved her. Finally, Kate said, "Ben wanted to get . . . serious."

Savannah frowned in confusion. "And you don't want to?"

"Hell no!"

"Why not?"

"At my age, Savannah?" Kate scoffed. "I'm too set in my ways to go that route." She shook her spiky head hard. "Besides, I enjoy my independence. Ben and I need to just, you know, have fun." She swung her arm in an arc. "Why be *serious* for heaven's sake?" Her tone was hard and firm, but Savannah wasn't buying it. For all of her bravado Kate was scared out of her wits; Savannah just knew it. Ben was a wonderful man, and Savannah was afraid that Kate was making a huge mistake, but didn't have a clue as to what to do about it.

"So, did you talk to Ben about how you feel?"

"Yeah, I explained to him that I wasn't ready to be in a committed relationship. I like things the way they are. As the old saying goes, if it ain't broke don't fix it."

"And how did he take your suggestion?"

"Ben was under the impression that we already were serious, but I set him straight. What's wrong with just having fun? Like I said, why throw a monkey wrench into the whole thing?"

"Did he buy into that idea?"

Kate chewed on the inside of her lip for a second. "I don't think so."

"Oh, meaning a great big fat *no*. So what are you going to do? Break it off with him?"

Kate nodded slowly. "It's best."

"Oh, Kate . . ."

"So what's going on with you and Tristan?"

"No fair changing the subject," Savannah protested.

"So, in other words, you're as scared as me." Kate gave her a knowing look.

"Well at least you finally admit it."

"And you're in denial?" Kate folded her arms across her chest and waited.

Savannah finally shrugged.

"Look, Savannah, your situation is much different from mine."

"How so?"

"Well, for starters, you're young. You have a lifetime ahead of you."

"Are you going to tell me that your ship has already sailed again?"

"No. More like my ship just sank."

Savannah didn't laugh. "Kate, you're hardly ancient and besides, age *shouldn't* matter when it comes to loving someone," Savannah said with more emotion than she intended, but she remembered being a lonely ten-year-old hoping to be adopted when all that everyone wanted was cute babies and toddlers.

"I thought we were talking about you and Tristan?" Kate deftly changed the subject once more, meaning that Savannah had hit a nerve.

"You seemed to have some reservations about him," Savannah reminded her.

"I've been known to be wrong, and like I said, I'm overly cautious where you're concerned. I can tell you that Tristan has approved every expense that I've asked for, and we're finally getting a much-deserved raise!"

"What?" Savannah sat up straighter. "Really?" Savannah had to wonder if his generosity had anything to do with Tristan being sweet on her.

Kate nodded. "I'll admit that I had my doubts about his motives for buying Whisper's Edge but his heart seems to be in the right place."

Savannah felt hope blossom in her chest and couldn't hold back a smile. "I fully admit that I had my doubts too. He gave up a lot for a struggling retirement community."

"Well, so far Tristan has come through for us."

Savannah frowned. "But Whisper's Edge is still struggling. Where is the extra money going to come from to pay for all of this?"

Kate tapped her pen onto a pile of papers. "Well, I was reading through all of that information. Tristan proposes that we do some creative thinking and rent the community center out for local meetings or events. Things like Boy Scouts and Girl Scouts meetings, local craft shows, those kinds of things. He's been talking to the county about leasing the back five acres for sports fields. The county would put up the cost of keeping it maintained. There's a real need for soccer fields for practice and weekend games and we currently don't use the area for anything."

"How do you feel about all of that?"

Kate tapped her pen on the stack of papers. "Well, I

don't want our quiet little community to become inundated with outsiders and traffic, but if we keep it under control I can see how these suggestions could work. We could generate much-needed cash flow without a whole lot of effort on our part. Going this route would eliminate raising the HOA fees and upping the rent for those who don't own their lots."

"Well, that sure is a plus." Savannah's brain started buzzing with additional ideas. "Maybe we could offer some craft classes of our own? You know, for other seniors living in Cricket Creek."

"A good idea, but Savannah you're overworked as it is." She shrugged. "We'll see."

"I'll keep my thinking cap on." Savannah smiled. "Well, I say that we should head up to Violet's later on and spend some of our raise money on something fun. I want a cute cowgirl outfit for the . . ."

"Hoedown?" Kate finally grinned if only slightly. "We could call it a barn dance if you like, but if you ask me I like hoedown."

"Then Whisper's Edge is about to have our first ever hoedown! We could have a horseshoe tournament before the dinner and call it the Hoedown Throw Down."

This drew a small chuckle from Kate. "I like it. Call Jeff and book him for next Thursday."

"So, do you want to go shopping later?" Savannah persisted.

Kate's smile vanished. "I'm not feeling all that well, Savannah, and I'm not sure I'd make for good company. In fact, I believe I'm going to call it an early day and head home for a nap."

Savannah felt a flash of alarm. Kate never went home early.

"Oh, sugar, don't look so stricken. I haven't been sleeping well and I just need some time to myself to regroup. Hey, why don't we close the office and you can head on up to Violet's to shop. Take a well-deserved half day off. Okay?"

No, it wasn't okay, but Savannah nodded. "All right, but if you change your mind and want to join me, let me know."

"Thanks, sweetie."

"I'm worried about you."

"Oh, shush. I'll survive. I always do."

Savannah nodded but then said, "You know, Kate, I truly don't think that falling in love has any age boundaries. We see evidence of that every day right here in Whisper's Edge. In other words, it's never too late."

"I know that," Kate admitted. "And I hate that Ben's wounds are a lot fresher than mine and he's the one willing to take a leap of faith and not me."

"But why aren't you willing?" Savannah asked gently.

Kate's shoulders rose and then fell as she sighed. Finally, she said, "I guess I had resigned myself to the fact that, I don't know, that my life was going to remain pretty much the same."

"But change can be a good thing."

"Yeah, and scary as hell."

"Maybe we both need to quit running scared and put our big-girl panties on."

"No fair quoting me," Kate grumbled. But when she tried to make a face at Savanna she failed.

"Talk to Ben, Kate. You owe him that much, at least," Savannah gently urged. She was fond of Ben and hated to think of him hurting.

Kate closed her eyes and inhaled deeply. "I hate that I'm acting this way," she admitted in a shaky voice. "I'm just one big ole hot mess."

"That's where the big-girl panties come into play," Savannah reminded her.

"Okay, but if I put on my big-girl panties, you have to do the same. Deal?"

Savannah scooted from behind her desk, walked over and extended her hand toward Kate. "Deal."

Kate came around from behind her desk and shook Savannah's hand, but then drew her close for a hug. "Ah, sugar, what would I do without you?" Because Savannah had spent her childhood feeling in the way and unloved, Kate's words felt like a validation of worth. "Feeling needed and wanted is something I've never had, and I feel it every day here at Whisper's Edge."

"Because you *are*, Savannah."

Savannah put her hands on Kate's shoulders. "Call me later, okay?"

Kate nodded. "I will. Now scoot on out of here and buy yourself something pretty."

"Okay. But try to get some rest. You look tired."

"I will. Now run along." Kate made shooing motions toward the door.

After giving Kate one last worried glance over her shoulder, Savannah left the office. She would have liked to have walked and enjoyed the pleasant weather but didn't want to have to lug packages home and so she opted to drive up into town. She smiled as she drove past the Cougars stadium. Flags were up, indicating a home game. Cricket Creek continued to build on the success of the baseball complex, and she knew that more development was yet to come. But as Savannah turned down Main Street she was glad that the renovations hadn't changed the charm of the small town. In fact, City Hall kept a careful eye on the historic buildings, and even the new strip mall had the appearance of old-fashioned brownstones. As luck would have it she found a parking spot on the street right in front of Violet's Vintage Clothing.

After getting out of her car she looked down the street, thinking that she'd like to pop into the used bookstore and browse and then perhaps pick up some baked goods at Grammar's. She paused at the sale rack that Violet always had outside in the nice weather. Fifty percent off would always entice Savannah to pause. When she didn't find anything that caught her eye she tugged the front door open.

"Well, hello there, stranger!" Violet shouted when Savannah entered the shop. Spry as ever, she came from around the counter and gave Savannah a quick hug. "Looking for anything in particular on this fine day?"

"Mmm, well, we're going to have a good old-fashioned country music hoedown at Whisper's Edge in a couple of weeks. If you have any cute cowgirl-looking stuff, that would be great. Boots would be even better."

Violet waved a hand. "Oh, what fun! I'll look around for you. And I've got some pretty jewel-toned blouses over on the sale rack. Perfect for your gorgeous auburn hair." She pointed to an artful display of shoes. "And just so you know those shoes were all donated for Mia Monroe's Heels for Meals charity. All of the proceeds will go directly to needy families right here in Cricket Creek."

"Oh, what a great idea!" Savannah knew all too well the importance of charity for those in need and she was so glad that she wasn't the only one in Cricket Creek who enjoyed giving back.

Violet nodded her white head. "I'm on the committee and I'm happy to say that we've already done a lot of good in the community. I sure hate to think of anyone, especially a child, going hungry."

"I couldn't agree more," Savannah said. "If you have a flier or anything like that, I'll be glad to post it on the bulletin board in the community center at Whisper's Edge."

"Well, now," Violet said, smiling, "it just so happens that I do! Remind me to give you a few as you leave." She tapped her red, glossy-tipped fingernail against her cheek. "I don't believe I have any boots right this minute but I'll call you first thing if I get any."

"Oh, thanks, Violet. I'm a size eight."

"I'll make a note of it. Now, you browse while I look around for some cowgirl attire. Maybe a denim skirt and tank beneath a Western-cut blouse? Oh, and I bet you can pick up a cowboy hat pretty cheap over at Wilson's. They carry a bit of everything there." She rubbed her hands together and grinned. "You'll make such a cute little ole cow-girl, Savannah."

Savannah laughed. "Why, thank you."

"The dance seems like such a fun time! I wish I could go. There are not many activities for seniors around these parts."

"Well, Kate and I have actually been talking about expanding some of our activities at Whisper's Edge to include Cricket Creek seniors. So, do you think that having craft classes, dances, and, you know, things like that, would go over?"

Violet nodded firmly. "Oh, without a doubt! In fact, I would have moved there a while ago but y'all didn't have anything available for sale. I know Whisper's Edge needs a little updating but the river setting is so pretty and within walking distance of everything up here in town. If you'd add some new homes they'd be snatched up in nothing flat." Violet snapped her finger.

"Really?"

"Absolutely."

"That's good to know." Savannah felt a surge of excitement. Did Tristan realize this? Savannah knew that there was occasional interest from local seniors but not how much. With a happy heart Savannah walked over to the shoe display and picked up a pair of cream-colored wedge-heeled espadrille sandals edged in black. They were surprisingly comfortable and made her feel tall . . . well, taller, anyway.

"Oh, I have the perfect dress to go with those shoes!" Violet hurried over to a rack of dresses with a sign that read: JUST IN. She held it up. "What do you think?" Violet was so excited that she could barely stand still.

Savannah walked over and looked at the crisscross halter-topped dress in soft cream eyelet lace. Her heart pounded a little bit harder. "Oh . . . do you think I could pull something like this off?"

Violet frowned. "Child, whatever do you mean?"

"My shoulders and, lordy, Violet, half of my back would be . . . *exposed*." Her other dresses were much more conservative.

"Savannah, this style is classic and feminine. The flared flirty skirt is so flattering. I think it will be a perfect fit too." She skimmed her hand down the dress. "You could wear this out on a date or dress it down for a picnic. Wear a floppy straw hat!"

Savannah pressed her lips together and hesitated. "But I'm, you know . . . a bit top heavy." She rolled her eyes and laughed. "Well, and bottom heavy too."

Violet shook her white head so hard that her curls bounced. "Girl, show off what God gave ya. There's nothing wrong with a little bit of cleavage or some junk in the trunk. Look, there's even a built-in bra so you don't have to bother with one of those strapless things that can slide down and be so annoying." She thrust the garment at her. "Do me a favor and try it on, okay, sweetie?"

"Okay . . ."

"Goody!" Violet ignored Savannah's hesitation with a wave of her hand. "In the meantime, I'll look for some cowgirl attire and anything else that I think would flatter your hourglass figure. Who wants to be built like an ole stick anyway? Back in my heyday women were proud of their curves. Marilyn Monroe is a prime example. 'Give a girl the right shoes and she can conquer the world . . .' and that's a direct quote. Marilyn was a lot smarter than she ever got credit for." Violet tapped her head.

Savannah smiled with more conviction than she felt and headed to the dressing room. Developing ample curves at an early age had been uncomfortable for her and she'd always tried to play them down. Being ogled by strangers or, worse, by people you lived with always made her blush hotly and run for cover. She'd dressed in big sweatshirts whenever possible, so showing her body off never really occurred to Savannah.

Savannah slipped into the dress and looked at her reflection in the mirror. "Oh my." She put a hand to her throat.

The crisscross neckline exposed her collarbone and the soft slope of her shoulders. While the cut was lower than she'd ever worn, it wasn't too sexy. . . . *Was it?* Violet said it was classic. She sucked in her bottom lip and turned to the side. Oh, and Violet was right. The nip of the waistline and flare of the skirt was a style that was tailor made for Savannah's body. After putting on the shoes, her legs appeared long! Well almost, but it was as good as it was going to get.

"May I look?" Violet asked.

"Sure." Savannah pushed back the dressing room curtain and shyly looked at her for approval.

"Oh . . . sweetie." She put down the armful of clothes draped over her arm on a nearby chair and sucked in a breath. "I declare!"

"That's good, right?" Savannah might have lived in Cricket Creek for a long time but the Southern way of speaking still gave her pause once in a while.

"Oh, you are stunning! The dress is per-*fect*. You need ten of them in all different colors!" She reached up and twisted Savannah's curls up into a French knot. "If you pull your hair up like this the delicate curve of your neck will make the dress look even more graceful and feminine. Just let a few tendrils trail down. My . . . *my*, you pull off both classy and sexy at the same time. You'd throw any man for a loop dressed like this."

"You think so?" Savannah immediately wondered what Tristan would think. "Really?"

"No doubt in my mind. Girlie, I'm not trying to sell you a bill of goods. I mean it."

Savannah chuckled. "I came in for cowgirl stuff, remember?"

Violet's eyebrows shot up. "Put on a pair of cute boots and you could pull that off with this outfit too. Hey, this dress might be a resale but it was made for you." Violet pointed at Savannah. "You must have it. I'll even mark it down twenty percent for you—that's how strongly I feel about it."

"Oh . . . I don't know." Savannah caught her bottom lip between her teeth. This was a bit of a splurge, but then again her thirtieth birthday was coming up. Maybe she needed to treat herself to a little early present.

"Say *yes* to the dress!" Violet said with a laugh.

"Yes!" Savannah raised her fist in the air and laughed with Violet. By the time she left the store, in addition to the cream-colored sundress and sandals, she had two pretty sleeveless blouses, a flared denim skirt, and a Western-cut shirt in teal plaid that she thought was a little bit too snug but Violet thought fit perfectly.

"I'll keep an eye out for the boots," Violet promised and then gave Savannah a hug.

"Thanks, Violet. Hey, why don't you come to the Hoe-down Throw Down as my guest?"

Violet sucked in a breath. "You mean it?"

"Sure, we have it planned for next Thursday."

"Why, thank you." Violet wiggled her eyebrows. "Are any eligible bachelors going to be there?" she asked in a low, excited tone.

Savannah laughed. "Why, yes, I'm sure there will be. Most of the events are attended by the entire community. Just watch out for the Camden brothers. They're players."

"I can be quite a flirt myself," Violet told her. She formed her very red lips into a pout.

"I don't doubt it for a minute." Savannah grinned as she hefted the bag of clothes from the counter and then picked up the dress that Violet had sheathed in plastic. "Talk to you soon."

After putting the packages in her car she decided to come back another day to shop for books. She did glance longingly over at Grammar's Bakery but at this time of the day Mabel probably wouldn't have much left on the shelves anyway.

As Savannah drove back to Whisper's Edge she tried not to feel guilty about her shopping spree. She rarely bought herself anything other than necessities, and the bag perched on the passenger seat seemed extravagant even though pur-chased at a secondhand store. But it was the sexy dress hanging from the garment hook in the backseat that made her heart pound harder. She wondered what Tristan would think if he saw her in it.

Hopefully, she would find out.

22

Take the Money and Run

$\mathcal{T}$RISTAN SLIPPED BACK INTO BED AND THEN PULLED SAVAN- nah into his arms. She made sweet moaning sounds and snuggled into his embrace. He could definitely get used to this. "Good morning, sleeping beauty."

"Is it time to milk the cows already?"

Tristan chuckled. "Have you ever milked a cow?"

"No," she mumbled. "And I think I would probably suck at it."

He brushed her hair to the side and kissed her bare shoulder. "No, you have a little time."

"Mmm . . . good."

Tristan could feel her smile and pulled her warm, naked body even closer. He fully understood. He used to be an early riser, but waking up next to Savannah had changed all of that. He could stay in bed with her all day. "I went in the kitchen and put on a pot of coffee a little while ago."

"Ahhh, my hero."

Tristan chuckled but the endearment hit him hard in the gut. "As you wish, my princess."

Savannah rolled over to face him. "You make me feel

like a princess, Tristan," she said, but then suddenly lowered her gaze.

"What is it?"

She hesitated but then raised her gaze to him once more. "Life has never been this ... good," she said softly. "This past week has been, well, amazing."

"And that's a bad thing?" he tried to joke but her eyes remained serious.

"I'll be honest. Sometimes I feel like Cinderella waiting for the clock to strike midnight."

Tristan traced the edge of her full bottom lip with his fingertip. "But you know that fairy tale ended with a happily ever after, right?"

She nodded and then let out a small sigh. "I know this stems back to my childhood, but whenever I started to feel a glimmer of hope it would be snatched from me." A frown furrowed her forehead and more than anything in the world Tristan wanted to erase it. She licked her bottom lip and then said, "I guess what I'm saying is that what we have feels so wonderful that I'm afraid to get my hopes up."

Tristan tucked an auburn curl behind her ear. "That's not going to happen this time. Nothing will be snatched away from you. Trust me, I won't let it."

Her eyes widened a fraction.

"Savannah, I've fallen in love with you." There, he said it.

She swallowed hard and her mouth worked but nothing came out. "Y-you have?"

Tristan nodded. "Yes, I sure have." He didn't want to say those three little words until he had all of the details worked out with Whisper's Edge, but he simply had to reassure her. Seeing the deer-in-the-headlights look on Savannah's pretty face clawed at his heart. "I love you," he repeated firmly.

Savannah sucked in a breath. "Tristan, I wasn't fishing ... trying to wrangle that out of you." A tear slid out of the corner of her eye. "Damn, I *hate* my insecurities."

"We all have them," he told her gently. "Me included."

"You do? But how? Tristan, you're smart, successful ...

handsome as sin and ooze confidence. What in the world would you have to be insecure about?"

Tristan propped up on one elbow. "Well, remember, I was a nerdy little kid being raised by a single mom. I wasn't an outcast or anything but certainly not your typical rough-and-tumble little boy."

"You said that you didn't sit at the cool table. I still find that difficult to believe."

"Oh, I can show you pictures."

"I bet you were so cute," she insisted, but then her grin faded. "But it couldn't have been easy on your mother."

"It wasn't. Her father sure did shame her when he found out she was pregnant." He ground his teeth together. "Even as a little kid, I remember that every time she'd call him for help she would end up in tears and finally she just stopped calling."

"Horrid man! You were his flesh and blood. It's hard for me to understand turning away family. People don't know how lucky they are to have one another," she added hotly.

"I agree, Savannah. He should have stood behind her no matter what. Instead, he pushed her away when she needed him the most."

"That's horrible!"

"Tell me about it." Tristan shook his head. "My grandfather was too caught up in his anger over his wife leaving him when my mother was still a baby."

"Where is she now?"

"I don't know. I do believe that my grandfather knows something about her disappearance that he isn't telling. I've always felt that. Anger as deep-seated as his usually revolves around guilt and denial as well." Tristan sighed. "But like I said, he didn't have the right to take any of it out on my mother or me." Tristan shook his head sadly. "I just don't get it."

"Well, he certainly must be grateful that you've stepped in and are taking over Whisper's Edge, keeping it from going under. Given what you just revealed, I think it's pretty amazing of you. I don't know that I could have been so generous."

"It was a good business opportunity for me," Tristan said carefully.

"Still, maybe saving Whisper's Edge will shake some sense into him."

Tristan felt a bit of unease at her assumption. "I don't think my grandfather has room in his black heart for anything but hatred and resentment."

"That's so sad."

"I agree." Tristan managed a small smile. "But a lot of my accomplishments were in an effort to prove my worth to him. I figured if I worked hard enough he would be proud and welcome my mother back with open arms, but he barely even did that when she battled cancer. I was determined to make sure that my mother wouldn't have to worry about money or ask him for anything ever again. So I guess I owe him that."

"You don't owe him anything. Love isn't something that you have to earn," Savannah said hotly. "Although I never met your grandfather, I'm sorry to say that nobody ever has anything nice to say about him. Whisper's Edge is much better off in your capable hands."

The unease crept up his throat.

"In fact, everybody here likes you. Miss Patty even said that the next time I come over for dinner that I should bring . . . 'that handsome studmuffin.'"

"Are you sure she meant me?" Tristan tried to joke but his voice came out a bit strained.

"Yes, silly." She arched her head up off the pillow and kissed his cheek.

Tristan felt his heart swell at her simple gesture. Everything she did was honest and pure. He longed to tell her the truth about why he purchased Whisper's Edge, but he couldn't until he had his ducks in a row. He had another meeting coming up later that morning with Mitch Monroe, and Tristan intended to run a few new ideas past him.

Savannah reached up and touched his chest. "Tristan, are you okay?"

He nodded, even though he really wasn't anywhere near okay.

"Oh, and I have something to tell you"—she lifted one shoulder slightly—"for what it's worth."

"Savannah, anything you have to say is important to me."

"Well, when I was shopping at Violet's Vintage Clothing up on Main Street, we started talking about some of the stuff I have planned here at Whisper's Edge. Now, mind you, Violet is a senior too and she expressed interest in attending some events that we're planning to offer in an effort to make extra revenue just like you suggested to Kate."

"That's good news."

Savannah scooted up to a sitting position, pulling the sheet up to cover her breasts but the lush outline made it difficult for Tristan to stay focused. "Well, there's more to it than that. Violet said that she's had an interest in buying a home here but there's never anything available."

Savannah's comment caught his full attention ... well almost. "Well, there was more land to develop but my grandfather dropped the ball with that when some poor investments forced him to cut back. There simply wasn't any money left to add on."

"I understand, but Violet reminded me that there really isn't any other retirement community anywhere in Cricket Creek, so there is a real need. She loves the river view and the peaceful surroundings. Plus, although Violet enjoys running her shop, she would like to have activities to attend and more of a social life. In fact, I felt so bad that I invited her to the Hoedown next Thursday. You're coming, aren't you?"

"Are you asking me?"

"Yes, and I'll even get you a cowboy hat."

"Well, then how could I refuse?"

Savannah laughed. "You'll make a handsome cowboy.

But anyway, I think that you could add some lots or even homes and sell them pretty quickly. She isn't the first person to express interest."

"Thanks, Savannah. You have a very good point."

"Not that I'm trying to tell you what to do. I know you have your hands full simply getting this place back up to snuff, but I thought it was worth mentioning, you know, maybe for the future."

"I value your opinion. Don't ever doubt that."

"I won't, and I don't mean to add to your burden. Are you really okay? I don't mean to be so pushy!"

He looked at the concern in her expressive eyes and reached over to touch her cheek. "Yes, I'm okay," he said gruffly. "And listen, you didn't wrangle anything out of me but the truth. I've wanted to tell you how I feel about you for a while now." He smiled. "Now, over a candlelit dinner would have been nice on my part. Hey, how about going out with me tonight and I can say it all over again?"

"Okay," Savannah said shyly. She pressed her lips together and then said, "Tristan . . . I love you too." She put a hand to her chest, but he saw something flash in her eyes that gave him pause.

"Hey, what's wrong?"

"Nothing. Everything is . . . right."

"Savannah, don't hold back. You can tell me anything."

"It's just that . . . and believe me, I *know* it's my insecurity rearing its ugly head but . . ."

"But what? Tell me."

She lowered her gaze. "Our backgrounds are so vastly different. You're so doggone smart."

"How many years I went to school doesn't matter."

"Oh, Tristan, sometimes I don't know the meaning of words you use so casually."

"I told you that's the geek in me coming out. Savannah, look, knowledge, whether from books or learned from life, is all the same thing in the end. You don't have any reason to feel inferior to me or *anyone* for that matter . . . *ever*. You are one smart lady and I've learned a lot about so many things since spending time with you." He tilted her head up. "Truly. Hey, my mother never made it back to college because she had to raise me. She learned about real estate on her own. Maggie McMillan doesn't know a word of Latin or Greek, and she's one of the smartest people I know. I respect and love her. We all put our pants on one leg at a time. That's what she instilled in me and I agree."

Savannah's eyes filled with tears. "And she chose to keep you under tough circumstances." She swiped at her cheek. "Unlike my own mother."

"I am so very grateful for her decision, but you don't know what your mother was faced with or what life was throwing her way. Sometimes tough decisions are made out of love, Savannah. It doesn't mean you weren't wanted or loved. She most likely did what she felt was best for you and has to live with her decision every day."

"Oh, Tristan . . ." Savannah dabbed at her eyes with the corner of the sheet. "I've thought about that too. It might be nice for her to know that I turned out okay."

"You turned out more than *okay*. You're a wonderful, loving human being." He smiled at her. "For whatever reason, the two of us were meant to be born."

"Maybe for each other?"

Her simple statement went straight to his heart and for a moment Tristan couldn't find his voice. "Yes," he said softly. He cleared his throat. "I'll help you find your birth mother if you want me to. I have resources that would help expedite your search."

Savannah swallowed and then nodded. "Thank you. I'm . . . I'm not sure if I want to do that but I appreciate the gesture."

Tristan leaned over and kissed her softly on the lips. "All you have to do is say the word."

"I'll keep that in mind." Savannah put her hand to his cheek and then, true to her usual form, she gave him a bright smile. "The coffee smells divine."

"Then stay for a while." He leaned over and gave her a lingering kiss. "I've got more sugar to go with your coffee."

"Tristan!" Savannah giggled. "Mmmm, well that sounds divine too, but I have a water aerobics class to teach in a little while and paperwork to do for Kate."

"Damn . . ."

"But I'll take a rain check."

"How about that romantic dinner tonight? Candlelight and the whole nine yards."

"I'd love it."

"Is seven too early?"

"No."

Tristan smiled. "Good. If you don't mind, I'm going to take a quick shower and take my coffee to go. I've got some work to get done today too."

"Okay, help yourself to my shampoo."

"Great, I'm going to smell like peaches again."

Savannah laughed. "I'll have to buy some manly stuff for you."

"You don't have to do that," he said, but he knew that she would.

A little while later when Tristan got inside his car he sat there for a moment and gripped the steering wheel. His temporary move to Cricket Creek had taken a turn that he least expected. Falling in love with Savannah wasn't part of the plan. In fact, he was feeling more and more at ease in the small-town atmosphere, and Plan B was starting to take shape in his brain.

He thought about the meeting he had with Mitch Monroe in a couple of hours. Mitch might either offer him a lump sum for Whisper's Edge or simply invest. If he did, Tristan had to decide how to handle the situation. What had first been so clear in his head was beginning to rapidly change and evolve.

After heading back to his condo, Tristan sat down on the leather sofa and opened his briefcase. He removed the Whisper's Edge file and started reviewing his notes. But the suggestion Savannah made kept creeping into his thoughts. Even in the run-down state the property was in, the residents still loved living there. And there was definitely plenty of land to develop. His mind started to race. The small marina that was already built could be expanded for public use, but still service the residents if a parking lot was paved along with another access road. There was a second small marina next to the baseball stadium that could actually be expanded to more of what he originally had in mind for Whisper's Edge, and if he wasn't mistaken, Noah Falcon might now own it. Tristan pored over the map of the grounds and started making notes and making estimates and crunching numbers.

Tristan didn't look up until it was nearly time to meet with Mitch Monroe, but luckily his office was directly across the parking lot. With a long sigh, Tristan leaned back against the pillows on the sofa. His heart thumped as he thumbed through his notes one last time. "Wow . . ." It just might be possible to develop the surrounding property, creating jobs and opportunity with a marina that abutted but didn't take the heart of Whisper's Edge. And yet he could expand like Savannah suggested, adding more housing for more residents and improve the grounds. Damn . . . all he needed was some financial backing.

Was it going to be possible to have his cake and eat it too?

He would have to sell Mitch Monroe on his new proposal, but Tristan certainly hoped it would be the case.

After stuffing the notes into his briefcase Tristan picked up his laptop in case he needed it and headed out the door. A few minutes later he was in the elevator taking him up to Mitch's office. When he stepped into the hallway he saw a tall man speed by him like the hounds of hell were after him.

"Benjamin, Daddy says to stop!"

Tristan saw a little guy dressed in a tiny baseball uniform tearing down the hallway.

"I mean it!"

The response was a wild giggle as he turned a corner.

"I'm warning you! Stop right there and bring Daddy the baseball."

Tristan realized that the man in hot pursuit of the toddler must be Ty McKenna. He grinned. Triple Threat Ty McKenna was a baseball superstar who would likely end up in the Hall of Fame someday, and was having trouble keeping up with a towheaded little boy. Tristan had to admit that the little guy had some serious speed.

"Noah? Mia? Baby Ben is on the loose!"

"Again?" The feminine voice must belong to Mia.

"Catch him! He's got my home-run baseball that won the National League playoffs."

"I'll try!"

"Gotcha!" Mia exclaimed with a laugh.

"No!" shouted Benjamin. "Let me go Meee-aaah!" he squealed but giggled.

"Oh, you can't wiggle away from Mia. Don't even try."

Tristan headed down the hallway just in time to see Ty McKenna shake his finger at Benjamin, who was doing his best to look blue-eyed innocent, even though he had a baseball clutched in two chubby hands. "I want to play!"

"Benjamin, you have to use your own baseball, not Daddy's. We talked about that."

Benjamin pouted. "I like dis one bedder!"

Mia laughed. "He wants the real deal, Ty, not some plastic toy."

"And he climbed his way up my bookcase to get it. Scared the crap out of me. I can't take my eyes off of him for a second." Ty sighed. "Don't tell Jessica that he got away from me again. Baby Ben, you're harder to chase than a line drive."

Mia chuckled but then nodded toward the hallway. "I think you're about to be relieved of your daddy duties."

Tristan turned to see a pretty young blonde walking down the hallway.

"Maddie!" Benjamin shouted and managed to wiggle away from Mia.

The pretty blonde laughed. "You're the only one allowed to call me that, baby brother."

Baby brother? Tristan could see the resemblance but, wow, that was some age difference between them.

"Hi, Madison," Ty said a bit sheepishly.

"Lose him again, did ya?" Madison asked with a grin.

"Don't tell your mother. And for the record, it sucks that he's figured out how to unlock doors. It's a recent achievement."

Madison hefted Benjamin up in the air, making him giggle. "What can I say, he's smart like his big sister." She gave Ty a look of sympathy. "Hey, Mom will tell you that it took a village to raise me. I was a wild child too."

Ty smiled. "And look how good you turned out."

"Ah, flattery will get you everywhere. Your secret is safe with me, Ty." She gave Benjamin a kiss on the cheek.

"You wouldn't want to take the little tiger to the park would you?" Ty asked and put his hands together in prayer. "I love my son but I have to get the lineup set for tonight."

"I'd never turn down a playdate with my baby brother. It took me long enough to get one!" Madison tossed the baseball to Ty. "We might even get an ice cream at the Dairy Hut if you're good for Maddie."

"Ice caa-weam! Yea!" He clapped his hands and gave Madison a loud, sloppy kiss. "I lub you, Maddie."

"I lub you too, sweet pea."

"I'm not a pea. I'm a boy, silly."

They all laughed, including Tristan.

"Oh, I'm sorry," Mia said when she noticed him standing in the background. "Benjamin tends to take center stage whenever he's around. I didn't see you standing there. My father is in his office, the last one on the left. He's expecting you and said to go on in when you arrive."

"Thanks," Tristan said and then took the outstretched hand from Ty.

"Ty McKenna," he said and of course had an iron grip.

"It's a pleasure to meet you, Mr. McKenna. I'm a big fan."

Ty grinned. "Good, then you'll keep it to yourself that I can be outrun by a toddler."

Tristan laughed. "A future star, I'm sure."

"I hope so," Ty said, "but he likes to bang around in the kitchen at Wine and Diner with his mother. Whatever he wants to be is okay with me. And you'll notice that Noah has stayed hiding in his office. Benjamin scares him," he said loudly.

"I'm not scared, I'm busy," Noah shouted from his office.

They all laughed once more.

"Sure you are," Madison called to him and got a grunt as an answer.

"Hi, I'm Madison. I'd shake your hand, Tristan, but he'd escape again."

"I understand," Tristan said. "Nice to meet you . . . and you too, Benjamin."

"Let's go, Maddie!" Benjamin put his hands on her cheeks and forced her attention back to him.

"Okay!" she said and twirled him in a circle. "To the park we go!"

Tristan made his way down the hallway but smiled at the easy camaraderie and chatter going on behind him. When he reached the last office on the left the door was open but he knocked, getting the attention of Mitch Monroe, who sat behind a big desk.

"Come on in, Tristan." He took off his reading glasses and rubbed the bridge of his nose.

"Hello, Mitch."

"Have a seat."

"Thanks," Tristan said and sat down in a plush leather chair. Out of a picture window a nice view of the Ohio River spanned nearly the width of the room. To the left was the Cougars' stadium. He opened his briefcase and took out his notes. "I know we talked about a couple of ideas for the

Whisper's Edge property but I want to run something different past you."

Mitch leaned back in his chair and nodded. "Well, before you go through all of that I want to make you an offer to purchase Whisper's Edge outright."

Tristan's heart pounded. "Really?" Tristan really hadn't expected Mitch to go that route.

Mitch nodded. "Look, if you sat on the property a little while it would go up in value because of the riverfront location, but if you want a quick turnaround I'm prepared to offer you five hundred thousand."

"Oh . . ." Several thoughts went through his head. A half a million dollars was quite a haul no matter how you sliced it. He could make that much money work for him in so many ways. His mother could immediately retire, for starters. He could hang out a shingle in Cricket Creek and practice law at a leisurely pace. Oh, and not to mention that his grandfather would be livid that he'd sold Whisper's Edge at a fraction of Tristan's selling price.

"Well . . ." His heart thudded and a trickle of sweat slid down his back. How could he turn this down? *Because you love Savannah,* slid into his brain and calmed him down. Then he thought of Kate and Ben . . . Miss Patty and even the Camden brothers. This was their home. And all of them were Savannah's extended family. "I've been doing some thinking about the property, and it's worth more than that to me."

"Ah . . . you drive a hard bargain." At Tristan's hesitation, Mitch said, "Okay, six hundred fifty thousand but that's the best I can do. I've got a lot invested in the strip mall and don't want to stretch myself too thin." He grinned. "I'm not out there making money hand over fist anymore so I have to learn to be a little bit conservative."

"Then why not listen to my proposal and invest instead of purchasing?"

Mitch angled his head. "Well, because I know for sure

that the land itself is a good investment that will eventually pay off. Anything else has a risk factor."

"You don't want to hear me out?"

"I want you to consider my offer first."

"Okay," Tristan said but couldn't help but feel a bit deflated.

"You don't have to answer me right this minute, Tristan. Sleep on it. Quite frankly, I'd like to have access to the land for my own purposes instead of a joint venture. At this point I don't know if I could even consider anything else. As I said, I like to make money but taking a risk has lost the allure."

Tristan nodded. "Okay, fair enough." He stood up and leaned over to shake Mitch's hand. But as he headed for the door he turned around and said, "To fully consider selling I'd like to know what you would plan to do with Whisper's Edge."

Mitch pressed his lips together and then replied, "At the moment I'm not entirely sure, but like you, I know that the property could be developed into something more than the run-down retirement community that it's been for a long time."

Tristan felt a flash of alarm.

"Is there something else you want me to know?"

Nodding slowly, Tristan said, "I hope you'll consider that Whisper's Edge is much more than a neglected piece of land. It's a community of seniors enjoying their twilight years being active and productive in Cricket Creek."

"I'll certainly keep that in mind. And I'll e-mail you the details of my offer. If you accept, I'll have the official contract drawn up and we'll go from there."

"Thanks." Tristan nodded briskly and then opened the door. As he rode down on the elevator he didn't think he'd ever been so confused in his entire life. Mitch Monroe had just offered him a sweet deal and yet he just didn't feel happy or even proud of the accomplishment. He cared about Kate and Ben, and he was fond of Miss Patty, the crazy Camdens, and even Willie! Tristan inhaled a deep breath. And this was home to Savannah. He wished that Mitch had heard him out!

Instead of going back to his condo Tristan decided to head up into town for a bite to eat. After arriving at his car, Tristan slid behind the wheel and shoved his fingers through his hair. But just as he was about to start his car his cell phone rang. It was his mother.

"Hi, Mom, what's up?"

"Sweetie, I have a bit of a legal issue concerning a piece of property I just sold. Do you think you could come home and take care of it for me?"

Tristan frowned. "Can't you just e-mail it to me?"

"I could, but it's an excuse to have you home for a few days. I won't lie. I miss you, Tristan."

"I miss you too, Mom." Tristan smiled and felt a tug at his heart. "I'll head up there later today."

"Oh, it's a long drive. I don't want to rush you."

"No, that's okay. I could use a long road trip to do some thinking. I have something I'd like to discuss with you, anyway."

"Oh, you have your mother curious, Tristan! Spill!"

"Not over the phone."

"Okay, well in that case I'll throw together your favorite lasagna."

"Oh, that's a deal I can't pass up. See you tonight."

"Have a safe trip."

"I will, Mom. Don't worry."

"It's my job to worry," she said with a laugh. "Call when you're close."

"Will do."

A moment later he called Savannah.

"Hey, what's up?" she asked brightly.

"Savannah, I'm sorry but I have to cancel dinner tonight. My mother needs me to help her with a real estate contract so I'm going to have to head to Cincinnati tonight."

She hesitated slightly. "Oh . . . How long do you think you'll be gone?"

"A few days at the most."

"Oh, okay." She sounded confused, and he didn't blame her one bit. "I'm sorry. This was unexpected," he said lamely.

"Don't be. Things come up. It's fine."

"Thanks for being understanding." Guilt stabbed him in the gut, and he dearly wished he had been honest with her from the beginning.

"Will you be home in time for the Hoedown?"

"I would think so, but I'll let you know. Damn, I'm going to miss you."

"Me too," she said softly. "A lot."

"I'm really sorry." Hearing the disappointment in her voice tore him up.

"Hey, you have to help your mother, Tristan. I'm going to be busy getting ready for the event. The days will pass in the blink of an eye."

"Not fast enough but you always manage to look at the bright side of things. Another reason I've fallen in love with you."

"And you caring so much about your mother is another reason I love you. Do what you have to do but get back here as soon as you can, okay? I miss you already."

"I'll do my best."

When Tristan hung up the phone he vowed to get everything straightened out with the Whisper's Edge property as soon as possible so he could come clean with Savannah. But, damn, he wasn't kidding. He was going to miss her terribly.

23

Sealed with a Kiss

BEN LOOKED DOWN AT HIS CHEESEBURGER AND FRIES AND frowned at the golden brown bun. Wine and Diner served up a bodacious burger, and he thought that ordering it would make his appetite return but he seriously didn't know if he could get the sandwich past his lips.

"Something wrong, sugar?"

Ben looked at Sunny and attempted to smile. "No, Sunny, everything looks fine, but I think I'll have a Coke instead of just water."

Sunny gave him a wink. "Coming right up."

It was well past lunch and the diner was nearly empty. Ben was glad. He didn't want to run into anybody who wanted to make small talk. Hopefully, the fizz in the Coke would help to settle his stomach. He missed Kate so much that sleeping and eating were becoming damned difficult. He even snapped at sweet little Savannah when she stopped over to ask him to replace the mailbox in front of the office. After Kate broke his already battered heart he didn't want to go anywhere near the woman. Deep down he knew that her reaction was out of some sort of misplaced fear, but Ben was too wounded to muster up the energy to sort all of that out.

He just felt so damned tired, and had tumbled right back into his old grumpy self. Ben didn't like it. And yet he just couldn't sleep. He was hungry and couldn't eat. His body was running on caffeine and anger. In other words, he was one big-ass mess.

"Thanks," Ben said when Sunny brought him the Coke. He took a sip and let the cold liquid slide down his throat and splash into his empty stomach. He knew he had to eat something and so he popped a hot, crispy French fry into his mouth, but chewing and swallowing took an effort. To give himself something to do, he lifted the lid of his bun, put the fresh bib lettuce and thick slice of tomato onto the melted cheddar cheese, and then squirted some brown mustard in a circle on top of the burger. He sliced the sandwich in half and noticed that the meat was cooked medium just like he requested. Ben had never gotten a bad meal at Wine and Diner, and all he wanted to do was enjoy the pleasure of eating something really tasty. His last few attempts at preparing a meal at home had been pitiful at best.

Ben didn't indulge in a big burger and salty fries often, and he got annoyed with himself for not being able to enjoy something as simple as lunch. He glanced at the round clock mounted on the wall. Okay, a very late lunch. Hours and then days had started to blend together in a meaningless lump of unhappiness. He took a bite of the pickle spear and winced. *Wow*, that was a bad idea! The tart taste shocked his system, and he had to take a bite of the burger to try to settle his stomach down. This wasn't going nearly as well as he had hoped. He couldn't even touch the hot sauce.

And then it hit him.

Ben sat up straighter and nearly knocked his drink over. This was stupid! He loved Kate, damn it! All of this feeling-sorry-for-himself stuff was a crock. He couldn't control what happened to Anna, but he could fight to keep Kate in his life. As soon as he finished lunch he was going to march into her office and . . . kiss some sense into the stubborn woman! Despite his lack of sleep, he suddenly felt energized. Alive! Ben thought about leaving right then and there but his stomach suddenly growled. He was hungry! He picked up a French fry, popped it into his mouth and delighted in the salty goodness. Next, he took a giant bite of the burger. God, it was delicious! With a grin, he shook some hot sauce onto his plate and dipped the next bite into the spicy sauce.

Ben smiled at Sunny when she paused at his booth to refill his glass. He wasn't one to eavesdrop but when he heard the man in the booth behind him talking on his cell phone, he listened absently while swirling a few fries in the puddle of ketchup. When Ben heard him say the name Nicolina, he realized the man was Mitch Monroe, the bigwig who'd moved here from Chicago and played a big part in revitalizing Cricket Creek. As they chatted about business at the jewelry store, Ben zoned out since it made him think of the unopened gift he bought there for Kate. But as Ben took another tentative bite of the burger, his ears suddenly perked up when Whisper's Edge was mentioned.

"Nicolina, I made Tristan McMillan an offer for Whisper's Edge," Mitch said to her. "He wanted to propose another joint venture to me but I decided that I'd like to have the land to myself. The riverfront property will only go up in value if we sit on it." Mitch paused as if listening, and then said, "Yes, I already discussed a marina and restaurant and maybe even a microbrewery with him, but Nicolina, I don't know. With the Wedding Row shops still not fully rented out I want to move a little bit slowly." He paused again. "Yes, the bakery will be opening in a couple of weeks and I'm hoping to have a photography studio and wedding boutique in place soon. I know it will help your business thrive too but you're already stretched to the limit. Sweetie, you truly need a personal assistant." He sighed. "I know . . . I know, but Bella is away at Logan's baseball games too much. We'll chat over a bottle of red tonight." After another pause he said, "No, Tristan is going to mull the offer over and give me an answer in a day or two." Silence, and then, "I love you too."

For a moment Ben just sat there while the realization that Tristan wasn't remotely who he represented himself to be slowly sank in. Ben ground his teeth together. Kate was going to be pissed.

And Savannah was going to be devastated.

Ben absently munched on the pickle while he decided what to do with the information. After a few minutes he knew he was going to have to break the news to Kate. And he'd better not cross paths with Tristan McMillan, or the hot-shot lawyer pretending to be a hero to a bunch of trusting senior citizens would get a much-deserved roundhouse to the jaw.

After polishing off what little he could of his meal, Ben paid his tab and left Sunny a hefty tip after she worried once more that he was unhappy with his meal or service.

But he drove back to Whisper's Edge with a heavy heart for so many reasons. After parking his truck in his driveway he started slowing strolling toward the office. This wasn't going to be easy. As he passed through the neighborhood, smiles and waves came his way. Little did they know that their community was at risk, and Ben felt another shot of anger toward Tristan McMillan.

"Hey there, Ben!"

Ben looked over to see Clovis Camden motion for him to cross the street. "Hi, Clovis." Ben forced a smile.

"Where you been keepin' yourself?"

"Ah, been busy."

Clovis leaned on his rake. "How about coming over tonight for some brats and beer and baseball? Clyde is making some of his killer tater salad. I'll be doing the grillin'. I don't do any of that girly kitchen stuff."

"Ah, sounds good but I have to pass," Ben said, but he truly appreciated the offer. "I've got some paperwork to do."

"If you change your mind, let me know," Clovis said. "The invitation will remain open."

"Thanks."

"We've been missing ya playin' horseshoes."

"I've been really busy," Ben lied. "I'll try to make it this week."

"Okay," Clovis said and swiped a hand across his forehead. "Whew," he said and, to Ben's horror, swayed just a bit.

"Clovis, are you feeling okay?"

"Aw, just this danged heat." He swiped at his forehead again. "I'll be fine in a minute."

Ben wasn't having it. "Let's get you inside where it's cooler." He was truly worried.

"I need to finish this yard work," he said with a stubborn lift of his chin.

"The weeds can wait, Clovis."

"Once I start a job, I like to finish."

Luckily, Willie and Miss Patty came walking by and overheard the exchange. "Hey there, is everything all right?" Miss Patty hurried across the lawn, followed closely by Willie.

"Clovis had a dizzy spell," Ben explained.

"I'm fine, I tell ya!" Clovis puffed out his chest with male pride that would have had Ben grinning if he hadn't been so concerned.

Miss Patty shushed him. "Don't be so danged stubborn, Clovis Camden. Have you hydrated? And I don't mean beer."

"Do you always have to be so bossy?" Clovis grumbled, but if Ben wasn't mistaken there just might be a bit of a spark between those two.

Miss Patty pressed her lips together. "I'll take that as a big fat no!" She grabbed him by the elbow. "Let's get you inside. Where's Clyde?"

"Grocery shoppin'. He's making some tater salad later. It's surprisingly tasty."

"Do you have this handled?" Ben asked hopefully and got a nod from Miss Patty.

"I'll take care of the stubborn old coot."

"I'm not an old coot. And that dog isn't coming in my house," he grumbled.

"You're as stubborn as the day is long," Miss Patty shot back as they entered the neat little house. Willie followed them.

Ben made a mental note to check on Clovis later and then felt another flash of anger at Tristan McMillan. The residents might gripe at one another from time to time but they were a community and cared about one another as friends and neighbors. Some of them had kids or grandkids that came over to check in on them from time to time, but many of them were on their own. They depended upon one another. Where would they go if Whisper's Edge was shut down?

Ben was thinking so hard on the subject that he forgot to be nervous about swooping in and kissing Kate until he found himself on the front steps to the office. The door was usually unlocked during the day for residents to come and go if they needed assistance for any reason. Ben normally entered without knocking, but when he got to the doorway of Kate's office and was about to make his presence known, his pulse kicked into high gear and he stopped in his tracks.

Intent on whatever she was doing, Kate failed to look up and notice him standing there like a lovesick fool. She swiveled in her seat in order to peck on the keyboard while peering intently at the monitor, giving Ben a view of her profile. Even wearing her crazy polka-dotted reading glasses, she looked gorgeous to Ben. Just last week, before everything had gone to hell in a handbasket, he'd bought a half dozen of the glasses for her since she was forever looking for them, most often finding them perched on top of her head.

Kate typed for a minute and then made a growling sound. "Whew!" She sighed, picked up a magazine, and started fanning her flushed face, even though the room was, as always, as cold as a meat locker.

As she fanned her face he noticed a bracelet dangling from her wrist. Ben narrowed his eyes.

Wait a minute.

Was it the coral and turquoise bracelet that he'd bought her? The sun caught the silver heart-shaped charm. Well damn . . . He must have made some kind of noise, because she suddenly stopped fanning and looked over in his direction. When her eyes widened in surprise, he said, "You're wearing the bracelet."

"Isn't that why you gave it to me?" she asked with false innocence.

"So . . . do you like it?"

"No." She rubbed the charm with her thumb and fingertip. "I love it," she admitted softly.

Ben took a step into the room. "Why didn't you call and tell me?"

She pushed her glasses up on top of her head. "I was waiting for you to show up."

"So that's all I had to do? Show up?"

She nodded.

Ben shoved his fingers through his hair. "So, I haven't been able to eat or sleep and all I had to do was walk through the door and everything would be just peachy?"

She nodded again. "I had a change of heart after I finally opened the gift. I realized that I was wrong. I want to be serious. Committed . . ."

"My emotions are warring with being really relieved and super pissed. I'm leaning toward super pissed."

This time she pressed her lips together as if warding off her own emotions.

"Kate, for the love of God, why didn't you call me or come over and put me out of my misery? Why did you choose to put me through hell?"

"I wanted you to come back after me, Ben."

His anger rose. "So this was a game to you?"

She tossed the magazine down. "I don't play games," she replied hotly.

"It sure feels like it."

"Look, in my lifetime I've been disappointed by those I

loved and trusted the most. I needed to be sure. I figured that if you gave up that easily then your words were ... *hollow*. I wanted for you to *show* how much you wanted me in your life."

"Great. So this wasn't a game but a *test*?" He voice sounded tight and strained but he couldn't help it. Ben was on the verge of shouting, something he almost never did.

"It wasn't easy for me not to call you."

"And that's supposed to make me feel better?" Ben took a step closer. When he saw the dark circles beneath her eyes some of his hot anger cooled. "In other words you were scared."

"No, petrified." She fingered the charm as if gathering strength from the silver heart. "But right now my plan seems shallow and mean." She blinked as if warding off tears.

"Ah, Kate." Ben softened. "You are neither of those things. But what if I hadn't shown up?"

"I had a backup plan." She grinned slightly.

"And what was that?"

"I was going to fake a leaky faucet or some such nonsense. Come up with a reason to call you."

Ben felt the tension leave his body. "I'm trying to stay pissed, especially since your devious plan, test, whatever it was worked like a charm."

"And?"

He sighed. "It isn't working. All I want to do is kiss you."

Kate pushed back her chair and walked over to him. She put her arms around his neck and said, "Then do it."

"After what you put me through, I shouldn't make it so damned easy on you," he growled but he dipped his head and captured her lips with his. Ben felt her tremble and held her tightly. After pulling his mouth from hers he said, "I love you, Kate. I missed you and I'm miserable without you in my life. You lifted me out of a deep depression and gave me back the will to live ... to laugh." He reached down and touched the silver charm. "Strength," he read softly. "We're both strong individuals but even stronger together."

"I agree." She looked into his eyes. "And I do love you, Ben. With all my heart." She pressed her palms to his cheeks. "I'm so sorry for the way I reacted. I want to explain . . ."

"You don't have to be sorry. We both have some pain in our past. I understand." He kissed her again and hugged her like he was never letting her go . . . because he wasn't. "But you are my future."

"Oh, Ben!" When her smile trembled with emotion Ben dipped his head and captured her lips with his and kissed her like there was no tomorrow. But there was a tomorrow. Lots of them and Ben wasn't going to waste one more minute without her in his life. But when he finally pulled back he frowned. "Unfortunately, I have some disturbing news to tell you."

Her eyes widened at his solemn expression. "Should I sit down?"

"Yeah, I think you should," he admitted. They took a seat on the sofa against the far wall. "I'm not one to listen in on other people's business, but I overheard Mitch Monroe talking on the phone. From what I gathered, Tristan McMillan is selling Whisper's Edge to him for future development." Ben relayed the conversation he'd overheard.

Kate put a hand to her mouth. "Why, that little weasel!"

"My thoughts exactly," Ben said darkly. "Now, mind you, I don't know if it's a done deal and I don't want to jump to conclusions, but Tristan certainly had other intentions for this property other than to make improvements."

"I had my doubts at first, but he sure won me over and had me fooled."

"He had us all fooled, Kate."

"That explains why he called earlier and said he'd be out of town for a few days. He must be finalizing the deal!" Kate shook her head slowly. "My God, Savannah is going to be simply devastated."

"Are you going to tell her?"

"I'm going to have to," she replied tearfully. "Oh . . . God."

"What?"

"It's Savannah's thirtieth birthday this coming weekend, remember? I met with some of the residents last night, and, Ben, it's been a huge secret but they're sending her to Maui! It's her ultimate dream destination. She's talked about it forever."

"You're kidding? How did I not know this? I mean I knew they were saving for a gift, but Hawaii?"

"Only a few people know. Otherwise, keeping it a secret would have been nearly impossible." Kate shook her head. "And we were going to send Tristan with her as an added surprise. I was working out the last-minute details when you walked in."

"Where is the money coming from?"

"Well, this has been in the works for quite a while. The Camden brothers own a time share in Florida that they switched out for a condo on Maui. All they would take as payment is the maintenance fee. Miss Patty has a granddaughter who is a flight attendant, and she's getting buddy passes. The rest of the money came from the residents pooling their resources for the past few months. But all they know is that it was for a present, not the details." She grinned. "It added up fairly quickly. The hard part has been keeping it a big secret. Not an easy feat around here, but they've all chipped in. Joy is a seasoned traveler, and she's been to Maui several times. She helped put together a few fun extras like an overnight stay in Hana, whale watching, a sunset cruise, a luau, . . . that sort of thing. Since Savannah was going to be traveling by herself we planned lots of excursions where she would be with people. Ben, it's a really awesome vacation but having Tristan along was going to make it so much more fun for her. And now this!" She raised her hands in the air. "What am I going to do? I know there's the bigger picture at stake but for now I don't want her birthday to be ruined. To think I'd grown to trust that boy and encouraged Savannah to not be afraid to follow her heart. I was so wrong."

Ben winced. "Let's think this through." He reached for one of her hands and gave it a gentle squeeze, wanting her to know she wasn't in this alone.

"You know these residents treat Savannah like the family she never had. This is her home. This is just horrible for everyone."

"I say you get her out of here before Tristan comes back. Can you possibly move her departure up a few days?" He paused for a moment and then an idea hit him. "Hey, why don't you go with her instead of Tristan?"

"We both can't be gone from Whisper's Edge at the same time."

Ben sighed. "Well, I'd get her out of here before she finds out about Tristan's plans. Savannah needs to be able to enjoy her trip and not ruin the fun the residents will have giving it to her. She can deal with the rest of the mess as it unfolds."

Kate nodded. "I agree. Let's work on it." She smiled and rubbed her hand up his arm. "Together."

"I like the sound of that. Look, whatever happens to Whisper's Edge, we'll deal with it as a team." He leaned down and sealed his promise with a kiss.

24

Cry Me a River

SAVANNAH OPENED THE DOOR TO THE COMMUNITY CENTER and sighed. With the Hoedown Throw Down the next day she should have been excited. Everything, from Jeff singing to the catered roasted pig, was in place. Joy headed up a team to decorate, and the community center had been transformed into a barn-dance atmosphere—from the red-and-white-checkered tablecloths dotted with terracotta pots of fresh flowers to the decorative bales of hay. Miss Patty was in charge of desserts, and a table was already starting to fill up with homemade pies, cupcakes, and cookies. Savannah peeled back the plastic wrap from a plate of snicker-doodles and was about to pick one up, but the sweet treat suddenly held no appeal and she put the wrap back in place.

Savannah knew why.

Although the past week had been busy, time had crawled by like molasses on a cold winter day. She missed Tristan something fierce. She'd spoken with him on the phone every evening, but he couldn't be sure that he'd be back in time for the dance although he promised to do everything in his power to do so.

His phone call telling her that he had to leave Cricket Creek to go to Cincinnati to help his mother with a real estate contract had come as a big disappointment after they'd finally expressed their feelings to each other. The timing couldn't be worse. While she believed him, a lingering sense of unease hovered over her like a dark cloud. Maybe he would go home and decide to move back to Cincinnati. Maybe he would see his sophisticated friends and realize that there was a big social gap between them after all. Maybe absence wouldn't make his heart grow fonder but bring him to his senses!

A few other maybes filtered into her brain, leaving Savannah feeling lost and uncertain.

But then she chided herself. Tristan had insisted that their backgrounds didn't matter. He loved her. He'd said so at the end of each phone call. Although she hadn't mentioned her birthday, maybe Kate had told him and he was going to come home with a big surprise? Oh, so many maybes . . .

And Savannah knew that even though no one had said a peep about her birthday that something must be in the works. She could just feel it. A buzz of excitement was in the air, and there were times when Savannah would walk in and the room would suddenly go silent, as if they had been talking about her. There was no way the Whisper's Edge residents would forget her thirtieth birthday. Kate had casually brought it up last week, and there had been a sparkle in her eye that said something big was going down. Otherwise they would already be fighting over who was having her over for dinner on her big day. Although she had insisted that she didn't want a big party, Savannah had to admit that thirty was hitting her pretty hard. Her bucket list didn't have hardly anything crossed off of it, and the years were slipping by. Thirty suddenly seemed . . . old.

"Stop it," Savannah said and stomped her foot like a little kid. "Everything in your life is finally going right and you're being nothing but a great big scaredy cat."

"Who are you talking to?"

Savannah looked up to see Miss Patty walk into the room with a plate full of brownies. Willie followed her.

"Myself," she admitted and felt heat creep into her cheeks. "I guess you think I'm some kind of crazy."

Miss Patty laughed. "No more than me talking to Willie."

"I talk to Willie too." She reached down and scratched Willie's head. "Don't I?"

"Woof!" It appeared an effort but he rolled his rotund body over for a belly rub. When Savannah kneeled down and rubbed his soft skin Willie made wheezing sounds of appreciation. Savannah chuckled softly. Willie had a way of chasing away her blues. Perhaps she needed a dog of her own.

"Wow, there's hardly any more room for desserts already, and the Hoedown isn't until tomorrow," Savannah commented as she came to her feet.

Miss Patty nodded. "I figured whatever is left over we can sell and put the money toward something good."

"Smart thinking," Savannah said and mustered up a smile.

Miss Patty put a hand on Savannah's arm. "Something wrong, honey child?"

"No . . ." she said but glanced away.

"Ah, man trouble?"

"Why would you say that?"

"Well, Tristan is gone. I can put two and two together."

Savannah quickly turned the tables. "Speaking of, I heard that you took dinner over to Clovis Camden and that you've been spending some time over there."

Miss Patty waved a casual hand through the air, but the color in her cheeks betrayed her. "Oh, the old coot had a dizzy spell a few days ago and refuses to go to the doctor. I'm just keeping an eye on him. You know, just being neighborly."

"If you say so."

"Savannah, you know as well as I do that Clovis is a piece of work! Both of those Camden brothers are."

"And so are you."

Miss Patty laughed. "True." She gave Savannah a slight shrug. "The man drives me nuts but he has his moments."

"Etta Mae sure would be jealous."

"An added bonus, I must admit," Miss Patty said with a laugh and then gave Savannah a sly wink. "Hey, I might be old but I'm not dead yet."

"You go, girl." Savannah gave her a sassy head bop coupled with a finger wave. Suddenly, thirty didn't seem over the hill after all and her mood lightened. "I have to lock up, but if you have any more desserts bring them over in the morning."

"Sure thing. I'm looking forward to the Hoedown, Savannah. We all are. Clovis and Clyde are putting together the horseshoe tournament to get the evening rolling. It's coming along nicely."

"Thanks!"

"Oh no, sugar, we should be thanking you. You keep all of us here at Whisper's Edge lively and having fun. I was worried but I'm so glad that Tristan McMillan rode in on his white horse and saved the day. We'd all survive without it but I sure do love this place. I'd surely hate to have to move at my ripe old age. I know we all feel the same way. Oh, and I hope he makes it back in time for the dance tomorrow."

"Me, too. See you tomorrow."

"Woof!"

"Oh, you too, Willie! Keep out of trouble now, would ya?"

Willie gave her an innocent look but Miss Patty laughed. "Not likely." She gave Savannah a wave. "Keep your chin up, Savannah. I hate to see a frown on your pretty face."

"I will." With that thought in mind Savannah decided to think positive and take the cowboy hat over to Tristan's condo and leave it there for him to find along with a note. . . . Maybe she could get up the nerve to write something suggestive? *Save a horse, ride a cowboy*, popped into her mind and she snorted with laughter. Okay . . . um . . . *no*. But leaving the hat would be fun and would put a smile on his face as soon as he saw it. Although Savannah didn't have a key, she was pretty sure that Madison or Bella would let her in if she hurried and got there before the office closed. It was worth a try.

After grabbing the cowboy hat Savannah drove over to the condo complex and parked in the visitor section of the lot. Luckily, Bella Diamante was manning the front desk. "Hi, Bella. I'm Savannah Perry, Tristan McMillan's . . . um, friend."

"Hi there. Sure, I've seen you around. So, Savannah, what can I do for you?"

"Um   Tristan is out of town, but I'd like to leave this hat in his condo. He's coming to a dance at Whisper's Edge, and I promised I'd pick this up for him. Could I do that?"

Bella smiled. "No problem, but I'd have to go with you if that's okay? Without his permission I can't let you in there without me."

"Oh, that's fine." She'd only been to his place a few times so she understood.

"Okay, follow me." Bella picked up a set of keys and then headed to the elevator. "So, you're having a dance?"

"Our first ever Hoedown. Music, pig roast, and so on. Jeff Greenfield is singing."

"Oh, I heard him sing at Sully's. He has an amazing voice! Sounds like a blast," Bella said as she opened the door to Tristan's place. "A lot of the Whisper's Edge residents come into Wine and Diner. They seem to love it there."

"It's a fun community. They might be seniors but they keep me hopping, for sure." Savannah followed Bella inside and looked around, trying to decide where to leave the hat and opted for the dining area table that was part of the great room. "I'm just going to write a short note," Savannah said.

"No rush."

Savannah put the hat on the table and then found a sticky notepad in her purse. She wrote a simple, *I missed you*, on the paper and was about to muster up the nerve to add *I love you*, when a drawing lying on the table caught her eye. She frowned. It was a map of Whisper's Edge. She angled her head. No, it was Whisper's Edge but . . . there were notes. *Marina here. Restaurant overlooking the river* was written where the community center now stood. Savannah's heart pounded and she felt light-headed. The rest of the notes blurred from the tears swimming in her eyes. She swallowed hard.

"Savannah, are you okay?" Bella asked from the doorway.

No, she wasn't okay at all. "Um, yes," she answered gruffly. She had to leave the hat or have Bella wonder what she was up to, but she grabbed the note and crushed it in her hand.

"Are you sure?" Bella locked the door and looked closely at Savannah.

"Yeah." Savannah managed a nod and a slight, wobbly smile.

Bella punched the Down button and then put a gentle hand on Savannah's arm. "Oh, I get it. You *miss* him! Believe me, I understand. My boyfriend is a baseball player and when he's gone, which is basically, like, all summer, unless I go to visit him, I'm a basket case. She sighed. "It seems like I'm living out of a suitcase, and I'm not helping my mom with her shop nearly as much as I should."

"Oh, that has to be hard."

Bella nodded firmly. "Sure is, but I love him and it's part of what he does and who he is." She sighed. "The smell of his aftershave on his laundry makes me crazy." She squeezed Savannah's arm. "I totally get it."

"Thanks."

"I sure hope he makes it back for the Hoedown."

"Me too," Savannah said and then headed to her car. But as soon as she slid behind the wheel she lost her composure. The drive home was like looking through a windshield covered in rain, clearing only when she blinked away the tears.

The radio played country music but she barely noticed, and when she pulled into her driveway she didn't even remember how she got there. Luckily, no one was around to see her walk like a wooden soldier to keep her knees from knocking.

Once she was inside Savannah made a beeline for her room. She flopped facedown onto her bed, dropping her purse next to her and beating her fists on the mattress.

And she cried a river . . .

Buckets and buckets leaked from her eyes and felt as if they were squeezed directly from her heart. When she was a child she had learned to keep emotion bottled up inside, and it suddenly seemed as if the cork had been blown from a champagne bottle of emotion, flowing out of her like a geyser and spilling everywhere. She cried for every hurt, every disappointment carelessly tossed her way. She cried for her mother, whom she never knew. She sobbed for the years of loneliness and fear that had led her to Whisper's Edge, where she finally felt at home . . . and at peace. And now, the solid foundation that she had here with people she adored and loved was splitting wide open, and she felt as if she were free-falling down a dark hole like Alice in Wonderland.

But most of all, she cried for the residents of Whisper's Edge. These were their twilight years, and the upheaval of moving was going to be so very stressful and sad. Like Kate, Savannah would survive. She always did, but this was a blow—no, make that a knockout punch—that she hadn't seen coming.

Finally, Savannah rolled over and stared at the paddle fan. Shadows fell across the walls as the sun set. She felt so tired, so drained, but just when she thought there couldn't possibly be another tear left in her body, more moisture leaked out of her eyes, sliding into her ears and dampening the pillows. She sniffed hard and felt something in her hand. Looking down she realized she still had the note squeezed in her palm. With an outcry of pure sorrow she tossed the note to the floor and wept all over again. Her eyeballs burned and her nose was stuffy. She was dimly aware of hunger pangs but the thought of food made her feel sick. Besides, moving her tired body from the bed wasn't an option.

As the darkness grew, Savannah had to wonder . . . why? What was Tristan's motive for letting her believe that he loved her? And then it hit her. Like her, many of the residents actually owned their little lots and mobile homes. Tristan might own everything else, but they would have to sell if he wanted to do something else with the property like the restaurant and marina. He wanted their cooperation. That had to be it. Why else would he do this to her? For his amusement? "Oh God . . ." Savannah whispered into the shadows. Was she simply a hot little roll in the hay while he was stuck in Cricket Creek doing his dirty business? The thought was simply too much to bear.

Savannah put her fist to her mouth, suddenly feeling like the lost little girl at the adoption fairs that nobody wanted. She stifled a sob and turned her head into the pillow. Her breath came quick as she tried to hold herself together. "You're not that little girl," she whispered into the darkness. She sat up. "You're not that little girl!" she repeated with conviction and then smacked the pillow for good measure. Kate adopted her. The residents loved her. She deserved to be loved fully and without reservation! Anything less was . . . unacceptable.

Exhausted, Savannah slid back down beneath the covers. She must have dozed, because when her phone rang the sudden sound had her nearly levitating off the bed. Dazed, she shoved her hair out of her eyes and blinked in the dark before she remembered that her phone was still in her purse. She dug around until she found it. Her heart thudded. It was Tristan.

Savannah blinked at his name until the phone went quiet and dark. She flopped back down onto the pillows and released a shaky sigh. She was going to have to tell Kate about Tristan's real plans for Whisper's Edge. But it could wait until after the dance tomorrow night. They might as well enjoy one last hurrah without the knowledge that all of their lives were going to be changed forever.

Savannah clenched her fists into the comforter. Putting on a happy face was going to be difficult but she was strong. She was a survivor. She could do it.

25
All the Right Reasons

TRISTAN TRIED TO FOCUS ON HIS BACON-AND-EGGS BREAKfast but his mind kept wandering.

"Something wrong with your food?" his mother asked with a frown.

"No, I'm just not used to such a big breakfast, I guess."

"Since when?" she asked with a gentle smile.

"Since Savannah failed to answer my call again."

Maggie McMillan pressed her lips together. "Oh, Tristan, I'm so sorry. This is all my fault! I kept you here much longer than I anticipated."

Tristan took a drink of his orange juice and then shook his head. "Mom, please don't beat yourself up. You didn't know that this would get so complicated or that you would be personally named in the lawsuit."

She sighed. "My sellers definitely didn't know that the furnace was faulty when we listed the house." She raised her hands in the air. "It was just unfortunate timing." She looked over at Tristan. "You know I'd never do something as underhanded as that."

Tristan sighed. "Unfortunately, juries are so difficult to

predict these days. Losing would have meant the full cost of replacement plus court costs. The compromise we worked out was the best I could do."

"And I'm grateful. But I'm so sorry that Savannah is upset with you for not making it back for the dance."

Tristan toyed with his scrambled eggs. "I know that she must be disappointed, but it isn't like her not to be understanding."

Maggie raised her eyebrows. "So you never got the chance to actually talk to her about it?"

"No. Since last night she hasn't answered my calls."

"Maybe she's just busy preparing for the dance? Or her phone could be on the blink. Cell phones can be temperamental," she offered with a soft smile. "Did you try calling the landline at her office?"

Tristan ran a hand down his face. "Yes, but her hours are sporadic. No luck there either."

"Well, Tristan, it's only been since last night since you haven't connected with her. I'm sure everything will be okay. And maybe you can make it back in time to surprise her by showing up at the dance after all. We should be able to wrap this headache up this afternoon."

"I know. I've just never felt this way about a woman before. The thought of losing her terrifies me."

Maggie took a sip of her coffee and nodded slowly. "That's why you need to rethink what's important you."

"I want you to be able to retire."

She raised her palms upward. "Do I look ready to retire?"

Tristan sighed. His mother was a beautiful, vibrant woman. Although she was over fifty you'd never know it. "No, but this lawsuit is a glaring example of why you deserve to relax and enjoy life without the stress of selling homes in a depressed market."

She arched an eyebrow.

"Oh no, I know that expression. What?"

"You know me all too well." She laughed but then gave

him a serious look. "We'll get to that in a minute but first I want to ask you a couple of things."

Tristan leaned back in his chair. "Shoot."

"Do you miss your fancy condo?"

"No, not really."

"Do you miss your law firm?"

After inhaling a deep breath he said, "I don't miss the crazy long hours or the stress, that's for sure."

"What do you miss, Tristan?"

"I've missed living near you."

Maggie's eyes misted over. "Me too . . ." she said but then cleared her throat. "Go on."

"Savannah," he admitted gruffly and then angled his head. "Even more than I thought I would."

"That's pretty evident."

"And I do miss practicing law. Helping people. It's why I went to law school in the first place. Well, that and I wanted you to have a secure future and early retirement." He frowned. "That's why I needed to consider Mitch Monroe's offer."

"And to show your grandfather up."

Tristan ground his teeth together. "I'm sorry, but he needs to be put in his place."

"Oh, Tristan . . ." Maggie rubbed her lips together and then gave Tristan a level look. "Whatever you do in life, do it for the right reasons."

"And showing Max McMillan up can't be a reason?" Tristan didn't want to even call the man grandfather. He wasn't a good father and there was nothing grand about the man.

"No. Tristan, my father is a miserable man. You have always done the right thing. Don't let his hatred suck you down."

"Easier said than done."

"Not really."

"Mom, some of the things he did . . . said, have stuck in my craw since I was a kid."

"Purge it." She flipped a hand in the air. "You'll feel better."

Tristan sighed.

"Look, if it helps, living well is the best revenge."

"And how do you do that?"

Maggie pointed to a decorative plaque hanging on her wall. "Live, laugh, love."

Tristan gave her a level look.

"Okay, you have to make money," she said with a crooked grin.

"That's the problem. I either have to sell Whisper's Edge or find an investor and then develop the property. I've made some basic improvements, but I don't have the funds to do what I really want to do."

"And that is?"

"I want to do what Savannah suggested. I want to add streets and lots to sell. Maybe even add some more homes. Remodel the community center and the pool. In other words, expand."

"I think that's an excellent idea."

"I can only do that if Mitch Monroe comes on board, and he wants to buy it outright." He sighed. "Well, that or find another investor."

Maggie McMillan gave him a wide smile.

"What?"

"There's a little something that you don't know about your mother."

"That you won the lottery?"

She tilted her head back and laughed. "No, but I saved a bit of a nice nest egg during the boom years."

"Look, I know I got some scholarship and grant money but you still had to help pay for law school."

"Mmm, not all of it. And even when the market got so tough, I worked my tail off and managed to make a decent living. I stayed in this little house and lived frugally." She smiled. "And it's paid off."

"Mom, what are you telling me?"

"I've always wanted to have the opportunity to develop property. I want to invest in Whisper's Edge."

Tristan blinked at her. "Really?"

"Absolutely. I've given it some thought. And you know, even though my father was a tyrant, I always loved it there. It was more of a fishing camp back then, but everyone treated me with kindness, something I was lacking in my home life. It would do my heart good to keep Whisper's Edge a retirement community. So what do you say?" She gave him a wink. "I know a thing or two about selling real estate."

Tristan jumped up so fast that his chair almost tumbled backward. "So, then you'd move to Cricket Creek?"

"I'd have to list my house, wrap things up, but yes, that would be the plan." She stood up and gave Tristan a big hug. "This way you can practice law while I lay the groundwork for expanding and improving Whisper's Edge."

"This is too good to be true."

Maggie laughed. "When you were a little boy and we'd be at a baseball game or something like that, you would often turn to me and say, 'Mom, this is the best day ever.'" Her eyes filled with tears.

"I think this qualifies."

"Yes, as long as you get back to Savannah early enough to make it to the dance. Let's wrap things up here so you can get on the road." She put her hands to her chest. "Tristan, she sounds wonderful. I can't wait to meet her."

"You'll love her," Tristan said with a smile. "Now, I've got to hightail it back so I can make it to the Hoedown Throw Down."

After wrapping up the final paperwork, Tristan was finally on the road. He tried calling Savannah several times with no luck and his exuberant mood dulled a bit. She knew that there was a chance that he wouldn't make it back in time, and her lack of response could no longer be shrugged off. This wasn't like her at all.

Something wasn't right.

But as luck would have it, pouring rain made for slow going. Still, he turned on the radio and tried to keep his spirits up. He gobbled up the miles as fast as the weather would allow and sang along, very poorly, with the radio.

"He went skydiving . . ." Tristan was belting out the Tim McGraw song when his car started feeling . . . weird. Frowning, Tristan turned off the music and listened.

Thwap, thwap, thwap.

"Please be the road," he prayed but deep down he knew what was wrong. "I think I've got a damned flat tire!" he grumbled beneath his breath. After easing off to the side of the road he got out into the pouring rain and confirmed his suspicion. Uttering an oath, he opened the trunk and hefted the spare tire out. Water sluiced down his back and soaked his jeans. "Ahhh! Damn!" he shouted when mud splattered the side of his face. Cars whizzed by, unnerving him as he worked as fast as he could, considering the circumstances.

Forty-five minutes later Tristan was wet to the core and splattered with mud and grime. He had about an hour to go but hopefully he would make it there for the last part of the Hoedown. Shivering, he turned on the heat, only to have the windows steam up. But he forged on and smiled despite his discomfort. Whatever reason Savannah had for not returning his calls would fly out the window when he gave her the news that his mother was going to be his investor in expanding Whisper's Edge.

"Ah, finally!" Tristan exclaimed when he came to the Cricket Creek exit. A hot shower was calling his name, big-time. As soon as he pulled into the parking lot, he hit the ground running. Once he was inside his condo he made a beeline for the shower, pausing only to text Savannah that he was home and would head over to the dance as soon as he could.

A few minutes later he was warm and clean but a glance at the clock had him grimacing. The digital numbers said that it was nearly midnight. Tristan sighed. The dance would surely be over by the time he got there. But he wanted to see Savannah, and so he decided to head over to her place instead. He picked up his phone and called her. The no answer once again sent a shot of alarm up his spine but he left a message, sat down on the bed, and decided to wait for her to call back.

When Tristan opened his eyes, rays of sunlight were reaching through his blinds. "What the hell . . ."

He glanced at the clock. "Damn, it's almost seven o'clock in the morning." How could he have fallen asleep? He looked down and realized that he was in the jeans and shirt he had changed into after his shower. In a bit of a panic he picked up his cell phone and frowned. Savannah hadn't called or texted him. Something was definitely wrong. Without waiting, he decided to drive over to her house and find out what was going on with her in person.

As he headed through his condo he spotted the cowboy hat she had promised, sitting on his dining room table. He hadn't seen it last night. Tristan grinned. If she left the hat, surely she wasn't angry, just disappointed, and he sighed in relief.

Ten minutes later Tristan stood on her doorstep, knocking. Her car was in the driveway but she failed to answer. Thinking she must already be working, he drove his car over to the front office. Tristan's first clue that something was terribly wrong was when he waved at Clyde Camden across the street and Clyde—or maybe it was Clovis—flipped Tristan the bird! Then Miss Patty walked by and didn't even wave, and damned if Willie seemed to give him the snub.

Perplexed, Tristan entered the office. Savannah's desk was empty, but Kate plunked away at the keyboard. When she looked up and spotted him, she glared.

"What are you doing here?"

"Um, I own the place, remember?" he said lightly as a joke but her eyes remained narrowed.

"Unfortunately."

"Where's Savannah?"

"Gone."

Icy fear slid down his spine. "Gone?" He walked closer to Kate. "What do you mean . . . gone?"

"On vacation."

"Where?"

Kate's chin came up. "None of your business."

"When did she leave?"

"Yesterday evening."

"But yesterday was the Hoedown."

"The residents surprised her with a birthday gift."

Tristan felt his heart sink. "Her birthday?"

"It's Saturday. She turns thirty. It was a bit tough on her so everybody got together and got her a nice gift."

"Why didn't you tell me her birthday was coming up?" Why hadn't she told him? A cold ball of fear formed in his gut. Something wasn't adding up.

"We were keeping it on the down low so the gift would be a surprise."

"So the gift was a trip?"

Kate nodded. "Some people care about her."

Tristan ran his fingers through his hair, quickly losing patience. "Are you going to tell me what's going on here, Kate?"

"I don't have to do anything more than my job."

Ben entered the room and gave Tristan a dirty look. He walked over and stood next to Kate's desk like he was her bodyguard. "Is there a problem?"

"You tell me," Tristan said tightly.

Kate threw down her pen. "We know what you're doing."

"And what's that?"

"Selling Whisper's Edge to Mitch Monroe!" Kate spat at him. "Tristan, how could you let us believe you were saving this place when you were selling all along?"

"I'm not selling."

Kate glanced at Ben and then back at Tristan. "What do you mean?"

"Mitch Monroe made me an offer but I turned it down. Well, at least I'm going to."

Kate blinked at him. "Go on."

"Look, I'll be honest. I bought Whisper's Edge with the intention of selling it for a quick profit or developing it into something different, like a bigger marina and a riverfront restaurant." He shrugged. "I only knew this as a fishing camp as a kid. I didn't realize that it was a tight-knit community." He smiled. "And I didn't have a clue that I would fall in love with the social director." Oh wait. They weren't smiling back.

Kate looked up at Ben.

"What's going on here?" Tristan wanted to know, and then his eyes widened. "Wait. So everybody really thinks I'm selling? Why?"

Ben cleared his throat. "Um, well, I overheard Mitch Monroe talking to his wife about buying Whisper's Edge. Seems we might have jumped the gun a little."

"A little?"

Ben gave him a sheepish look. "Okay, a lot. But in my defense I only repeated what I heard."

Tristan sighed. "And thought the worst of me."

"Sorry. I really am. But hey, you weren't forthcoming either, Tristan. You should have let us know what was going on and we wouldn't have jumped to conclusions."

Ben had a point. "So where is Savannah? Let's clear all this up."

Kate winced. "Hawaii."

"Hawaii!"

"Two nights on Oahu and then to Maui." Kate's chin came up. "Look, Tristan, the residents have scrimped, saved, and planned this for her for over a year. We whisked her away early before you could give her the news about selling Whisper's Edge."

"I didn't sell it!"

"We didn't know that," Kate explained.

"Well that explains why one of the Camden brothers flipped me the bird."

She winced again. "Only a few people were told so we could get Savannah out of here a couple of days early. But news might have . . . *spread*."

"Oh, goody."

"You were supposed to go with her," Kate said sadly.

"Sorry, Tristan," Ben said in such a sad voice that some of his anger actually cooled.

Kate raised her eyebrows. "The good news is that she doesn't know that you were selling the place."

"You *thought* I was selling," he corrected. Tristan drew in a deep breath. "I would remain super pissed but I know you did this out of sheer love for her. But if she doesn't know this false truth of yours, why doesn't she answer my calls?"

"Well, she was probably on the flight," Kate explained.

Tristan shook his head. "No, I tried way before that," he said and then groaned when he remembered the hat sitting on his table. "Oh, no." He scrubbed a hand down his face.

"What?" Kate asked.

"She brought a cowboy hat over to my condo. There was a map of Whisper's Edge that I'd made notes on. It indicated a marina, restaurant . . ." His voice trailed off.

"Oh shit," Kate muttered. She looked up at Ben, "Oh, Ben, she knew all along but didn't realize that we knew! She didn't want to ruin the Hoedown or the birthday presentation. Bless her heart. How did she ever keep it together?"

"May I remind you that I'm not selling the place?!" Tristan nearly shouted.

"You're not?" Miss Patty asked from the doorway. "Did I hear that right?"

"You heard right!" Tristan said loudly, but then grinned at the utter joy on Miss Patty's face. "Now, go and tell everybody so I don't get tarred and feathered."

"Let's go, Willie! We've got some damage control to do."

"Woof!"

"But Savannah still thinks so," Kate wailed. "Oh, her trip is going to be ruined!"

"Not if I join her," Tristan said, determinedly. "Let me fix this debacle."

"Good idea," Ben said.

"Where in Hawaii is she?" Tristan asked and then grinned. "Let me guess. Maui?"

"On Saturday. We had to add a little excursion on Oahu since she couldn't get into the condo until Saturday."

"Her birthday," Tristan said. "I've got to get on a flight there."

Kate nodded. "Joy arranged it all. We'll get her in here, and if luck is with us you can beat her to Maui and give her the surprise of her lifetime!" She put up a finger. "Hold on. I'm calling Joy."

"I'm so sorry about all of this, Tristan," Ben said while Kate chatted with Joy.

"Like I said, you did it out of love and caring. And I'm mostly to blame as well. I should have told Savannah . . . and all of you . . . what my plans were. Secrets always come out."

Ben nodded. "No matter how old we get, we still live and learn."

"Well," Kate said when she hung up the phone. She grinned at Tristan. "Here today . . . gone to Maui!"

26
Aloha!

SAVANNAH DROVE HER CUTE LITTLE RENTAL AWAY FROM THE Maui airport and felt a sense of personal pride. She had never flown on an airplane or traveled out of the country before, and doing this on her own was scary! But she ignored her fear and forged ahead. Of course, Joy's extensive and detailed itinerary was almost like having a tour guide traveling right along with her.

Her stay at the beautiful pink Royal Hawaiian Hotel, overlooking Diamond Head and the Pacific Ocean, had been breathtaking! And visiting Pearl Harbor was an emotional experience she would never forget. Savannah took a deep breath of sea-scented air drifting in through the windows that she had rolled down. As much as the knowledge of Tristan's betrayal had knocked her world right off its axis, she was determined to make the most of this trip. She was so touched that the residents had pulled this vacation of a lifetime together. So she pushed away the sadness that tugged at her heart, and lifted her chin.

"Life will go on. It always does," she said in a firm voice, even though her lips trembled. When she thought about

Whisper's Edge being plowed over for a restaurant her eyes filled with tears. Maybe they could fight it and win, she thought. "Don't think about it today. You're in Maui!" she shouted and smiled, even though she really felt like crying. But she'd conquered her sadness before and she'd do it again. After all, what choice did she have?

Savannah glanced at the map and then took a skinny road that led up a bluff overlooking the ocean. The condo complex was at the top. When sadness crept back into her thoughts she reminded herself that tomorrow she'd be lounging at the beach sipping on a mai tai, a drink she'd already tried. After drinking two last night at the Royal Hawaiian lounge, she'd almost called Tristan. Savannah shook her head. Perhaps she'd better stick to soft drinks.

After checking in, she rolled her suitcase down the sidewalk behind her. The pretty luggage was part of her birthday gift and had been filled with a vacation wardrobe, courtesy of Violet's Vintage Clothing. The residents had thought of everything from packing her bags to a Visa card loaded up with spending money. Savannah sighed as she rolled the suitcase to a stop at unit 40. She looked at the number and frowned. Ten years from today she would be forty years old. How many more things would she scratch off her bucket list by then?

Savannah opened the door and lugged the heavy suitcase inside. She smiled when she glanced to the left and saw a pretty vase of fresh exotic flowers sitting on the table. An envelope was perched against the vase and had her name on it. Curious, Savannah put her purse down, leaned her suitcase against the wall, and walked over to the table.

"Don't open that yet."

"Eeeee!" Savannah squeaked and spun around. Her eyes rounded when she saw Tristan sitting on a floral and rattan sofa in the shadows of the living room.

"Aloha."

"W-what are you doing here?"

"People keep asking me that." He shook his head and stood up. "I came here to celebrate your birthday."

Savannah's heart hammered against her ribs. "Well, I think you should ... go." She pointed toward the door, but her finger trembled.

"Sorry. That's not going to happen."

"Then I'm leaving," she announced, trying so hard not to be happy to see him.

"You're on an island. It's not that easy to leave."

"Watch me!"

Tristan walked across the room to face her. "Savannah, I'm not selling Whisper's Edge ... despite popular belief."

"But you're turning it into a marina! And a ... a restaurant!"

Tristan shook his head slowly. "No."

Savannah's knees went weak with relief but she wasn't fully convinced. "But I saw that map...."

"That map is no longer valid."

Savannah wanted to believe him, but fear crept up into her throat and she backed away. "When did you have this sudden change of heart? Before or after you told me that you loved me?"

Tristan closed his eyes and inhaled a deep breath. "Oh, Savannah. I didn't do everything right. I should have been more forthcoming from the very beginning but I liked being the hero." He smiled softly. "Especially your hero. I knew pretty quickly that I had to change my plans. I just didn't know how I was going to do it. But I fell in love with you along the way and that changed my way of thinking."

"Like feeling the need to impress your grandfather?" she asked gently.

Tristan nodded.

"And making piles of money?"

He nodded again. "Savannah, falling in love with you has softened my hard edges. I look at life from a whole different angle. In a nutshell, my mother is moving to Cricket Creek and will invest in the expansion of Whisper's Edge Retirement Community. She's taking care of selling her house and my condo too. I only hope that I can move into your home until we can pick out a lot and build our own home. Unless, of course, you want to keep that little bungalow that's such a reflection of you? It's totally up to you."

Her heart sang with joy. "For real?"

Tristan chuckled. "For real. Instead of tearing it down I'm going to build it up. You were the one who planted that seed."

She put her hands on his chest. "And together we'll watch it grow."

"I'll explain everything over the sunset dinner cruise that's on Joy's extensive itinerary."

Savannah felt another burst of happiness. She wrapped her arms around neck. "Oh, and Joy booked a whale-watching cruise, a trip to Hana, Tristan! And Laihana! Tomorrow there's a luau and—"

"All of that can wait, Savannah. For now all I want is to be with you." He silenced her with a long and luscious kiss that took her breath away. A moment later he scooped her up and carried her to a big bedroom that had a picture-perfect view of the ocean below.

"I've missed you so much," Tristan said as he untied the knot at the back of her halter-top sundress. When her breasts tumbled free he dipped his head and took one into his mouth, making her gasp. "I love the taste of your skin."

"Mmmm, I love the feel and taste of you too," she said and tugged his shirt over his head. She splayed her hands on his chest. "Luckily, while we're here very little clothes are required."

"And I plan on taking full advantage."

They made quick work of shedding the rest of their clothes and then fell into bed in a tangle of arms and legs. Tristan slid his naked body against her skin, moving erotically while he kissed her on and on. He explored every inch of her with hot kisses, nibbles, licks until she arched her back, needing more. She threaded her fingers through his hair and gently tugged his head up and looked into his eyes. "I'm so glad you're here with me."

"Ah, Savannah, me too." He captured her mouth in a passionate but tender kiss and then moved down to her neck. Her body tingled . . . ached with wanting him, but he took his sweet time.

When he finally parted her thighs and took her with his mouth, she all but melted into the mattress. He kissed her and licked her until she fisted her hands into the covers and climaxed with a burst of lingering pleasure that left her gasping with the wonder of it all.

"Happy birthday," he said and kissed her again.

"Better than cake," she managed in a breathless voice. "Although we know what to do with the ice cream."

"Oh, you'll have that too." And while her body was still reeling with the aftershocks of her orgasm, he rolled on a condom and then entered her. She loved the glorious feeling of being intimately connected. "It feels so good to have you in my arms again." He moved with slow strokes, bringing her body back to wanting him, needing him. Savannah wrapped her arms and legs around him and closed her eyes. She loved him with her heart and her body, and when he found his sweet release she came right along with him.

Savannah sighed with satisfaction when he rolled over and pulled her against his body. After a moment she said, "I'm so happy."

Tristan kissed the top of her head. "I intend to keep you that way."

"I was worried about turning thirty, Tristan. I thought to myself that I have so many things on my bucket list to cross off!"

"We'll do all of them," Tristan promised.

"I hope we do." Savannah leaned up and kissed him softly. "But in truth none of that really matters anymore. I was searching for happiness in meaningless pictures in magazines." She put a gentle hand on his chest. "This . . . *This* is real and nothing compares."

"Ah, Savannah . . ." He leaned down and kissed her so tenderly that more tears were squeezed from her heart. "I couldn't agree more."

Epilogue
Cricket Creek

"WHOA!" SAVANNAH TEETERED BACK AND FORTH ON A ROCK in the middle of the creek she was attempting to cross. "I almost joined the bullfrogs and crawdads in Cricket Creek."

"Watch your step," Tristan warned belatedly with a laugh. He reached over and offered his hand.

"Where are you taking me, anyway? We couldn't still be on Whisper's Edge property."

"Patience," Tristan said calmly, but there was an underlying excitement in his tone that had Savannah's heart beating faster. He helped her hop over to the grassy bank. While still holding her hand he pointed at a fairly steep embankment. "Just a little bit farther."

"Up there?"

"I'll help you," he promised with a grin that she found sexy.

"Okay . . ." Savannah held tightly to his hand while she struggled to keep from sliding backward. "But if I fall I'm taking you with me," she warned him but he only laughed. He held back sticker bush branches as he led her down a narrow path through the woods. Savannah was glad she'd worn jeans and sneakers for what Tristan told her was going to be a casual date. When a thorn snagged at her hair she made grumbling noises about beady-eyed creatures hiding in the trees.

"I thought you liked hiking? We did a lot of it in Maui."

"Yes, on trails."

"Sometimes you have to take the road less traveled."

She smiled. "True."

"Don't worry. I'll check you all over for ticks."

Savannah wrinkled her nose at him but there was excitement buzzing in the air. "There'd better be a really amazing spread at the end of this path, you know, like the destination dates they have on the *Bachelorette*. Champagne and caviar." She looked at him, hoping to get a clue as to why he was taking her on this hike.

"Do you like caviar?"

"I don't know but . . ." She paused when they reached an open field dotted with wildflowers. "Oh . . . my!" To the left was a barn that must have once been red but had faded to a rusty orange. And on the right was a two-story fieldstone farmhouse. She looked at Tristan in question and he gave her a slow smile.

"Do you like it?"

"W-what do you mean? Did you buy this for the expansion of Whisper's Edge?"

"No. I'll buy it for us if you want it. But first I have something to ask you."

Savannah felt her eyes widen and her mouth open, but no words would come out. She put her hand to her chest when Tristan reached inside the pocket of his cargo pants and pulled out a blue velvet ring box. He got down on one knee, crushing a few daisies in the process.

"Savannah, will you marry me?" He opened the lid, revealing a delicate but stunning solitaire diamond ring. He looked up at her with hope, longing, and such love in his eyes that she wanted to shout her answer, but her throat clogged with emotion, not letting the words out. Instead, she nodded vigorously. He smiled and came to his feet. His fingers trembled as he removed the ring and then slid it onto her finger. Sunlight caught the sparkle of the diamond, and for a moment Savannah could only stare at her finger wearing an engagement ring.

She was engaged to be married! To Tristan!

Savannah suddenly found her voice and let out a whoop. Laughing, Tristan picked her up and spun her around in the field of flowers. It was like a scene in a romantic movie ... well, until he stumbled and took them both tumbling and laughing to the ground. And then he gave her a slow, long, hot, sweet kiss that stole her breath and went straight to her heart.

Tristan smiled at her tenderly and then pulled a twig from her hair. "Do you want to see the house?"

"Yes!"

He grinned and tugged her to her feet. They all but ran over to the front steps that led to a porch. "It needs some work," he warned and then looked at her expectantly as she peeked into the front windows.

Savannah turned and beamed at him. "My favorite kind!"

"I've got the key," he said and dug inside his pocket.

"Sweet!" Savannah all but jumped up and down in her eagerness to get inside. Hand in hand they walked around while Savannah exclaimed in delight over every little detail. "Oh, look at the stone fireplace! And Tristan, I love the plank hardwood floors!" She sucked in a breath. "The glass doorknobs are gorgeous." She tugged him into the kitchen. "Oh, exposed beams! A pantry!" She tugged his hand and pulled him up the narrow steps leading to the second floor. "A claw foot bathtub?" Her voice raised an octave. She pulled him down the hallway and into each of the three bedrooms. "Tristan, this house is perfect."

"Not perfect, Savannah. It needs updating and lots of renovation."

She turned and smiled at him. "It will be perfect. We'll make it perfect." She hugged him but then pulled back. "Wait. Is this what you want? It's a far cry from a high-rise condo."

Tristan trailed a fingertip down her cheek. "I came here looking for land to expand Whisper's Edge. But when I saw the farmhouse I immediately pictured you on the porch waving to me. And cooking in the kitchen. Planting a garden. This house has heart and soul." He tilted her chin up. "Like you." He looked into her eyes. "It was then that I knew I wanted to be your husband. So yes, this is what I want. Now . . . and forever."

Savannah put her palms on his cheeks. "I love you, Tristan." She went up on tiptoe and kissed him tenderly.

"Do you want to see the barn?"

She gave him a bright smile. "I want to see everything!"

They headed out the back door and explored the backyard on the way to the barn. "Tomatoes over there and a flower garden next to the shed. Oh, and a bird bath."

Tristan chuckled. "A bird bath?"

"I want it all!" She waved her hands upward and laughed.

"And you shall have it."

When they reached the barn Tristan pulled the big door open. Dust motes danced in the air, and the earthy smell of hay and animals wafted their way. Sunshine cut through the darkness, illuminating a slice of the floor and beyond. A few forgotten tools were scattered here and there, and a weathered-looking ladder led up the hayloft.

"Just needs a little sprucing up," Savannah commented.

"I'm not sure what we'd do with a barn but I like having one," Tristan said with a grin. "Well, we'd better get going since we have a little hike back. And I have an offer to make."

Savannah nodded but put a hand on Tristan's arm. "Did you hear that?"

"What?"

"That!" Savannah said when she heard a whine. "Something is in here," she whispered and crept forward.

"Cats usually live in barns, I think," Tristan said. But it wasn't a cat that was hiding behind a pile of hay—it was a dog. He was skinny with matted hair and big eyes.

"Come here," Savannah coaxed. When the dog scooted backward, she dug in her purse and found some peanut butter crackers. She showed the dog a cracker but he didn't move. "Oh, Tristan, he's scared."

"Be careful, Savannah. It's obviously a stray. He must have gotten in through a hole somewhere."

Savannah nodded but she crept forward and finally tossed the cracker in front of the scared dog, who hesitated but then wolfed the treat down. "Oh, it's hungry!" She tossed another cracker closer so that the dog would come into the light. God, she knew just how he felt . . . lost and alone. Desperate.

"Savannah," Tristan warned, but she somehow knew the dog wouldn't harm her.

The pooch became less frightened, and Savannah tossed the remaining crackers until they were out of the barn. "Are you thirsty? Because I know where there's a creek," she said over her shoulder. The dog trotted up beside them as if he understood. Savannah looked over at Tristan and chuckled. "I talk to dogs, remember?"

"And save them from drowning."

Savannah laughed at the memory.

"He's coming home with us, isn't he?" Tristan asked with a shake of his head but he was grinning.

"He?"

Tristan tilted his head and looked. "Yep, I do believe it is a . . . him."

She nodded and turned to the dog. "Come on, Sandy. My friend Willie will show you the ropes. Let's go home."

"Home . . . I like the sound of that."

Savannah reached out and took Tristan's hand. "Me too."

Read on for a sneak preview of
LuAnn McLane's charming
Cricket Creek novella,

"MISTLETOE ON MAIN STREET,"

appearing in the anthology
CHRISTMAS ON MAIN STREET
Available in November 2013 wherever
books and eBooks are sold.

"OH, NO!" AVA WHIMSY GRIPPED THE HANDLE OF HER BIG wicker basket tightly as she dodged past dancing elves and then cut through a Girl Scout troop decked out in cookie costumes. The lineup for the Cricket Creek Christmas parade was organized chaos at best and this was no time to be running late.

"Santa, where are you . . . ?" Ava stopped and twirled around so fast that the red velvet skirt of her Mrs. Claus dress billowed out like an umbrella before settling down around her calves. The basket tilted, sending a few candy canes sliding to the concrete, but she didn't have time to pick them up. Ava knew the Santa's sleigh float brought up the rear, but seriously, the end of the line was nowhere in sight.

"Where in the world is Santa's sleigh?" Ava shouted to Noah Falcon, owner of the Cricket Creek professional baseball team and grand marshal of the parade. Even though the weather had a threat of snow flurries, the top of the flashy red convertible was down, allowing Noah and his wife, Olivia, to wave and toss Cougar baseball caps to the eager crowd.

"Back . . ." Noah began but the high school marching band started playing "Jingle Bells," drowning out his answer. Ava looked in the direction of Noah's thumb, jammed over his head. *Finally* she spotted the flying reindeer jutting up in the air all the way over at the other end of the parking lot.

The jolly old man might have to ride in the sleigh solo this year. But after taking a deep breath to ready herself, Ava lifted her red velvet skirt with one hand, put one dainty laced-up boot in front of the other, and then hurried as fast as she could past floats and other Christmas-themed participants. Her basket, laden with tiny toys and candy canes, swung back and forth.

A last-minute customer at Ava's toy store, just a few blocks away on Main Street, had had her running behind, and then to make matters worse, her dog had decided to shred her white wig to pieces. Apparently, Rosie—her usually sweet little rescue mutt—didn't take kindly to Ava's recent long hours stocking A Touch of Whimsy in preparation for the holiday rush. In a panic, Ava had pulled her chestnut brown hair into a bun and sprayed it with the fake snow she'd been using for the front window display. Judging by the crusty white flakes falling from her head, it wasn't her best idea. Although she considered herself a creative person, she was normally a casual dresser and not really equipped for situations like this. The label at least *said* the contents were nontoxic, so she hoped her hair wouldn't fall out.

For the past ten years she and Pete Sully had played Santa and Mrs. Claus during the three-day celebration filled with food and festivities along Main Street in Cricket Creek. Pete also made Santa appearances at her store throughout the holiday season. With his real beard, round belly, and booming voice, Pete played the part well. And although perhaps more suited to play a cute elf, Ava dressed up and portrayed Mrs. Claus at Sully's Tavern when Pete hosted Toys for Tots and Teens, a charity event to benefit local children in need. She just couldn't fathom any child not having a toy on Christmas morning.

"Finally!" Ava muttered when she reached the row of plastic reindeer. Sure, they had seen better days, but the worn rosy cheeks and chipped paint somehow added a nostalgic appeal that Ava found endearing. Rudolph's red nose blinked as if in welcome and Ava sighed in relief. She'd made it.

"Hey there!" Ava waved to Braden Greenfield sitting on the big green tractor that was going to pull the float. A huge red bow adorned the front grille. When Braden tipped his cowboy hat at Ava, she grinned and tossed him a candy cane, which he deftly caught.

"You took your sweet time getting here, Ava," Braden called over to her.

"Long story," she shouted back. The Greenfield farm butted up to her family's farm and Braden was like a little brother to her. "Catch ya later!" Ava turned and accepted Santa's white-gloved hand as she took the big step up and slid onto the black leather seat.

"Sorry I'm late," Ava apologized a little breathlessly, and set her basket down onto the floor. She leaned over to pick up a few candy canes that had tumbled around her feet. "I had a customer who couldn't decide whether to purchase trains or airplanes." Sitting back up, she arranged her velvet skirt just so and brushed away a mist of white flakes that continued to flutter from her head as she moved. "And then a wardrobe situation complicated matters." She pointed to her head. "So, how's it going, Pete?"

"Pretty good, but, um . . . I'm not Pete."

Ava chuckled as she tugged at her tight gloves. "Sorry. . . . Right, you're Santa. I forgot that you like to stay in character." After flicking another powdery flake from her skirt, she reached down for a handful of candy canes and finally glanced his way. "Would you like one?"

"Thanks," Santa said, reaching for the treat. But when their fingers brushed, for some odd reason Ava felt a little tingle.

"You're welcome." Ava smiled. . . . *Whoa. Wait a minute.*

She peered at Santa over the top of her granny glasses and her heart started to thud. "W-why do you have a fake beard?"

"Shhh, I'm not the real Santa," he replied in a stage whisper. "Only a helper. I'm a very big elf."

Ava looked into light blue eyes accentuated by tan cheeks visible above the beard and felt another tingle of awareness. She swallowed hard. No, it couldn't be. The candy canes slid from her hand and into her lap. *Clint?* The name slammed into her brain but got caught in her throat and stayed there.

"Dad couldn't make it, so I'm filling in," he explained, confirming her suspicions.

"Clint?" The single word that was a tangle of so many emotions tumbled out of her mouth. Of course it was Clint. Pete had only one son.

And she hadn't spoken to him since he'd broken her heart twenty years ago.

Missed the first book
in LuAnn McLane's
Cricket Creek series?
Here's an excerpt from

PLAYING FOR KEEPS

Available now.

$\mathcal{W}$ELCOME TO CRICKET CREEK, KENTUCKY, BIRTHPLACE OF NOAH FALCON, Noah read as he drove his red Corvette convertible past the city-limits sign. He had won several awards as a major-league relief pitcher, but this little bit of hometown recognition never failed to bring a smile to his face. Of course, he'd never dreamed he would be returning home to audition for the community theater. His life wasn't exactly going as planned.

Noah's smile faded as he turned onto Main Street. The once-thriving little town was all but deserted, even on a Saturday afternoon. Several of the shops had FOR LEASE signs in the windows, and other storefronts were looking rundown.

He supposed that the sluggish economy had taken its toll on the small river town where the locals earned a living on charter boating and tourism. He guessed that here, like everywhere else, it was difficult for the local stores and restaurants to compete with nearby suburban chains. Some of the antiques shops had survived, and he smiled when he stopped at the red light and spotted Myra's Diner, where he had consumed many a cherry Coke, double cheeseburger, and giant onion rings with his rowdy teammates after high school baseball games.

As Noah idled there at the light, he remembered Myra Robinson, as feisty as she was tiny, who had somehow managed to keep Noah and his cronies pretty much in line. All she had to do was raise one eyebrow in their direction and they would pipe down . . . well, at least for a minute or two. He also recalled Myra's niece, Jessica, who had caused quite a stir when she had shown up on her aunt's doorstep pregnant at sixteen. But free-spirited Myra lived by her own rules. She had taken her niece in, and after sweet little Madison was born, she charmed the town with her mop of blond curls and big blue eyes. Noah shook his head, thinking that here he was, twenty years later, auditioning for a play that Jessica's daughter wrote. As he passed the diner he did notice that there seemed to be some construction going on inside and hoped it meant that the restaurant remained on solid ground.

"Yes!" Noah shot a celebratory fist into the air when he saw that Grammar's Bakery, home of the best butter cookies on the planet, was still in business. "Thank God for small favors!" he said to the blue sky and then slid his sleek red car into a parking spot directly in front of the bakery. He glanced at his watch. If he was lucky they would still have a few cookies left. He unfolded his jeans-clad legs from the driver's seat and eased his road-weary body to a standing position before stretching. At least nobody in here would poke fun at his cowboy boots or Western-cut flannel shirt. It was a bit on the cool side to have the top down, but on a bright, sunshiny day like this, Noah couldn't resist. "You can take the boy out of the country . . ." he said under his breath, and then grinned. Man, it felt good to be back home.

A bell jingled when Noah tugged the door open, and he had to stop in his tracks and take a deep breath of air scented with cinnamon and yeast. "Please tell me you have some butter cookies left."

"I think so." A teenage girl with a lopsided pale blond ponytail glanced up from wiping the counter and gave him a bored smile.

"Sweet. I'll take them all." Since it was Saturday afternoon the shelves were already mostly bare, but he glanced in the glass display case and breathed a sigh of relief when he spotted a couple dozen butter cookies dotted with pastel icing. A fat cinnamon cake topped with mounds of crumble called his name, and so did a flat, crispy elephant ear. Oh, and he needed a loaf of white and a loaf of marble rye . . .

"Well, I'll be a monkey's uncle!" boomed the big voice of Mabel Grammar. She stood there with her hands on her ample hips and grinned while the double doors to the kitchen swung back and forth behind her. "Noah Falcon?"

Noah pushed his mirrored aviators up onto his head and grinned back. "The one and only."

"No truer words were ever spoken." Mabel laughed, causing her double chin to jiggle. "Well, aren't you just a sight for sore eyes?" She dusted floured hands on her apron and ambled out from behind the counter.

"And so are you, Mabel," Noah told her, and gave her a big bear hug. "It sure smells good in here." After he stepped back he noticed that the teenager's jaw had dropped.

"Noah, this is Chrissie."

"Uh-uh . . ."

"You mean you're not Chrissie?" Noah asked with a grin.

"No, I mean . . . yes. Really? You're *Noah Falcon*?" She stood up from her slouch and suddenly appeared less bored.

"Yep." Although Noah bestowed his best Dr. Jesse Drake soap-opera smile upon her, it grated a little that he wasn't worth the time of day until she knew he was famous. He had experienced much of the same after he was no longer a major-league baseball player, and now that he had been booted off *Love in the Afternoon*, his net worth had taken a nosedive once again. His personal life had taken a tumble too. No one wants a has-been, only a *right-now*, and it was beginning to wear on him—but he kept his smile in place and gave her a wink. She was just a kid and meant no harm.

Chrissie's eyes widened. "Dude, my mom was so upset when you got all blown up in that car wreck."

"What?" Mabel took another step back and gave him a once-over. "What's this about a car wreck?"

"On television," Noah explained. He hadn't seen his untimely death coming either, but before he could elaborate Chrissie interrupted with an excited wave of her hands.

"He plays Dr. Jesse Drake on *Love in the Afternoon*."

Mabel slapped her leg. "Oh, that's right. I'm never home in the afternoon to watch."

"You should totally TiVo it."

"Chrissie, honey, I have no idea what in the world you're even talkin' about. I have a tough enough time workin' my remote."

"My mother never misses it," Chrissie gushed. "She said she knew you back in high school. She said you were superhot."

"Thanks . . . I think."

"N-not that you aren't now," Chrissie quickly amended, and then blushed. "You know, for an old dude."

"Oh, Chrissie, good one," Mabel said, and slapped her leg again.

"What?" Chrissie frowned for a second, and then she said in a rush, "Oh, not *old* . . . old."

"Chrissie, honey, you'd better quit while you're ahead." Mabel chuckled but then pressed her lips together when Noah gave her a look. "Oh, Noah, I think you're still cute as a button with those dimples and all." She reached up and pinched his cheeks.

"You meant ruggedly handsome, right?"

Mabel patted his cheeks. "You betcha. Well, except you could use a shave."

"That's my sexy soap-opera stubble, I'll have you know." When he playfully arched one eyebrow and struck a pose, Chrissie whipped out her cell phone and snapped a picture. Great—he looked like a total asshat. Plus, he wanted to keep his presence here on the down low for a while. He would have asked her to delete it, but she seemed so thrilled that he didn't have the heart.

"Camera didn't break, did it?" Mabel asked Chrissie, who looked at her like she was one taco short of a combo.

"Miss Mabel!"

"Oh, Noah knows I'm just yanking his chain," she said with a wink in his direction.

"My mom is gonna freak," Chrissie announced when she looked at the picture.

Noah laughed. Although his hometown had always showered him with pride, Noah's friends and family also made certain that he checked his ego at the door. What they didn't know was that except when he was on the baseball field or in front of the camera, his hotshot persona was just that—an act that he wasn't always comfortable with. He'd much rather be noshing on chili cheese fries at Myra's Diner than eating sushi at a fancy restaurant, but if he wanted to continue with his acting career he had to keep up his over-the-top image.

"Well, now . . ." Mabel waved her hand toward the glass cases just as the bell above the door tinkled. Noah turned to see a tall, slender woman enter the bakery. "Noah, do you see anything that strikes your fancy?" Mabel asked.

"Um . . ." Noah opened his mouth to answer but paused when the woman's eyes widened a fraction before she pushed her rimless glasses up and sort of looked down her nose at him. Not understanding what he had done to deserve such a reaction, he tried to coax a smile from her but failed. When she abruptly turned away, Noah studied her profile, thinking that she looked a bit familiar, but he couldn't quite put his finger on it. He was used to getting smiles instead of snubs, and he racked his brain but came up empty.

"Well, hey there, Olivia," Mabel said to the woman, and

got a warm smile in return. Her brown hair was pulled back into a tight, controlled bun, and from her creased slacks to her ironed oxford shirt everything about her screamed prim and proper. Oh ... but she had a full, sensual mouth that was shiny with pale peach gloss, making Noah fantasize that she was wearing black lace lingerie beneath her neatly pressed pants. He could just imagine her loosening her bun and shaking her hair free ...

"Noah?" Mabel persisted. "Have you decided what you want?"

"Yeah ..." he answered, but cookies were no longer on his mind. "I have."

When he failed to elaborate, Mabel shook her head and turned to Olivia. "What brings you in today?"

"Do you have any butter cookies left?" Olivia asked hopefully. Like her appearance, her voice seemed all business but possessed an unexpected throaty edge along with a hint of the South.

"I believe we do," Mabel answered, and then glanced at Chrissie.

"Um, Miss Lawson, I'm afraid that Dr. Jesse Drake— I mean, Noah, um, *Mr. Falcon* already spoke for them."

"Oh," she said in a disappointed tone, and glanced down into the glass case.

When she licked her bottom lip Noah heard himself say, "I'll share them with you."

"Thanks ... but no," Olivia replied in a gracious but not overly friendly tone. She smiled, but it was a tight little smile that matched her tight little bun. By rights Noah should have been totally put off.

But he wasn't. Not even a little.